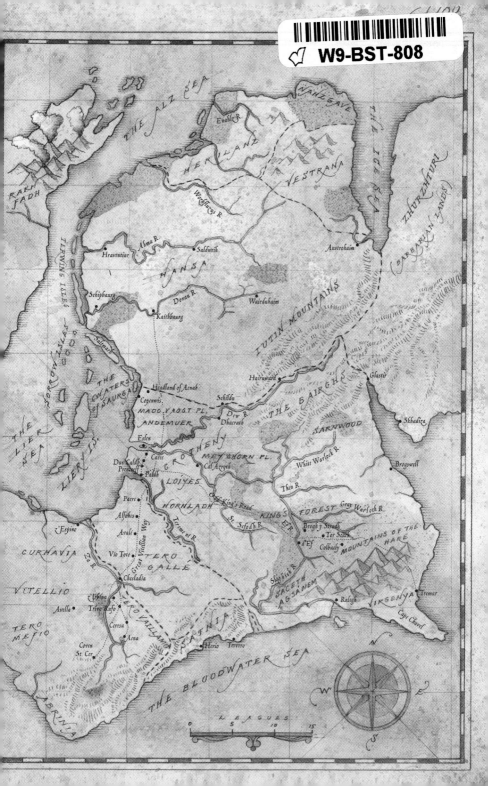

THE ALZ SEA

RAKH FADH

TERWING ISLES

THE SORROW ISLES

THE LIER SEA

LIERI IS.

THE CRATERS of NAURGA

VITELLIO

CURHAVIA

TERO MEFIO

ABRINIA

Hraventiur

Schipbaurg

Salauer

Copenwis

Duv Caldh
Prenhaff

Paldh

Cares

Eslen

Pacre

Alsohes

Avale

l'Espine

Vio Toto

Chesladia

Urbina

Trivo Rufo

Avella

Ceresa

Acna

Coven
St. Cer

Abma R.

Saldweth

HANSA

Donau R.

Kaithbaurg

HERILANZ

Enable R.

Wadfleurs R.

Headland of Aenah

MAOG VAOST PL.

ANDEMUER

GROHENY

LOIYES

HORNLADH

TERO GALLE

Great Vitellian Way

Tevento

VESTRANA

WANLGAVE

Austrohaim

THE ICE SEA

ZHURHTURI
(BARBARIAN LANDS)

IUTIN MOUNTAINS

Hairusward

Schildu

Dew R.
Dhacrath

Cat Azroth

METGHORN PL.

White Warlock R.

Then R.

Old King's Road

St. Sefodh R.

THE BAIRGHS

Glastir

SARNWOOD

Skhadira

Brogswell

Gray Warlock R.

Brogh y Stradh

Tor Scath

d'Ef

Colbaely

KING'S FOREST

Treront R.

Tor R.

Ynis

Cresta

TERO VAILLAMO

Herio

Teverro

SACETH
AG SANEM

Slaghish R.

Raleigh

MOUNTAINS OF THE HARE

VIRGENYA

Tremar

Cape Chavel

THE BLOODWATER SEA

LEAGUES

0   5   10   15

N
W   E
S

Wairduhaim

THE
CHARNEL
PRINCE

By Greg Keyes

The Chosen of the Changeling
THE WATERBORN
THE BLACKGOD

The Age of Unreason
NEWTON'S CANNON
A CALCULUS OF ANGELS
EMPIRE OF UNREASON
THE SHADOWS OF GOD

The Psi Corps Trilogy
BABYLON 5: DARK GENESIS
BABYLON 5: DEADLY RELATIONS
BABYLON 5: FINAL RECKONING

Star Wars®: The New Jedi Order
EDGE OF VICTORY: CONQUEST
EDGE OF VICTORY: REBIRTH
THE FINAL PROPHECY

The Kingdoms of Thorn and Bone
THE BRIAR KING
THE CHARNEL PRINCE

GREG KEYES

THE CHARNEL PRINCE

The Kingdoms of Thorn and Bone

BALLANTINE BOOKS • NEW YORK

The Charnel Prince is a work of fiction. Names, places, and incidents either are products of the author's imagination or are used fictitiously.

A Del Rey® Book
Published by The Random House Publishing Group
Copyright © 2004 by J. Gregory Keyes

ISBN 0-345-44067-6

Endpaper maps by Kirk Caldwell

Manufactured in the United States of America

For Elizabeth Bee Vega

PROLOGUE

Had laybyd hw loygwn eyl
Nhag Heybeywr, ayg nhoygwr niwoyd.

The Forest speaks with many tongues
Listen well but never answer.

—*Nhuwd nhy Whad* proverb, given as a warning to young children

"I HEAR A NOISE," Martyn murmured, reining in his dappled gray stallion. "It is an unnatural sound." The monk's predatory blue eyes strained, as if trying to burn through the huge-girthed ironoaks and rocky slopes of the King's Forest. Ehawk could see by the set of the man's shoulders beneath his bloodred robe that every muscle in his body was tensed.

"No doubt," Sir Oneu replied jovially. "This forest chatters like a woman who is half-mad with love."

But despite his tone, Sir Oneu's black eyes were serious when he turned to speak to Ehawk. As always, Ehawk was surprised by the older man's face—soft and tapered it was, the corners of his eyes crinkled by fifty years of laughter. The knight hardly seemed to fit his reputation as a fierce warrior.

"What do you say, m' lad?" Oneu asked.

"From what I've seen," Ehawk began, "Brother Martyn can hear a snake breathe over the next hill. I haven't such ears, and at this moment hear little. But sir, that's strange of itself. There ought to be more birds singing."

"Saint Rooster's balls," Oneu scoffed, "what do y'mean? There's one warbling right now, so loud I can scarce hear myself."

"Yes, sir," Ehawk replied. "But that 'un is an *etechakichuk*, and they—"

"In the king's tongue, boy, or in Almannish," snapped a dour, sallow-faced man. He wore robes of the same color as Martyn's. "Don't gabble at us in your heathen language."

That was Gavrel, another of the five monks traveling with the party. His face looked as if it had been cut into an apple and left to dry.

Ehawk didn't like Gavrel much.

"Mind your own tongue, Brother Gavrel," Sir Oneu said mildly. "I'm the one speaking to our young guide, not you."

Gavrel glared at the reprimand, but he did not challenge the knight.

"You were saying, m' lad Ehawk?"

"I believe you call 'em crow-woodpeckers," Ehawk replied. "Nothing frightens them."

"Ah." Oneu frowned. "Than let's have quiet, while Brother Martyn listens more closely."

Ehawk did as he was told, straining his own ears to the limits, feeling an unaccustomed chill as the hush of the forest sank in. It was strange.

But these were strange days. Only a fortnight before, the crescent moon had risen purple, a dire portent indeed, and a weird horn had sounded on the wind, heard not just in Ehawk's village but everywhere. The old oracle-women muttered prophecies of doom, and tales of awful beasts roaming and slaying in the King's Forest grew more common each day.

And then these men had come from the west, a knight of the

Church, resplendent in his lord's plate, and five monks of the order of Saint Mamres—warriors all. They'd arrived in Ehawk's village four days ago and bargained for a native guide. The elders had appointed him, for though Ehawk was scarcely beyond his seventeenth summer, there was no man more keenly gifted at hunting and tracking. He'd been excited to go, for strangers were uncommon here near the Mountains of the Hare, and he'd hoped to learn something of foreign lands.

He hadn't been disappointed. Sir Oneu de Loingvele loved to talk of his adventures, and he seemed to have been everywhere. The monks were quieter and somewhat frightening—except Gavrel, who was outspoken and frightening—and Martyn, who was kind in his own brusque way. If he spoke laconically of his training and his life, what he did have to say was usually interesting.

But one thing Ehawk had not learned—what these men were searching for. Sometimes he thought they themselves did not know.

Sir Oneu doffed his conical helm and rested it under one arm. A stray beam of sunlight glinted from his steel breastplate as he patted the neck of his warhorse to calm it. He shifted his gaze back to Martyn.

"Well, Brother?" he asked. "What are the saints whispering to you?"

"No saints, I think," Martyn said. "A rustling, many men moving over the leaves, but they pant like dogs. They make other strange sounds." He turned to Ehawk. "What people live in these parts?"

Ehawk considered. "The villages of the Duth ag Paé are scattered through these hills. The nearest is Aghdon, just up the valley."

"Are they warriors?" Martyn asked.

"Not usually. Farmers and hunters, same as my people."

"Are these sounds drawing nearer?" Sir Oneu asked.

"No," Martyn replied.

"Very well. Then we'll go on to this village and see what the local people have to say."

"Not much to look at," Sir Oneu observed half a bell later, when they reached Aghdon.

To Ehawk's eyes, Aghdon wasn't that different from his own village—a collection of small wooden houses around a common square and a high-beamed longhouse where the chieftain lived.

The greatest difference was that his own village bustled with people, chickens, and pigs. Aghdon was empty as a Sefry's promise.

"Where is everyone?" Sir Oneu asked. "*Hallo?* Anyone there?"

But there was no reply, and not a soul stirred.

"Look here," Martyn said. "They were trying to build a stockade."

Sure enough, Ehawk saw that a number of fresh-cut timbers had been erected. Others logs had been cut, but never set up.

"On your guard, fellows," Sir Oneu said softly. "Let's ride in there and see what happened to these folk."

But there was nothing to be found. There were no bodies, no signs of violence. Ehawk found a copper kettle with its bottom scorched out. It had been left on the cookfire, untended, until its contents had boiled away.

"I think they all left suddenly," he told Martyn.

"Yah," the monk replied. "They were in a hurry for certain. They didn't take anything."

"But they were afraid of something," Ehawk said. "Those wreaths of mistletoe above their doors—that's to ward against evil."

"Yes, and the stockade they began," Sir Oneu said. "The praifec was right. Something is happening here. First the Sefry abandon the forest, now the tribesmen." He shook his head. "Mount up. We'll continue. I fear our mission is more urgent than ever."

They left Aghdon and struck off across the uplands, leaving the largest of the ironoaks behind them and entering a forest of hickory, liquidambar, and witaec.

Still they rode in eerie silence, and the horses seemed nervous. Brother Martyn wore a slight but perpetual frown.

"Ride up with me, lad," Sir Oneu called back. Obediently, Ehawk trotted his own dun mare until he was abreast of the knight.

"Sir Oneu?"

"Yes. Now would you like to hear the rest of that story?"

"Yes, sir. Indeed I would."

"Well, you'll recall that I was on a ship?"

"Yes, sir. On the *Woebringer.*"

"That's right. We'd just broken the siege at Reysquele, and what was left of the Joquien pirates were scattering to the sea winds. The *Woebringer* was badly damaged, but so were a lot of ships, and no dearth of them ahead of us for repairs at Reysquele. The weather was calm, so we reckoned we could make Copenwis, where fewer ships go for dry-dock." He shook his head. "We didn't make it to Copenwis, though. A squall came up, and only the favor of Saint Lier brought us to a small island none of us knew, somewhere near the Sorrows. We made land in a longboat and gave offering to Saint Lier and Saint Vriente, then sent out parties to search for habitants."

"Did you find any?"

"In a manner of speaking. Half the pirate fleet was camped on the leeward side of the island."

"Oh. That must have been trouble."

"Indeed. Our ship was too badly damaged for us to leave, and too big to hide. It was a matter of little time before we were discovered."

"What did you do?"

"I marched over to the pirate camp and challenged their leader to a duel of honor."

"He accepted?"

"He had to. Pirate chieftains must appear to be strong, or their men will not follow them. If he had refused me, the next day he would have had to fight ten of his own lieutenants. As it was, I relieved him of that worry by killing him."

"And then what?"

"I challenged the second-in-command. And then the next, and so on."

Ehawk grinned. "Did you kill them all?"

"No. While I fought, my men took possession of one of their ships and sailed away."

"Without you?"

"Yes. I'd ordered them to."

"And so what happened?"

"When the pirates discovered what had happened, they took me prisoner, of course, and the dueling stopped. But I convinced them the Church would pay my ransom, and so they treated me pretty well."

"Did the Church pay?"

"They might have—I didn't wait to see. I had a chance for escape, later, and took it."

"Tell me about that," Ehawk pleaded.

The knight nodded. "In time, lad. But you tell me now—you grew up in these parts. The elders at your village told many strange tales of greffyns, manticores—fabulous monsters, never seen for a thousand years, now suddenly everywhere. What do you make of that, Ehawk, m' lad? Do you credit such talk?"

Ehawk considered his words carefully. "I've seen strange tracks and smelled weird spore. My cousin Owel says he saw a beast like a lion, but scaled, and with the head of an eagle. Owel don't lie, and he's not like to scare or see things wrong."

"So you do believe these tales?"

"Yah."

"Where do these monsters come from?"

"They've been t'sleep, they say—like how a bear sleeps the winter, or the cicada sleeps in the ground for seventeen year before comin' out."

"And why do you think they wake now?"

Ehawk hesitated again.

"Come, m' lad," the knight said softly. "Your elders were tight-lipped, I know, I suspect for fear of being labeled heretics. If that's your fear, you've no worry about me. The mysteries of the saints are all around us, and without the Church to guide, folk think odd things. But you live here, lad—you know things I don't. Stories. The ancient songs."

"Yah," Ehawk said unhappily. He glanced at Gavrel, wondering if he, too, had keener hearing than a normal man.

Sir Oneu caught the look. "This expedition is my charge," he said, softly still. "I give you my word as a knight, no harm will come to you for what you tell. Now—what do the old women say? Why do unholy things stalk the weald, when never they did before?"

Ehawk bit his lip. "They say 'tis Etthoroam, the Mosslord. They say he woke when the moon was purple, as was foretold in ancient prophecy. The creatures are his servants."

"Tell me about him, this Mosslord."

"Ah . . . it's only old stories, Sir Oneu."

"Tell me nevertheless. Please."

"In shape, they say he is a man, but made of the stuff of the forest. Antlers grow from his head, as on an elk." Ehawk looked frankly at the knight. "They say he was here before the saints, before anything, when there was only the forest, and it covered all the world."

Sir Oneu nodded as if he already knew that. "And why does he wake?" he asked. "What does prophecy say he will do?"

"It's his forest," Ehawk said. "He'll do what he wants. But it's said when he wakes, the forest will rise against those who have done it harm." He cut his eyes away. "It's why the Sefry left. They fear he will kill us all."

"And do you fear that?"

"I don't know. I only know . . ." He broke off, uncertain how to put it.

"Go on."

"I had an uncle. A sickness came to him. There was little to see— no sores nor open wounds, no marks of fever—but he grew more tired as the months passed, and his eyes dulled. His skin paled. He died very slowly, and it was only near the end that we could smell the death in him."

"I'm sorry to hear that."

Ehawk shrugged. "The forest—I think it's dying like that."

"How do you know?"

"I can smell it."

"Ah." The knight seemed to mull that over for a few minutes, and so they rode in silence.

"This Mosslord," Sir Oneu said at last. "Have you ever heard him called the Briar King?"

"That's what the Oostish call him, Sir Oneu."

Sir Oneu sighed, and looked older. "I thought as much."

"Is that what you're looking for in the forest, sir? The Briar King?"

"Yes."

"Then—"

But Martyn cut him off suddenly. "Sir Oneu?" the monk's face was set in hard lines.

"Yes, Brother?"

"I hear them again."

"Where?"

"Everywhere. In all directions now. Coming closer."

"What is it, Martyn? Can you tell me what we face? Minions of the Briar King?"

"I don't know, Sir Oneu. I only know we are surrounded."

"Ehawk? Is there aught you can tell us?"

"No, sir. I can't hear anything yet."

But soon enough he did. The wood stirred all around them, as if the trees themselves had come alive. Ehawk felt as if the forest was tightening, the trees standing ever closer together, a great trap closing on the company. The horses began to whicker nervously, even Airece, Sir Oneu's warsteed.

"Ready yourselves, lads," Sir Oneu muttered.

Ehawk caught glimpses of them now, the figures in the trees. They grunted and growled like beasts, they croaked and mewed, but they looked like men and women, naked or wearing only the uncured skins of beasts.

Sir Oneu increased his pace to a trot, indicating that the others in the party should do the same. He lifted his heavy ashe spear. Ahead, on the trail, Ehawk saw that someone was awaiting them.

His heart was a cricket in his breast as they drew near. There were seven of them, some men, some women, cut and bruised and naked as the day they were born—all save one. He stood in front, a lion-skin thrown over one shoulder like a cloak. From his head grew spreading antlers.

"Etthoroam!" Ehawk gasped. He could no longer feel his knees clasping his horse.

"No," Martyn said. "It is a man. The antlers are part of a head-dress."

Ehawk, trying to control his growing terror, saw that Martyn was right. But that didn't mean anything. Etthoroam was a sorcerer. He could take any form.

"You're certain?" Sir Oneu asked Martyn, perhaps sharing Ehawk's doubts.

"He has the smell of a man," Martyn said.

"They're everywhere," Gavrel muttered, jerking his head from side to side, peering at the forest. The other three monks, Ehawk noticed, had strung their bows and formed a loose perimeter around the group.

Martyn brought his mount alongside Ehawk's. "Keep near me," he said, voice very low.

"Ehawk, m' lad," Sir Oneu said. "Could those be the villagers?"

Ehawk studied the faces of those who stood with the antlered man. Their eyes were very strange, unfocused, as if they were drunk or entranced. Their hair was matted and tangled.

"I reckon they might be," he answered. "It's hard to say, them lookin' like that."

Sir Oneu nodded and drew to a halt ten yards from the strangers. It was suddenly so still, Ehawk could hear the breeze in the highest branches.

"I am Sir Oneu de Loingvele," the knight called in a clear, carrying voice, "a peer of the church on a holy mission. Whom do I have the honor of addressing?"

The stag-horned figure grinned and raised his fists so they could see the snakes he held writhing in them.

"Look at their eyes," Gavrel said, drawing his sword. He sounded grim. "They are mad."

"Hold your hand," Sir Oneu said. He rested his palm on his pommel and leaned forward. "That's a clever reply," the knight said loudly. "Most would give a name or speak some vapid greeting. You, with your deer-horn cap, you're too clever for that. Instead, you shake snakes at me. Very cunning, I must say. A most excellent reply. I await your next witticism with utmost eagerness."

The antlered man merely blinked, as if Sir Oneu's words were so many raindrops.

"You're quite senseless, aren't you?" Sir Oneu asked.

This time the horned man crooked his head back, so his mouth opened to the sky, and he howled.

Three bows hummed together. Ehawk jerked around at the sound and saw that three of the monks were firing into the forest. The naked and half-naked figures that had been drifting through the trees were suddenly charging. Ehawk watched as one of them fell, an arrow in her neck. She was pretty, or had been. Now she spasmed on the ground like a wounded deer.

"Flank me, Brother Gavrel," Sir Oneu said. He dropped his lance level to the party on the trail. Like their brethren in the woods, they were unarmed, and the sight of a fully armored knight ought to have shaken them, but instead, one of the women sprang forward and ran upon the spear. It hit her with such force that the spearhead broke through her back, but she clawed at the shaft as if she might drag herself up its length to the knight who had killed her.

Sir Oneu cursed and drew his broadsword. He hacked down the first man leaping for him, and the next, but more and more of the madmen came pouring from the woods. The three monks kept firing at a rate Ehawk deemed impossible, yet already most of their shafts were hitting almost point-blank, and the sides of the trail were quickly heaped with dead.

Martyn, Gavrel, and Sir Oneu drew swords, now trading places with the archers, forming a circle around them to give them space to fire. Ehawk was crowded into the center of the ring. Belatedly, he took out his own bow and put an arrow to it, but with all the jostling chaos, it was hard to find a shot.

They had more attackers than Ehawk could count, but those were all unarmed.

Then that changed, suddenly, as someone seemed to remember how to throw a stone. The first rock belled from Sir Oneu's helm and did no damage, but soon there came a hail of them. Meanwhile, the enemy had begun a kind of wordless chant or keening. It rose and fell like the call of the whippoorwill.

Brother Alvaer staggered as a stone struck his forehead and blood sprayed from the cut. He raised a hand to wipe his eyes, and in that brief pause, a giant of a man yanked at his arm, pulling him into the sea of rabid faces.

Ehawk had never seen the sea, of course, but he could imagine it from Sir Oneu's vivid descriptions—like a lake that rose and fell. Alvaer was like a man drowning in such water. He fought his way above the waves and was pulled down again. He reappeared once more, farther away and very bloody. Ehawk thought the monk was missing an eye.

Alvaer struggled back up a final time—and then was gone.

Meanwhile, the other monks and Sir Oneu continued the slaughter, but bodies were piling too thick for the horses to move. Gavrel was next to die, pulled into the throng and torn limb from limb.

"They will overwhelm us!" Sir Oneu shouted. "We must break free." He urged Airece forward, his sword arm rising and falling, hewing limbs that grappled at him and his mount. Ehawk's pony screamed and pranced, and suddenly a man was there, tearing at Ehawk's leg with filthy, ragged nails. He shouted, dropped his bow, and yanked out his dirk. He stabbed and felt rather than saw the blade cut. The man ignored him and leapt up, caught Ehawk by the arm, and began to pull with hideous strength.

Then suddenly Martyn was beside him, and the attacker's head bouncing on the ground. Ehawk watched with detached fascination.

He looked back up in time to see Sir Oneu go down, three men attached to his sword arm and two more tugging at him. He shouted in anguish as they pulled him from his horse. The monks fought forward, moving with absurd speed, striking, it seemed, in all directions at once.

They did not reach Sir Oneu in time. A rock hit Ehawk in the shoulder; several struck Martyn, one in the head. He swayed for just an instant, but kept in his saddle.

"Follow me," Martyn told Ehawk. "Do not flinch."

He wheeled his horse away from his two brothers and plunged off the trail. Dazed, Ehawk never considered disobeying. Martyn's sword whirled too quickly to be seen, and the monk had chosen his direction wisely, picking the point where the attackers were thinnest. Beyond the battle was a broad stream.

They plunged into the water, and their steeds sank deep and began to swim. They managed the other side, where the slope was gentle and their mounts found purchase.

A look back showed their attackers already following.

Martyn reached over and took Ehawk by the shoulder. "News of this must reach the praifec. Do you understand? Praifec Hespero, in Eslen. It's much for me to ask of you, but you must swear to do it."

"Eslen? I can't go to Eslen. It's too far, and I don't know the way."

"You must. You must, Ehawk. I lay it as a dying *geos* on you."

Several of their pursuers splashed into the stream, swimming clumsily.

"Go with me," Ehawk desperately begged. "I cannot do it without you."

"I'll follow if I can, but I must hold them here, and you must ride as hard as that horse will take you. Here." He detached a pouch from his belt and thrust it into Ehawk's hand. "There's coin there, not much. Spend it wisely. Within is also a letter with a seal. That will get you before the praifec. Tell him what we've seen here. Do not fail. Now *go!*"

Then he had to turn to meet the first of the madmen emerging from the stream. He split the fellow's skull like a melon, then shifted his footing and prepared to meet the next.

"Go!" he shouted, without looking back. "Or we all have died in vain."

Something snapped in Ehawk then, and he spurred his horse and rode until the mare stumbled in exhaustion. Even then, he did not stop, but kept the poor beast at what pace it could maintain. Sobs tore from his chest until it ached, and then the stars came out.

He rode always west, for he knew it was somewhere in that direction that Eslen lay.

PART **I**

SHADOW DAYS

The Year 2,223 of Everon
The Month of Novmen

The last day of Otavmen is the day of Saint Temnos.
The first six days in Novmen are, in their turn, Saint
Dun, Saint Under, Saint Shade, Saint Mefitis, Saint
Gavriel, and Saint Halaqin. Taken together, these are
the Shadow Days, where the World of the Quick meets
the World of the Dead.

—FROM *THE ALMANACK OF PRESSON MANTEO*

And after twelve long months he grieved
His lover's ghost rose from the deep
What do you want from me my love
That troubles my eternal sleep?

I want a kiss, oh love of mine
A single kiss from thee
And then I'll trouble you no more
I'll let you sleep in peace

My breath is ice and sea my love
My lips are cold as clay

And if you kiss my salt wet lips
You'll never live another day

—FROM "THE DROWNED LOVER," A FOLK SONG OF VIRGENYA

He shall be cursed to live, and thus bring ruin to life.

—TRANSLATED FROM THE *TAFLES TACEIS* OR *BOOK OF MURMURS*

CHAPTER ONE

THE NIGHT

NEIL MEQVREN RODE WITH his queen down a dark street in the city of the dead. The tattoo of their horses' hooves was drowned by hail shattering on lead cobbles. The wind was a dragon heaving its misty coils and lashing its wet tail. Ghosts began to stir, and beneath Neil's burnished breastplate, beneath his chilled skin and cage of bone, worry clenched.

He did not mind the wind or frozen rain. His homeland was Skern, where the frost and the sea and the clouds were all the same, where ice and pain were the simplest facts of life. The dead did not bother him either.

It was the living he feared, the knives and darts the dark and weather hid from his merely human eyes. It would take so little to kill his queen—the prick of a tiny needle, a hole the size of a little finger in her heart, a sling-flung stone to her temple. How could he protect her? How could he keep safe the only thing he had left?

He glanced at her; she was obscured in a wool weather-cloak, her face shadowed deep in the cowl. A similar cloak covered his own lord's plate and helm. They might appear to be any two pilgrims, come to see their ancestors—or so he hoped. If those who wanted the queen dead were grains of sand, there would be strand enough to beach a war galley.

They crossed stone bridges over black water canals that caught bits of the fire from their lantern and stirred them into gauzy yellow webs. The houses of the dead huddled between the waterways, peaked roofs shedding the storm, keeping their quiet inhabitants dry if not warm. A few lights moved elsewhere between the lanes—the queen, it seemed, was not the only one undeterred by the weather, determined to seek the company of the dead this night. The dead could be spoken to on any night, of course, but on the last night of Otavmen—Saint Temnosnaht—the dead might speak back.

Up the hill in Eslen-of-the-Quick, they were feasting, and until the storm came, the streets had been filled with dancers in skeleton costume and somber Sverrun priests chanting the forty hymns of Temnos. Skull-masked petitioners went from house to house, begging soulcakes, and bonfires burned in public squares, the largest in the great assembly ground known as the Candle Grove. Now the feasts had gone inside homes and taverns, and the procession that would have wound its way to the Eslen-of-Shadows had shrunk from a river to a brooh in the fierce face of winter's arrival. The little lamps carved of turnips and apples were all dark, and there would be little in the way of festival here tonight.

Neil kept his hand on the pommel of his broadsword, Crow, and his eyes were restless. He did not watch the moving light of the lanterns, but the darkness that stretched between. If something came for her, it would likely come from there.

The houses grew larger and taller as they passed the third and fourth canals, and then they came to the final circle, walled in granite and iron spears, where the statues of Saint Dun and Saint Under watched over palaces of marble and alabaster. Here, a lantern approached them.

"Keep your cowl drawn, milady," Neil told the queen.

"It is only one of the scathomen, who guard the tombs," she answered.

"That may or may not be," Neil replied.

He trotted Hurricane up a few paces. "Who's there?" he called.

The lantern lifted, and in its light, an angular, middle-aged face appeared from the shadows of a weather-cloak. Neil's breath sat a little easier in his lungs, for he knew this man—Sir Len, indeed, one of the scathomen who dedicated their lives to the dead.

Of course, the appearance of a man and what was inside him were two different things, as Neil had learned from bitter experience. So he remained wary.

"I must ask you the same question," the old knight replied to Neil's question.

Neil rode nearer. "It is the queen," he told the man.

"I must see her face," Sir Len said. "Tonight of all nights, everything must be proper."

"All shall be proper," the queen's voice came as she lifted her lantern and drew back the deep hood of her cloak.

Her face appeared, beautiful and hard as the ice falling from the sky.

"I know you, lady," Sir Len said. "You may pass. But . . ." His words seemed to go off with the wind.

"Do not question Her Majesty," Neil cautioned stiffly.

The old knight's eyes speared at Neil. "I knew your queen when she wore toddling clothes," he said, "when you were never born nor even thought of."

"Sir Neil is my knight," the queen said. "He is my protector."

"Auy. Then away from here he should take you. You should not come to this place, lady, when the dead speak. No good shall come of it. I have watched here long enough to know that."

The queen regarded Sir Len for a long moment. "Your advice is well-intended," she said, "but I will disregard it. Please question me no more."

Sir Len bowed to his knee. "I shall not, my queen."

"I am queen no longer," she said softly. "My husband is dead. There is no queen in Eslen."

"As you live, lady, there is a queen," the old knight replied. "In truth, if not in law."

She nodded her head slightly, and they passed into the houses of the royal dead without another word.

They moved under the wrought-iron pastato of a large house of red marble, where they tethered the horses, and with the turn of an iron key left the freezing rain outside. Within the doors they found a small foyer with an altar and a hall that led into the depths of the building. Someone had lit the hall tapers already, though shadows still clung like cobwebs in the corners.

"What shall I do, lady?" Neil asked.

"Keep guard," she answered. "That is all."

She knelt at the altar and lit the candles.

"Fathers and mothers of the house Dare," she sang, "your adopted daughter is calling, humble before her elders. Honor me, I beg you, this night of all nights."

Now she lit a small wand of incense, and an aroma like pine and liquidambar seemed to explode in Neil's nostrils.

Somewhere in the house, something rustled, and a chime sounded.

Muriele rose and removed her weather-cloak. Beneath was a gown of boned black safnite. Her raven hair seemed to blend into it, making an orphan of her face, which appeared almost to float. Neil's throat caught. The queen was beautiful beyond compare, and age had done little to diminish her beauty, but it was not that which twisted Neil's heart—rather, it was that for just an instant she resembled someone else.

Neil turned his gaze away, searching the shadows.

The queen started up the corridor.

"If I may, Majesty," he said quickly. "I would precede you."

She hesitated. "You are my servant, and my husband's kin will see you as such. You must walk behind me."

"Lady, if there is ambush ahead—"

"I will chance it," she replied.

They moved down a hall paneled in bas-reliefs depicting the deeds of the house Dare. The queen walked with measured step, head bowed, and her footsteps echoed clearly, despite the distant hammering of the storm on the slate roof.

They entered a great chamber with vaulted ceilings where a long table was prepared, thirty places set with crystal goblets. In each, wine as red as blood had been poured. The queen paced by the chairs, searching, until she found the one she sought, and then she sat, staring at the wine.

Outside the wind groaned.

Long moments passed, and then a bell sounded, and another. Twelve in all, and with the midnight stroke, the queen drank from the cup.

Neil felt something pass in the air, a chill, a humming.

Then the queen began to speak, in a voice deeper and huskier than usual. The hairs on Neil's neck prickled at the sound of it.

"Muriele," she said. "My queen."

And then, as if answering herself, she spoke in her more usual tone. "Erren, my friend."

"Your servant," the deeper voice replied. "How fare you? Did I fail?"

"I live," Muriele answered. "Your sacrifice was not in vain."

"But your daughters are here, in this place of dust."

Neil's heartbeat quickened, and he realized he had moved. He was standing near one of the chairs, staring at the wine.

"All of them?"

"No. But Fastia is here, and sweet Elseny. They wear shrouds, Muriele. I failed them—and you."

"We were betrayed," Muriele replied. "You did all you could, gave all you could. I cannot blame you. But I must know about Anne."

"Anne . . ." The voice sighed off. "We forget, Muriele. The dead forget. It is like a cloud, a mist that eats more of us each day. Anne . . ."

"My youngest daughter. Anne. I sent her to the coven of Saint Cer, and no word has come from there. I must know if the assassins found her there."

"Your husband is dead," the voice called Erren replied. "He does not sleep here, but calls from far away. His voice is faint, and sad. Lonely. He did love you."

"William? Can you speak to him?"

"He is too distant. He cannot find his way here. The paths are dark, you know. The whole world is dark, and the wind is strong."

"But Anne—you cannot hear her whisper?"

"I remember her now," Erren crooned, in the queen's voice. "Hair like strawberry. Always trouble. Your favorite."

"Does she live, Erren? I must know."

Silence then, and to his surprise Neil found the glass of wine in his hand. It was only distantly that he heard the reply.

"I believe she lives. It is cold here, Muriele."

More was said, but Neil did not hear it, for he raised the cup before him and drank.

He set the cup on the table as he swallowed the bitter sip he'd taken. He stared into the remaining wine, which calmed and became a red mirror. He saw himself in it; his father's strong jaw was there, but his blue eyes were black pits and his wheat hair ruddy, as if he examined a portrait painted in blood.

Then someone stood behind him, and a hand fell on his shoulder. "Do not turn," a feminine voice whispered.

"Fastia?"

But now he saw her face instead of his mirrored in the wine. He smelled her lavender fragrance.

"I was called that, wasn't I?" Fastia said. "And you were my love."

He tried to face her then, but the hand tightened on his shoulder. "Do not," she said. "Do not look at me."

His hand trembled the wineglass, but the image of her in it remained untroubled. She smiled faintly, but her eyes were lamps burning sadness.

"I wish . . . ," he began, but could not finish.

"Yes," she said. "So do I. But it could not have been, you know. We were foolish."

"And I let you die."

"I don't remember that. I remember you holding me in your arms. Cradled, like a child. I was happy. That is all I remember, and soon I will not even remember that. But it is enough. It is almost enough." Fingers traced chills on the back of his neck. "I must know if you loved me," she whispered.

"I have never loved anyone as I loved you," Neil said. "I shall never love another."

"You will," she said softly. "You must. But do not forget me, for I will forget myself, in time."

"I would never," he said, vaguely aware that tears were coursing down his face. A drop fell into the wine, and the shade of Fastia gasped. "That is cold," she said. "Your tears are cold, Sir Neil."

"I am sorry," he said. "I'm sorry for everything, milady. I cannot sleep—"

"Hush, love. Quiet, and let me tell you something while I still remember. It's about Anne."

"The queen is here, asking about Anne."

"I know. She speaks to Erren. But there is this, Sir Neil, a thing I have been told. Anne is important. More important than my mother or my brother—or any other. She must not die, or all is lost."

"All?"

"The age of Everon is ending," she said. "Ancient evils and fresh curses speed it. My mother broke the law of death, did you know?"

"The law of death?"

"It is broken," she affirmed.

"I don't understand."

"Nor do I, but it is whispered in the halls of bone. The world is now in motion, rushing toward its end. All who live stand at the edge of night, and if they pass, none shall follow them. No children, no generations to come. Someone is standing there, watching them pass, laughing. Man or woman I do not know, but there is little chance they can be stopped. There is only the smallest opportunity to set things right. But without Anne, even that possibility does not exist."

"Without you, I do not care. I do not care if the world goes into oblivion."

The hand came onto his shoulder and stroked across the back of his neck. "You must," she said. "Think of the generations unborn and think of them as our children, the children we could never have. Think of them as the offspring of our love. Live for them as you would for me."

"Fastia—" He turned then, unable to bear it any longer, but there was nothing there, and the touch on his shoulder was gone, leaving only a fading tingle.

The queen was still staring at her wine, whispering.

"I miss you, Erren," she said. "You were my strong right hand, my sister, my friend. Enemies surround me. I don't have the strength for it."

"There is no end to your strength," Erren replied. "You will do what must be done."

"But what you showed me. The blood. How can I do that?"

"You will make seas of blood in the end," Erren said. "But it is necessary. You must."

"I cannot. They would never allow it."

"When the time comes, they cannot stop you. Now hush, Muriele, and bid me peace, for I must go."

"Do not. I need you, especially now."

"Then I've failed you twice. I must go."

And the queen, who these past months might have been forged of steel, put her head down and wept. Neil stood by, his heart savaged by Fastia's touch, his mind burning with her words.

He wished for the simplicity of battle, where failure meant death rather than torment.

Outside, the sounds of the storm grew stronger as the dead returned to their sleep.

Sleep never came, but morning did. By the sun's first light the storm was gone, and they began the ascent from Eslen-of-Shadows to Eslen-of-the-Quick. A clean, cold sea wind was blowing, and the bare branches of the oaks lining the path glistened in sheaths of ice.

The queen had been silent all night, but while they were still some distance from the city gates she turned to him.

"Sir Neil, I have a task for you."

"Majesty, I am yours to command."

She nodded. "You must find Anne. You must find the only daughter I have left."

Neil gripped his reins tighter. "That is the one thing I cannot do, Majesty."

"It is my command."

"My duty is to Your Majesty. When the king knighted me, I was sworn to stay at your side, to protect you from all danger. I cannot do that if I am traveling afar."

"The king is dead," Muriele said, her voice growing a bit harsher. "I command you now. You will do this thing for me, Sir Neil."

"Majesty, please do not ask this of me. If harm should befall you—"

"You are the only one I can trust," Muriele interrupted. "Do you think I *want* to send you from my side? To send away the one person I know will never betray me? But that is why you must go. Those who killed my other daughters now seek Anne—I'm certain of it. She remains alive because I sent her away, and no one at the court knows where she is. If I trust any other than you with her location, I compromise that knowledge and open my daughter to even greater danger. If I tell only you, I know the secret is still safe."

"If you believe her secure where she is, should you not leave her there?"

"I cannot be sure. Erren intimated that the danger is still great."

"The danger to Your Majesty is great. Whoever employed the assassins that slew your husband and daughters meant to kill you, as well. They still do, surely."

"Surely. I am not arguing with you, Sir Neil. But I have given my command. You will make ready for a long journey. You will leave tomorrow. Pick the men who will guard me in your absence—I trust your judgment more than my own in such matters. But for your own task you must travel alone, I fear."

Neil bowed his head. "Yes, Majesty."

The queen's voice softened. "I am sorry, Sir Neil. I truly am. I know how badly your heart has been hurt. I know how keen your sense of duty is and how terribly it was wounded at Cal Azroth. But you must do this thing for me. Please."

"Majesty, I would beg all day if I thought you would change your mind, but I see that you won't."

"You have good vision."

Neil nodded. "I will do as you command, Majesty. I will be ready by morning."

z'Espino

Anne Dare, youngest daughter of the Emperor of Crotheny, Duchess of Rovy, knelt by a cistern and scrubbed clothes with raw and blistered hands. Her shoulders ached and her knees hurt, and the sun beat her like a golden hammer.

Only a few yards away, children played in the cool shade of a grape arbor, and two ladies in gowns of silk brocade sat sipping wine. Anne's own dress—a secondhand shift of cotton—hadn't been washed in days. She sighed, wiped her brow, and made sure her red hair was secure beneath her scarf. She sneaked a longing glance at the two women and continued her work.

She cast her mind away from her hands, a trick she was becoming quite adept at, and imagined herself back home, riding her horse Faster on the Sleeve or eating roasted quail and trout in green sauce, with gobs of fried apples and clotted cream for desert.

Scrub, scrub, went her hands.

She was imagining a cool bath when she suddenly felt a sharp pinch on her rump. She turned to find a boy about four or five years younger than she—perhaps thirteen—grinning as if he'd just told the best joke in the world.

Anne slapped the clothes onto the scrubbing board and spun on him. "You horrible little beast!" she shouted. "You've no more manners than—!"

She caught the women looking at her then, their faces hard.

"He pinched me," she explained. And just to be sure they understood, she pointed. "*There.*"

One of the women—a blue-eyed, black-haired casnara named da Filialofia—merely slitted her eyes. "Who exactly do you think you are?" she asked, her tone quite flat. "Who, by all the lords and ladies in earth and sky, do you think you are that you can speak to my son in such a manner?"

"Wherever do you find such servants?" her companion Casnara dat Ospellina asked sourly.

"But h-he—," Anne stuttered.

"Be silent this instant, you little piece of foreign trash, or I will have Corhio the gardener beat you. And he will do quite more to you *there* than pinch it, I daresay. Forget not whom you serve, whose house you are in."

"A proper lady would raise her brat to have better manners," Anne snapped.

"And what would you know of that?" da Filialofia asked, crossing her arms. "What sort of manners do you imagine you were taught in whatever brothel or pigsty your mother abandoned you to? Certainly, you did not learn to mind your place." Her chin tilted up. "Get out. Now."

Anne picked herself up from her kneeling position. "Very well," she said, facing them squarely. She held out her hand.

Da Filialofia laughed. "Surely you don't think I'm going to pay you for insulting my house, do you? Leave, wretch. I've no idea why my husband hired you in the first place." But then she cracked a faint smile that didn't even hint at good humor. "Well, perhaps I do. He might have found you entertaining, in a barbaric sort of way. Were you?"

For a long moment Anne was simply speechless, and for a moment longer she was poised between slapping the woman—which she knew *would* earn her a beating—and simply walking away.

She didn't quite do either. Instead she recalled something she learned in her last week working at the triva.

"Oh, no, he has no time for *me*," she said sweetly. "He's been much too busy with Casnara dat Ospellina."

And then she did walk away, smiling at the furious whispers that began behind her.

The great estates lay on the north side of z'Espino, most of them over-looking the azure water of the Lier Sea. As Anne passed through the gate of the house, she stood for a moment in the shade of chestnut trees and gazed out across those foam-crested waters. North across them lay Liery, where her mother's family ruled. North and east was Crotheny, were her father sat as king and emperor, and where her love, Roderick, must be giving up hope by now.

Just a little water separating her from her rightful station and everything she loved, and yet that little bit of water was expensive to cross. Princess though she was, she was penniless. Nor could she tell anyone who she was, for she had come to z'Espino with terrible danger on her heels. She was safer as a washerwoman than as a princess.

"You." A man on a horse rode up the lane and sat looking down at her. She recognized by his square cap and yellow tunic that he was an *aidilo,* charged with keeping order in the streets.

"Yes, casnar?"

"Move along. Don't tarry here," he said brusquely.

"I've just come from serving the casnara da Filialofia."

"Yes, and now you're done, so you must go."

"I only wanted to look at the sea for a moment."

"Then look at it from the fish market," he snapped. "Must I escort you there?"

"No," Anne said, "I'm going."

As she trudged down a lane bounded by stone walls topped with shards of broken glass to prevent climbing, she wondered if the servants who worked on her father's country estates were treated so shabbily. Surely not.

The lane debouched onto the Piato dachi Meddissos, a grand court of red brick bounded on one side by the three-story palace of the meddisso and his family. It wasn't so grand as her father's palace in Eslen, but it was quite striking, with its long colonnade and terrace gardens. On the other side of the piato stood the city temple, an elegant and very ancient-looking building of polished umber stone.

The piato itself was a riot of color and life. Vendors with wooden carts and red caps hawked grilled lamb, fried fish, steamed mussels, candied figs, and roasted chestnuts. Pale-eyed Sefry, hooded and wrapped against the sun, sold ribbons and trifles, stockings, holy relics, and love potions from beneath colorful awnings. A troop of actors had cleared a space and were performing something involving sword fighting, a king with a dragon's tail, Saint Mamres, Saint Bright, and Saint Loy. Two pipers and a woman with a hand-drum beat a fast melody.

In the center of the piato, a stern-eyed statue of Saint Netuno wrestled two sea serpents, which twined about his body and spewed jets of water into a marble basin. A group of richly dressed young men lounged at the edge of the fountain, fondling their sword hilts and whistling at girls in gaudy dresses.

She found Austra near the edge of the square, almost on the steps of the temple, sitting next to her bucket and scrub brush.

Austra watched her approach and smiled. "Finished already?" Austra was fifteen, a year younger than Anne, and like Anne she wore a faded dress and a scarf to cover her hair. Most Vitellians were dark, with black hair, and the two girls stood out enough without advertising their gold and copper tresses. Fortunately, most women in Vitellio kept their heads covered in public.

"In a manner of speaking," Anne said.

"Oh, I see. Again?"

Anne sighed and sat down. "I try, truthfully I do. But it's so difficult. I thought the coven had prepared me for anything, but—"

"You shouldn't have to do these things," Austra said. "Let me work. You stay in the room."

"But if I don't work, it will take us that much longer to earn our passage. It will give the men who are hunting us that much more time to find us."

"Maybe we should take our chances on the road."

"Cazio and z'Acatto say the roads are much too closely watched. Even the road officers are offering reward for me now."

Austra looked skeptical. "That doesn't make sense. The men who tried to kill you at the coven were Hansan knights. What do they have to do with Vitellian road officers?"

"I don't know, and neither does Cazio."

"If that's the case, won't they be watching the ships, as well?"

"Yes, but Cazio says he can find a captain who won't ask questions or tell tales—if we have the silver to pay him off." She sighed. "But that's not yet, and we have to eat, too. Worse, I was paid nothing today. What am I going to do tomorrow?"

Austra patted her shoulder. "I got paid. We'll stop at the fish market and the carenso and buy our supper."

The fishmarket was located at the edge of Perto Nevo, where the tall-masted ships brought their cargoes of timber and iron, and took in return casks of wine, olive oil, wheat, and silk. Smaller boats crowded the southern jetties, for the Vitellian waters teemed with shrimp, mussels, oysters, sardines, and a hundred other sorts of fish Anne had never heard of. The market itself was a maze of crates and barrels heaped with gleaming sea prizes. Anne looked longingly at the giant prawns and black crabs—which were still kicking and writhing in tuns of brine—and at the heaps of sleek mackerel and silver tuna. They couldn't afford any of that and had to push deeper and farther, to where sardines lay sprinkled in salt and whiting was stacked in piles that had begun to smell.

The whiting was only two minsers per coinix, and it was there the girls stopped, noses wrinkled, to choose their evening meal.

"Z'Acatto said to look at the eyes," Austra said. "If they're cloudy or cross-eyed, they're no good."

"This whole bunch is bad, then," Anne said.

"It's the only thing we can afford," Austra replied. "There must be one or two good ones in the pile. We just have to look."

"What about salt cod?"

"That has to soak for a day. I don't know about you, but I'm hungry now."

A low feminine voice chuckled over their shoulders. "No, sweets, don't buy any of that. You'll be sick for a nineday."

The woman speaking to them was familiar—Anne had seen her

often on their street, but had never spoken to her. She dressed scandalously and wore a great deal of rouge and makeup. She'd once heard z'Acatto say he "couldn't afford that one," so Anne figured she knew the woman's profession.

"Thanks," Anne said, "but we'll find a good one."

The woman looked dubious. She had a strong, lean face and eyes of jet. Her hair was put up in a net that sparkled with glass jewels, and she wore a green gown, which, though it had seen better days, was still nicer than anything Anne owned at the moment.

"You two live on Six-Nymph Street. I've seen you—with that old drunkard and the handsome fellow, the one with the sword."

"Yes," Anne replied.

"I'm your neighbor. My name is Rediana."

"I'm Feine and this is Lessa," Anne lied.

"Well, girls, come with me," Rediana said, her voice low. "You'll find nothing edible here."

Anne hesitated.

"I'll not bite you," Rediana said. "Come."

Motioning them to follow, she led the two back to a table of flounder. Some were still flopping.

"We can't afford that," Anne said.

"How much do you have?"

Austra held out a ten-minser coin. Rediana nodded.

"Parvio!" The man behind the tray of flounder was busy gutting a few fish for several well-dressed women. He was missing one eye, but didn't bother to cover the white scar there. He might have been sixty years old, but his bare arms were muscled like a wrestler's.

"Rediana, *mi cara*," he said. "What can I do for you?"

"Sell my friends a fish." She took the coin from Austra's hand and passed it to him. He looked at it, frowned, then smiled at Anne and Austra. "Take whichever pleases you, dears."

"*Melto brazi,* casnar," Austra said. She selected one of the flounders and put it in her basket. With a wink, Parvio handed her back a five-minser coin. The fish ought to have cost fifteen.

"*Melto brazi,* casnara," Anne told Rediana, as they started toward the carenso.

"It's nothing, dear," Rediana said. "Actually, I've been hoping for a chance to talk to you."

"Oh. About what?" Anne asked, a tad suspicious of the woman's goodwill.

"About a way you could put fish like that on the table every day. You're both quite pretty, and quite exotic. I can make something out of you. Not for those oafs on our street, either, but for a better class of client."

"You—you want us to—?"

"It's only difficult the first time," Rediana promised. "And not so hard as that. The money is easy, and you've got that young swordsman to look out for you, if you come across a rough customer. He works for me already, you know."

"Cazio?"

"Yes. He looks after some of the girls."

"And he put you up to this?"

She shook her head. "No. He said you would turn your noses up at me. But men often don't know what they're talking about."

"He does this time," Anne said, her voice frosty. "Thank you very much for your help with the fish, but I'm afraid we must decline your offer."

Rediana's eyes sharpened. "You think you're too good for it?"

"Of course," Anne said, before she could think better of it.

"I *see*."

"No," Anne said. "No, you don't. I think you're too good for it, too. No woman should have to do that."

That put a queer little smile on Rediana's face. But she shrugged. "Still you don't know what's best for you. You could earn more in a day than you do now in a month, and not ruin your looks with scrubwork. Think about it. If you change your mind, I'm easy enough to find." With that, she sauntered off.

The two girls walked in silence for a few moments after Rediana left them. Then Austra cleared her throat. "Anne, *I* could—"

"No," Anne said angrily. "Thrice no. I would rather we never made it home, than on those terms."

◇ ◇ ◇

Anne was still fuming when they reached the carenso at the corner of Pari Street and the Vio Furo, but the smell of baking bread put everything from her mind but her hunger. The baker—a tall, gaunt man always covered in flour—gave them a friendly smile as they entered. He was slashing the tops of uncooked country loaves with a razor while behind him his assistant slid others into the oven on a long-handled peel. A large black dog lying on the floor looked up sleepily at the girls and put his head back down, thoroughly uninterested.

Bread was piled high in baskets and bins, in all shapes and sizes— golden brown round loaves the size of wagon wheels and decorated with the semblance of olive leaves, rough logs as long as an arm, smaller perechi you could wrap one hand around, crusty egg-shaped rolls dappled with oats—and that was just at first glance.

They spent two minsers on a warm loaf and turned their feet toward the Perto Veto, where their lodgings were located.

There they walked streets bounded by once-grand houses with marble-columned pastatos and balconied upper windows, picking their way through a shatter of unreplaced roof tiles and wine carafes, breathing air gravid with the scents of brine and sewage.

It was four bells, and women with low-cut blouses and coral-red lips—ladies of Rediana's profession—were already gathered on the upper-story balconies, calling to men who seemed as if they might have money and taunting those who did not. A knot of men on a cracked marble stoop passed around a jug of wine and whistled at Anne and Austra as they went by.

"It's the Duchess of Herilanz," one of the men shouted. "Hey, Duchess, give us a kiss."

Anne ignored him. In her month quartered in the Perto Veto, she had determined that most such men were harmless, though annoying.

At the next cross-street they turned up an avenue, entered a building through an open door, and climbed the stairs to their second-floor apartment. As they approached, Anne heard voices above— z'Acatto and someone else.

The door was open, and z'Acatto glanced up as they entered. He was an older man, perhaps fifty, a bit paunchy, his hair more gray than black. He sat on a stool talking to their landlord, Ospero. The men were of about the same age, but Ospero was nearly bald, and stockier yet. They both looked pretty drunk, and the three empty wine carafes that lay on the floor confirmed that impression. There was nothing unusual about that—z'Acatto stayed drunk most of the time.

"*Dena dicolla,* casnaras," z'Acatto said.

"Good evening, z'Acatto," Anne returned, "Casnar Ospero."

"You're home early," z'Acatto noticed.

"Yes." She didn't elaborate.

"We brought fish and bread," Austra said brightly.

"That's good, that's good," the old man said. "We'll need a white with that, perhaps a vino verio."

"I'm sorry," Austra said. "We didn't have money for wine."

Ospero grunted and produced a silver menza. He squinted at it, then flipped it toward Austra. "That for the wine, my pretty della." He paused a bit to leer at the two girls, then shook his head. "You know the place by Dank Moon Street? Escerros? Tell him I sent you. Tell him that will buy two bottles of the vino verio, or I'll come crack his head."

"But I was—," Austra began.

"Go on, Austra. I'll cook the fish," Anne said. She didn't like Ospero. There seemed something vaguely criminal about him and his friends. On the other hand, z'Acatto had somehow managed to convince him to rent them their rooms on credit for a week, and he had never done more than leer at her. They relied on his good graces, so she held her tongue.

She went to the cramped pantry and took out a jar of olive oil and a pouch of salt. She put a little of the oil into a small earthenware *crematro*, sprinkled both sides of the fish with salt, and placed it in the oil. She stared despondently at the preparation, wishing for the hundredth time that they could afford—or even *find*—butter for a change. Then she sighed, put the lid on the crematro, and carried it back down the stairs, then through an inner first floor door into the small courtyard that was shared by the building's inhabitants.

A few women were gathered around a small pit of glowing coals. There wasn't yet room for her dish, so she took a bench and waited, gazing absently around the dreary walls of flaking stucco, trying to imagine it as the orchard courtyard in her father's castle.

A male voice foiled her attempt. "Good evening, della."

"Hello, Cazio," she said without turning.

"How are you this evening?"

"Tired."

She noticed there was room at the fire now, and stood to take the crematro over to it, but Cazio interposed himself.

"Let me," he said.

Cazio was tall and lean, only slightly older than Anne, dressed in dark brown doublet and scarlet hose. A rapier in a battered scabbard hung at his side. His dark eyes peered down at her from a narrow, handsome face. "Your day didn't go well?"

"Not as well as yours, I'm sure," she replied, handing him the crematro.

"What do you mean by that?"

"I mean the work you've chosen must give you ample opportunity for refreshment."

He looked puzzled.

"And don't try to look coy," she said. "I spoke with Rediana today. She told me what you've been doing."

"Ah," he said. He went over to place the roasting pan on the ashes and used a charred stick to bank them up around the edges. Then he came back and sat next to her. "You don't approve?"

"It's nothing to me."

"It ought not to be. I'm doing this for you, remember? I'm trying to earn passage for us to escort you home."

"And yet we seem no nearer to departing than we were a month ago."

"Sea passage does not come cheap, especially when the cargo must remain secret. Speaking of which, take especial care. There are more men searching the streets for you than ever. I wonder if you know why."

"I've told you, I don't." It wasn't exactly a lie. She had no idea why there was a price on her head, but she figured it had to do somehow with her station and the dreams that troubled even her waking hours. Dreams that she knew came from—elsewhere.

"I took your word for silver," he said, "and I still do. But if there is any suspicion you have . . ."

"My father is a wealthy and powerful man. That's the only cause I can imagine."

"Do you have some rival who vies for his affections? A step-mother, perhaps? Someone who would prefer not to see you return?"

"Oh, yes, my stepmother," Anne said. "How could I have forgotten? There was that time when she sent me out with the huntsman and told him to bring my heart back. I would have died, then, if the old fellow hadn't taken a shine to me. He took her back the heart of a boar instead. And then there was that other time, when she sent me to fetch water, never mentioning the nicwer that lived in the stream, waiting to charm me and eat me. Yes, those events should have been clues to my present situation, but I suppose I didn't suspect her because dear father assured me she has changed so."

"You're being sarcastic, aren't you?" Cazio guessed.

"This isn't a phay story, Cazio. I don't have a stepmother. There's no one in the family who would wish me ill. My father's enemies might, on the other hand, but I couldn't say exactly who they are. I'm not very political."

Cazio shrugged. "Ah, well." Then a smile brightened his face. "You're *jealous*," he accused.

"What?"

"I've just figured it out. You think I'm sleeping with Rediana's ladies, and you're jealous."

"I am not jealous," Anne said. "I already have a true love, and he is not you."

"Oh, yes, the fabled Roderick. A wonderful man, I hear. A true prince. I'm sure he would have answered your letter, if given another few months to get around to it."

"We've been around this before." Anne sighed. "Escort whomever you wish, do with them what you will. I am grateful to you, Cazio, for all your help, but—"

"Wait." Cazio's voice was clipped now, his face suddenly very serious.

"What is it?"

"Your father sent you to the coven Saint Cer, didn't he?"

"It was my mother, actually," she corrected.

"And did your true love Roderick know where you were bound?"

"It all happened too quickly. I thought I was going to Cal Azroth, and told him that, and then that very night my mother changed her mind. I had no way to send him word."

"He couldn't have discovered it through gossip?"

"No. I was sent away in secret. No one was supposed to know."

"But then you dispatched a letter to your beloved—a letter I delivered to the Church cuveitur myself—and in a matter of ninedays those knights came to the coven. Doesn't that strike you as suspicious?"

It did strike—it struck like tinder in Anne's breast.

"You go too far, Cazio. You have slandered Roderick before, but to suggest—to imply . . ." She stammered off, too angry to continue, all the more because it made a sort of sense. But it couldn't be true, because Roderick loved her.

"The knights were from Hansa," she said. "I knew their language. Roderick is from Hornladh."

But silently she remembered something her aunt Lesbeth once told her. It seemed long ago, but it was something about Roderick's house being out of favor at court because they had once supported a Reiksbaurg claim to the throne.

No. It's ridiculous.

She was about to tell Cazio that when Austra suddenly burst into the courtyard. She was out of breath, and her face was flushed and wet with tears.

"What's wrong?" Anne asked, taking Austra's hands.

"It's horrible, Anne!"

"What?"

"I s-s-saw a cuveitur. He was giving out the news in the square, by the wine shop. He'd just come from— Oh, Anne, what shall we do?"

"Austra, *what*?"

Her friend bit her lip and looked into Anne's eyes. "I have terrible news," she whispered. "The worst in the world."

CHAPTER THREE

THE COMPOSER

Leovigild Ackenzal stared at the spear with a mixture of fear and annoyance.

The fear was entirely rational; the sharp end of the weapon was poised only inches from his throat, and the man holding the shaft was large, armored, and mounted on a ferocious-looking steed. His iron-gray eyes reminded Leoff of the pitiless waters of the Ice Sea, and it seemed to him that if this man killed him, he would not even remember him in the morning.

There was certainly nothing he could do to stop the fellow if murder was on his mind.

That he should also be annoyed was quite irrational, he supposed, but in truth it had little to do with the armored man. Days before—in the hill country—he'd heard a faint melody off in the distance. No doubt it had been some shepherd playing a pipe, but the tune had haunted him ever since, the worse because he'd never heard the end of it. His mind had completed it in a hundred ways, but none of them were satisfactory.

This was unusual. Normally, Leoff could complete a melody without the slightest effort. The fact that this one continued to elude him made it more tantalizing than a beautiful, mysterious—but reluctant—lover.

Then, this morning, he'd awoken with a glimmer of how it ought to go, but less than an hour on the road brought this rude interruption.

"I have little money," Leoff told the man truthfully. His voice shook a bit as he said it.

The hard eyes narrowed. "No? What's all that on your mule, then?"

Leoff glanced at his pack animal. "Paper, ink, my clothes. The large case is a lute, the smaller a croth. Those smallest ones are various woodwinds."

"Auy? Open them, then."

"They won't be of any value to you."

"Open them."

Trying not to take his gaze off the man, Leoff complied, opening first the leather-bound case of the lute, which sounded faintly as the gourd-shaped back bumped against the ground. Then he proceeded to unpack the rest of his instruments; the eight-stringed rosewood croth inlaid with mother-of-pearl that Mestro DaPeica had given him years ago. A wooden flute with silver keys, an hautboy, six flageolets of graded sizes, and a dark red krummhorn.

The man watched this with little expression. "You're a minstrel, then," he said at last.

"No," Leoff replied. "No, I'm not." He tried to stand taller, to make the most of his average height. He knew there was little intimidating about his hazel eyes, curly brown hair, and boyish face, but he could at least be dignified.

The fellow raised an eyebrow. "Then what exactly are you?"

"I'm a composer."

"And what does a composer do?" the man asked.

"He composes music."

"I see. And how does that differ from what a minstrel does?"

"Well, for one thing—"

"Play something," the man interrupted.

"What?"

"You heard me."

Leoff frowned, his annoyance growing. He looked around, hoping to find someone else, but the road stretched empty so far as the eye could see. And here in Newland, where the terrain was as level as a sounding board, that was very far indeed.

Then why hadn't he seen the approach of the man on a horse?

But the answer to that lay in the melody he'd been puzzling over. When he heard music in his head, the rest of the world simply didn't matter.

He picked up the lute. It had gone out of tune, of course, but not badly, and it was only a moment's work to set it right again. He plucked out the melody line he'd been working on.

"That's not right," he murmured.

"You *can* play, can't you?" the mounted man challenged.

"Don't interrupt me," Leoff said absently, closing his eyes. Yes, there it was, though he'd lost the end.

He started into it, a single line on the top string, rising in three notes, dropping into two, then tripping up the scale. He added a bass accompaniment, but something about it didn't fit.

He stopped and started again.

"That's not very good," the man said.

That was too much, spear or no. Leovigild turned his eyes on the fellow. "It would be *quite* good if you hadn't interrupted me," he said. "I almost had this in my head, you know, perfect, and then along you come with your great long spear and . . . What do you want with me, anyway? Who are you?" He noticed distantly that his voice wasn't shaking anymore.

"Who are *you*?" the man asked placidly.

Leoff drew himself up straight. "I am Leovigild Ackenzal," he said.

"And why do you approach Eslen?"

"I have an appointment to the court of His Highness, William the Second, as a composer. The emperor has a better opinion of my music than you do, it seems."

Bizarrely, the man actually smiled. "Not anymore, he doesn't."

"What do you mean?"

"He's dead, that's what I mean."

Leoff blinked. "I . . . I didn't know."

"Well, he is. Along with half the royal family." He shifted in his saddle. "Ackenzal. That's a Hanzish-sounding name."

"It is not," Leoff replied. "My father was from Herilanz. I myself was born in Tremar." He pursed his lips. "You aren't a bandit, are you?"

"I never said I was," the fellow replied. "I haet Artwair."

"You are a knight, Sir Artwair?"

Again, that ghost of a smile. "Artwair will do. Do you have a letter proving your claim?"

"Ah, yes. Yes, I do."

"I would very much like to see it."

Wondering why Artwair should care, Leoff nevertheless rummaged through his saddle pack until he found a parchment with the royal seal. He handed it to the warrior, who examined it briefly.

"This looks in order," he said. "I'm returning to Eslen just now. I'll escort you there."

Leoff felt the muscles of his neck unknotting. "Very kind of you," he said.

"Sorry if I gave you a fright. You shouldn't have been traveling alone, anyway—not in these times."

By noon, the infant-eyed sky of morning was cataracted an oppressive gray. This did nothing to improve Leoff's mood. The landscape had changed; no longer totally flat, the road now ran alongside some sort of embankment or ridge of earth. It was so regular in shape, it seemed to him that it must be man-made. In the distance he could see similar ridges. The strangest things were the towers that stood on some of them. They looked as if they had huge wheels fixed to them, but with no rims, only four big spokes covered in what looked like sailcloth. They turned slowly in the breeze.

"What is that?" Leoff asked, gesturing at the nearest.

"First time in Newland, eh? It's a malend. The wind turns it."

"Yes, I can see that. For what purpose?"

"That one pumps water. Some are used to grind grain."

"It pumps water?"

"Auy. If it didn't, we'd be talking fishling right now." Sir Artwair gestured broadly at the landscape. "Why do you think they call this Newland? It used to be underwater. It would be now, but the malenden keep pumping it out." He pointed to the top of the embankment. "The water is up there. That's the great northern canal."

"I should have known that," Leoff said. "I've heard of the canals, of course. I knew that Newland was below the level of the sea. I just— I suppose I thought I wasn't that far along yet. I thought it would be more obvious, somehow."

He glanced at his companion. "Does it ever make you nervous?"

Sir Artwair nodded. "Auy, a bit. Still, it's a wonder, and good protection against invasion."

"How so?"

"We can always let the water out through the dikes, of course, so any army marching on Eslen would have to swim. Eslen itself is high and dry."

"What about the people who live out here?"

"We'd tell them first. Everyone knows the way to the nearest safe birm, believe me."

"Has it ever been done?"

"Auy. Four times."

"And the armies were stopped?"

"Three of them were. The fourth was lead by a Dare, and his descendents sit yet in Eslen."

"About that—about the king—," Leoff began.

"You're wondering if there's anyone left to sing to for your supper."

"I'm not unconcerned with that," Leoff admitted, "but clearly I've missed a great deal of news while on the road. I'm not even sure of the date."

"It's the Temnosenal. Tomorrow is the first of Novmen."

"Then I've been on the road longer than I thought. I left in Seftmen."

"The very month the king was killed."

"It would be a kindness . . . ," Leoff began, and then, "Could you please tell me what happened to King William?"

"Surely. He was set upon by assassins while on a hunting expedition. His entire party was slain."

"Assassins? From where?"

"Sea reavers, they say. He was near the headland of Aenah."

"And others of the royal house were slain with him?"

"Prince Robert, his brother, was slain there, as well. The princesses Fastia and Elseny were murdered at Cal Azroth."

"I don't know that place," Leoff said. "Is it near to where the king was killed?"

"Not at all. It's more than a nineday's hard riding."

"That seems a very strange coincidence."

"It does, doesn't it? Nevertheless, it is the case, and it doesn't go well for those who suggest otherwise."

"I see," Leoff said. "Then can you tell me—who rules in Eslen now?"

Artwair chuckled softly. "That depends on whom you ask. There is a king—Charles, the son of William. But he is, as they say, touched by the saints. He must be advised, and there's no lack of advice available to him. The nobles of the Comven give it most freely and at every opportunity. The praifec of the Church has much to say, as well. And then there's William's widow, the mother of Charles."

"Muriele Dare."

"Ah, so you know something, at least," Artwair said. "Yes, if you had to pick one person to say rules Crotheny, she would be the best choice."

"I see," Leoff said.

"So you say you're worried about your position?" the knight said. "Are positions for your sort rare?"

"There are other patrons who would have me," Leoff admitted. "I am not without reputation. I last served the Greft of Glastir. Still, a royal appointment . . ." He looked down. "But that's a small thing, isn't it, in all this mess."

"At least you have some sense, composer. But cheer up—you may have your position yet—the queen may honor it. Then you'll be right in the thick of things when the war starts."

"War? War with whom?"

"Hansa—or Liery—or perhaps a civil war."

"Are you joking with me?"

Artwair shrugged. "I have a sense for these things. All is chaos, and it usually takes a war to sort things out."

"Saint Bright, let's hope not."

"You don't fancy marching songs?"

"I don't know any. Can you sing some?"

"Me, sing? When your mule is a warhorse."

"Ah, well," Leoff sighed. "Just a thought."

They traveled in silence for a time, and as evening came, a mist settled, made rosy by the waning sun. The lowing of cattle sounded in the distance. The air smelled like dried hay and rosemary, and the breeze was chill.

"Will we reach Eslen tonight?" Leoff asked.

"Only if we travel all night, which I don't fancy," Sir Artwair replied. He seemed distracted, as if he were searching for something. "There's a town where the road crosses the canal up here. I know an inn there. We'll take a room, and with an early start we'll be in Eslen by midday tomorrow."

"Is something wrong?"

Artwair shrugged. "I've an itchy feeling. It's likely nothing, as in your case."

"Were you searching for anything in particular when we met?"

"Nothing in particular and everything out-of-place. You were out-of-place."

"And what's out-of-place now?"

"Did I say anything was?"

"No, but something is—it shows in your face."

"And what would a minstrel know about my face?"

Leoff scratched his chin. "I told you, I'm not a minstrel. I'm a composer. You asked what the difference was. A minstrel—he goes from place to place, selling songs, playing for country dances, that sort of thing."

"And you do it for kings."

"There's more. You're from hereabouts? You've been to dances?"

"Auy."

"Minstrels might travel in a group as large as four. Two bowing on the croth, one on a pipe, and another to play the hand-drum and sing."

"I'm with you so far."

"There's a tune—'The Fine Maid of Dalwis.' Do you know it?"

Artwair looked a bit surprised. "Yah. It's a favorite at the Fiussanal."

"Imagine it. One crother plays the melody, then another comes in, playing the same tune, but starting a bit after, so it makes a round. Then the third joins, and finally the singer. Four voices as it were, all at counterpoints to one another."

"I don't know counterpoint, but I know the song."

"Good. Now imagine ten croths, two pipes, a flute, an hautboy, a greatpipe, and every one playing something different."

"I reckon it would sound like a barnyard full of animals."

"Not if it's written right and the musicians perform it fair. Not if everything is in its place. I can hear such a piece, in my head. I can imagine it before it's ever been played. I have a fine sense for things like that, Sir Artwair, and I can see when someone else does, whether it's for music or not. There's something bothering you. The trick is, do you know what that thing is?"

The knight shook his head. "You're a strange man, Leovigild Ackenzal. But, yes—this town I mentioned, Broogh—it's just ahead. But what do you hear, with those musician's ears of yours?"

Leoff concentrated for a moment. "Sheep bleating, far away. Cows. Blackbirds."

"Raeht. By now we ought to hear children hollering, wives yelling at their men to lay off the ale and come home, bells and horns sounding in the field, workers. But there's none of that." He sniffed the air. "No smell of cooking, either, and we're downwind."

"What could it mean?"

"I don't know. But I think we won't go in by the main road." He cocked his head. "What use are you if there's trouble? Can you use a sword or spear?"

"Saints, no."

"Then you'll wait here, up at the malend. Tell the windsmith that Artwair said to look after you for a bell or so."

"Do you think it's that serious?"

"Why would a whole town go silent?"

Leoff could think of a few reasons, all bad. "As you say," he sighed. "I'd only be in the way if there's trouble."

After ascending to the birm of the dike, Leoff stood for a moment, mazing at what a few feet in altitude did to transform Newland.

Mist collected in the low places like clouds, but from his heightened vantage he could see distant canals dissecting the landscape, coral ribbons that might have been cut from the dusky sky and laid on those amber fields by the saints themselves. Here and there he could even make out moving slivers that must be boats.

Lights were beginning to appear, as well, faint clusters of luminescence so pale, they might be the ephemeral dwellings of the Queerfolk rather than what they must be—the candlelit windows of distant towns and villages.

At his feet lay the great canal itself, broader than some rivers— but indeed, it must be a river, probably the Dew, caught here in walls built by human hands, kept here by ingenuity. It was indeed a wonder.

Finally he studied the malend, wondering exactly how it worked. Its wheel was turning in the breeze, but he couldn't see how it was keeping the water from drowning the land below. It squeaked faintly as it rotated, a pleasant sound.

A cheerful yellow light shone through the open door of the malend, and the smell of burning wood and fish grilling wafted out. Leoff got down off his mule and rapped on the wood.

"*Auy?* Who is it?" a bright tenor voice asked.

A moment later a face appeared, a small man with white hair sticking out at all angles. Age seemed to have collapsed his face, so wrinkled it was. His eyes shone, though, a pale blue, like lapis bezeled in leather.

"My name is Leovigild Ackenzal," Leoff replied. "Artwair said to kindly ask if I might rest here a bell or so."

"Artwair, eh?" The old man scratched his chin. "Auy, Wilquamen. I haet Gilmer Oercsun. Be at my home." He gestured a bit impatiently.

"That's very kind," Leoff replied.

Inside, the lowest floor of the malend tower was a single cozy room. A hearth was set into one wall, where a cookfire crackled. An iron pot hung over the flame, as well as a spit that had two large perch skewered on it. A small bed was butted up against the opposite wall, and two three-legged stools sat nearer the fire. From the roofbeams hung nets of onions, a few bunches of herbs, a wicker basket, swingle-blades, hoes, and hatchets. A ladder led to the next floor.

In the center of the room, a large wooden shaft lifted in and out of a stone-lined hole in the floor, presumably driven somehow by the windwheel above.

"Unburden 'zuer poor mule," the windsmith said. "Haveth-yus huher?"

"I beg your pardon?" Artwair's dialect had been strange. The windsmith's was nearly unintelligible.

"Yu's an faerganger, eh?" His speech slowed a bit. "Funny accent you have. I'll try to keep with the king's tongue. So. Have you eaten? You have hungry?"

"I don't want to inconvenience you," Leoff said. "My friend ought to be back soon."

"That means you've hungry," the old man said.

Leoff went back out and took his things off the mule, then let her roam on the top of the dike. He knew from experience that she wouldn't go far.

When he reentered the malend, he found one of the fish awaiting him on a wooden plate, along with a chunk of black bread and some boiled barley. The windsmith was already sitting on one of the stools, his plate on his knees.

"I don't have a board just now," he apologized. "I had to burn it. Wood from upriver has been a little spotty, these last few nine-days."

"Again, thank you for your kindness," Leoff said, picking at the crisp skin of the fish.

"Nay, think nothing of it. But where is Artwair gang, that you can't go?"

"He's afraid something's wrong in Broogh."

"Hm. Has been quiet there this even', that's sure. Was wonderin' about it minself." He frowned. "Like as so, don't think I even heard the vespers bell."

If that brought Gilmer any further thoughts, he didn't share them, but tucked into his meal. Leoff followed suit.

When the meal was done, Gilmer tossed the bones in the fire. "Where've you come from, then?" he asked Leoff.

"Glastir, on the coast," he replied.

"That's far, auy? Mikle far. And how do you know Artwair?"

"I met him on the road. He's escorting me to Eslen."

"Oh, gang to the court? Dark times, there, since the night of the purple moon. Dark times everywhere."

"I saw that moon," Leoff said. "Very strange. It reminded me of a song."

"An unhealthy song, I'll wager."

"An old one, and puzzling."

"Sing a bit of it?"

"Ah, well . . ." Leoff cleared his throat.

Riciar over fields did ride
Beneath the mountains of the west
And there the palest queen he spied
In lilies fair taking her rest

Her arms shone like the fullest moon
Her eyes glimed like the dew
On her gown rang silver bells
Her hair with precious diamonds strewn

All hail to thee, oh my great queen
All hail to thee he cried
For thou must be the greatest saint
That ere a man has spied

Said she truly I am no saint
I am no goddess bright
But it's the queen of Alvish lands
You've come upon tonight

Oh Riciar welcome to my fields
Beneath the mountains of the west
Come and take with me repose
Of mortal knights I love thee best

And I will show thee wonders three
And what the future holds
And I will share my wine with thee
My arms wilt thou enfold

And there beneath the western sky
She showed him wonders three
And in the after bye and bye
She gave him Alvish eyes to see

Oh Riciar stay with me awhile
Keep here for an age or two
Leave the lands of fate behind
And sleep with oak and ash and yew

Here's my gate of earth and mist
Beyond my country fair
Of all the knights upon the earth
Thou art most welcome there

I will not go with thee great queen
I will not pass thy gate
But will return unto my liege
In the lands of Fate

If thou wilt not stay with me
If thou art bound to leave
Then give to me a single kiss
And I'll remember thee

So he bent down to kiss her there
Beneath the mountains of the west
She pulled a knife out from her hair
And stabbed it through his chest

He rode back to his mother's home
His heart's blood pouring true
My son, my son, you are so pale
What has become of you

O mother I am wounded sore
And I shall die today
But I must tell you what I've seen
Before I've gone away

A purple scythe shall reap the stars
An unknown horn shall blow
Where regal blood spills on the ground
The blackbriar vines shall grow

Leoff finished the song, Gilmer listening in evident pleasure.

"You've a fine voice," the old man said. "I don't cann of this Riciar fellow, but all he said has come to pass."

"How so?"

"Well, the purple scythe—that was the crescent moon that rose last month, as you said. And a horn was blown—it was heard everywhere. In Eslen, at the bay, out on the islands. And the royal blood was spilled, and then the brammel-briars."

"Briars?"

"Auy. You aens't heard? They sprang up first at Cal Azroth, where the two princesses were slain. Sprouted right from their blood, it's said, just as in your song. They grew so fast, they tore down the keep there, and they creep still. They spell the King's Forest is full of 'em, too."

"I haven't heard that at all," Leoff said. "I've been on the road from Glastir."

"Sure the news has been up the road by now," Gilmer said. "How did it miss you?"

Leoff shrugged. "I traveled with a Sefry caravan, and they spoke to me very little. This past nineday I was alone, but I was preoccupied, I suppose."

"Preoccupied? What with the end of the world coming, and all?"

"End of the world?"

Gilmer's voice lowered. "Saints, man, don't you know anything? The Briar King has wakened. That's his brammels eating up the land. That was *his* horn you heard blaw."

Leoff stroked his chin. "Briar King?"

"An ancient demon of the forest. The last of the evil old gods, they say."

"I've never—no, wait, there *is* a song about him."

"You're right full of songs."

Leoff shrugged. "Songs are my trade, you might say."

"You're a minstrel?"

Leoff sighed and smiled. "Something like that. I take old songs and make them into new ones."

"A songsmith, then. A smith, like me."

"Yes, that's more the case."

"Well, if it's a song about the Briar King, I don't want to hear it. He'll kill us all, soon enough. No need to trouble over him before it happens."

Leoff wasn't sure how to react to that, but he felt sure that if the world were about to end, Artwair would probably have mentioned it. "Very well," he said at last, gesturing above. "Your malend. May I ask, how does it work?"

Gilmer brightened. "You saw the saglwic outside, auy? The wind spins it, which turns a shaft up there." He pointed toward the roof. "Then there's wooden cogs and gears, takes that turning and makes this shaft go up and down. That runs the pump, down under. I can show you tomorrow."

"That's very nice of you, but I won't be here tomorrow."

"You may be. Artwair has had time to gang and come from Broogh twice now, so something must be keeping him there. And I'm needin' min rest. And judging by the way the Kuvoolds are pulling at your eyelids, I'd say you need a rest, as well."

"I am rather tired," Leoff realized.

"You're welcome to stay until Artwair gets back, as I said. There's another bed, on the next floor, for just such a purpose. Take it, if you'd like."

"I think I shall, even if it's only for a short nap."

He climbed the ladder to the next level and found the bed, just under a window. It was well dark now, but the moon was out, and up the canal some half a league he saw what must be Broogh, a collection of house-shaped shadows, a wall, and four towers of varying height. He saw no light, however, not even so much as he had made out in the far more distant—and probably smaller—villages.

With a sigh he lay on the rough mattress, listening to the wolf-wings and nighthawks singing, tired but not sleepy. Above, he could hear the gears Gilmer had mentioned clattering and clucking, and somewhere near, the trickling of water.

The end of the world, eh? That was just his luck. At the age of thirty-two he had a royal appointment in his grasp, and the world was going to end.

If he still had a royal appointment.

His thoughts on the matter were interrupted by the sudden breathy voice of a recorder. It was so clear and beautiful, it might have been real, but he'd lived long enough with his gift to know it was in his head.

A melody began, and he smiled as his body relaxed and his mind went to work.

The malend was teaching him its song.

It came easily, first the alto recorder, the wind coming along from the east across green plains. And now the drum, as the wheel—

saglwic?—began to turn, and croths—plucked here rather than bowed—began playing the melody in unison with the flute. Then joined the low strings of the bass croths, the vast waters beneath the earth responding, but still all melody, of course—and now water flowing into the canal, a merry trickling on a flageolet, as the malend became the union of air, earth, water, and craft.

Now the variations began, each element acquiring its own theme—the earth a slow pavane on the deep instruments, but on the pipes a mad, happy dance as the wind quickened, and the strings bowing nearly glissando arpeggios . . .

He blinked. His candle had gone out, and it was pitch-black. When had that happened?

But the concerto was finished, ready to go to paper. Unlike the melody in the hills, the dance of the malend had come to him whole.

Which was perhaps why he only now realized that someone was in the room below, talking.

Two voices, and neither belonged to Gilmer Oercsun.

" . . . don't see why we had got picked to do *this* job," a voice said. It was a tenor voice, scratchy.

"Don't complain," another said. This one was a booming baritone. "Especially don't complain around *him*."

"It's just that I wanted to *see*," the first replied. "Don't you want to be there, when they bust through the dike, and the water goes all a rushin' out?"

"You'll see it," the baritone replied. "You'll see it well enough. You'll be lucky not to swim in it."

"Yah, I suppose. Still." A cheerful tone crept into his voice. "But won't it be fun, rowing a boat over all of that down there? Over the roofs of the houses? I'm going to row right over . . . what was the town?"

"Where the girl said you had a nose like a turtle's prickler?"

"That's the one."

"Reckhaem."

"Right. Hey, a turtle's prickler is the best she'll be getting, after tonight."

"Still better than yours, from what I've heard," the baritone said. "Now let's be done here. We've got to burn every malend for four leagues before morning."

"Yah, but why?"

"So they can't pump the water back up, you dumb sceat. Now, come on."

Burn? Leoff's heart did a triple-quick-step.

The top of the stairway suddenly appeared, an orange rectangle, and he smelled burning oil.

CHAPTER FOUR

THE PRAIFEC

ASPAR WHITE FOUGHT TO draw a breath, but he felt as if a giant hand were clenched around his throat. "*Sceat,* this *can't* be right," he managed to gasp out. "Winna—"

Winna rolled her blue eyes and shook her honey locks. "Hush, Asp," she admonished, "don't be such a kindling. Haven't you ever worn a Farling collar before?"

"I've never worn any damn sort of collar before," Aspar grunted. "What's the point?"

"The point is, you're in Eslen, in the royal palace, not tramping through a heath in the uplands, and before the next bell you're going to see His Grace, the Praifec of all Crotheny. You've got to dress for the occasion."

"But I'm just a holter," he complained. "Let me dress like one."

"You killed the Black Warg and his bandit band, alone, with nothing but your bow, ax, and dirk. You fought a greffyn and lived. You mean to say now you're afraid to wear a simple set of weeds?"

"They aren't simple, I look stupid, and I can't breathe."

"You haven't even seen yourself, and if you've got enough breath to whinge so, I'd say you're doing fine. Now here, come to the mirror."

He raised his eyebrows. Winna's young face was broad with smile. Her hair was caught up in a black net of some sort, and she wore an azure gown that—to his mind—was cut far too low at the bodice. Not that the view didn't please, but it would please every other man who saw it, too.

"Well, you look—ah—pretty, at least," he said.

"Surely I do. And so do you. See?" She turned him toward the mirror.

Well, he recognized the face, even with it shaved clean. Burned dark by the sun, scarred and worn by forty-one years of hard living, it might not be pretty, but it was the sort of face the king's holter ought to have.

From the neck down, he was a stranger. The tight, stiff collar was merely the most torturous part of a doublet made of some sort of brightly patterned cloth that ought to have ended up as a drape or a rug. Below that, his legs felt naked, clothed as they were in tight green hose. He felt altogether like a candied apple on a stick.

"Who ever thought of dressing like this?" He grunted. "It's as if some madwoman tried to think of the most ridiculous outfit imaginable, and—Grim's eye—succeeded."

"Mad*woman*?" Winna asked.

"Yah, well, no man would ever invent such a clownish suit. It must have been some sort of evil trick. Or a dare."

"You've been at court long enough to know better," Winna said. "The men here love their plumage."

"Yah," he conceded, "and I'm damn ready to be away from here, too."

Her eyes narrowed a little, and she wagged an accusing finger. "You're *nervous* about meeting the praifec."

"I'm no such a thing," he snapped.

"You *are* such a thing! A nervous little kindling thing!"

"I haven't had much to do with the Church, that's all," he grumbled. "Other than killing a few of their monks."

"Outlaw monks," she reminded him. "You'll do fine, just try not to blaspheme—in other words, try not to talk at all. Let Stephen do the talking."

"Oh, yah, that will be a comfort," Aspar muttered sarcastically. "He's the soul of tact."

"He's a churchman, though," Winna pointed out. "He ought to know more about talking to a praifec than you do."

That brought a sharp little laugh from near the door. Aspar glanced over to see that Stephen had entered and was leaning against the frame, clad much as he was but appearing far more comfortable. His mouth was quirked in a smile, and his brown hair was swept back in something approaching courtly fashion. "I *was* in the Church," Stephen said. "Before committing heresy, disobeying my fratrex, getting him killed, and fleeing my monastery. I doubt much that His Grace the Praifec will have many good things to say to me."

"Like as not," Aspar agreed, "we'll end this meeting in a dungeon."

"Well," Winna said, primly, "at least we'll go well-dressed."

Praifec Marché Hespero was a tall man of upper middle years. He had a narrow face made sharper by a small black goatee and mustache. His black robes were draped on a body to suit—thin, almost birdlike. His eyes were like a bird's, as well, Aspar reflected—like a hawk's or an eagle's eyes.

He received them in a somber, spare room of gray stone with low-beamed ceilings. In the baroque splendor of Eslen Castle, it seemed very much out-of-place. The praifec sat in an armchair behind a large table. To his left sat a dark-complexioned boy of perhaps sixteen winters, looking at least as uncomfortable in his courtly garb as Aspar felt. Other than that, Aspar, Winna, and Stephen were the only people in the chamber.

"Sit, please," the praifec said pleasantly.

Aspar waited until Stephen and Winna took their chairs, then settled in the one that remained. Grim knew if it was the right one. If there was a right one. He still smarted from an incident with spoons at a banquet the nineday before. Who needed more than one sort of spoon?

When they were seated, the praifec rose and clasped his hands behind his back. He looked at Aspar. "Aspar White," he said in a soft voice, soft as the fabric of Winna's dress. "You've been the royal holter for many years."

"More years than I care to remember, Your Grace."

The praifec smiled briefly. "Yes, the years chase us, do they not? I put you at a man of some forty winters. It's been some time since I saw that age." He shrugged. "What we lose in beauty, we gain in wisdom, one hopes."

"Ya—yes, Your Grace."

"You've a distinguished career up until now, all in all. Several acts of an almost impossible sort—did you really sort out this Black Warg all by yourself?"

Aspar shifted uncomfortably. "That's been made a bit much of," he said.

"Ah," the praifec said. "And the affair of the Relister?"

"He'd never fought a man with dirk and ax, Your Grace. His armor slowed him down."

"Yes, I'm sure." He glanced at a paper on the table. "I see a few complaints, here, as well. What's this about the Greft of Ashwis?"

"That was a misunderstanding," Aspar said. "His lordship was mad with drink, and taking a firebrand to the forest."

"Did you really bind and gag him?"

"The king saw it my way, sir."

"Yes, eventually. But there's this thing with Lady Esteiren?"

Aspar stiffened. "The lady wanted me for a holiday guide, Your Grace, which is in no way my charge. I tried to be polite."

"And failed, it seems," the praifec said, a touch of amusement in his voice.

Aspar started a reply, but the praifec held up his hand, shook his head, and turned to Stephen.

"Stephen Darige, formerly a fratir at the monastery d'Ef." He peered down his nose at Stephen. "You've made quite an impression on the Church during your very brief tenure with it, haven't you, Brother Stephen?"

Stephen frowned. "Your Grace, as you know, the circumstances—"

The praifec cut him off. "You're from a family of good standing, I see. Educated at the college in Ralegh. An expert in antique languages, which you put to use at d'Ef translating forbidden documents, which translation—as I understand it, correct me if I get this wrong—

led both to the death of your fratrex and the commission of unspeakable acts of dark sorcery."

"This is all true, Your Grace," Stephen replied, "but I did my work at the command of the fratrex. The dark sorcery was practiced by renegade monks, led by Desmond Spendlove."

"Yes, well, you see, there's no proof of any of that," the praifec pointed out. "Brother Spendlove and his compatriots are all dead, as is Fratrex Pell. This is convenient for you, as there is no one to contradict your story."

"Your Grace—"

"And yet you admit to summoning the Briar King, whose appearance is said to foretell the end of the world."

"It was an accident, Your Grace."

"Yes. That will be small comfort if the world is actually in the process of ending, will it not?"

"Yes, Your Grace," Stephen replied miserably.

"Nonetheless, your admission of guilt in that case goes far to suggest that you're telling the truth. Privately, I confess I had long suspected something was awry at d'Ef. The Church, after all, is made up of men and women, all of whom are fallible, and as prone to corruption as anyone. We are doubly on the watch now, you may be assured."

He turned at last to Winna.

"Winna Rufoote. Hostler's daughter from Colbaely. Not a holter, not in the Church. How in Heaven did you become involved in all this?"

"I'm in love with this great lump of a holter, Your Grace," she replied.

Aspar felt his face color.

"Well," the praifec said. "There's no accounting for such things, is there?"

"Likely not, Your Grace."

"Yet you were with him when he tracked the greffyn, and at Cal Azroth when the Briar King appeared. You were also a captive of the Sefry, Fend, said to be responsible for much of what happened."

"Yes, Your Grace."

"Well." His lips pressed into a thin line. "I give you a choice, Winna Rufoote. We are about to speak of things that cannot go beyond the walls of this room. You may remain and become a part of something which could prove quite dangerous in several different ways—or you may leave, and I will have you escorted safely back to your father's inn in Colbaely."

"Your Grace, I'm a part of this. I'll stay."

Aspar found himself standing suddenly. "Winna, I forbid—"

"Hush, you great bear," Winna said. "When could you ever forbid me?"

"This time I do!" Aspar said.

"Silence, please," the praifec said. He focused his raptor eyes on Aspar. "It's her choice."

"And she's made it," Winna said.

"Think carefully, my dear," the praifec said.

"It's done, Your Grace," Winna replied.

The praifec nodded. "Very well."

He placed his hand on the shoulder of the boy, who had sat silent through all of this. He had black hair and eyes to match, and his skin was dark, darker than Aspar's.

"Allow me to present Ehawk, of the Wattau, a tribe from the Mountains of the Hare. You know of them, perhaps, Holter White."

"Yah," Aspar answered curtly. His mother had been Wattau, his father an Ingorn. The child they bore had never been welcome in either village.

The praifec nodded again. "The events you three have been a part of are of great concern to the Church, most especially the appearance of the so-called Briar King. Up until now, we have considered him to be nothing more than a folktale, a lingering superstition, perhaps inspired by an illiterate memory of the Warlock Wars or even the Captivity, before our ancestors broke the shackles of the demons who enslaved them. Now that he has appeared, of course, we must reassess the state of our knowledge."

"If I may, Your Grace, my report—," Stephen began.

"I have read your reports, of course," Hespero said. "Your work on the subject is laudable, but you lack the full resources of the

Church. There is, in holy z'Irbina, a certain set of volumes which may be read only by His Holiness the Fratrex Prismo. Immediately on hearing of the events at Cal Azroth, I sent word to z'Irbina, and word has now come back to me." He paused.

"Word and more," he continued. "I will explain that later. Anyway, at the time I did not feel that I could wait to hear from z'Irbina. I sent, under Church auspices, an expedition to track this—*creature*, and to learn more of it. The expedition was a strong one; a knight of the Church and five monks of Mamres. They hired Ehawk in his village to act as a guide. Ehawk will now relate what he saw."

"Ah," Ehawk said. His accent was thick, and it was that of someone not used to speaking the king's tongue. "Hello to you." He fixed his eyes on Aspar. "I've heard of you, Sir Holter. I thought you'd be taller. It's said your arrows are the size of spears."

"I've shrunk down for His Grace," Aspar grunted. "What did you see, boy, and where did you see it?"

"It in the territory of the Duth ag Paé, near Aghdon. One of the monks—Martyn—heard something. And there they were."

"They?"

"Men and women, but like beasts. They wore nothing; they carried no weapons. They tore up poor Sir Oneu with their bare hands and teeth. A madness was upon them."

"Where did they come from?"

"They were the Duth ag Paé, I'm sure of it. Maybe all of them, except no children. There were old people, though." He shuddered. "They ate the monks' flesh as they killed them."

"Do you know what might have driven them to madness?"

"It's not just them, Sir Holter. As I fled, I came across village after village, all abandoned. I hid in holes and under leaves, but they found my horse and tore her up. I heard them at night, singing songs in no speech of the mountains."

"But you escaped them."

"Yah. When I left the forest, I left them. I came here because Martyn wished it."

"Martyn was one of my most trusted servants," the praifec amplified, "and very powerful in Mamres."

"What sort of madness sweeps whole villages?" Stephen wondered.

"The old women . . . ," Ehawk began; then his voice trailed off.

"It's all right, Ehawk," the praifec said reassuringly. "Speak what you will."

"It's one of the prophecies. They said that when the Etthoroam wakes, he will claim all in the forest for his own."

"Etthoroam," Stephen said. "I've seen that name. It's what your people name the Briar King."

Ehawk nodded.

"Aspar," Winna murmured. "Colbaely is in the King's Forest. My father. My family."

"Colbaely is far from the country of the Duth ag Paé," Aspar said.

"How does that matter, if what this boy says is true?"

"She has a point," Stephen said.

"They are not confined to the depths," the praifec said. "We've had reports of fighting in towns all along the edge of the King's Forest, at least in the east."

"Your Grace, you must pardon me," Aspar said.

"For what crime?"

"Pardon me to leave. I'm the king's holter. The forest is in my charge. I have to see this for myself."

"Yes, to that second point I agree. As to the first—you are no longer the king's holter."

"What?"

"I petitioned His Majesty to have you placed under my command. I need you, Aspar White. No one knows the forest as you do. You've faced the Briar King and lived—not once, but twice."

"But he's been a holter all his life!" Stephen exploded. "Your Grace, you can't just—!"

The praifec's voice was suddenly not soft. "I most certainly can, Brother Darige. I can and I have. And in point of fact, your friend is still a holter—the Church's holter. What greater honor could he hope for?"

"But—," Stephen began again.

"If it's all the same, Stephen," Aspar said quietly, "I can speak for myself."

"Please do," the praifec urged.

He looked the praifec straight in the eye. "I don't know much about courts or kings or praifecs," he admitted. "I'm told I have few manners, and those I have are bad ones. But it seems to me, Your Grace, that you might have *asked* me before telling me."

Hespero stared at him for a moment, then shrugged. "Very well. You have a point. I suppose I was letting my anxiety for the people of Crotheny and the greater world muddy my concern for the personal wishes of one man. I can always ask the king to change his decree—so I'll ask you now."

"What exactly is it Your Grace is requesting?"

"I want you to go to the King's Forest and discover what is really happening there. I want you to find the Briar King, and I want you to kill him."

A moment's silence followed the praifec's words. He sat there, watching them as if he had just asked that they go hunting and return with some fresh deer meat.

"Kill him," Aspar said carefully, after a moment.

"Indeed. You killed the greffyn, did you not?"

"And it nearly killed Aspar," Winna interjected. "It *would* have killed him, except that the Briar King somehow healed him."

"You're sure of that?" the praifec said. "Do you discount the saints and their work so easily? They do keep an eye on human affairs, after all."

"The point is, Your Grace," Stephen said, "that we do not know precisely what happened that day, what the Briar King is, or what he truly portends. We don't know that the Briar King should be slain, and we do not know if he *can* be slain."

"He *can* be slain, and he must be slain," Hespero said. "This can slay him." He lifted a long, narrow leather case from behind his desk. It looked old, and Aspar saw some sort of faded writing stamped on it.

"This is one of the most ancient relics of the Church," the praifec said. "It has been waiting for this day, and for someone to wield it. The

Fratrex Prismo cast the auguries, and the saints have revealed their will."

He opened one end of the case and gingerly withdrew an arrow. Its head glittered, almost too brightly to be looked at.

"When the saints destroyed the Old Gods," Hespero said, "they made this and gave it to the first of the Church fathers. It will kill anything that has flesh—beast canny or uncanny, or ancient, pagan spirit. It may be used seven times. It has already been used five."

He replaced the arrow in the case and folded his hands before him.

"The madness Ehawk witnessed is the doing of the Briar King. The auguries say it will spread, like ripples in a pool, until all the lands of men are engulfed by it. Therefore, by command of the most holy senaz of the Church and the Fratrex Prismo himself, I am ordered to see that this shaft finds the heart of the Briar King. That, Aspar White, is the charge and the duty I am asking you to take up."

CHAPTER FIVE

THE SARNWOOD WITCH

W E CAN'T TAKE THEM all," Anshar said grimly as he drew back the string of his bow. There was nothing to hit—the wolves were nothing more than shadows in the trees, and he was certain every shaft he had fired thus far had missed its mark. The Sarnwood was too dense, too tangled with vines and creepers for a bow to have much worth.

"Well, no," the one-eyed Sefry to his left said coolly. "I don't imagine we can. But we didn't come here to fight wolves."

"Perhaps you haven't noticed, Fend," Brother Pavel said, pushing wet brown bangs from his gaunt face. "We haven't a choice."

Fend sighed. "They aren't attacking, are they?"

"They tore Refan to shreds," Brother Pavel observed.

"Refan left the path," Fend said. "We won't be so foolish, will we?"

"You really think we're safe if we stay on the path?" Anshar asked, looking down dubiously at the narrow trail they all three stood on. There seemed no real boundary between it and the howling wild of the forest, just a muddy mingling of earth and leaves.

"I didn't say we were safe," Fend amended with a grim sort of humor. "Only that the wolves won't get us."

"You've been wrong before," Brother Pavel pointed out.

"Me?" Fend wondered. "Wrong?"

"At Cal Azroth, for instance," Pavel persisted.

Fend stopped suddenly, focusing his single eye upon the monk. "In what way was I wrong?" the Sefry asked.

"You were wrong about the holter," Pavel accused. "You said he wasn't a threat."

"Me, claim Aspar White wasn't a threat? The one man who ever gave me a real wound in single combat? The man who took my eye? I don't think I ever claimed, in anyone's dreams, that Aspar White wasn't a threat. I believe that might have been your friend Desmond Spendlove, who swore he would stop the holter ere he reached Cal Azroth."

"He ruined our plans," Pavel grumbled.

Well, let's see," Fend said. "I'm confused by your word *ruined*. We killed the two princesses, didn't we?"

"Yes, but the queen—"

"Escaped, I grant you that. But it wasn't because I was wrong about anything—it was because we were outfought."

"If we had stayed—"

"If we had stayed, we'd both be dead, and our cause would have two fewer champions," Fend said. "Do you think you know the mind of our master better than I, Brother?"

Pavel kept his brow clenched, but finally he nodded. "No," he admitted.

"No. And see? While we've been arguing, where are the wolves?"

"Still out there," Anshar answered, "but not coming any closer."

"No. Because *she* wants to know what we've come for. As long as she's curious about us—as long as we obey her rules and stay on the path—we'll be fine." He clapped Pavel on the back. "Now will you stop worrying?"

Brother Pavel managed a fretful smile.

Anshar had heard about the business at Cal Azroth, but he hadn't been there. Most of the monks involved in that conflict had been from d'Ef. He'd taken his training at the monastery of Anstaizha, far to the north in his native Hansa. He'd been sent south only a few ninedays ago, told by his fratrex to lend whatever aid he could to the strange Sefry and Brother Pavel.

He'd been told specifically that the Sefry, though not a churchman, was to be obeyed at all times.

So he had followed Fend here, to the place where all the most frightening children's stories of his youth were supposed to have taken place—to the Sarnwood—in search of none other than the Sarnwood Witch herself.

The trail took them deeper, into a cleft between two hills which soon became a gorge rising in sheer walls on either side. He'd been raised in the country and was familiar with trees, and at the outskirts of the Sarnwood, he'd been able to name most of them. Now he knew almost none of them. Some were scaled and looked as if they were made of smaller snakes joined to larger ones. Others soared incredibly high before spreading spidery foliage. Yet others were less strange in appearance, but just as unidentifiable.

At last they came to a spring-fed pool of clear water whose banks were thick with moss and pale—almost white—ferns. The trees here were black and scaled, with drooping leaves that resembled sawtoothed blades. Empty gazes stared down at him from the human skulls nestled in the crooks of the branches. Anshar felt himself trying to back away, and he crushed the instinct with his will.

He smelled something musky and bitter.

"This is it," Fend murmured. "This is the place."

"What do we do now?" Anshar asked.

Fend drew a wicked-looking knife. "Come here, both of you," he said. "She'll want blood."

Obediently, Anshar stepped to the Sefry's side. Pavel did, too, but Anshar thought he saw hesitation there.

Meanwhile, Fend drew his blade across his palm. Blood welled from the line, and Anshar was half-surprised to see it was red as that of any human.

He glanced at the two of them. "Well?" he said. "She'll want more than this."

Anshar nodded and drew his own blade, and so did Brother Pavel.

Anshar was cutting his palm when he caught a peculiar motion from the corner of his eye.

Brother Pavel still stood there, his knife across his palm, but he was jerking oddly. Fend was facing him, holding his hand to Pavel's head, as if to hold him up . . .

No. Fend had just thrust a knife through Brother Pavel's left eye. Now he removed it and wiped it on Pavel's habit. The monk continued to stand there, twitching, the remaining eye fixed on his half-cut palm.

"A lot more blood," Fend amplified. He gave Pavel a push, and the monk toppled facefirst into the pool. Then the Sefry looked up at Anshar. He felt a chill, but stood his ground.

"You aren't worried you might be next?" Fend asked.

"No," Anshar said. "If my fratrex sent me here as a sacrifice, a sacrifice I'll be."

Fend's lips twisted in a grudging smile. "You Churchmen," he said. "You have such belief, such loyalty."

"You don't serve the Church?" Anshar asked, surprised.

Fend just snorted and shook his head. Then he sang something in a peculiar language Anshar had never heard.

Something moved in the trees. He didn't actually see the motion, but he felt and heard it. He had the impression of vast, scaly coils dragging themselves through the forest and contracting around the pool like a great Waurm of legend. Soon, he knew, it would poke its head through the tree trunks and open its vast, toothy mouth.

But what did step from the trees was very different from what his impressions had led him to imagine.

Her skin was whiter than milk or moonlight, and her hair floated about her like black smoke. He tried to avert his eyes because she was naked, and he knew he shouldn't gaze upon her, but he couldn't help it.

She was so slim, so exquisitely delicate, that he first thought she was a child. But then his eyes were drawn to the small cups of her breasts and the pale blue nipples that tipped them. To his surprise he saw she had four more, smaller nipples arranged down her belly, like on a cat, and he suddenly understood that she was Sefry.

She smiled, and to his shame, he felt a surge of lust equaled only by his terror. She lifted a hand toward them, palm up, beckoning, and he took a step forward.

Fend stopped him with a hand on his chest.

"She's not calling you," he said, pointing to the pool.

Pavel suddenly gathered his arms and legs beneath him and pushed himself clumsily to his feet. He turned to face them.

"Why have you come, Fend?" Pavel croaked.

"I've come to speak to the Sarnwood Witch," Fend replied.

"You've found her," Pavel said.

"Really? I'd always heard that the Witch was a terrible ogress, a giant, a thoroughly ugly creature."

"I have many appearances," Pavel's corpse said. "And there are many foolish stories told of me besides." The woman cocked her head. "You killed the Dare princesses," she said. "I smell it on you. But there were three daughters. Why didn't you kill the third?"

Fend chuckled. "I thought my sacrifice entitled *me* to have *my* questions answered."

"Your sacrifice only ensures that I won't slay you without hearing what you have to say. From here on out, you'll have to stay in my good graces if you want anything more than that."

"Ah," Fend said. "Very well. The third daughter—I believe her name was Anne—was not present at Cal Azroth. Unknown to us, she was sent away."

"Yes," the corpse said. "I see. Others found her in Vitellia, but they failed to kill her."

"So she's still alive?" Fend asked.

"Was that one of your questions?"

"Yes, but it sounds as if it's someone else's problem now."

"Earth and sky are being bent to find her," Pavel said. "She must die."

"Yes, well, I know that," Fend replied. "But if, as you say she has been found—"

"And lost again."

"Can you tell me where she is?"

"No."

"There, then," Fend said. "The others lost her—they can find her again."

"You had the queen in your grasp and did not kill her," Pavel said.

"Yes, yes," Fend replied. "It seems someone is always reminding me of that. An old friend of mine showed up and put something of a damper on the whole business. But as I understand it, the queen is not as important as Anne."

"She is important—and have no fear, she will die. Your failure there will cost you little. And you are correct in one thing—the daughter is *everything,* so far as your master is concerned."

For the first time, Fend seemed surprised. "I wouldn't call him a *master*—you know whom I serve?"

"He came to me once, long ago, and now I smell him on you." The woman lifted her chin, as did Pavel, in grotesque parody.

"Is the war begun?" the corpse asked.

"How is it you know so much concerning certain matters and nothing concerning others?"

"I know much of the large, but little of the small," Pavel said, and chuckled at the word play. Behind him, the woman just stood there, but Anshar could see her eyes now, a startling violet color.

"I can see the sweep of the river, but not eddies and currents, not the ships upon it or the leaves following it seaward. Your words supply me with that. You say one thing, and I see those things connected to it—and thus I learn the small things. Now. Has the war begun yet?"

"Not yet," he replied, "but soon, I'm told. A few more pieces are moving into place. Not really my focus, that."

"What is your focus, Fend? What did you really come here to discover?"

"They say you are the mother of monsters, O Sarnwood Witch. Is it true?"

"The very earth is pregnant with monsters. What do you seek?"

Fend's smile spread, and Anshar felt an involuntary chill. When Fend answered her, he felt another, deeper one.

CHAPTER SIX

THE EYES OF ASH

I T WAS ONLY MOMENTS before smoke started boiling up through the stairwell and the crackling of flame rose over all other noises. The floor began to heat, and Leoff realized that if the malend were an oven, he was just where the bread ought to be.

He went to the window, wondering if the fall would break his leg, but jerked his head back when he saw two figures watching the malend burn, their faces ruddy in the light spilling from the door.

The brief glimpse he got wasn't reassuring. One of them was nearly a giant, and Leoff could see the glint of steel in both their hands. They hadn't searched the malend—they were letting the fire do it for them.

"Poor Gilmer," he murmured. They had probably killed the little man in his sleep.

Which would probably be an easier fate than what lay in store for Leoff. It was already getting difficult to breathe. The flame was climbing for him, but the smoke would surely find him first.

He couldn't go down; he couldn't go out the window. That left only up, if he wanted to live even another few moments.

He found the ladder and climbed it to the next level. It was already smoky there, too, but not nearly so much as the level he had just left.

And it was dark, very dark. He could hear the gears working again, and something squeaking nearby. He must be in the machinery of the thing now.

He found the final ladder and went up it with trembling care. He had an image of getting a hand—or worse, his head—caught in an unseen cog.

The final floor wasn't very smoky at all. He faintly made out a window and went to it hopefully. But they were still down there, and now the drop was ridiculous.

Trying to calm himself, Leoff felt around in the dark, and nearly shrieked when he touched something moving. He caught himself as he realized it was a vertical beam, turning—probably the central shaft that drove the pump.

Except that the shaft he'd seen on the first floor wasn't rotating; it was moving up and down. The motion must be translated somehow on the floor just below.

That still didn't seem right. The axis of the—what had Gilmer called it? The big veined spokes? Saglwic. Their axis would have to be horizontal, so *that* motion must be translated to *this* shaft.

Which meant that there was something still above him.

Groping carefully above, he found a great-toothed wheel of wood at the top of the shaft. It was rotating. A little more feeling about, and he discovered the second wheel, set above the first and at right angles, so that the teeth meshed at the bottom of the second wheel to turn the first. Leoff figured that the shaft turning the second wheel must be connected to the windwheel itself.

He found that and followed it, not sure what he was looking for. The smoke had discovered him again, as had the heat.

The shaft passed through a greasy hole in the wall only incrementally larger than the smoothed beam itself.

He began to understand what he was looking for.

"There must be *some* way to repair the saglwic— Yes!"

Below the shaft he found a latch, and lifting it allowed him to open a small square door. He cracked it open and peered out.

A pale moon sat on the horizon, and by its light he saw the spokes of the malend turning in the wind, and beyond that the waters of the

canal, shining like silver. He saw no one below, but there were shadows enough to hide anything.

A shudder ran through the building, then another. Beams were
collapsing below. The tower ought to stand, though, since it was made
of stone.

A blast of hot air and a fist of flame followed the thought and came
punching up through the ladder hole.

Saints, I don't want to do this! he thought. *But it's this or burn.*

Holding his breath, he followed the slow rhythm of the rotating
spokes until he felt it with everything he had. The song of the malend
came back to him, filled him up, and now he breathed in time with it.

He jumped on the downbeat. His legs jerked when he did it, and
he nearly didn't make it, but one hand caught the wooden latticework
of the windsail. Without warning he found himself turning upside
down, but he managed to claw his other hand into the fabric. His
stomach churned with fear and disorientation as the landscape retreated impossibly far below him. Then it was rushing back at him
again, and he started climbing down the vane.

As it dipped near the ground, he hastened his pace, fearing to
make another rotation, but it was still too far away. He clung tight as
his perch swung up again, and oddly enough, his fear began to turn
into a sort of exhilaration. His head was toward the axis now, and
something seemed to be tugging at his feet, even when his feet were
pointed toward the sky, as if the saints didn't want him to fall. He went
with the tug, climbing on even while upside down, and when next the
vane moved earthward, he was low enough to drop.

He hit the ground hard, but not breaking hard, and lay there in
the grass for a moment.

But not for long. Keeping low, he moved away from the burning
malend and toward the canal. He had almost reached it when a strong
hand gripped his arm.

"Ssh!" a low voice commanded. "Quiet. It's just me, Gilmer."

Leoff closed his eyes and nodded, hoping his heart would not explode through his breastbone.

"Follow," Gilmer said. "We've got to get away from here. The men
who did this—"

"I saw them, on the other side of the malend."

"Auy. Stupid, they are."

"Well, there are no windows on this side to watch."

They reached the canal. Leoff saw that a small rowboat was moored there.

"Quickly," Gilmer said, untying the rope. "Get in."

Only a few moments later they were out in the center of the canal, with Leoff pulling on the oars as hard as he could. Gilmer had taken the tiller.

"I was afraid you were dead," Leoff said.

"Nay. I'd stepped outside to watch her turn. Heard 'em come in and what they were talking about. I didn't reckon I could stop 'em." He looked back at the malend. Flames were bursting from the top, and the windsails had caught like torches. They were still turning. "Sorry, love," Gilmer said softly. "Rot 'em for doing that to you. Rot 'em." Then he turned away.

"What now?" Leoff asked.

"Now we go to Broogh and see what mischief is goin' on there."

"But Artwair didn't come back."

"Then he may need our help."

It seemed to Leoff that any trouble Artwair couldn't get himself out of was likely to be *far* too much for the likes of a composer and a windsmith. He started to say as much, but then another thought occurred.

Gilmer must have seen it on his face.

"What?" the old man asked.

"My instruments. My things!"

The old man nodded sadly. "Auy. We've both lost today. Now think about what those folk down there will lose if these villains break the dike."

"I just wonder what we can do. I can't fight. I know nothing of weapons."

"Well, me neither," Gilmer replied, "but that doesn't mean I'll just let it happen."

As if mourning the malend, the wind dropped, and stillness settled on the canal, broken only by the liquid pull of oars through water. Leoff watched the banks anxiously, fearing that the men might be following them along it, but nothing stirred through the stately silhouettes of the elms that bordered the waterway.

Soon the trees were joined by larger shadows—cottages at first, then tall buildings. The canal narrowed.

"The gate is ahead," Gilmer whispered. "Be ready."

"For what?" Leoff asked.

"I've no cann," the elder man said.

The watergate was a simple one made of wrought iron, and it was open. They passed almost noiselessly through it and into the town of Broogh.

The strange silence of the night was thicker there than it had been farther down the canal, as if Broogh were the very heart of the still-ness. Neither did the faintest candle illumine the windows. They were filmed with moonlight like the eyes of the blind.

Quietly, Gilmer guided the small boat to a quay.

"You first," he told Leoff. "Careful not to rock me."

Leoff stepped gingerly from the boat and onto the stone landing, and a shiver ran up his spine as his feet touched solid ground.

Artwair had been right—something was terribly wrong here.

"Hold her steady for me," Gilmer said. "Be useful, auy?"

"Sorry," Leoff whispered. Even his faint reply seemed to echo in the silent town. He held the edge of the boat while the windsmith tied her off, feeling the pulse in his throat.

Broogh was beautiful, cloaked in moonlight. The tall, narrow build-ings were leafed in silver, and the cobbles of the streets seemed liquid while the waters of the canal had become a sheet of mica. The bridge that must have given the town its name arched strong and elegant a few paces away, a saint sleeping in stone at each pillar. Beyond, across and down the canal, rose the bell tower of the church.

Just next to him, on the street parallel to the canal, a wooden sign was barely readable in faint light. It proclaimed the door beneath as the entrance to the PAITER'S FATEM. Beneath the words was a small wooden bas-relief of a fat sacritor filling a cup from a cask of wine.

When Gilmer finished with the boat, he pointed at the Paiter's

Fatem. "There," he said. "That's the busiest tavern in town, and it should be awful busy right now."

Like every other building in Broogh, it was quiet and dark.

"We'll have a look inside," Gilmer murmured. "If everyone is hiding, you can bet half the town is hiding in there. In the cellar, maybe."

"Hiding from what? A few rascals like the ones who burned your windmill?"

"No," Gilmer said. "Broogh has a reputation."

"What do you mean?"

"Evildoers have sought out this town in the past. Its location is perfect—break the dike here, and the water won't stop for sixty leagues. It's been tried. Thirty years ago, a renegade Hansan knight— Sir Remismund fram Wulthaurp—came here with twenty horse and a hundred foot. He installed himself in this very inn and sent letters to Eslen, threatenin' to open the waters unless he was given ransom."

"But he didn't?"

"Nay. A girl, the daughter of a boatwright, the fairest in town, was to be married the next day. She put on her weddin' gown and went to Wulthaurp, up there, in that topmost apartment. She kissed him, and as they kissed, there, near that window, she wound the train of her dress about his neck and threw herself from the buildin'. They made a bloody mess almost where you're standin'. At that signal, the rest of the folk turned against his men. The army had to fight its way out the gate, leaving nearly a hundred Brooghers dead in the streets." He shook his head. "Nor was that the first time such a thing has happened. No, every boy and girl who grows up in Broogh thinks of the dike and the bridge as a holy trust. They all yearn to be the hero of the next story."

"And yet you think something has frightened them into hiding?"

Gilmer shook his head. "No," he said sadly, "I fear they're nay hidin' at all."

The door opened with no more protest than a faint creak, but their entry drew no response. Muttering to himself, Gilmer took out his tinderbox and struck light to a candle.

"Holy saints!" Leoff gasped, when the light fell about them.

There were indeed a lot of people in the Paiter's Fatem, or what had once been people. They lay or slumped in groups, unmoving. Leoff had no doubt whatever that they were dead. Even in the warm light of fire, their flesh was whiter than bone.

"Their eyes," Gilmer said, his voice thick with emotion.

Leoff noticed then, and he doubled to the floor, retching. The very earth seemed to reel beneath him and the sky to press down.

None of the dead in the tavern had eyes, only ashy pits.

Gilmer clapped his hand on Leoff's shoulder. "Easy," he said. "We don't want them as did this to hear us, do we?" The old man's voice was quavering.

"I can't . . ." Another wave of nausea came over Leoff and he pressed his forehead to the hardwood floor.

It was many long moments before he could look up again.

When he did, it was to find Gilmer studying the corpses.

"Why would they burn out their eyes?" Leoff managed.

"Saints know. But they didn't do it with brands or hot irons. The eyes are still there, just gone to charcoal."

"Shinecraft," Leoff whispered.

"Auy. Shinecraft most foul."

"But why?"

Gilmer straightened, his face grim. "So's they can break the dike and have no hindrance or witness." His lips puckered. "But they aens't broken it yet, have they? There's still time."

"Time to do what?" Leoff asked incredulously.

Gilmer's face went flat. "These people were my friends," he said. "You stay here, if you please."

He searched through the corpses for a moment and finally came up with a knife.

"Whoever did this aens't counted on anyone living now. They don't know about us."

"And when they do, we'll end just like these," Leoff said desperately.

"Auy, could well be," Gilmer said, and walked toward the door.

Leoff looked again at the dead and sighed. "I'm coming," he said.

When they were back on the street, he glanced again at the cobbles. "What was her name?" he asked.

"Eh?"

"The bride."

"Ah. Lihta. Lihta Rungsdautar."

"And her fiancé? What became of him?"

Gilmer's mouth quirked. "He never married. He became a wind-smith, like his father. Hush, now—the floodgate isn't far."

They passed more dead in the streets, all with the same empty gaze. Not just people, but animals, as well—dogs, horses—even rats. Some had expressions of terror frozen on their faces, while others looked merely puzzled. Some—the worst somehow—seemed to have died in rapture.

Leoff noticed something else, as well—a smell, a faint odor of putrefaction. Yet it did not have the scent of the grave or butcher shop. There was no hint of maggots or sulfury gases. It reminded him of dry rot—subtle, not really unpleasant, with a faint perfume of burnt sugar.

As he progressed, he made out a noise, as well—a rhythmic hammering—not like a single hammer, but like many, all beating the bass line of the same dirge.

"That's them working at the wall!" Gilmer said. "Hurry."

He led them to the city wall and the stone stairs that went up it. They stepped over dead guardsmen to reach the top. From there they looked down.

Newland was moon-frosted to the horizon, but just below them, the wall cast a shadow down the embanked dike it stood upon. Torches burned there, flames straight and unwavering in the windless dark. Five men stripped to their waists were working at a stone section of the dam, hacking away with picks. Another five or six looked on—it was hard to tell exactly how many.

"Why is that one section made of stone?"

"It's a cap. Most of the dyke is banked earth. It would take too long to dig through it if the king *needed* to have Newland flooded, as has happened now and then. But it's never been done at royal behest without warning to the low-dwellers."

"But won't they be drowned when they cut through?"

"Nay. They're digging a narrow hole, see? The water will come out in a jet and tear the hole bigger as it goes, but it'll give them time to move."

"Who do you think it is?"

"Saints know."

"Well, what can we do?"

"I'm thinking."

Leoff strained his eyes to understand more of the scene. There was a pattern down there. What was it?

He settled his mind. There was the landscape, and the dike. They were like the staff that music was written on. Then there were the men digging, like the melody line, and the men silently standing guard, like the low throbbing bass notes of a pavane.

And that was all . . .

"No," he whispered.

"Eh?"

Leoff pointed. "Look, there are dead down there, too."

"Not surprising. Anyone alive would try to stop 'em." The windsmith squinted. "Right, see? They came around from the gate and attacked 'em from behind."

"But see how they're lying, in a sort of arc? As if something simply struck them down when they got too close."

Gilmer shook his head. "Aens't you ever seen battle? If they formed their line there, that's where they'd fall."

"But I don't see any signs of a fight. We haven't seen any signs of battle *anywhere* in town, yet everyone is dead."

"Auy. I noticed that," Gilmer said dryly.

"So they form an arc. Look to the center of the arc."

"What do you mean?"

"A lantern casts light in a circle, yes? Pretend where the corpses are is the edge of a circle of light. Now look for the lantern."

With a skeptical grunt, Gilmer did that. After a moment, he whispered, "There *is* something. Some sort of box or crate with a cloak over it."

"I'm willing to bet that it's what struck down the people of

Broogh. If we go down there—if they see us at all—they'll turn it on us."

"Turn *what* on us?"

"I don't know. I don't have any idea. But it's covered up, and there has to be some reason. Something tells me we can't do anything as long as they have that."

Gilmer was silent for a long moment. "You may be right," he said, "but if you're wrong . . ."

"I don't believe I am."

Gilmer nodded solemnly and peered back down. "It aens't far from the wall, is it?"

"Not too. What do you have in mind?"

"Follow me."

The little man gingerly searched the guardsmen for weapons, but found their scabbards empty—small wonder, considering the cost of a good sword. Then he guided Leoff along the top of the wall to a small storehouse. They had to step over six dead bodies along the way.

Gilmer opened the door, stepped into shadow, and stepped out again, grunting. He held a rock the size of Leoff's head. "Help me with this."

The two of them wrestled the stone to the parapet.

"Reckon we can toss it out far enough?" Gilmer asked.

"There's a slope," Leoff replied. "Even if we miss, it will roll."

"Might not destroy that shinecrafting box, then. We'll have to heave together."

Leoff nodded and put both hands on the stone. When they had it aimed, Gilmer said very softly, "On three. One, two—"

"Hey! Hey there!" A shout went up, farther along the wall, not far from them at all.

"Go!" Gilmer shouted.

They heaved. Leoff wanted to watch, but someone was running along the battlement toward them, and he didn't think it was for a friendly chat.

CHAPTER SEVEN

DISCOVERED

T HE RIVER ZA DISSOLVED Anne's tears and swept them
gently toward the sea.

Canaries sang in the olive and orange trees that struggled up
through the ancient cracked flagstones of the terrace, and the wind
was sweet with baking bread and autumn honeywands. Dragonflies
whirred lazily in the pour of golden sunlight, and somewhere nearby
a man strummed liquid chords on a lute and crooned softly of love. In
the city of z'Espino, winter came gently, and this first day of Nova-
menza was especially kind.

But Anne's reflection in the river looked as cold as the long, bleak
nights of northernmost Nahzgave. Even the red flame of her hair
seemed a dark shadow, and her face as pallid as the ghost of a drowned
girl.

The river saw her heart and gave her back what was in it.

"Anne," someone behind her said quietly. "Anne, you should not
stay out in the open so."

But Anne did not look up. She saw Austra in the river, too, looking as spectral as she did.

"I don't care," Anne said. "I can't go back to that horrible little
place, not now, not like this."

"But it's safer there, especially now . . ." Her voice faltered as Austra began to cry, too. She sat next to Anne, and they held each other.

"I still can't believe it," Austra said after a time. "It seems impossible. Maybe it's not true. Maybe it's a false rumor. After all, we are far and far from home."

"I wish I could believe that," Anne said. "But the news came by the Church cuveiturs. And know that it's true. I can feel it." She wiped at her eyes with the back of her hand. "It happened the same night they tried to kill us, you know. The night of that purple moon, when the knights burned the coven. I was meant to die with them."

"Your mother lives yet, and your brother Charles."

"But my father is dead. And Fastia, Elseny, Uncle Robert, all dead, and Lesbeth is missing. It's too much, Austra. And all the sisters of the coven Saint Cer, killed because they stood between me and—" She shuddered back off into sobs.

"Then what shall we do?" Austra said after a time.

Anne closed her eyes and tried to sort through the phantoms that whirled behind her lids. "We have to go home, of course," she said at last. It sounded like a weary stranger talking. "Everything she said . . ." She stopped.

"Who?" Austra asked. "Who said? What's this, Anne."

"Nothing. A dream I had, that's all."

"A dream?"

"It's nothing. I don't want to talk about it." She tried to smooth her cotton dress. "I don't want to talk about anything for a while."

"Let's at least go someplace more private. A chapel, perhaps. It's almost three bells."

The city was already waking up around them from its daily siesta. Traffic along the riverside was picking up as people returned from naps and long lunches to their shops and work, and the illusion of solitude was wiped away.

The Pontro dachi Pelmotori spanned the Za a few tens of perechi to their right. Quiet a few moments before, it was already humming with activity. Like several of the bridges in z'Espino, it was really more like a building, with shops of two and three stories lining both sides, so they couldn't actually see the people walking on the span. All that was visible was the red-stuccoed outer facade with its dark mouths of windows. The bridge belonged to the butcher's guild, and Anne could hear their saws cutting, their boys haggling prices. A bucket of something bloody flew out one of the windows and splashed into the river, narrowly missing a man in a boat. He began shouting up at the bridge, waving his fist.

When another bucket of the same stuff came even closer, he seemed to think better of it and returned to earnestly rowing.

Anne was about to agree with Austra when a shadow fell across them. She looked up and saw a man, dark of complexion—like most Vitellians—and rather tall. His green doublet was faded and a little threadbare. He wore one red stocking and one black. His hand rested on the pommel of a rapier.

"*Dena dicolla, casnaras,*" he said, with a little bow. "What makes such beautiful faces so long and sorrowful?"

"I do not know you, casnar," Anne replied. "But good day to you and the saints bless you."

She looked away, but he did not take the hint. Instead, he stood there, smiling.

Anne sighed. "Come," she said, plucking at Austra's dress. The two of them rose.

"I mean you no harm, casnaras," the man said hastily. "It's just that it is so unusual to see hair of copper and gold here in the south, to hear such charming northern accents. When such treasures of the eye present themselves, it behooves a man to offer whatever services he may."

A small chill ran up Anne's spine. In her grief, she had forgotten to keep her head covered, and so had Austra.

"That's very kind of you," she said quickly, "But my sister and I were just returning home."

"Let me escort you, then."

Anne let her gaze travel around. Though the streets above were now beginning to bustle, this part of the terrace was something like a park, and it was still relatively quiet. To reach the street, she and Austra had to travel some ten yards and climb a dozen stone stairs. The man stood between them and the nearest stair. Worse, another fellow sat on the stairs themselves, taking a more than casual interest in the conversation.

There were probably others she didn't see at all.

She stood straighter. "Will you let us pass, casnar?"

He looked surprised. "Why shouldn't I let you pass? I told you, I mean no harm."

"Very well." She started forward, but he backed away.

"Somehow we've started off on an ill footing," he said. "My name is Erieso dachi Sallatotti. Won't you tell me yours?"

Anne didn't answer, but kept walking.

"Or perhaps I should guess?" Erieso said. "Perhaps one of the birds will tell me your names?"

Anne was now certain she heard someone behind them, as well. Rather than panicking, she felt a swift anger take her grief for wings and rise high. Who was this man, to bother her on this day, to interrupt her mourning?

"You are a liar, Erieso dachi Sallatotti," she said. "You most certainly mean me harm."

The humor vanished from Erieso's face. "I mean only to collect my reward," he said. "I do not see what anyone would want with such a pale and disagreeable catella, but there is silver to be had. So come, will you walk or be dragged?"

"I will call out," Anne replied. "There are people all around."

"That might deprive me of my reward," Erieso said, "but it will not save you. Many in the streetguard seek you, as well, and they might well use you before claiming their silver. That I will not do, I swear by Lord Mamres." He proffered his hand. "Come. Take it. It is the easiest way for you, and for me."

"Is that so?" Anne said, feeling her anger blacken. But she reached for his hand. As their fingers touched, she felt his pulse, the wet flow of his insides.

"Cer curse you," she said. "Worms take you."

Erieso's eyes widened. "Ah!" he croaked. "Ah, no!" He clutched at his chest and sank down to one knee, as if bowing. He vomited.

"Be glad you did not meet me by the light of the moon, Erieso," she said. "Be gladder still that you did not meet me in the dark of it." And with that she stepped past him. The man on the steps stood and stared at her wide-eyed. He said nothing, and he didn't bar their way as they went up to the street.

"What did you do?" Austra asked breathlessly as they slipped into the crowd on the Vio Caistur.

"I don't know," Anne replied.

By the time they reached the stairs, almost all her anger and courage had burned out of her, leaving only fear and confusion.

"It was like that night at the coven, when the men came," Anne said.

"When you blinded the knight."

"Something in me—it frightens me, Austra. How can I do these things?"

"It frightens me, too," Austra agreed. "Do you think you killed him?"

"No, I think he will recover. We must hurry."

They turned from the Vio Caistur into a narrow avenue, hurrying past stocking shops and a tavern that smelled of grilled sardines, through the Piata da Fufiono with its alabaster fountain of the goat-legged saint and on until the streets grew smaller and more tangled until at last they reached the Perto Veto. The women were already out on their balconies, and several groups of men sat drinking on the stoops, just as they had been the day before.

"They're still following us, I think," Austra said, glancing behind.

Anne looked, too, and saw a group of men—five or six of them—rounding the corner.

"Run," Anne said. "It's not far."

"I hope Cazio is there," Austra said.

"Figs for Cazio," Anne muttered.

The girls started running. They had gone only a few yards when Erieso stepped from a side street, pale but angry, another man by his side.

Erieso drew his rapier, a narrow, wicked length of steel. "Sorcel this, witch," he snarled. "I've word that they'll pay every bit as much for you dead, and my goodwill is all worn away."

"What a big prickler for such little girls," a woman taunted down from her balcony. "It's good to see that *real* men have come to our street."

"Rediana!" Anne called up, recognizing the woman. "They mean to kill us!"

"Oh, the duchess likes me now, does she?" Rediana called down. "Not like at the fish market yesterday, eh?"

Erieso snorted. "You'll get no help here, *cara*," he said.

An instant after he said it, an earthen crock full of something odious struck his companion squarely in the skull. The fellow dropped, squealing and pressing his head with his hands. Erieso yelped and began to dodge as he was pelted with rotten fruit and fish bones from more than one window.

His other men had arrived now, though, and they spread out to encircle the girls. They were forced to the middle of the street, where heavy objects couldn't be thrown.

All the women on the street were shouting now.

"I'll wager he's got a limpet in his breeches," one shouted. "Or a wet little snail, all curled for fear in its shell."

"Go back to Northside, where you belong!"

But Erieso, safely out of range of anything dangerous, had ceased paying attention to the ladies of the neighborhood. He advanced on Anne and Austra once more.

"You can't kill us, not in front of all these people," she said.

"There are no people in the Perto Veto," he said. "Only vermin. Even if someone here bothered to tell the tale, no one would listen."

"A pity," a new voice said. "For this tale shall have an interesting ending."

"Cazio!" Austra cried.

Anne didn't look—she could not take her gaze from the tip of Erieso's sword, and she knew Cazio's voice well enough by now.

"And who in the name of Lord Ondro are you?" Erieso asked.

"Why, I'm Cazio Pachiomadio da Chiovattio, and I'm the protector of these two casnaras," he said. "And this is turning out to be a fine day, for I have someone to protect them from. I only wish you were not so clearly cowards—it cheapens my joy. But, no matter."

Anne heard steel snick free of leather.

"Caspator," Cazio said, speaking to his sword, "let's us to work."

"There's six of us, you fool," Erieso said.

Anne heard a quick motion behind her, a gasp, a gurgle.

"You count poorly," Cazio said. "I make only five. Anne, Austra, come back. Quickly."

Anne did as he instructed, nearly brushing Cazio as he slid past her, his sword held out in a level guard.

"Stay behind me," he said.

Now the women were cheering. The fellow Cazio had already run through was dragging himself pitifully off the street as the swordsman engaged Erieso and the rest of his men. Anne wasn't fooled by Cazio's bravado, though—five were too many, even for him. As soon as they surrounded him . . .

But he showed little concern, fighting languidly, almost as if he were bored. He danced in, out, around, and for a moment actually had his opponents standing in a clump, all defending themselves at the same time.

But then their advantage sank in, and they began to flank him. Cazio parried one attack and did a strange sort of twist, binding up his opponent's blade and forcing the point out to the side, where it pricked another of Erieso's men. At the same time, Cazio's point drove hard into his original target's shoulder. Both men cried out and backed away, but neither seemed mortally injured.

"*Za uno-en-dor*," Cazio told them, "my own invention. I—"

He broke off to parry a furious attack by Erieso, then quickly ducked a thrust from another quarter. He scuttled back, but wasn't fast enough to avoid a third thrust, which hit him in the left shoulder. Cazio grunted and grabbed the blade to hold it there, but didn't have time to run the fellow through, for they were all converging on him again.

"Cazio!" Austra cried in pure anguish.

Then a bottle struck one of the men in the head, bursting his ear into a red mess.

Anne looked to see who had thrown it and discovered around thirty men of the neighborhood standing behind her, armed with knives and wooden clubs.

One of them was Ospero. He flicked his thumb at Erieso.

"You there!" Ospero grated. "What do you want with these girls?"

Erieso's lips tightened. "That's my business."

"You're in the Perto Veto, pretty boy. That makes it our business."

Erieso's able men had withdrawn to stand near him. One held his ear, and blood flowed between his fingers. Anne suddenly felt as if she were caught between a pair of lions.

Erieso's face worked through several expressions before he finally sighed. "That one, the one with red hair. She's betrothed to Prince Latro, but the stupid little catella is smitten with this fellow here and ran off. I've been sent to get her back."

"Is that so?" Ospero said. "Is there a reward for her return?"

"No."

"Then why would you be so stupid as to follow her down here?"

"My honor demands it. I promised to get her back."

"Uh-huh. Prince Latro, eh? The same Prince Latro that put the tariff on our fish, so he can sell his cheaper? The same Prince Latro that hanged Fuvro Olufio?"

"I know nothing of these things."

"Then you don't know much. But I'll tell you this—if cutting off my nose would bring pain to Latro da Villanchi, I'd do it gladly. He'll get his girl back. From us. In pieces."

Erieso's face reddened even further. "You won't do that. The prince's wrath would be terrible. He would have the meddisso send troops here. You want that?"

"No," Ospero allowed. "But we're modest, down here in the Perto. We don't much care if we get credit for this sort of thing, only that it happens."

"But how will you—" Erieso's eyes widened as the men suddenly surged forward. "No!"

He turned and ran, and his men ran with him.

Ospero laughed as he watched them vanish from sight. Then he turned back to Anne, Austra, and Cazio.

"He was lying, so I guess there *is* a reward for you," he said to Anne. "I think you'd better tell me what it is, and I think you'd better do it now."

As if to emphasize his point, Ospero's men drew nearer.

CHAPTER EIGHT

THE BASIL-NIX

I'M GOING TO DIE, Leoff thought. It seemed a slow thought, as everything seemed slow, and limned in a peculiar golden light. He could see everything about the man who was approaching him all at once. His hair was light, cut in uneven bangs. It was too dark to tell the color of his eyes, but they were set wide on his face. His jerkin was open almost to his belly. His ears stuck out. He had a rag tied around his head.

And there was the sword, lovely as a viper in the moonlight.

He'd meant to run, but when he looked up and saw how close death was already, he knew he didn't want it in the back.

Then something came sailing past him, another shard of moonlight, and it hit the man high in the chest. That stopped him. He yelped and looked down. Something metal hit the ground and sang a perfect note. It seemed to hang there, undergirded by a strange set of harmonies.

"Damn," Gilmer said.

"Silly bugger," the man said, lifting his sword again. "I'll have your testicles for that before you die." But then he hesitated.

The singing Leoff had heard hadn't been in his head. It was there, below the wall, a spine-chilling sound. It was only reluctantly that he recognized it as men screaming—or crying out, at least, at the tops of their lungs.

The man with the sword was standing just next to the edge, and he looked over.

Then he tried to join the song. His mouth gaped, and the cords of his neck stood out like wire. Finally, he simply collapsed.

"What?" Gilmer started forward to look, as well, but Leoff tackled him to the stone and lay there, trying to hold him down.

"Don't," he gasped. "*Don't*. I don't know what was in that box, but I know we mustn't look at it."

The man with the sword had fallen so his head was turned toward them. Even in the moonlight they could see that his eyes had gone to ash, just like the eyes of the other dead in Broogh.

There was still shouting below.

"Don't look at it!"

"Cover your eyes! Let Reev and Hilman get it."

"It didn't get them all," Leoff whispered.

"*What* didn't get them all?" Gilmer asked.

Leoff noticed that the old man was trembling.

A stronger, more commanding voice rose over the others: "That came from the wall. Someone's still in there. Find them. Kill them."

"That means us," Leoff said. "Come on. And don't look!"

The two men scrambled down the stairs and back into the silent town.

"How long will it take them to come around?" Leoff huffed, as they raced over rough cobblestones.

"Not long. They'll come in by the south gate. We'd better hide. Come on, this way."

He led Leoff through several turns, across the square below the bell tower, and up another street.

"I wonder how many it got, whatever it was?"

"No telling."

"Shsst!" Gilmer said. "Stop. Listen."

Leoff did, and though the sounds of his breath and heart cloyed in his ears, he could make out what Gilmer had stopped for—the footsteps of several men approaching the spot where they stood.

"Come on, in here," Gilmer said. He unlatched the door of a three-story building, and they entered it. They took the stairs to the second story, to a room with a bed and a curtained window. Gilmer went to the window.

"Take care," Leoff said. "They might have it with them."

"Auy, raeht. I'll just peek."

The smaller man went to the window. Leoff was watching him nervously when a hand clapped over his mouth from behind.

"Shh," a voice said in his ear. "It's me, Artwair."

Gilmer turned at even that faint sound.

"My lord Artwair!" he gasped.

"Hello, windsmith," Artwair said. "What sort of trouble have you gotten us into?"

"My *lord*?" Leoff repeated.

"You didn't know?" Gilmer said. "Sir Artwair is our duke, cousin to His Highness, Emperor Charles."

"No," Leoff said. "I did not know that. My lord—"

"Hush," Artwair said. "This is of no importance now. They're coming, close on your heels, and they will find you. The basil-nix has a keen nose."

"Basil-nix?"

"Auy. Our darkest legends come to life, these days."

"That's what was in the box?"

"Auy." He grinned tightly. "When I arrived, they were walking the streets with it, shining it about like a lantern. I saw the last of the townspeople die. I have my old nurse to thank for my life, for only from her tales did I understand what was happening. I averted my eyes before its gaze turned my way. Of course, when you burst its cage, I nearly died again, because I was watching. Still, that was clever. I think you killed more than half of them before they got the thing covered again."

"You saw?"

Artwair nodded. "I was watching from the south tower."

"How did they manage to capture and cover the thing?"

"They have two blind men with them," he said. "They serve as its handlers. The rest walk behind. The cage is like an aenan lamp, closed on all sides but one. It makes a light, this thing, and once you have seen it, you can resist only through the greatest contest of will."

"But the cage is shattered now."

"Auy. And so they must take greater care, and so must we."

"We must flee, before they find us."

"No," Artwair said softly. "I think we must fight. Two men remain at the dike. It will take them longer, but they will still open it if we give them time. We can't allow that."

"No," Gilmer agreed. "Not after Broogh gave its life."

"But how can we fight something we cannot look at?" Leoff wondered.

Artwair lifted something near the door. Two flasks of blue glass, filled with liquid. Rags had been stuffed in the top.

"Here is my plan," Artwair said.

Moments later, Leoff stood facing down the stairs. Artwair stood below him on the first landing, a shadow with a bow held before him, and an arrow nocked. Gilmer crouched behind Leoff at the window, with his eyes squeezed tightly shut.

"They're here," Artwair's voice came up. "Be ready."

Leoff nodded nervously. He gripped a candle in one hand and one of the flasks of oil in the other. Gilmer was similarly armed.

Leoff heard the door open, and the bow sang a low pitch.

"They have a bow!" someone yelped.

"Move up!" another voice commanded. "They can't hit what they can't see. If they open their eyes, they'll die."

Footsteps started up the stairs. The bow whined again, and again, and someone shouted in pain.

"A lucky shot," shouted the person who seemed to be their leader. "Up, and quickly."

"Now!" Artwair hollered, and ran back up the stairs.

Leoff lit the oil-soaked rag.

And he saw a light suffusing the landing. It was beautiful, golden, the most perfect light he had ever seen. A promise of absolute peace filled him, and he knew that he could not live without seeing the source of that light.

"Now, I say!" Artwair shouted.

Distantly, Leoff heard glass breaking and a renewal of shouts from below. Gilmer must have thrown his flask, aiming for the entrance to the house. But Gilmer didn't see the light, didn't understand . . .

Leoff suddenly remembered the corpses in the inn. He remembered their eyes.

He threw the flask at the landing Artwair had just vacated. The light was brighter now, more beautiful than ever. Even as flame blossomed like a many-petaled rose, Leoff leaned out to catch a glimpse, just a small glimpse—

And then Artwair knocked him roughly to the floor.

"By all the saints, what do you think you're doing? You *cannot* look!" he snarled.

More screams. It was a night for screams. The oil burned quickly, and so did the mostly timber house.

"Gilmer!" Artwair shouted. "Did you hit the doorstep?"

"Auy, that I did," Gilmer replied. "I reckoned it was worth risking a peek, since they had the thing on the stairs. My aim was true." He scratched his head. "Course, now we're trapped in a burning house."

"So are they," Artwair said. He went to the window, pushed open the curtain, and set an arrow on the bow. "Now is the reckoning," he said. "Watch the stairs. If any get through, call out."

The stairwell was already an inferno, and choking smoke boiled up. This was also a night for fire, Leoff mused. He was destined to burn, it seemed.

He heard the bow twang over the roar and over the screaming. And again, as Artwair fired at something in the street.

A shadow came up through the flame then, something the size of a small dog, but serpentine. The flames turned golden.

Leoff snapped his eyes shut.

"Close your eyes," he screamed. "It's come up."

"Follow my voice," Artwair returned. "The window. We have to jump."

"Here," Gilmer said. He grasped Leoff's hand and pulled him up. The smell from earlier was all around, and he felt his skin tingle from more than the heat.

Then he touched the window frame, and driven by terror he

gripped it, stepped through, hung for an instant by his fingers, and dropped.

His belly rose to his head, and then the ground seemed to explode under his feet. A pain brighter than any sun lit him up.

Someone tugged at him. Gilmer, again.

"Get up," the small man said.

Leoff tried to answer, but he gagged on his tongue instead.

Artwair's face appeared in the ruddy firelight.

"He's broken his leg. Help me move him."

They dragged him away from the fire, which had begun to spread. Darkness crept in with the pain, and Leoff lost track of what was happening a time or two. The next thing he knew clearly was that they were in a boat, on the canal.

"Stay with him, Gilmer," Artwair said grimly. "I've two more to deal with. Then we can go."

"Go where?" Gilmer said, and for the first time despair colored his voice. "My malend, my town . . ." He was weeping now.

Leoff lay his head back, watched the smoke rise against the stars as the boat rocked gently on the canal. He tried not to think about the pain.

"How's the leg?" Artwair asked.

"A dull ache," Leoff replied, glancing at his limb. It had been splinted tight, but even so, every jounce the wagon made in the deeply rutted road sent a throb up his thigh, even with the hay bales to cushion it. Artwair had hired the cart and the untalkative fellow who drove it.

"It was a clean enough break, and should heal well," Artwair said.

"Yes, I suppose I'm lucky," Leoff said glumly.

"I mourn for Broogh, too," Artwair said, his voice gentling. "The fire claimed only a few buildings."

"But they're all dead," Leoff said.

"Most are, auy," Artwair allowed. "But some were afar, or late in the fields."

"And the children," Leoff said. "Who will look after them?"

Gilmer and Artwair had made a house-to-house search the morning after the fire. Thirty children they had found in all, still in cribs or abed. Those old enough to be out had shared their parents' fate.

"They will be cared for," he said, "Their duke will see to it."

"Yes, that," Leoff sighed. "Why did you not tell me who you were, my lord?"

"Because one learns more, sees more, lives more when people aren't constantly calling him 'my lord,'" Artwair replied. "Many a greffy and kingdom has come to ruin because its lord had no knowledge of what went on in its roads and on its streets."

"You're an unusual duke," Leoff said.

"And you're an unusual composer—I suppose, though I'd never heard of one before I met you. You've done me—and this empire—a great service."

"It was Gilmer," Leoff said. "I didn't understand. I would have run far away, if it had been just me. I'm no hero, no man of action."

"Gilmer has lived here all his life. His obligations and duty are rooted deep in his bones. You are a stranger, and owe this place nothing—and as you say, you aren't a warrior. Still you risked all for it. You are a hero, sir, the more because you wished to run and did not."

"And yet we saved so little."

"Are you mad? Do you have any idea how many would have perished had they broken the dike? What cost to the kingdom?"

"No," Leoff said. "I know only that an entire town has died."

"It happens," Artwair said. "In war and famine, in flood and fire."

"But why? What were those men about? Where did they get that terrible creature?"

"I wish I knew," Artwair said. "I *very* much wish I knew. When I returned to the dike, the last two men had fled. The rest were killed by the fire or by the basil-nix."

"And the creature," Leoff asked. "Did it escape?"

Artwair shook his head. "It burned. That's it on Galast, there."

Leoff looked. The packhorse had an irregular bundle on it, wrapped in leather.

"Is it safe?" he asked.

"I wrapped it myself, and have suffered no ill."

"Where did such a thing come from?"

The duke shrugged. "Some months ago a greffyn was slain at Cal Azroth. A year ago I would have sworn all such creatures were nothing but children's alvspellings. But now we have a basil-nix, as well. It's as if a whole hidden world is waking around us."

"A world of evil," Leoff said.

"The world has always had plenty of evil in it," Artwair said. "But I'll admit, its face seems to be changing."

By noon, Leoff saw what he thought at first was a cloud hunkered on the horizon, but he gradually made out the slim towers and the pennants upon them and realized that what he saw was a hill rising up from the great flat bottom of Newland.

"Is that it?" he asked.

"Auy," Artwair replied. "That's Ynis, the royal island."

"Island? It looks like a hill."

"It's too flat here to see the water. The Warlock and the Dew meet on this side of Ynis, and divide around it. On the other side is Foambreaker Bay, and the Lier Sea. The castle there is Eslen."

"It looks big."

"It is," Artwair said. "They say Eslen Castle has more rooms than the sky has stars. I don't know—I've never counted either."

Soon they came to the confluence, and Leoff saw that Eslen was indeed on an island of sorts. The Dew—the river they had crossed at poor, doomed Broogh—ran into another bediked river, the Warlock. The Warlock was enormous, perhaps half a league in width, and together the rivers formed a sort of lake from which the hills of Ynis rose precipitously.

"We'll take the ferry across," Artwair said. "Then I'll make certain the right introductions are made. I've no way of knowing if your position is secure, but if it is, we'll find out. If it isn't, come to my estates at Haundwarpen, and I'll find a place for you."

"Thank you, my lord."

"Call me Artwair—it's how you came to know me."

❖   ❖   ❖

When they came in sight of the ferry crossing, Leoff feared they had come up on an encamped army. As they drew nearer, he saw that if it was an army, it was a terribly patchwork and unorganized one. Tents and wagons had formed themselves into a sort of maze with narrow avenues and squares, almost a makeshift city. Smoke curled from a few cookfires, but not as many as he might have expected. He remembered what Gilmer had said about wood being scarce.

People certainly weren't scarce, though. Leoff guessed that several thousand were gathered there, and most of them weren't in wagons and tents but were disposed upon blankets or the bare ground. They watched the cart pass, and their faces showed many expressions—most commonly greed, anger, and hopelessness.

At the heart of this ragtag encampment was a more orderly one, with tents all flying the king's colors and no lack of armed men wearing them. As they approached the camp, a man of middle years stepped out into the road, a hard look of determination reflected in his eyes.

"Clear off," the driver said.

The man ignored him, looking up instead at Artwair. "My lord," he said. "I know you. I worked in your city guard when I was younger."

Artwair peered down at him. "What do you want?" he asked.

"My wife, my lord, and my children. Take them into the city, I beg you."

"And put them where?" Artwair asked softly. "If there were room in the city, you wouldn't have been stopped here. No, they're better off outside, my friend."

"They are not, my lord. Terrors stalk this land. Everyone talks of war. I am not a man easily frightened, my lord Artwair, and yet I fear. And it's damp here. When the rains come, we will have no shelter."

"You would have none in the city, either," Artwair said regretfully. "Here you have the water to drink, and soft ground, and some food at least. In there you would have nothing but beds of stone and piss thrown from windows to lick up for your thirst."

"But we would have the wall," the man said, his voice pleading now.

"The things you fear will not be stopped by walls," Artwair said. Then he straightened. "Remind me of your name, sir."

"Jan Readalvson, my lord."

"Come into the city with me, Fralet Readalvson. You'll see for yourself it's no place for your family, not at the moment. Furthermore, I'm going to give you a charge—distributing food, clothing, and shelter to these people. I trust that after you provide for your family, you will be fair in your disbursements. I will check on you, from time to time. It is the best I can do."

Readalvson bowed. "You are very generous, lord."

Artwair nodded. "We'll move along, now."

They boarded the ferry and began their short journey across the water. Above them, the castle rose like a mountain, and the city rolled down like its slopes, an avalanche of black-roofed houses stopped only by the great wall that encircled it.

As they neared the broad stone quay, Leoff saw conditions there were much as they were on the side they'd just left. Hundreds of people were huddled on the far side of the quay, though these were without wagons or tents, and their expressions held less hope.

"You said you served in my guard." Artwair spoke to their new companion. "From whence do you hail now?"

"I heard there was steading in the east, near the King's Forest. I took a wain there ten years ago and built a farm." His voice seemed broken. "Then the Briar King woke, or so they say, and the black vines came—and worse." He looked up. "There are times I can still hear the shrieks of my neighbors."

"They were killed?"

"I don't know. The tales—I could not risk to see, do you understand? I had my children to think of. I still feel them at my back, though, I still feel the shiver in my bones."

Leoff felt a shiver in his bones, as well. What was become of the world? Was the end truly at hand, when the heavens would splinter and fall like shards of a broken pot?

When they reached the quay, the crowd pressed toward them, but the city guard pushed them back, and a path cleared. A few moments later, the gate creaked wide, and they entered the city itself.

Their way led them into a courtyard, and beyond that, through a second gate. The walls above them bristled with guards, but clearly they recognized Artwair, and so the inner gate was opened.

The main thoroughfare to the castle wound through the city as if it were a great snake crawling up the hill. Leoff propped his back against the wagon to sit for a better view as they jounced past chapels of ancient marble streaked and decayed by a thousand years of rain and smoke, houses with steepled roofs stabbing skyward, low cottages with white walls and red trim crammed tightly together save where narrow alleys divided them. Most buildings were of two stories, with the upper stories overhanging a bit—some few were of three.

They rolled into another plaza, in the center of which stood a weathered bronze statue of a woman with her foot upon the throat of a winged serpent. The beast coiled and writhed beneath her boot, and her face was as cold and imperious as the north wind.

Near a hundred people were gathered in the square, and for a moment, Leoff thought it a mob, but then he heard a bright soprano and pulled himself up farther. On the broad pedestal of the statue, a troop of players was performing, accompanied by a small ensemble of instrumentalists and singers. The instruments were simple—a lesser and bass croth, a drum and three pipers. When Leoff arrived, a woman had just finished singing as another woman in a green gown and gilt crown acted out her words. The player seemed to be addressing a man on a throne. Leoff had missed the words of the song, for the crowd roared in response and drowned her out, but the tune was a simple one, a well-known tavern ballad.

The man on the throne drew himself up, grinning stupidly.

"Hold a moment," Leoff said. "Can I hear a bit of this?"

Artwair shot him an ironic look. "You may as well have your introduction to the court, I suppose. The lady in green represents our good queen Muriele, I believe."

The man coughed, as if to clear his throat. Down among the musicians, a chorus of three men sang.

He is the King,
Ha, ha, ha,
He is the King,
Tee, hee, hee
What shall he do,
Ha, ha, ha
Touched by the Saints,
Tee, hee, hee

The player broke off into the helpless laughter of an idiot and gamboled a bit while the chorus repeated its verse. A ridiculous figure in a huge hat joined the "king" in his dance.

"Our good king Charles," Artwair said wryly. "And his jester."

The instruments fell silent, and the player acting the king suddenly spoke what seemed to Leoff to be gibberish.

A sinister figure in black robes with a long, ridiculous goatee ran onto the stage. He fawned up to the queen. He did not sing, but spoke in a theatrical fashion that resembled chant.

"Let me interpret!" the black-robed figure cried. "Good Queen, your son has proclaimed, in the voice of the saints, that I should be given the whole of the kingdom. That I should be handed the keys to the city, that I should have leave to fondle your—"

The audience finished his sentence for him in a roar.

"Our beloved praifec Hespero," Artwair explained.

"What's this!" A group of three men dressed as ministers rushed up, tripping and bumbling into one another. Below them, a chorus began singing,

Here, here are nobles three
Who claim the Praifec wrong, you see
Charles speaks in Fing, not Churchalees,
And they say that his thoughts are these . . .

They paused, and the music changed meter, became a rather jolly dance.

Raise the taxes,
Draw the gates,
Bring them damsels, bring them cakes
War's a bother
They don't see,
They are nobles foolish three!

The "nobles" covered their eyes, and the chorus began another verse as they capered around the queen.

"Our wise and beloved Comven," Artwair said.

The queen drew herself up in the midst of this.

"The Queen implores!" she chanted. "Is there no one to save us in our time of darkness?"

The chorus then launched into a song of loss and mourning for the queen's children, while she danced a pavane for the dead, and the other songs came back as counterpoint.

"Is that the sort of thing you compose?" Artwair asked.

"Not really," Leoff murmured, fascinated by the spectacle. "Is that the sort of thing that's common around here?"

"The *lustspell*? Auy, but it's a thing for the street, you understand. The common folk like it. The aristocracy pretends it doesn't exist— save when it goes too far in mocking them. Then the players might have a more tragic end to their play."

He glanced back at the singers. "We'd best move on."

Leoff nodded thoughtfully as Artwair spoke to the driver and the wagon creaked back to life, climbing through steadily wealthier neighborhoods.

"The people seem to have scant faith in their leaders," Leoff remarked, reflecting on the content of the tale.

"Times are hard," Artwair answered. "William was only a middling good king, but the kingdom was prosperous and at peace, and everyone liked him. Now he's dead, along with Elseny and Lesbeth, who were truly beloved. The new king, Charles—well, the portrayal you just saw of him was not unfair. He's a nice enough lad, but saint-touched.

"Our allies, even Lier, have turned against us, and Hansa threatens war. Demons come from the woodwork, refugees crowd the streets, and the marshwitches all foretell doom. People need a strong leader in times like this, and they don't have one." He sighed. "Would that unflattering portrayals of the court were the worst of it, but the guilds are up in arms, and I fear bread riots are not far away. Half the crops withered in the field the night of the purple moon, and the sea catch has been bad."

"What of the queen? You said she was strong."

"Auy. Strong and beautiful and as distant from her people as the stars. And she's Lierish, of course. In these times, with Liery making renegade noise, some don't trust her."

Leoff absorbed that. "The news from Broogh won't make things any better, will it?"

"Not a bit. But better than if Newland had been drowned." He clapped Leoff on the shoulder. "Worry not. After what you've done, we'll find you a stipend of some sort."

"Oh," Leoff said. He hadn't been thinking about his own worries. The eyes of Broogh would not let him.

CHAPTER NINE

PROPOSALS

THE VIEW FROM THE throne was a long one, a vista of knife-points and poison.

The buttresses of the greater hall rose like the massive, spreading trunks of trees into a pale haze of cold light coming from the high window slits. Above that smoky atmosphere lay another, deeper vault of darkness. Pigeons cooed and fluttered there, for they were impossible to keep out of the vast space, as were the cats that prowled behind the curtains and tapestries in search of them.

Muriele often wondered how such an immense space could feel so *heavy*. It was as if—in entering the great bronze valves that were its entrance—one were transported so far beneath the earth that the very air itself became a sort of stone. At the same time, she felt perilously high, as if in stepping through one of the windows, she might find herself falling from a mountaintop.

It seemed like all the worst of Heaven and Hell were present in the symmetries of the place.

Her husband—the late King William—had seldom used the great hall, preferring the lesser court for his audiences. It was easier to heat, for one thing, and today the great hall was freezing.

Let them freeze, Muriele thought of the assembled faces. *Let their teeth chatter. Let pigeon shit fall upon their brocades and velvets. Let this place crush them down.*

Examining the people who had gathered before the throne, she hated them all. Someone—probably someone who was out there staring up at her now—had arranged or helped to arrange the murder of her children. Someone out there had killed her husband. Someone out there had left her with *this*, a life of fear and grief, and as far as she was concerned, it might as well have been all of them.

Knifepoints and poison. Five hundred people, all wanting something from her, some wanting her very life.

A few of the latter were easy to spot. There was the pale face of Ambria Gramme, the black lace of mourning on her head, as if *she* had been the queen and not merely the king's mistress. There was Ambria's eldest bastard, Renwald, dressed as a prince might dress. There were Gramme's three lovers from the Comven, pressed near as if to hold her up above the crowd, blissfully unaware—or perhaps uncaring—that each was cuckold to the other.

Gramme would kill her in a heartbeat if she thought she could get away with it.

To Muriele's left stood Praifec Hespero in his black robes and square hat, hand lifted idly to stroke his narrow goatee, his eyes nearly unblinking as he absorbed each word around him and arranged them in his plans. What did he want? He played the friend, of course, the advocate, but those who had slain her daughters had worn churchly robes. They were said to have been renegade, but how could she take anything for granted?

And here, just approaching her feet, a new pack of dogs dressed in silk were crouching, peering at her, looking to see if her neck was exposed to their teeth. She wished she could have them killed out of hand, slaughtered like animals and fed to pigs.

But she could not. Truly, she had few weapons.

And one of them was her smile.

So she smiled at the leader of the pack and nodded her head, and to her left, her son on the emperor's throne copied her by nodding his head, indicating that the dog could rise from his bended knee and bark.

"Your Majesty," he said, speaking to her son, "it is pleasing to see you in good health."

Charles, the emperor—her son—widened his eyes. "Your cloak is pretty," he said.

It was indeed. The archgreft Valamhar af Aradal liked his clothes. The cloak her son so admired was an ivory-and-gold brocade worn over a doublet of sea green that matched the archgreft's eyes. It did not, however, match his florid pink face with its standing veins or his corpulent form.

His guard, in black-and-sanguine surcoats, were trimmer but no less garish.

"Thank you, Your Majesty," he said in a tone of absolute seriousness, ignoring the snickers, as if that were a perfectly reasonable response from an emperor.

But she saw the ridicule hiding in his eyes.

"Queen Mother," Aradal purred, bowing now to Muriele, "I hope I find you well."

"Very well indeed," Muriele said brightly. "It is always a pleasure to welcome our cousins from Hansa. Please convey my delight at your presence to your sovereign Marcomir."

Aradal bowed again. "In that I will not fail. I hope to convey more to him, however."

"Indeed," Muriele said. "You may convey my condolences on the recent death of the Duke of Austrobaurg. I believe the duke was a close friend to His Majesty."

Aradal frowned, very briefly, and Muriele watched him closely. Austrobaurg and her husband had died together on the windswept headland of Aenah in some sort of secret meeting. Austrobaurg was a Hansan vassal.

"That is most gracious, Your Majesty. The whole matter is as puzzling as it is tragic. Austrobaurg will be missed, as shall Emperor William and Prince Robert. I hope—as I know you hope—that the villains behind that atrocity will be brought soon to light."

As he said it, he cast a brief glance at Sir Fail de Liery. The corpses on the headland had been riddled by Lierish arrows.

Sir Fail purpled, but said nothing—which for him showed admirable and nearly unheard-of restraint.

Muriele sighed, wishing she still had Erren by her side. Erren would have known in an instant whether Aradal was concealing something. To Muriele he sounded sincere.

"There has been much regrettable loss of life, these past months," he continued, glancing back at Charles. He bowed. "Your Majesty, I know your time is valuable. I wonder if I might come directly to the point."

"So I command," Charles said, looking slightly aside at Muriele to see if he had spoken properly.

"Thank you, Your Majesty. As you well know, these are unsettling times in many other ways. Uncanny things walk in the night, terrible prophecies seem to be fulfilled. Tragedy looms everywhere, most terribly for your family."

My face is stone, Muriele told herself.

But even stone would melt if it contained her fury. She didn't know for certain who had arranged the slaughter of her husband and daughters, but there could be little doubt that Hansa was involved, despite the puzzle of Austrobaurg. Hansan kings had once sat the throne her son now occupied, and they never ceased dreaming of taking it back and placing it once more beneath their buttocks.

But if there was little doubt of their involvement, there was also little proof. So she did her best to keep her composure, but worried that she was not entirely succeeding.

"His Majesty sent me here to offer our friendship in these troubled times. We are all one beneath the eyes of the saints. We would hope to put any past unpleasantness behind us."

"It is a commendable gesture," Muriele said.

"My lord offers more than gesture, milady," Aradal said. He snapped his fingers, and one of his servants placed a box of polished rosewood in his hands. He bowed, and handed it toward Muriele.

"Surely that is meant for my son, archgreft," Muriele said.

"Present?" Charles mumbled.

"No, milady. It is for you. A token of affection."

"From King Marcomir?" she said. "A married man? Not too affectionate, I should hope."

Aradal smiled. "No, milady. It is from his son, Prince Berimund."

"Berimund?" She had last seen Berimund when he was five, and it didn't seem that long ago. "*Little* Berimund?"

"The prince is now twenty and three, Queen Mother."

"Yes, and so I could easily be *his* mother," Muriele said.

A chuckle went around the court at that. Aradal's face reddened. "Milady—"

"Dear Aradal, I am only joking," she said. "Let us see what the prince has sent us."

The servant opened the box, revealing an exquisite chatelaine of formed gold set with emeralds. Muriel widened her smile, allowing her teeth to show a bit. "It is exquisite," she said. "But how can I accept it? I already wear the chatelaine of the house Dare. I cannot wear two."

Aradal's face finally colored a bit. "Your Majesty, let me be frank. The friendship my lord Berimund offers is of the most affectionate sort. He would make you his bride, and one day Queen of Hansa."

"Oh, dear," Muriele said. "More and more generous. When did the prince conceive this great love for me? I am flattered beyond all words. That a woman of my years can excite such passions—" She broke off, knowing that she was only seconds away from saying the words that might start a war. She stopped, and breathed deeply before continuing.

"The gift is exquisite," she said. "Yet I fear that my grief is too fresh for me to accept it. If the prince is honest in his intentions, I beg that he give me time to recover before pressing his suit."

Aradal bowed, then stepped nearer, lowering his voice. "Majesty," he whispered, "do not be unwise. You may not believe me, but I not only respected your husband, I liked him. I am only a messenger—I do not set in motion the affairs of state in Hansa. But I know something of your situation here, and it is a tenuous one. In these times, you must look to your security. It is what William would have wanted."

Muriele dropped her voice low to match the archgreft's. "Do not presume to speak for my husband's ghost," she said. "He has not been cold for very long. This offer, at this time, is inappropriate. You know that, Aradal. I have told you I will consider it, and I will. That is the best I can do, for the moment."

Aradal's voice dropped still lower, as everyone in the chamber strained to perceive the faint conversation. Muriele felt five hundred gazes needling at her, looking to see what new advantage they might find in this.

"I agree, lady, that the timing is inopportune," Aradal admitted. "It is not how I would have chosen to do things. But time is against us all. The world brims with war and treachery. If you will not think of your security, think of your people. With everything that has happened, does Crotheny need a war?"

Muriele frowned. "Is that a threat, archgreft?"

"I would never threaten you, lady. I feel nothing but compassion for your situation. But it is not a threat to look at dark clouds and guess that a storm is coming. It is not a threat to council a friend to seek shelter."

"You are a friend," Muriele lied. "I see that. I will consider your council most sincerely, but I cannot, will not give you an answer today."

Aradal looked grim, but he nodded. "As you wish, Majesty. But if I were you, Your Highness, I would not delay for long."

"You will not delay another second," Sir Fail de Liery roared, his face so red with fury that his hair might have been a plume of white smoke drifting up from it. "You will tell that puffed-up oyster from Hansa that you utterly reject any overture from his thimble-headed prince."

Muriele watched her uncle pace like a chained birsirk for a moment. The court was over, and they were in her private solar, a room as airy and open as the court was cold and hard.

"I must appear to consider all offers," she said.

"No," he replied, pointing a finger, "that is certainly not true. You cannot contemplate delivering—or even *appear* to consider delivering—the Kingdom and Empire of Crotheny to Marcomir's heir."

Muriele rolled her eyes. "What heir? Even if I were to marry him,

I would still have to produce one. Even if I had a mind to—and I do not—do you honestly think I could, at my age?"

"It doesn't matter," Sir Fail snapped. "There are wheels within wheels turning here. Marrying you gives them the throne in all but name." He pounded the casement of the window with the heel of his hand. "You must marry Lord Selqui," he snapped.

Muriele raised an eyebrow. "Must I?" she said coldly.

"Yes, you must. It is entirely the best course of action, and I should think you would see that."

She rose, her fists balling so tightly that her nails cut into her palms. "I have listened now to five marriage proposals, with William's breath still warm on the wind. I have been as patient and gracious as I can be. But you are more than a foreign envoy, Fail de Liery. You are my uncle. My blood. You put me on your knee when I was five and told me it was the waterhorse, and I laughed like any child and loved you. Now you have become just one of *them*, another man coming into my house, telling me what I must do. I will not have this from *you*, Uncle. I am no longer a little girl, and you will *not* impose upon my affection."

Fail's eyes widened, and then his features softened a bit. "Muriele," he said, "I'm sorry. But as you say, we are blood. You are a de Liery. The rift between Crotheny and Liery is growing. It isn't your fault—something William was up to. Did you know he lent ships to Saltmark in their battles against the Sorrow Isles?"

"That is a rumor," Muriele said. "It is also rumored that Lierish archers killed my husband."

"You cannot believe that. The evidence for that was obviously contrived."

"At this point, you cannot imagine what I would believe," Muriele said.

Fail seemed to bite back a retort, then sighed. He suddenly looked ancient, and for a moment she wanted nothing more than to hug him, feel that rough old cheek against hers.

"Whatever the cause," Fail said, "the problem remains. You can heal this wound, Muriele. You can bring our nations back together."

"And you think Liery and Crotheny together can stand against Hansa?"

"I know that alone, neither of us can."

"That isn't what I asked."

He puffed his cheeks out and nodded.

"I am a de Liery," she said. "I am also a Dare. I have two children left, and both are heirs to this throne. I must protect it for them."

Fail's voice gentled further. "It is well known that Charles cannot get a child."

"Thank the saints, or I should be dealing with proposals for *his* hand."

"Then when you speak of heirs, you mean Anne. Muriele, William's legitimization of his daughters has little precedent. The Church is against it—Praifec Hespero has already begun a campaign to annul the law. Even if it stands, what if Anne . . ." He stumbled, his lips thinning. "What if Anne is also dead?"

"Anne is alive," Muriele said.

Fail nodded. "I dearly hope Anne is still alive. Nevertheless, there are other heirs to consider, and you know they *are* being considered."

"Not by me."

"It may not be up to you."

"I will die long before I see one of Ambria Gramme's bastards put on the throne."

Fail smiled grimly. "She is a very political animal," he said. "She has won over more than half the Comven to her cause, as you must know. Muriele, you must be reconciled, both with the Comven and with your father's people. This is not the time to further divide Crotheny."

"Nor is it the time to return it to Lierish rule," she said.

"That is not what I am proposing."

"That is precisely what you are proposing."

"Muriele, dear, something must be done. Things cannot continue as they are. Charles does not—will never—hold the people's trust. They know the saints have touched him, and in gentler times, they might not care. But terrible things are happening, things beyond our understanding. Some say the end of the world is upon us. They want a strong leader, a certain one. And there is still the fact that he cannot father an heir."

"Anne could be a strong leader."

"Anne is a willful child, and all the kingdom knows it. Besides, with each passing day, the rumor is growing that Anne shares her sisters' fate. The dangers on your borders are multiplying. If you do not give Hansa the throne by marriage, they will take it by force. Only their hopes and the feeble worry that the Church might intervene have delayed them this long."

"I know all of this," Muriele said wearily.

"Then you know you must act, before they do."

"I cannot act rashly. Even if I were to marry Selqui, it would anger as many as it would please. More. If I spurn the offer from Hornladh, they might well join Hansa against us. There is no clear course for me here, Sir Fail."

"*Your* course is made clear by your loyalties. Mine is made invisible by mine. I need real council, real options, not this continued pressure from every direction. I need one single person I can count on, one person who has no loyalties other than to me."

"Muriele—"

"No. You know you cannot be that. Lierish seawater flows in your veins. As much as I love you, you know I cannot trust you here. I wish I could, but I cannot."

"Then whom can you trust?"

Muriele felt a solitary tear start in her eye and roll down her cheek. She turned so he would not see it. "No one, of course. Please leave me, Sir Fail."

"Muriele—" She could hear his voice break with emotion.

"Go," she said.

A moment later, she heard the door close. She went to the window, gripped the frame with her fingers, and wondered how sunlight could seem so dark.

CHAPTER TEN

OSPERO

CAZIO STEPPED BETWEEN ANNE and Ospero. He didn't raise his sword to guard, but he did keep it in front of him.

"As I told those other fellows," he said firmly, "these ladies are under my protection. I am no more willing to give them up to you than I was to them."

Ospero's eyes tightened, and he suddenly seemed very dangerous indeed, even without the twenty-odd men gathered behind him.

"Careful how you talk to me, boy," he said. "There are many things you do not know."

"There certainly are," Cazio responded. "I do not know how many seeds there are in a pomegranate. I do not know what sort of hats they wear in Herilanz. I've no understanding whatever of the language of dogs, and I cannot tell you how a water pump works. But I know I have sworn to protect these two ladies, and protect them I will."

"I've made no threat to your charges," Ospero said. "On the other hand, they have become a threat to me. When swordsmen from Northside come into *my* town, I am very much concerned. When I am forced to act against them, it is even more my concern. Now I have to kill them all and sink their bodies in the marsh, and I need to know if anyone will miss them. I need to know *who* will miss them, and who, if anyone, will come to look for them. And most of all, I need to know why they came here in the first place."

"And the reward does not concern you?" Cazio asked skeptically.

"We haven't gotten to that yet," Ospero said.

"Nor shall we," Cazio replied. "Now, kindly send your men away."

"Boy—," Ospero began.

"I don't know who they were," Anne blurted. "I only know someone wants me dead and is willing to pay for it. I can't answer any of your other questions, because I don't *know* the answers. I thank you for your help against those men, Ospero. I believe you are a gentleman at heart, and that you will not take advantage of the situation."

Ospero graveled out a laugh, and many of his men echoed it. "I'm no gentleman," he said. "That, above all, you can be sure of."

Cazio raised his sword deliberately.

"You don't want to do that, boy," Ospero said.

"I think I know better than you what I want to do," Cazio replied haughtily.

Ospero nodded slightly. Then he moved with astonishing speed, dropping and whipping his leg out so that he clipped Cazio's leading foot. Cazio spun half around, and Ospero stood and almost lazily took his sword arm and twisted it so the sword fell clattering to the ground. As if by magic, a knife appeared in his other hand and flashed up to Cazio's throat.

"I think," Ospero said, "you've need of a lesson in respect."

"He's in need of many lessons of that sort," a new voice said.

"Z'Acatto!" Austra shouted.

It was indeed the old man, shuffling down the street toward them. "What do you plan to do with him, Ospero?" z'Acatto asked.

"I'm just deciding whether to bleed him out quickly or slowly."

"Do your worst," Cazio gritted.

"I'd say to do it quickly," z'Acatto advised. "He's likely to make a long-winded speech otherwise."

"I can see that," Ospero mused.

"Z'Acatto!" Cazio yelped.

The old man sighed. "You'd better let him go."

Anne braced herself. She knew that despite his appearance,

z'Acatto was a mestro of the sword, and also that he had a deep love for Cazio. He wouldn't let the younger man die without a fight. Could she summon the power of Cer again, blind Ospero, and make him drop the knife? She would have to try, for all their sakes.

But to her surprise Ospero took the knife away and stepped back. "Of course, Emratur."

Cazio looked shocked. "Emratur?" he asked. "What is this? Emratur?"

"Hush, boy," z'Acatto muttered. "Just be glad you're alive." He turned to Ospero. "We'll need to talk in private," he said.

Ospero nodded. "It would seem there are things you did not tell me."

Z'Acatto nodded, too. "Cazio, take the casnaras back to the room. I'll join you there shortly."

"But—"

"Don't argue for once," z'Acatto said bluntly.

Ospero's men dispersed as the two older men walked off together.

Cazio watched them go, sighed, and sheathed Caspator. "I wish I knew what that was about," he said.

"What was that name Ospero called z'Acatto?" Anne asked. "Emratur? I've never heard you call him that."

"Come on," Cazio said. "We'd better do what he said." He started walking.

Anne followed. "Cazio?" she persisted.

"Cazio's just saved our lives," Austra reminded her. "Again."

Anne ignored her. "You looked surprised," she said.

"It's not a name," Cazio grunted. "It's a title. The commander of a hundred men."

"You mean as in an army?"

"Yes, as in an army."

"Was z'Acatto an emratur?"

"If he was, I've never known it."

"I thought you had known him all your life."

They had reached the steps to their apartment, and Cazio started up. "I have. Well, sort of. He was a servant of my father's. He taught dessrata to my brothers and me. But sometimes, when I was young, he would leave for months at a time. I suppose he might have been off fighting. My father had many interests in those days. He might have commanded a hundred men."

"But z'Acatto still serves your father."

"No. My father fell on hard times, and eventually was killed in a duel. I inherited z'Acatto, along with a house in Avella. They are all that remain of my father's estate."

"Oh. I'm sorry." Tears welled in Anne's eyes. In the excitement, for just a few moments, she had forgotten to grieve.

Cazio stopped, looked a little puzzled at her expression, and put a hand on her shoulder. "It happened a long time ago," he said. "There's no reason for you to cry."

"I just recalled something," Anne murmured, "that's all. Someone I lost."

"Oh." He looked down at his feet and then brought his gaze back to hers. "I'm sorry to be so brusque," he said. "I'm just—well, I wish I knew what was going on. I thought something was strange when z'Acatto got us lodging here, that he must have known Ospero before—it was too easy, and he even gave us credit. Now I'm sure of it. I just don't know what it means."

"Then you don't trust z'Acatto?"

"I don't think he would ever betray me, if that's what you mean," Cazio said. "But his judgment is sometimes poor. He let my father get killed, after all."

"How was it z'Acatto's fault? What happened?"

"I don't know what happened, but I know that z'Acatto feels guilty about it. It was after that he started drinking all the time. And he doesn't have to stay with me—I haven't the money to pay him. Yet he does, and it must be out of guilt."

"Maybe he stays out of love," Austra suggested.

"Hah," Cazio replied, waving the possibility aside with his hand.

"But who is Ospero? I thought he was just our landlord."

"Oh, yes—he's landlord for most of the Perto Veto. He also controls a lot of what happens at the docks. And the ladies I escort. They call him *zo cassro*, around here—'the boss.' Not a pocket gets picked without him knowing about it."

"He's a criminal?"

"No. He's the prince of criminals, at least in this quarter."

"What are we going to do?" Anne said.

"Until the right ship comes along, and we have enough to pay passage for it, there's nothing we can do. They're looking for you everywhere now. We're safer here than anywhere. *If* z'Acatto knows what he's doing."

"I'm sure he does," Austra said.

"Let's hope so."

Anne didn't say anything. She knew very little about z'Acatto other than that he stayed drunk most of the time. Now, as it turned out, Cazio didn't know as much about the old man as he thought he did.

It might be true that z'Acatto would never betray Cazio. But that didn't mean Austra and Anne were safe—not in the slightest.

PART **II**

FRESH ACQUAINTANCES

The Year 2,223 of Everon
Late Novmen

*Prismo, the first mode, is the Lamp of Day. It invokes
Saint Loy, Saint Ausa, Saint Abullo, and Saint Fel. It evokes
the bright sun and the blue vault of Heaven. It provokes
optimism, ebullience, restlessness, brash behavior.*

*Etrama, the second mode, is the Lamp of Night. It invokes
Saint Soan, Saint Cer, Saint Artumo. It evokes the Moon in
all of her phases, the starry sky, gentle night breezes. It
provokes weariness, rest, and dream.*

—FROM THE CODEX HARMONIUM OF ELGIN WIDSEL

*Prismo, the first parry, is so called because it is the easiest
one to do on drawing the sword from its sheath. The
riposte is awkward.*

*Etrama, the second parry, is named this for no particular
reason, but it is a strong parry against flank attacks.*

—TRANSLATED FROM OBSAO DAZO CHIADIO ("WORK OF THE SWORD"),
BY MESTRO PAPO AVRADIO VALLAIMO

CHAPTER ONE

A JOUST

"I THINK THIS MAN wants to kill us, Hurricane," Neil told his mount, patting the stallion's neck. Then he shrugged, took a deep breath, and studied the sky.

He'd always reckoned the sky was the sky—changeable with weather, yes, but essentially the same wherever you went. But here in the south, the blue of it was somehow different, bolder. It went with the rest of the strangeness—the rambling sun-drenched fields and vineyards, the white-stuccoed houses with their red tiled roofs, the low, gnarly oaks and slender cedars that spotted the landscape. It was hard to believe that such a region existed in the same world as his cold, misty homeland—especially now, with the month of Novmen half-done. Skern was probably under a kingsyard of snow right now. Here, he was sweating lightly beneath his gambeson and armor.

The wonder of it did not escape Neil. He remembered his awe at first seeing Eslen, how big the world had seemed to a boy from a small island in the Lier Sea. And yet these last months the world had seemed to shrink around him, and Eslen Castle had become little more than a box.

Now the world seemed larger than ever, and that brought for him a sort of melancholy happiness. In a world this spacious, the sadness and fears of Neil MeqVren were not so large a thing.

Even that mixed pleasure brought with it a certain amount of guilt, however. The queen lived in constant danger, and leaving her for any reason felt wrong. But she had chosen this road for him, she and the shades of Erren and Fastia. Surely they knew better than he what was the right thing to do.

Still, he ought not to enjoy himself.

He heard shouting, and realized that the man in the road didn't care to be ignored in favor of the sky.

"I'm sorry," Neil called back, in the king's tongue, "but I can't understand you. I am not educated in the speech of Vitellio."

The man replied with something equally unintelligible, this time addressing one of his squires. At least Neil guessed they were squires, because he reckoned the shouting man to be a knight. He sat upon a powerful-looking horse, black with a white blaze on the forehead, and it was caparisoned in light barding.

The man also wore armor—of odd design, and awfully pretty, with oak leaves worked at the joints, but lord's plate nevertheless. He carried the helmet under his arm, but Neil could see that it was conical in shape, with a plume of bright feathers arranged almost like a rooster's tail. He wore a red-and-yellow robe instead of a tabard or surcoat, and that and his shield bore what might be a standard— a closed fist, a sunspray, a bag of some sort—the symbols meant nothing in the heraldry familiar to Neil, but he was, as he had been reflecting, very far from home.

The knight had four men with him, none in armor, but all wearing red tabards with the same design sewn on them as the shield. A large tent had been erected by the side of the road, flying a pennant with the sunspray alone. Three horses and two mules grazed in the pastures along the side of the rutted red road.

One of the men shouted, "My master asks you to declare yourself!" He had a long, bony face and a tuft of hair on his chin trying to pass for a beard. "If you can do so in no civilized language, then speak what babble you will, and I shall translate."

"I'm a wanderer," Neil replied. "I may tell you no more than that, I fear."

A brief conversation followed between the knight and his man; then the servant turned back to Neil.

"You wear the armor and bear the weapons of a knight. In whose service do you ride?"

"I cannot answer that question," Neil said.

"Think carefully, sir," the man said. "It is unlawful to wear the armor of a knight in this country if you do not have the credentials to do so."

"I see," Neil answered. "And if I am a knight, and can prove it, then what will your master say to that?"

"He will challenge you to honorable combat. After he kills you, he will take possession of your armor and horse."

"Ah. And if I am merely masquerading as a knight?"

"Then my lord will be forced to fine you and confiscate your property."

"Well," Neil said, "there is not a large difference in what I call myself then, is there? Fortunately I have a spear."

The man's eyes went round. "Do you not know whom you face?"

"I would ask, but since I cannot give my name, it would be impolite to require his."

"Don't you know his emblem?"

"I'm afraid I do not. Can we get this over with?"

The man spoke to his master again. For answer, the knight lifted his helmet onto his head, couched his lance beneath his arm and lifted his shield into position. Neil did the same, noticing that his own weapon was nearly a king's yard shorter than his foe's.

The Vitellian knight started first, his charger kicking up a cloud of red dust in the evening sun. Neil spurred Hurricane into motion and dropped the point of his spear into position. Beyond the rolling fields, a cloud of blackbirds fumed up from a distant tree line. For a moment, all seemed very quiet.

At the last moment Neil shifted in the saddle and moved his shield suddenly, so the enemy iron hit it slantwise rather than straight on. The blow rattled his teeth and scored his shield, but he swung his own point to the right, for his enemy was turning in a similar maneuver. He hit the Vitellian shield just at the edge, and the whole force of his blow shocked into the knight. Neil's spear snapped, its head buried in the shield. As he went by, he saw the Vitellian knight reel back in the saddle, but as he turned, he discovered that the fellow had somehow managed not to fall.

Neil grinned fiercely and drew Crow. The other knight regarded him for a moment, then handed his lance to one of his men and drew his blade, as well.

They came together like thunder, shield against shield. Crow beat over and rang against the Vitellian's helm, and the strange knight landed a blow on Neil's shoulder that would certainly have taken the arm off if not for the steel it was sheathed in. They tangled like that for a moment, horses crushing their legs between heaving flanks, but they were too close for hard blows.

Hurricane broke free, and Neil wheeled him around, cutting almost instinctively. He caught his foe right at the neck and sent him crashing to earth. The black horse stamped fiercely and stood to protect his master.

Amazingly, the knight came shakily to his feet. His gorget and the thick cloth wrapped beneath it had stopped the edge, but it was a miracle that his neck wasn't broken.

Neil dismounted and strode toward his opponent. The Vitellian cocked his sword back for a swing, but Neil shield-rushed him, sending him staggering back a step. Neil used the opening in distance to make a cut of his own, hitting the shoulder of the man's weapon arm. The armor rang like a bell, and the foe's blade clattered to the ground.

Neil waited for him to pick it up. Instead, the knight dropped his shield and pulled off his helmet, revealing a face rounded by middle age, tousled black hair streaked silver, a well-tended mustache and goatee. His nose was a bit shapeless, as if it had been broken too many times.

"You are a knight," the man admitted, in accented but comprehensible king's tongue. "Even though you will not name yourself, I must yield to you, for I believe you have broken my arm. I am Sir Quinte dac'Ucara, and I am honored to have faced you in combat. Will you guest with me?"

But before Neil could answer, Sir Quinte fainted, and his men rushed to his side.

Neil waited as Sir Quinte's men peeled him out of his armor and washed him with a perfumed rag. The shoulder bone was indeed broken, so they made a sling for the arm. Sir Quinte revived during the process, but if the shattered bone caused him pain, he showed it only a little, and only in his eyes.

"I did not speak your tongue before," he said, "because I did not know you, and it would not be meet to speak a strange language in my native land. But you have bested me, so Virgenyan shall be the language of this camp." He nodded at his dented armor. "That belongs to you," he managed. "As does *zo Cabadro*, my mount. Treat him well, I beg you—he is a fine horse."

Neil shook his head. "You are generous, Sir Quinte, but I have no need for either. I must travel light, and both would slow me."

Quinte smiled. "You are the generous one, sir. Will you not extend that generosity to telling me your name?"

"I may not, sir."

Sir Quinte nodded sagely. "You have taken a vow. You are on secret business."

"You may guess as you like."

"I respect your wishes," Sir Quinte said, "but I must call you something. Sir *zo Viotor* you shall be."

"I don't understand the name."

"It is no more than you named yourself, 'the wanderer.' I put it in Vitellian so you can explain who you are to less educated folk."

"Thank you then," Neil said sincerely.

Sir Quinte turned to one of his men. "Arvo, bring us food and wine."

"Please, I must be going," Neil told him. "Though I thank you for the offer."

"The hour is late. Lord Abullo dips his chariot to the world's end, and even you—great warrior though you may be—must sleep. Honoring my hospitality could not hinder your quest by much, and it would give me great pleasure."

Despite Neil's protests, Arvo was already spreading a cloth on the ground.

"Very well," Neil relented. "I accept your kindness."

Soon the cloth was covered in viands, most of which Neil did not recognize. There was bread, of course, and a hard sort of cheese, and pears. A red fruit revealed countless tiny pearl-like seeds when husked. They were good, if a bit of a bother to eat. A yellowish oil turned out to be something like butter, to be eaten with the bread. Small black fruits were salty rather than sweet. The wine was red and tasted strongly of cherry.

It occurred to Neil only after they began eating that the food might be drugged or poisoned. A year earlier, he would never have even imagined such a dishonorable thing. But at court, honor and the assumptions it carried were more a liability than anything else.

But Sir Quinte and his squires ate and drank everything Neil did, and the thought left him. However strange his appearance and standard, Sir Quinte was a knight, and he behaved like one—he would no more poison Neil than would Sir Fail de Liery, the old *chever* who had raised him after his father had died.

Vitellio suddenly did not seem so strange, after all.

The Vitellians ate slowly, often pausing to comment or argue in their own language, which to Neil's ears sounded more like singing than speaking. Dusk gave way to a pleasant, cool night. Stars made the heavens precious, and they, at least, were the same stars Neil remembered from home.

Except that in Eslen one rarely saw them. Here, they dazzled.

Sir Quinte switched back to the king's tongue somewhat apologetically. "I am sorry, Sir Viotor," he said, "to leave you outside of the conversation. Not all of my squires speak the Virgenyan tongue, nor does my historian, Volio." He gestured at the oldest of his men, a square-headed fellow with only a fringe of gray hair on his scalp.

"Historian?"

"Yes, of course. He records my deeds—my victories and losses. We were arguing, you see, about how my defeat today shall be written— and what it portends."

"Is it so important that it be written at all?" Neil asked.

"Honor demands it," Quinte said, sounding surprised. "Perhaps you have never lost a duel, Sir Viotor, but if you did, could you pretend that it never happened?"

"No, but that is not the same as writing it down."

The knight shrugged. "The ways of the north are different—there is no arguing that. Not every knight in Vitellio is answerable to history, either, but I am a Knight of the Mount, and my order demands records be kept."

"You serve a mountain?"

The knight smiled. "The mount is a holy place, touched by the lords—what you call the saints, I believe."

"Then you serve the saints? You have no human lord?"

"I serve the merchant guilds," Sir Quinte replied. "They are pledged to the mount."

"You serve merchants?"

The knight nodded. "You are a stranger, aren't you? There are four sorts of knight in Vitellio, all in all. Each overguild has its knights—the merchants, the artisans, the seafarers, and so on. Each prince—we would say *meddissio*—each meddissio also commands knights. There are the knights of the Church, of course. Finally, the judges are served by their own knights, so they cannot be intimidated by any of the others to render corrupt decisions."

"What about the king?" Neil asked. "Has he no knights?"

Sir Quinte chuckled and turned to his squires. *"Fatit, pispe dazo rediatur,"* he said. They took up his laughter.

Neil held his puzzlement.

"Vitellio has no king," Quinte explained. "The cities are ruled by meddissios. Some meddissios rule more than one city, but no one rules them all. No one has ruled them all since the collapse of the Hegemony, a thousand years ago."

"Oh." Neil could imagine a country with a regent, but he had never heard of a country without a king.

"And," Sir Quinte went on, "since I serve the merchant overguild, they want records to be kept. Thus I have my historian."

"But you also said something about portents?"

"Ah, indeed," Sire Quinte said, raising a finger. "A battle is like the casting of bones or the reading of cards. There is meaning in it. After all, it is the saints who choose which of us defeats the other, yes? And if you have defeated me, there is meaning in it."

"And what does your historian see in this?"

"A quest. You are on a most important quest, and much hangs upon it. The fate of nations."

"Interesting," Neil said, trying to keep his face neutral, though inwardly, his curiosity was aroused.

"Therefore, of course, I must join you. The saints have declared it."

"Sir Quinte, there is no need to—"

"Come," the knight said. "We have banqueted. I am injured and weary. You must at least be tired. I beg you, share the hospitality of my camp for the night. Tomorrow we shall make an early start."

"I must travel alone," Neil said, though more reluctantly than he might have expected.

Sir Quinte's face flattened. "Do you mistrust me? You have defeated me, sir. I could never betray you."

"Sir Quinte, I have learned to my great chagrin that not all men—and I mean no disrespect—but not all men who lay claim to honorable behavior do follow it. My destination is secret, and must remain so."

"Unless your destination is the hamlet of Buscaro, I cannot imagine what it might be, whether secret or no."

"Buscaro?" Neil had a map, but he wasn't very good at reading it. He had been a little uncertain of his route since leaving the Great Vitellian Way.

"That's the only place this road goes. Are you certain you don't need a native guide?"

Neil considered that a moment. If he was lost, he'd lost more than just his way—he'd also lost time. If he had gone astray, he would eventually have to ask directions of someone.

But not necessarily a group of armed men.

Still . . .

He returned his gaze to Sir Quinte's earnest-looking face and sighed. "You do not deceive me, sir?"

"*Echi'dacrumi da ma matir.* By my mother's tears."

Neil nodded. "I'm searching for the coven Saint Cer," he said reluctantly, "also known as the Abode of Graces."

Sir Quinte whistled. "Then you see, it is the will of the saints that you should meet me. You chose the wrong path several leagues ago." He waggled his finger at Neil. "It is no shame to admit you need a guide."

Neil considered that. If Sir Quinte was an enemy, he could easily follow him, and with his men take Neil whenever it was his pleasure—at night, with no warning. At least if he was among them, he knew where they were. And he would know if they sent a messenger with the news.

"I accept your offer, sir," Neil replied. "I would be happy of your help."

Still, he slept very lightly that night, with his hand on the pommel of Crow.

The next morning dawned cool and clear, with a slight frost on the grass. Sir Quinte's squires had his camp broken down and packed before the sun even cleared the horizon. They followed back down the road Neil had come up, and within two bells had turned onto a track that might have been left by a few goats.

"This is the road to the coven Saint Cer?" Neil asked, trying to hide his skepticism. He was still more than uneasy with his decision to confide in the Vitellian, and was careful not to let any of the knight's men entirely out of his sight.

"A shortcut," the knight explained. "You went wrong back at the crossroads after Turoci, on the river. This will take us to the proper road in half the time. And my guess is that time is not your ally."

"You are right there," Neil replied earnestly. The sooner he found Anne and returned to Eslen, the sooner he could resume his protection of the queen.

"Never fear, then. I'll have you at the coven before the stars come out tonight."

The cultivated landscape grew wilder as they went on. One of Sir Quinte's squires produced a stringed instrument that resembled a small lute with too few strings and began to sing a jaunty melody Neil understood not a word of. Still, the tune was pleasing, and when the lutist finished, he struck up another.

"It's a tragedy, this song," Sir Quinte explained, "about the doomed affair between a knight and a lady in a coven. Very sad."

Neil felt a melancholy smile flit across his face.

"Ah!" Sir Quinte exclaimed. "There is a lady involved then! In the coven?"

"No," Neil said. "A lady, yes, but she is very far from the coven."

"Ah." Sir Quinte chewed on that a bit. "I am sorry, Sir Viotor, for my questions. I did not see the pain in you before. Now it marks you like a coat-of-arms."

"It's nothing," Neil replied.

"It is far from nothing. I fear no sword or lance, Sir Viotor, not even yours. But love—that can lay the tallest giant low." He frowned and started to say something, then began again, much more softly. "Take care, Sir Viotor. I know nothing of your love, and would ask no further questions, but it seems to me that your lady must be forever lost, perhaps passed beyond these fields we know. If that is the case, you must be certain you know your heart, for your heart will hear her voice and try to answer. It may betray you to Lord Ontro and Lady Mefita and their dreary kingdom when you still have many deeds to accomplish here among us."

Neil felt a sudden catch in his throat, and for a terrible moment thought he might weep. He swallowed it down. "You seem to think you know a lot about me, Sir Quinte."

"I know that I presume. Let me presume one thing more, and then I shall remain silent. If you seek audience with the departed through the sisters of the coven, I would advise against it. The price is terrible."

"You've lost me entirely now," Neil admitted.

"Do you know nothing of where you go? Lady Cer and Lady Mefita are aspects of the same *sahto*, what you call a 'saint' in the king's tongue. The ladies who dedicate to her—while holy, and of the Church—learn the arts of murder and the language of the dead. You will never in your life want to cross even an initiate of that order, Sir Viotor."

Neil had a sudden vision of the lady Erren, in the fortress of Cal Azroth, surrounded by the slain bodies of her enemies, most with no visible mark upon them. He remembered that she had trained at Saint Cer.

"That I believe most sincerely, Sir Quinte," he replied.

They entered a region of vineyards, rows of vines that stretched to the tops of the hills surrounding them, and Sir Quinte changed the topic to wine, about which he seemed quite knowledgeable. Dusk approached, and Neil's doubts about his companions crept and faded, then crept back again. But, if they meant him harm, why had they not seized the opportunity? He was outnumbered.

Perhaps they still needed something from him. Anne, for instance. If the women of Saint Cer were all as fearsome as Erren, they could not walk or fight their way in. They would need Neil to bring her out with the queen's word.

That would be the time to be wary.

Sir Quinte was as good as his word on one issue, at least—before the sunset, they followed a curve around the base of a hill and came upon the coven Saint Cer.

Or, rather, the ruins of it, for the coven had been put to the torch. At first sight, Neil kicked Hurricane into a gallop, but he had ridden only a hundred paces when he slowed the horse to a walk.

There was no smoke. This place had burned long ago.

But was this even the coven Saint Cer? He had only Sir Quinte's word.

Behind him he heard the faint snick of steel coming from scabbard, and he realized that he had finally put Sir Quinte and the others at his back.

CHAPTER TWO

RETURN TO THE FOREST

WHEN THE PLAIN OF Mey Ghorn gave way to the King's Forest, Aspar White stopped and stared, and wished he were stone.

"We came this way just two months ago," Stephen whispered.

"I don't remember much of what happened then," Winna said. "But I would have remembered *this*."

"Quiet, the both of you," Aspar snapped.

Winna's eyes rounded with surprise and hurt, and he couldn't look at them.

Ehawk, the Wattau boy, just stared at the ground.

"I've got to . . ." Aspar tried to explain, but he couldn't think of anything to say. "Just wait here," he muttered instead. "I'll be back."

He gave Ogre a switch with the reins, and the massive horse started forward—reluctantly, it seemed. Aspar didn't blame him—Ogre was a killer, a beast with very little fear, but he and Aspar were alike in this. What they rode toward now ought not to be.

As Stephen had said, they had been here scarcely two months before. Then, it had been forest fringe, meadows and small trees, a few giant oaks and chestnuts, their leaves touched with fall color.

Now all was black. From a distance it looked almost like smoke, billowing yet strangely anchored to the ground. Close up, you could see what it really was. Vines as thick as ferry cables wound about the trees and writhed across the ground, sending thousands of smaller shoots to grapple with every limb and twig they could reach—which was all of them. The tops of the tallest trees had bent or snapped beneath their clinging weight. And everywhere, thorns—from stickers no longer than his fingernail to woody daggers more than a hand span long.

"Grim," Aspar muttered. "Haergrim Raver, what is happening to my forest?"

Stephen cast a glance at Winna. "He didn't mean—"

"I know," she said. "His hardness comes from habit, not from his heart. It's like those metal shells the knights in Eslen wear." She kept her eyes on the holter as his figure grew smaller against the loom of black. "He loves this forest," she said softer. "More than anything. More than he loves me."

"I doubt that," Stephen said.

"Don't," she replied. "It doesn't bother me. It doesn't make me jealous. It's good to know a man can feel so much, even one who has been through what Aspar has. It's good to know a man has a passion, and not just hollow bones in him." She glanced at Stephen, and her green eyes looked almost gray in the overcast morning. "I love these woods, too—I grew up at the other edge of them. But you and I can never know what he feels for this place. That's the only thing that I'm jealous of—not that he feels it, but that I don't."

Stephen nodded. "What about your family? Are you worried about them?"

"Yah," she said. "Oh, yah. I try not to think of it. But my father, he'd be the first to leave, if things went too wrong. If he had notice. If he had time."

Aspar had dismounted now, some distance away. Stephen heard the squeak of him coming off the leather saddle. As a novice priest, Stephen had walked the faneway of Saint Decmanis. The saint had improved his senses, his memory—and other things. He heard Aspar curse, too, invoking the Raver.

"Do you have an explanation for this?" Winna asked. "Why this is happening? What those thorns are, exactly? Did you find anything in the royal scriftorium?"

"I know little more than you do," Stephen admitted. "They are connected in folklore and legend to the Briar King, but that much we already know from experience."

The fortress of Cal Azroth was still visible behind them, across the Warlock River, a mass of twining thorns and little more. That was where they had last encountered the Briar King. A path of the vines led here, to the forest, where they seemed to have taken hold.

"Why would he destroy his own forest?"

"I don't know," Stephen said. "Some stories say he will destroy everything, make the world new from the ashes of the old." He sighed. "Half a year ago I considered myself learned, and the Briar King was no more than a name in a children's song. Now nothing I know seems true."

"I know how you feel," Winna replied.

"He's motioning us forward," Stephen said.

"Are you sure?"

"Yes."

Aspar watched his companions approach. He calmed his breathing.

Sceat on it, he thought to himself. *What is, is. No use getting all mawkin' about it. That won't help a thing. I'll find the Briar King, kill him, and put an end to this. That's that.*

By the time they'd arrived, he even managed to force a smile.

"Fast-growin' weed," he said, tilting his head at the dying forest.

"That it is," Stephen allowed.

"I reckon all of this sprang from his trail," Aspar said. "That makes him easy to track, at least. Unless this stuff has already spread everywhere."

It hadn't. Only a bell later, they found trees that were only half covered with the stuff, and finally not at all. Aspar felt relief sink down his body and toward his toes. There was still time to do something. It wasn't all lost yet.

"Let's see," Aspar said. "We've another two hours of daylight yet, but I expect rain at dusk. Stephen, since we're working for the praifec now, I reckon you ought to mark all this on your maps—how far this stuff has spread. Winna and I will set up camp, meantime."

"Where do you think we are?" Stephen asked.

Aspar took a slow look around. His bearings had been thrown off a bit by the unfamiliarity of what they had seen earlier.

The forest was more or less west of them, running north-south. East were the rolling fields of the Midenlands. He could make out five or six small farmsteads, a scattering of sheep, goats, and cows on the gentle hills. The tower of a small country church stood perhaps a league away.

"Do you know what town that is?" Stephen asked.

"I make it to be Thrigaetstath," Aspar said.

Stephen had his map out and was scrutinizing it. "Are you sure?" he asked. "I think its more likely Tulhaem."

"Yah? Then why ask me? I've only traveled these woods my whole life. You, *you've* got a map."

"I'm just saying," Stephen said, "that this is only the third town I've seen since passing Cal Azroth, which ought to make it Tulhaem."

"Tulhaem's bigger than that," Aspar replied.

"It's hard to tell how big a town is," Stephen said, "when you can only see the top part of a bell tower. If you says it's Thrigaetstath, I'm happy to mark it that way."

"Werlic. Do it then."

"Still, Thrigaetstath ought to be nearer—"

"Winna," Aspar asked, "where are you going?" She had quietly started her mount walking down the hill, away from the forest.

"To *ask*," she said. "There's a farmstead just down there."

"Bogelih," Aspar grunted. "Are you sure?"

The boy—a straw-headed lad of fourteen or so named Algaf—scratched his head and seemed to think hard about the question.

"Well, sir," he said at last, "I've spent my whole life here and never heard it called nothin' else."

"It's not on my map," Stephen complained.

"How far are we from Thrigaetstath?" Aspar asked.

"Ogh, near a league, I reckon," the boy said. "But ain't nobody living there now. Them black brammels grew over it."

"The whole town?" Winna said.

"I always said it was too near the forest," a female voice added.

Aspar's gaze tracked the sound to a woman of perhaps thirty who was clad in a brown homespun dress and standing near the stone-walled pigpen. Her hair was the same color as the boy's, and Aspar reckoned her for his mother.

"Pride, that's what it was," she went on. "They went over the boundary. Everyone knew it."

"How long ago was this?" Stephen asked.

"I don't know," she said. "Before my grandmother's grandmother. But the forest thinks slow, my grandmother said. It doesn't forget. And now the lord Brammel has waked, and he's taking back what was his."

"What happened to the folk of Thrigaetstath?" Aspar asked.

"Scattered. Went to their relatives, if they had any. Some went to the city, I reckon. But they're all gone." Her eyes narrowed. "You're him, aren't you? The king's holter?"

"I'm the holter," Aspar acknowledged.

The woman nodded her head at the small buildings of her farm. "We built outside the boundary. We respected his law. Are we safe?"

Aspar sighed and shook his head. "That I don't know. But I intend to find out."

"I've ney husband ner family that will take me," the woman said. "I've only the boy there. I can't leave this place."

Stephen cleared his throat. "Have you heard anything about other villages being abandoned? About people who run—pardon me—naked, like beasts?"

"A traveler from the east brought tales like that," the woman said. "But travelers often bring tales." She shifted uncomfortably. "Still, there *is* something."

"What?" Aspar asked.

"Things come out of the brammels. The animals smell them. The dogs bark all night. And yesterday I lost a goat."

"I saw it," the boy said eagerly. "I saw it at the edge of the woods."

"Algaf," the woman snapped. "I've told you not to go there. Ever."

"Yes, Mum. But Riqqi ran up there, and I had to go after him."

"We can get another dog, if it comes to that," the woman said. "Never, you hear me?"

"Yes, Mum."

"But what did you see, boy?" Aspar asked.

"I think it was an utin," the boy said cheerfully. "He stood taller than you, but he was all wrong, if y'kann me. I only saw him for a minute."

"An utin," Aspar grunted. Once he would have gruffly dismissed the boy's words. His whole life he had heard tales of utins and alvs and boygshinns and all manner of strange beasts in the King's Forest, and in almost four decades he had never seen any sign of them.

But he'd never seen a greffyn before this year, either, or a Briar King.

"I can take you there, master holter," Algaf said.

"Your mother just told you to stay away from the forest," Aspar said. "It's fine advice. You just tell me where, and I'll have a look before sundown."

"You'll stay with us, will you?" the woman asked.

"I wouldn't impose," Aspar said. "We'll pitch a camp in your field, if we may."

"Stay in the barn," the woman said. "It won't be an imposition—it'll be a comfort." She couldn't quite meet his eyes.

"Well enough," Aspar said. "Thank you for your kindness." He motioned to the Wattau. "Ehawk, you come with me. We'll go see if this thing left any sign."

Aspar wrinkled his nose at the smell.

"Don't touch it," Aspar warned Ehawk, who had bent to trace the track with his finger.

"Why, Master White?"

"I touched a greffyn track once, and it made me ill. Killed smaller creatures outright. I've no idea what left that, but it's nothing I know, and when I see things I don't know in the King's Forest, I've learned to be careful about 'em."

"It's big," Ehawk observed.

"Yah. And six toes, yet. Do they have anything leaves tracks like this up your way?"

"No."

"Mine either," Aspar said. "And that smell?"

"I've never smelled the like," the boy admitted. "But it is foul."

"I've known that scent before," Aspar said. "In the mountains, where I found the Briar King's barrow." He sighed. "Well, let's go back down. Tomorrow we'll track this thing."

"Something's tracking it already," Ehawk said.

"Eh? What do you see?"

The boy knelt and pointed, and Aspar saw he was right. There was another set of tracks, small, almost child-size, these in soft-soled shoes. The prints were so faint, even his trained eye had skipped over them.

"Those are good eyes you have there, Wattau," Aspar said.

"They might be traveling together," the boy allowed.

"Yah. Might be. Come along."

Brean was the woman's name, and she served them chicken stew, probably better than she and the boy had eaten in months. Aspar ate sparingly, hoping to leave them some when they'd gone.

That night they slept in the barn. The dogs, as Brean had claimed, did bark all night, for leagues in all directions and probably out of earshot, too. There was fear in their voices, and Aspar did not sleep well.

The next day they rose early and went utin hunting.

Unfortunately, the tracks didn't go far—they vanished about twenty yards into the woods.

"The ground is still soft," Aspar said. "And this beast is heavy. There ought to be tracks."

"In the stories I heard growing up, utins could shrink to the size of a gnat or turn into moss," Winna said. "It could be hiding right beneath our feet."

"That's just stories," Aspar said.

"Greffyns used to be just stories, too," she replied.

"But the stories didn't have it all right," Stephen pointed out. "Each tale and account I read of the Briar King had only a few words of truth about him. And the real greffyn was very different from phay-story greffyns."

"But real, yah?"

"Werlic," Aspar agreed. "I never trusted those stories."

"You never trust anything except what you see with your own two eyes," Winna shot back.

"And why should I? All it ever took to convince me there was such a thing as a greffyn was to see one. All it will ever take to convince me a beast that weighs half a ton can turn into moss is to see it. I'm a simple man."

"No," Stephen said. "You're a skeptical man. That's kept you alive when others would have died."

"Are we agreeing about this?" Aspar asked, one eyebrow raised.

"More or less. It's clear that many things we once considered legend have a basis in fact. But no one has actually seen a greffyn or an utin since ancient times. Stories grow and change in the telling, so no, we can't trust them to be reliable. The only way to sort out truth from invention is with our own senses."

"Well, use your senses," Winna said. "Where did it go?"

It was Ehawk who answered, solemnly pointing up.

"Good lad," Aspar said. He motioned to where Ehawk had indicated. "The bark is scraped there, see? It's traveling in the trees."

Stephen paled and stared up at the distant canopy. "That's almost as bad as being able to turn into moss," he said. "How will we ever see it?"

"Is that a riddle?" Aspar asked. "With our eyes."

"But how to track it?"

"Yah, that's a problem. But it seems to be going along the forest edge where the briars are, which is where we're going, as well. The praifec didn't send us out here to hunt utins. I reckon we'll keep on with what we were hired for, and if we run across it again, all well and good."

"That's not at all well and good by my sight," Stephen said, "but I take your point."

They traveled in silence for a time. Aspar kept his eyes searching the treetops, and his back itched constantly. The smell of autumn leaves was almost overpowering. Long experience had taught him that the smell was a sign that murder was coming. The Sefry woman who had raised him had told him the strange sense came from Grim, the Raver, for Aspar had been born at a place of sacrifice to Grim. Aspar didn't necessarily believe that, nor did he care—he cared only that it was usually true.

Except in autumn, when the smell was already there . . .

But once again, his nose was right. Approaching a clearing, the scent intensified.

"I smell blood," Stephen said. "And something very foul."

"Do you hear anything with those saint-blessed ears of yours?"

"I'm not sure. Breathing, maybe, but I can't tell where."

They advanced a little farther, until they saw the crumbled, torn body in the clearing.

"Saints!" Winna gasped.

"Saints bless," Stephen said. "The poor lad."

Blood soaked the leaves and ground, but the face was clean, easily recognizable as Algaf, the boy from the homestead.

"I guess he didn't listen to his mother." Aspar sighed.

Stephen started forward, but Aspar stopped him with an outstretched arm.

"No. Don't you see? The boy is bait. It wants us to walk in there."

"He's still alive," Stephen said. "That's him I hear breathing."

"Asp—," Winna began, but he hushed her. He walked his gaze through the treetops, but there was nothing but bare branches and a sigh of wind.

He sighed. "Watch the trees," he said. "I'll get him."

"No," Stephen said. "I will. I can't use a bow the way you can. If it's really hiding in the trees, you've got the best chance of stopping it."

Aspar considered that, then nodded. "Go, then. But be ready."

As Stephen advanced cautiously into the field, Aspar nocked an arrow to his bow and waited.

A flight of sparrows whirred through the trees. Then the forest was eerily silent.

Stephen reached the boy and knelt by him. "It's bad," he called to them. "He's still bleeding. If we bandage him now, we might have a chance."

"I don't see anything," Ehawk said.

"I know," Aspar said. "I don't like it."

"Maybe you were wrong," Winna suggested. "We don't know that an utin—or whatever it is—is smart enough to set a trap."

"The greffyn had men and Sefry traveling with it," Aspar reminded her. He remembered the footprints. "This thing might, too. It doesn't have to be smart enough itself."

"Yah."

He was missing something—he knew it. It had to have come into the clearing on foot. He had found only the one set of tracks in. He'd assumed it had left on the other side, then taken to the trees.

"Utins could shrink to the size of a gnat or turn into moss," Winna had said.

"Stephen, come here, *now,*" Aspar shouted.

"But I—" His eyes widened, and his head nearly spun from his shoulders; then he lurched to his feet.

He hadn't gone a yard when the ground seemed to explode, and in a cloud of rising leaves, something much larger than a man leapt toward Stephen.

CHAPTER THREE

MERY

LEOFF'S FINGERS DANCED ACROSS the red-and-black keys of the hammarharp, but his mind drifted into daymarys of corpses with eyes of ash and a town gone forever still beneath the wings of night. Darkness crept through his fingers and into the keyboard, and the cheerful melody he had been playing suddenly brooded like a requiem. Frustrated, he reached for his crutches and used them to stand, wincing at the pain from his leg.

He considered returning to his room to lie down, but the thought of that small dark chamber depressed him. The music room was sunny, at least, with two tall windows looking out across the city of Eslen and Newland beyond. It was well furnished with instruments, as well—besides the hammarharp, the were croths of all sizes, lutes and theorbos, hautboys, recorders, flageolettes and bagpipes. There was an ample supply of paper and ink, too.

Most of these things lay under a fine layer of dust, however, and none of the stringed instruments had been tuned in years. Leoff wondered exactly how long it had been since the court had employed a resident composer.

More pointedly, he wondered if the court employed one *now*.

When would he hear from the queen?

Artwair had as been as good as his word, finding Leoff quarters in the castle and getting him permission to use the music room. He'd had a very brief audience with the king, who had hardly seemed to know he was there. The queen had been there, beautiful and regal, and at her prompting, the king had commended him for his actions at Broogh. Neither had said anything about his appointment. And though a few suits of clothes had been made for him and meals came regularly to his chambers, in twice ninedays he had been given no commission.

So he had dabbled. He'd written down the song of the malend, arranging it for a twelve-piece consort and then—dissatisfied with the result—for thirty instruments. No consort so large had ever played, to his knowledge, but in his mind that was what he heard.

He'd made another stab at the elusive melody from the hills, but something kept stopping him, and he had laid that aside, instead beginning a suite of courtly dance music, anticipating the hoped-for commission—for a wedding, perhaps.

Through it all, the dead of Broogh haunted him, crying out for a voice. He knew what he needed to do, but he hesitated. He was afraid that the composition of so powerful a work as was forming in his mind might somehow drain him of his own life.

So he fretted, and poked about the music room, exploring the manuscrifts in its cabinets, tuning the stringed instruments, then tuning them again.

He was staring out the window at distant barges on the Dew when he heard a muffled sneeze. He turned to see who was there, but there was no one in the room. The door was ajar, and he could see ten yards of the hall beyond.

The hair on his neck pricking up, he walked slowly around the room, wondering if he had imagined the sound.

But then it came again, louder, from one of the wooden cabinets.

He stared at the source of the noise, fear waxing. Had they found him, the murderers from Broogh? Had they come for revenge, sent an assassin, fearing he might reveal them?

Carefully, he picked up the nearest thing at hand, an hautboy. It was heavy—and pointed.

He glanced back out into the hall. No guard was to be seen. He considered going to find one, and almost did, but instead, he steeled himself, advanced on the cabinet, and brandishing the hautboy, quickly grabbed the handle and yanked it open.

Wide eyes blinked up at him, and a small mouth gave a little gasp. The child within stared at him a moment, as Leoff relaxed.

The cabinet held a little girl, probably no more than six or seven years of age. She wore a blue satin gown, and her long brown hair was rather disarrayed. Her blue eyes seemed guileless.

"Hello," he said after a moment. "You gave me rather a fright. What's your name?"

"It's Mery, please," she replied.

"Why don't you come on out, Mery, and tell me why you're hiding in here."

"Yes, please," she said, and scooted out of the cramped space. She stood and then backed away from him.

"I'll go now," she said.

"No, wait. What were you doing in there?"

"Nobody used to be in here," she said. "I would come in and play with the hammarharp. I like the way it sounds. Now you're here, and I can't play it, but I like to listen to you."

"Well, Mery, you might have asked. I wouldn't mind you listening sometimes."

She hung her head a little. "I just try to stay quiet and not be seen. It's best that way."

"Nonsense. You're a beautiful little girl. There's no reason to be shy."

She didn't answer, but stared at him as if he were speaking Vitellian.

He pulled another stool up to the hammarharp. "Sit here. I'll play you something."

Her eyes widened further, and then she frowned, as if doubting him. "Truly?"

"Truly."

She did as he said, settling on the stool.

"Now, what's your favorite song?"

She thought for a moment. "I like 'Round the Hill and Back Again.'"

"I know that one," he said. "It was a favorite of mine when I was your age. Let's see—does it go like this?" He picked out the melody line.

She smiled.

"I thought so. Now let me play it with two hands." He started a simple bass line and played through again, and on the third pass added a counterpoint.

"It's like a dance now," she observed.

"Yes," he said. "But listen, I can change it into a hymn." He dropped the moving bass line and went into four-part harmony. "Or I can make it sad." He shifted into a more plaintive mode.

She smiled again. "I like it like that. How can you make one song into so many songs?"

"That's what I do," he said.

"But how?"

"Well—imagine you want to say something. 'I want some water to drink.' How many ways could you say that?"

Mery considered. "Some water I want to drink?"

"Right. How else?"

"I'd like some water to drink, please."

"Just so. Politely."

"I want some water, *now*."

"Commanding, yes. Angrily?"

"Give me some *water*!" She supressed a giggle at her feigned rage.

"And so on," Leoff said. "It's the same with music. There are many ways of expressing the same idea. It's a matter of choosing the right ones."

"Can you do it with another song?"

"Of course. What song would you like?"

"I don't know the name of it."

"Can you hum it?"

"I think so." She concentrated, and began humming.

Two things struck Leoff immediately. The first was that she was humming the main theme from the "Song of the Malend," which he'd just written down only a few days before.

The second was that she was humming it exactly in key, with perfect pitch.

"You heard that in here, didn't you?"

She looked abashed. "Yes, please."

"How many times?"

"Just once."

"Once." Interest went quicker in his chest. "Mery, would you play something on the hammarharp for me? Something you used to play when you came in here alone?"

"But you're so much better."

"But I've been playing longer, and I was trained. Have you ever had a lesson in music?"

She shook her head.

"Play something, then. I'd like to hear it."

"Very well," she said. "But it won't be good."

She settled onto the little stool and spread her tiny fingers on the keyboard and began to play. It was just a melody, a single line, but he knew it immediately as "The Fine Maid of Dalwis."

"That's really very good, Mery," he said. He pulled up another stool next to her. "Play it again, and I'll play with you."

She started again, and he added only chords at first, then a walking bass line. Mery's smile grew more and more delighted.

After they were done, she looked at him, her blue eyes glittering.

"I wish I could play with both hands," she said, "the way you do."

"You could, Mery. I could teach you, if you would like."

She opened her mouth, then hesitated. "Are you sure?" she asked.

"It would be my honor."

"I'd like to learn."

"Very well. But you must be serious. You must do what I say. You have an excellent ear, but the way you're using your hands is wrong. You must place them thusly—"

◊   ◊   ◊

Two bells passed almost without Leoff's realizing it. Mery picked up the exercises quickly. Her mind and ear were quite amazing, and it delighted him to see her progress.

He certainly didn't hear anyone approaching, not until they were rapping on the open door.

He swiveled in his chair. The queen, Muriele Dare, stood there. She wasn't looking at him, but at Mery. The girl, for her part, hopped down quickly and bent her knee. Belatedly, Leoff overcame his surprise and tried to do the same, though his splint spoiled the effect.

"Mery," the queen said in a soft, cold voice, "why don't you run along?"

"Yes, Majesty," she said, and started to scuttle off. But she turned and looked shyly at Leoff. "Thank you," she said.

"*Mery,*" the queen said, a little more forcefully.

And the little girl was gone.

The queen turned an icy eye on Leoff then. "When did Lady Gramme commission you to teach her child music?" she asked.

"Majesty, I know no Lady Gramme," Leoff said. "The child has been hiding here because she likes music. I discovered her today."

The queen's face seemed to relax a bit. Her voice softened incrementally. "I shall make certain she bothers you no more."

"Majesty, I find the child delightful. She has an excellent ear, and is quick to learn. I would teach her without compensation."

"Would you?" The chill was back, and Leoff suddenly began wondering who exactly Lady Gramme was.

"If it is permitted. Majesty, I know so little of this place. I do not even know, frankly, if I am employed here."

"That is what I have come here to discuss." She took a seat, and he stood watching her nervously, the crutches tight under his arms. In the hall, a guard stood at either side of the door.

"My husband did not mention hiring you, and the letter you had from him seems to have left your possession."

"Majesty, if I may, the fire in the malend—"

"Yes, I know, and Duke Artwair saw the letter, and that is good enough for me. Still, in these days, I must take great care. I made inquires about you in various places, and that took some time."

"Yes, Majesty. Of course I understand."

"I do not know much about music," the queen said, "but I am given to understand you have an unusual reputation, for a composer. The Church, for example, has censured your work on several occasions. There were even allegations of shinecraft."

"I assure you, Majesty," Leoff began quickly, "I have done nothing heretical, and am certainly no shinecrafter."

"Yet that opinion comes from the clergy in Glastir. They said that your works were often indecently orchestrated." She shrugged. "I do not know what that means. They also report that one of your concerts provoked violence."

"That is true in only the most abstract way, Majesty. Two gentlemen began arguing about the worth of one of my compositions. They did come to blows over it, and they had—friends—who joined them."

"So there was a brawl."

Leoff sighed. "Yes, Majesty."

"The attish of Glastir said your music had a corrupting influence on the crowd."

"I do not believe that to be true, Majesty."

She smiled faintly. "I think I understand why my husband offered you this position, though it went long unfilled. He was somewhat at odds with the Church, and especially with Praifec Hespero. I suppose he did this to devil him a bit." The smile vanished. "Unfortunately, my son is not in the position my husband was. We cannot afford to provoke the Church—at least not much. On the other hand, you did prove yourself a friend to this kingdom, and Duke Artwair's good word in your behalf is worth its measure in gold." Her brow creased slightly. "Tell me what the Church dislikes about your music. Precisely."

Leoff considered his words carefully. "Majesty, your last court composer—what was your favorite of his works?"

She blinked, and he suddenly felt cold, for presuming to answer her question with a question.

"I really cannot say," she said. "I suppose it may have been one of his pavanes."

"Can you hear it in your head? Can you hum it?"

Now she looked annoyed. "Is there a point to this?"

He balanced on the crutches so he could clasp his hands in front of him. "Majesty, music is a gift of the saints. It has the power to move the human soul. And yet for the most part it does not. For almost a hundred years, music has been written not with the heart, but with the mind, almost arithmetically. It has become sterile, an academic exercise."

"A pavane should sound like a pavane, should it not?" the queen asked. "And a requiem like a requiem?"

"Those are *forms*, Majesty. Within those forms, such sublime things could be done—"

"I don't understand. Why does the Church object to your philosophy?"

And now Leoff knew he must choose his words *very* carefully.

"Because some members of the clergy confuse habit with doctrine. There was a time before the invention of the hammarharp—it was hardly a hundred years old. Two hundred years ago, it was unheard of for two voices to sing different parts, much less four, yet hymns in the Church are now routinely written in four parts. And yet, for whatever reason, for the last hundred years, music has changed not at all. It has inertia, and familiarity. Some people fear change—"

"I asked you to be specific."

"Yes, Majesty. Forgive me. Take, for instance, the separation of instrumental and vocal music. The music of the Church is of the voice only. Instruments never accompany a requiem. A concerto, on the other hand, never has a human voice added to it."

"Minstrels play and sing," the queen said.

"Yes. And the Church mislikes it. Why? I have never been shown a written doctrine to explain it."

"Then you want to compose for both the voice and instruments?"

"Yes! It was done in ancient times, before the reign of the Black Jester."

"He banned it?"

"Well—no. He encouraged it, actually, but like everything else he touched, he corrupted the form. He made music a thing of terror—torturing singers to scream in unison, that sort of thing."

"Ah," the queen said. "And when the Hegemony defeated him and imposed the peace, they banned such music because of its association, just as they banned everything else associated with the Black Jester."

"Including artifice," Leoff said. "If all such bans were still in af-fect, the malends that drain your Newland would never have been in-vented."

The queen smiled again. "Don't think the Church didn't try to stop that," she said. "But to return to your own assertion—you say music has the power to move the human soul, and now you mention the Black Jester. It is said that in his reign, music was written which drove whole nations to despair, which could provoke madness and bestial behavior. If so—if music can move the human soul toward darkness—is it not better that it remain, as you say, sterile and harm-less?"

Leoff unclasped his hands and sighed. "Majesty," he said, "the world is already full of the music of despair. Songs of woe are always in our ears. I would counter that with joy, pride, tenderness, peace—and above all, hope. I would add something to our lives."

The queen looked at him for a long moment without showing a readable expression. "Move my soul," she said finally. "Show me what you mean. I will judge how dangerous it is."

He hesitated a moment, knowing this was the moment, wonder-ing what to play. One of the stirring airs he had written for the court at Glastir? The victory march of Lord Fell?

He had chosen that last, and set his fingers to the keyboard, but something else happened. He began playing the thing he had been avoiding, the part that had already formed in his head. Softly at first, a song of love and desire, a path to a bright future. Then the enemy, discord, terror, dark clouds blotting the sun. Duty, grim duty but through it all, the melody of hope returned again and again, uncon-querable, until in the end, after death and grief, only it remained, tri-umphant despite everything.

When he finished, he felt his own eyes were damp, and he gave silent prayer to the saints for what they had given him.

He turned slowly from the keyboard, and found the queen staring at him. A single tear was working down her cheek.

"What is it called?" she asked softly.

"I have never played it before," he said. "It is a part of something larger, a distillation of it. But I might call it the 'Tale of Lihta.'"

She nodded thoughtfully. "I see why the Church does not like your music," she said. "It does indeed move the soul, and they would claim our souls as their own. But the saints speak through you, don't they, Leovigild Ackenzal?"

"I believe so, Majesty. I hope so."

"So do I." She lifted her chin and stood. "You are in my employ," she said. "And I would like to commission something from you."

"Anything, Majesty."

"These are dark times. War threatens, and creatures of terror that should not exist walk the land. Much has been lost, and as you say, despair is all around us. I had thought to commission from you a requiem for the dead—for my husband and daughters. Now I think we need something greater. I want you to write something—something like I just heard—not for me, or the nobles of the court. I want you to write something for this country, something that will unite the most humble servant with the highest lord. I want something for all of my people, do you understand? A music that can fill this whole city, that can float into the countryside beyond and will be whispered of over the gray seas."

"That would be—" Leoff couldn't find words for a moment. "Majesty," he began again, "you have named my heart's desire."

"I'd like it performed on Wihnaht, in the Yule season. Could you have it ready by then?"

"Absolutely, Majesty."

She nodded, turned, and began to leave, but she stopped.

"You are dangerous, Mestro Ackenzal. I take a great risk with you, much greater than you can ever know, but since I take it, I take it fully and with conviction. If you do this, you cannot hold back from fear of the Church. You must do as I have asked to the best of your abilities and with all of your invention. Do it understanding that I may not be able to protect you, though I will do my best. If you are not willing to burn for this, tell me now."

A chill of fear went through Leoff, but he nodded. "I was, as you know, Majesty, in Broogh," he said. "I saw the price they paid there for your kingdom. I am no warrior. In my heart I am not brave. But for what you ask—for the chance to do what you ask—I will risk burning. I only hope I am worthy."

"Very well," she said. And then she was gone.

CHAPTER FOUR

GUEST OF THE COUNTESS

NEIL SPUN IN HIS saddle, fearing treachery in the sound of steel behind him, but the Vitellian knight and his retainers weren't threatening him. Instead, he realized, they had noticed what he had not—a group of armed horsemen off to the right, riding their way.

They were dressed all alike, in sable surcoats and crimson robes over armor. None had donned their helms.

Sir Quinte resheathed his sword, and his men did likewise. "Knights of the Church," he said. "The order of Lord Tormo."

Neil nodded and said nothing, but he kept his hand near his sword. While he trusted the saints, he'd learned the hard way that their human servants were as corruptible as anyone.

They sat their horses and waited for the knights to arrive.

The leader was a giant of a man, with bushy black beard and swell-green eyes. He held up his hand in greeting and spoke in clear Vitellian. Sir Quinte answered, and they seemed to have a brief argument. Then the knight of Tormo turned to regard Neil.

"I am Sir Chenzo," he said, in the king's tongue now, "a knight in service of our holy Fratrex Prismo in z'Irbina. Sir Quinte tells me you came in search of this coven?"

"I did," Neil replied.

"Did you know of its condition?"

"No, sir, I did not."

"Then for what purpose did you travel here?"

"I am sorry, Sir Chenzo, but I'm afraid I cannot tell you that. But please, I must know—what happened here? Where have the sisters of the coven gone?"

"They have gone to their lady Cer," the knight replied. "All were slaughtered."

Neil felt light, as if he were falling. "All, Sir Chenzo? None survived?"

Sir Chenzo narrowed his eyes. "A terrible crime has been committed here. I must ask you again, why did you come to this place?"

"Sir Viotor is sworn to secrecy," Sir Quinte explained, "but I will vouch that he is a most gentle and honorable knight."

"Come, come," Sir Chenzo said to Neil. "Tell me generally. Did you come to deliver a message? Did you come for one of the sisters? A rendezvous, perhaps?"

Neil felt his chest tighten. "I am sorry, sir. Sir Quinte is right. I have taken a vow."

"As have I," the knight replied. "I have vowed to find the perpetrator of this obscenity. Anything you know may be of use to me."

"Have you no clues?" Sir Quinte asked.

"A few. It was done by foreign knights bearing no standard or markings, like your friend here. They slaughtered the sisters and then rode off in different directions."

"As if they were searching," Neil muttered.

"Yes, as if searching for someone," Sir Chenzo affirmed. "But searching for whom, Sir Viotor? That is the question, and I suspect you have some inkling of the answer."

Neil averted his eyes, trying to think. He could not imagine that the slaughter at the coven and the murder of the royal family in Eslen were coincidence. Whoever had sent the assassins to slay his beloved Fastia had also sent killers here, to murder her sister.

If Anne were dead, then he could justifiably consider himself released from his vow. He could return to the queen and protect her.

But the queen's conversation with the shade of Erren indicated that Anne was still alive only two weeks ago. Judging from the ruins, the coven looked to have been burned longer ago than that. So she must have escaped the general slaughter, and was being pursued by the perpetrators.

That meant that her pursuers already knew who she was. The secret he was sworn to protect was no longer a secret at all.

If that was so, the only things that remained secret were his identity and what his mission was. He had to preserve his anonymity; if Anne was still alive, he might be her only hope. He could not allow himself to be waylaid.

And so, saying a silent prayer to Saint Freinte, Neil lied.

"I see that I must trust you with my seceret," he sighed. "My name is Etein MeqMerlem, from the isle of Andevoi. There is a young lady whom I love, but her parents disapproved of our affections. They sent her to a coven to keep us apart. I know not which coven, but for three years now I have searched for her, from Hansa to Safnia, thus far without success.

"Now I have come here, and you tell me of this terrible thing." He sat straighter in his saddle. "I know nothing of these murders, but I must know if she was here. If she lives, I will find her. If she is dead, then I will avenge her. I pray that you will help me in my quest."

"I knew it!" Sir Quinte said. "I knew your quest was for the sake of love."

Sir Chenzo studied Neil with one eyebrow upraised. "What was the lady's name?" he asked.

"Muerven de Selrete," he replied. Then, anxiously, "Please, was she here?"

The knight shrugged. "The records of the coven were burned along with everything else. I'm sorry, but there is no way of knowing."

"Yet the bodies—"

"Long buried, and—you'll forgive me—mostly unrecognizable, in any case."

"I know that she lives," Neil said. "I feel it in my heart. Can you at least tell me the direction the largest group of searchers went in?"

Sir Chenzo shook his head. "I am sorry, Sir Etein, I have my own vows and duties. But please, accompany us to the place where we are guested. Take ease for the night. Perhaps you will remember something there that will be of use to us."

"I'm afraid I must decline," Neil replied. "I must renew my search immediately, especially now."

"Please," Sir Chenzo said. "I insist."

The look in his eye made it clear to Neil that he was not merely being polite.

They rode from fields of yellowing grass and purple thistle into vast vineyards and finally up to a rambling white-walled estate roofed in red tile. By the time they reached the mansion, the sun had set, and only a faint glow remained in the west.

Servants in plum doublets and yellow hose took their horses, and they passed through a gate and into a large inner courtyard. A few servants in the same livery were sweeping it as they entered, and a page led them through another door and into a hall lit brightly by candles and hearth. A few people were gathered around a long table. The most notable of these was a woman of middle years and large girth, who rose from the head of the table as they entered.

"*Portate az me ech'ospi, casnar Chenzo?*" she said in a pleasant, jovial voice.

"*Oex,*" he answered, and then he proceeded to make some explanation in Vitellian.

The woman nodded, made various hand gestures, and then looked pointedly at Neil.

"*Pan tio nomes, me dello?*" she asked.

"I am sorry, my lady," Neil said, "I do not understand you."

The woman shot a mock-angry look at Sir Chenzo. "You've allowed me to be rude to a guest," she told him in the king's tongue. "You should have told me right away that he doesn't understand our tongue."

She turned back to Neil. "I only asked your name, my dello," she said.

"Lady, my name is Etein MeqMerlem, and I am at your service."

"I am the countess Orchaevia, and this is my house you've been brought to." She smiled again. "My. So *many* guests."

"I regret the lack of notice," Sir Chenzo rushed to say, "but we met them just now, near the ruins of the coven. My order will of course reimburse—"

"Nonsense," the woman said. "Do not become vulgar, Sir Chenzo. The countess Orchaevia does not need to be plied with Church silver to persuade her to host travelers." Her gaze settled on Neil. "Especially such a handsome young dello as this." Then she smiled at Sir Quinte. "Or one with the reputation of Sir Quinte."

Sir Quinte bowed. "Countess Orchaevia, the pleasure is mine. I had a mind to pay you a call, being in the region, even before these gentlemen escorted us here."

Neil bowed, too. He was reminded of the Duchess Elyoner of Loiyes, though physically there was no resemblance. The duchess was dainty, almost a child in size. Yet the countess Orchaevia had something of her flirting manner.

She set as lavish a table, as well. Fruit came out first, and a dark sweet wine, followed by an earthy yellow soup Neil did not recognize, roasted hare, tender flanks of kid stuffed with parsley, roasted pork with sour green sauce, and pasties filled with wild mushrooms. Next came partridge and capon served with dumplings of ground meat shaped and gilded so as to resemble eggs, then a pie of unlaid eggs and cheese and quail glazed with red honey and garlic.

By the time the fish course arrived, Neil was nearly too full to eat any more, but he persevered, not wishing to insult his host.

"Sir Etein is in search of his true love, Countess," Sir Quinte said as he plucked out the eyeball of a trout and popped it into his mouth.

"How delicious," the countess said. "I am an authority on true love. Do you have someone specific in mind, Sir Etein, or is the girl still unknown to you?"

"She—," Neil began, but Sir Quinte interrupted him.

"We believe she was in the coven," Sir Quinte explained.

"Oh," the countess said, her face falling. "So many girls, so young.

What a horrible thing. And just after the Fiussanal, too. They had just been here, you know."

"Here?" Neil asked.

"Oh, indeed. The sisters of the coven are—were—my neighbors. I held a feast for the girls each Fiussanal. It was that very night—"

"The night of the purple moon?" Neil blurted before he could think better. Again he saw poor Elseny, her throat cut ear to ear. He felt Fastia in his arms, her heartbeat no stronger than a bird's. He saw again the greffyn and the Briar King.

He realized that everyone at the table was watching him.

"Yes," the countess said, "the night of the purple moon." Her eyebrows descended, and she shook her head. "I hope you are mistaken, Sir Etein. I hope your love was not one of the girls in the coven."

"Is it possible—if they were here—that they did not all return?"

"I do not think so," Orchaevia said softly. "The sisters were quite strict about such things, and the attack came hours after the party had ended."

"Bless the saints that their attackers did not come here," Sir Quinte said, quaffing from a cup of dry red wine.

"Yes," Orchaevia said. "Thank the saints, indeed. What was your lady's name, Sir Etein? If she was here, I might have met her."

"Muerven de Selrete," he replied.

"Of course they did not go by their given names in the coven," Orchaevia said. "Can you describe her?"

Neil closed his eyes, still remembering Fastia. "Her arms are whiter than thistledown," he said. "Her hair as black as a raven's wing. Her eyes were darker yet, like orbs cut from the night sky." His voice shook as he said it.

"That does not help me much," the countess said. "You describe your love better than her appearance."

"I must find her," Neil said earnestly.

Sir Chenzo shook his head. "We've had a few reports of two girls who were seen fleeing with two men. One had hair like copper, the other like gold. Neither sounds like your lady, Sir Etein."

As he said this, he glanced rather casually at Neil, but something in that glance was searching, watching for him to react.

"I must hope," he said softly.

But inwardly, he felt a sudden fire. Sir Chenzo had just described Princess Anne and her maid, Austra.

He tried to look disappointed, and thought he succeeded.

After the meal, one of the countess' servants led him to what he reckoned would be a bedchamber, but he was wrong. The room he was shown to was decorated all in tile, with frescoes of leaping dolphins, eels, and octopi. Set into the floor was a huge tub, already full of steaming water.

The servant stood by, expectantly, as Neil stared at it, knowing how good it would feel.

Knowing also how vulnerable he would be. The room had only one entrance. "I am not in need of a bath," he said finally.

Clearly puzzled, the servant nodded and led him to a bedchamber. It was as lavish as the rest of the house, but it had a window, and the door could be barred.

The drop from the window was not a long one. He was considering this when a faint sound caused him to whirl about.

The countess was standing there in his chambers. He could not see how she had entered.

"First you refuse the hospitality of a warm bath, and now it looks as if you will refuse my bed, as well," she said.

"Countess—"

"Hush. Your suspicions are well advised. Sir Chenzo plans to take you into his custody this very night."

He set his mouth grimly. "Then I must leave at once."

"Rest a moment. Sir Chenzo is of no danger to you at this instant. This is *my* house."

When she said it, all frivolity dropped from her, and for a moment Neil felt a tingle of fear—not of something substantial, but of her very presence. It was as if he stood alone in the dark of the moon.

"Who are you?" he whispered.

"I am the countess Orchaevia," she said.

"You are something else."

A wan smile flitted across her face. "Not all of the sisters of Cer died in the razing of the coven. One lives yet."

He nodded in understanding. "Do you know what happened?" he asked.

"Knights came by dark, mostly Hanzish. They sought a girl, just as you do. The same girl, yes?"

"I believe so," Neil replied.

"Yes. She is important. More important than you could possibly know."

"I know only that my duty is to find her and keep her safe. It is all I need to know."

"I can see that. I watched you lie, and saw how it hurt you. You are not skilled at falsehood."

"I have not practiced it," he said.

"She lives, she and her maid. I believe two friends of mine, swordsmen who know the country, yet accompany them. My servants tell me they went north, probably to the port of z'Espino. I advise you to seek them there. I also advise you to leave tonight, and alone."

"Sir Chenzo. Is he a villain?"

"Not as such, though he may serve them. He was not involved in the murders at the coven. But mark this well, Sir Neil—someone in the Church *was*. Someone of importance. The knights that were here were saint-marked, and some were of a very special sort, a sort that the world has not seen in ages."

"What sort is that?"

"In one of my wine cellars there is a man whose head has been smitten off. He is still alive. He is not conscious, he cannot speak or see or feel, but his body continues to twitch." She shrugged. "I think Sir Chenzo knows nothing of this, but his superiors might. He was told to watch for someone like you. Your lies, as I said, are quite unconvincing."

"And Sir Quinte?"

"I don't know if he has any part in this, but it would be foolish to chance it."

"He has been a help to me. I do not know the language here. I was lost when he found me."

"Perhaps you were. Perhaps he merely convinced you that you were. I have a servant I will send with you. He is utterly trustworthy, and will act as your guide and interpreter. He will provision you, as well."

Then she smiled. "Go. You may leave by the front door. You will be neither seen nor hindered."

"What of you?"

"Do not fear for me. I can settle any trouble that may arise from your leaving."

Neil regarded her for a moment longer, then nodded.

As the countess had promised, he encountered no one in the halls or manse other than her own servants, who only bowed or nodded politely, always in silence.

Outside, in the courtyard, Hurricane was waiting, along with a smallish black mare and a brown gelding strapped with provisions. Near them stood a boy in brown breeches and white chemise with long black waistcoat and a broad-brimmed hat.

"If you please, sir," the boy said. His language was slightly accented king's tongue. His tone seemed ironic.

"Thank you—"

"You may call me Vaseto." He nodded at the horses. "All is ready. Shall we leave?"

"I suppose so."

"Good." He swung onto his mount. "If you will follow me."

The land was pale gold where the moon kissed it, but where she did not, the shadows were strange. Some were spread like dark rust, others like bronze blackened in flame or the green of rotted copper. It was as if a giant had wrought the world of metal and then left it too long to the weather. Even the stars looked like steel, and Vaseto— when his face came into view from beneath his brim—was red gold etched in deep relief.

Neil had never known such a night. He wished he could appreciate it, but the many colored shadows seemed to bristle with deadly quills, and nocturnal sounds parted around them, leaving space to hear something else—something following them.

"Do you hear that?" he asked Vaseto.

"It is nothing," the boy replied. "It's not your friends the knights, that's for sure. They would each be as noisy as you." He smiled thinly. "But you have good ears."

A few hours later they stopped at an abandoned house hidden by a copse of willows and took turns sleeping. Neil glumly stood guard, watching the shadows shift as the moon went down, now and then seeing one move in a way it shouldn't.

Dogs bayed in the distance, as if mourning the moonset.

A little after daybreak, they resumed their journey northward, Neil with weary eyes, his companion seeming cheerful and rested. Vaseto was a small, dark lad with large brown eyes and hair cropped in a bowl just above his ears. He rode as if born to the saddle, and his mount—though small—was spirited.

Midday they crossed a small river and passed a town on a hilltop. Three large towers stood up from the jumble of roofs, and fields spread to the road and beyond. Houses and inns became more frequent, until the road was nearly bounded by them; then they thinned again. Woodlands crept around the trail, sometimes forming dark, fragrant tunnels of cedar and bay.

"How far is z'Espino?" Neil asked restlessly.

"Ten chenperichi. We should reach it tomorrow."

"What did the countess tell you?"

"You're looking for two girls, one with red hair and another with golden. They might be with Cazio and z'Acatto."

"Who are Cazio and z'Acatto?" Neil asked.

"Former guests of the countess," Vaseto answered.

"Why would they be with these girls?"

"Cazio was courting one of them. The night the coven burned, Cazio and z'Acatto vanished, as well. I found some sign of their trail."

"You did?"

"Yes," Vaseto answered. "*I* did."

"And you think they were **together**?"

Vaseto rolled his eyes. "Three sets of tracks, two small, one large, all pursued by mounted men. They met at some ruins where a third man joined them—z'Acatto, by the torn sole of his boot. They fought the horsemen, and won after a fashion. All four left together."

Neil regarded Vaseto for a few moments, considered the authoritative ring of his voice.

"You're older than I thought," he said.

"Probably," Vaseto replied.

"And you're not a boy."

Vaseto gave him a small smirk. "I wondered if you would ever work that out," she said. "They must make you thick, up north. Not that men down here are generally any smarter."

"You're dressed like a boy. Your hair is cut like a boy's. And the countess called you male."

"So I am, and so it is, and so she did," Vaseto said. "And that's plenty of talk on that subject. Anyway, we've other things to worry about at the moment."

"Such as?"

For answer, an arrow thumped into the trunk of an olive tree, just a yard from Neil's head.

CHAPTER FIVE

THE UTIN

A SPAR LOOSED AN ARROW at the thing before he could even see what it was. It hit, he was certain, but the arrow didn't seem to have much effect. A long, clawed limb whipped out and struck Stephen to the ground.

As Aspar loosed his second arrow, a film of light seemed to settle on everything. The leaves that had concealed the pit where the creature had been hiding turned slowly as they fell, each distinct—ironoak, ash, haurnbagm, poplar.

As the leaves settled, the utin was revealed.

The first impression was of a huge spider—though it had only four limbs, they were long and spindly, attached to a torso so compact as to be boxlike, a mass of muscle covered in what looked like brown scales and sparse greenish hair that grew thicker on its upper spine and ruffed a short, thick neck. Yellow eyes glared from an enormous oblong of dark green horn with only slits for nostrils and holes for ears. Its mouth was the laugh of a Black Mary, a slit that cut the head in two and champed around wicked, black, uneven teeth.

The second arrow took it high in the chest, where its heart ought to have been. The creature turned away from Stephen and dropped to all fours, then sprang toward Aspar with terrible speed.

Aspar got off another shot, and so did Ehawk, and then the monster was on them. Its stench hit Aspar in the gut, and his gorge rose as he discarded the bow and yanked out his fighting dirk and throwing ax. He struck hard with the latter and dodged as the thing swept by. A six-clawed hand swiped at him and narrowly missed.

He whirled and fell into a fighting crouch.

The utin paused, bouncing slowly up and down on its two weird long legs, its body upright, fingers tapping at the ground. It towered a kingsyard above Aspar.

Aspar shifted back, hoping he was a little out of reach.

"Winna," he said. "Get away from here, now."

Ehawk, he noticed, was slowly creeping to get behind the beast.

"Wiiiiinaaah," the thing croaked, and Aspar's flesh went as crawly as if he'd stumbled into a nest of worms.

"Wiinaah gooh, yah. I find you later. Make fun."

The language was the local dialect of Almannish.

"Grim's eye," Aspar swore. "What the sceat are you?"

For answer, the utin swayed forward a bit, then plucked one of the arrows from its chest. Aspar saw the scales were more like bony plates, natural armor—the shaft hadn't penetrated deep. More and more he was reminded of the greffyn, which had also had much of the reptile about it.

If this thing was poisonous like the greffyn, Stephen was already as good as dead. So was he, if it touched him.

He waited for its next move, looking for soft spots. The head was plated, too, and was probably mostly bone. He might hit one of the eyes with a good throw. The throat, maybe?

No. All too far in. Its limbs were everywhere. He shifted his knife hand slightly.

The utin suddenly blurred toward him. Ehawk gave a cry and fired an arrow; Aspar ducked, leapt inside the reaching claws, and slashed at the inner thigh, then stabbed toward the groin. He felt flesh part at the first cut, and the thing howled. His thrust missed as the monster leap-frogged over him and then dealt him a terrific kick that sent him sprawling. It turned before he could even think about getting up, tore a branch from a tree, and hurled it. Aspar heard Ehawk cry out, and the thump of a body hitting the ground. Then the utin bounded toward him. From the corner of his eye, he saw Winna armed only with a dagger, rushing in to help.

"No!" Aspar shouted, levering himself up, lifting his ax.

But the utin struck Winna with the back of its hand, and as she staggered, it grabbed her with the other. Aspar hurled the ax, but it bounced harmlessly from the monster's head. In the next instant it leapt straight up, taking Winna with it. It caught a low-hanging branch, swung, clenched another branch with its handlike feet. It moved off through the trees faster than a man could run.

"No!" Aspar repeated. He pushed to his feet, retrieved his bow, and chased after the rapidly receding monster. A sort of shivering was in him, a feeling he had never known before.

He pushed the emotion down and ran, reached to his belt for the arrow case the praifec had given him, and extracted the black arrow.

The utin was quickly vanishing from sight, here-again-gone-again behind trunk and branch. Breath tore harshly through Aspar's lips as he set the relic to his string. He stopped, got his stance, and for an instant the world was quiet again. He felt the immensity of the earth beneath him, the faint breeze pushing itself over the land, the deep slow breath of the trees. He drew.

The utin vanished behind a bole, reappeared, and vanished again. Aspar aimed at the narrow gap where he thought it would appear again, felt the time come right, and released.

The ebony shaft spiraled out and away from him, hissing past leaf and branch, to where the utin's broad back was a brief occlusion between two trees.

The quiet stretched, but stillness did not. Aspar ran again, already taking out another shaft, cursing under his breath, his heart tightening like an angry fist.

He found Winna first. She lay like an abandoned doll in a patch of autumn-reddened bracken, her dress smeared with blood. The utin sprawled a few feet away, its back to a tree, watching him come. Aspar could see the head of the black arrow protruding from its chest.

Aspar knelt by Winna, feeling for her pulse, but he kept his gaze fixed on the utin. It gurgled and spat out blood, and blinked, as if tired. It raised a six-fingered hand to touch the arrowhead.

"Not fair, mannish," it husked. "Not weal. An unholy thing, yes? And yet it will slay you, too. Your doom is the same as mine."

Then it vomited blood, wheezed two more times, and looked beyond the lands of fate.

"Winna?" Aspar said. "Winna?" His heart tripped, but she still had a pulse, and a strong one. He touched her cheek, and she stirred.

"Eh?" she said.

"Stay still," Aspar said. "You fell, I don't know how far. Do you have any pain?"

"Yes," she said. "Every part of me hurts. I feel like I've been put in a bag and kicked by six mules." She suddenly gasped and jerked up to a sitting position. "The utin—!"

"It's dead. Still, now, until we're sure nothing's broken. How far did you fall?"

"I don't know. After it hit me, everything is cloudy."

He began inspecting her legs, feeling for breaks.

"Aspar White. Do you always get so romantic after killing an utin?" she asked.

"Always," he said. "Every single time." He kissed her then, from sheer relief. As he did it, he realized that in the past few moments he had known the greatest terror of his life. It was elevated so far above any fear he had ever known before, he hadn't recognized it.

"Winna—," he began, but a faint noise made him look up, and in the thicket behind the dead utin, he had a brief glimpse of a cowled figure, half hidden by a tree, face as white as bone, and one green eye—

"Fend!" he snarled, and reached for the bow.

When he turned, the figure was gone. He set the arrow and waited.

"Can you walk?" he asked softly.

"Yah." She stood. "Was it really him?"

"It was a Sefry, for certain. I didn't get a better look."

"There's someone coming behind us," she said.

"Yah. That's Stephen and Ehawk. I recognize their gaits."

The two younger men arrived a moment later.

Stephen gasped when he saw the dead creature. "Saints!"

Aspar didn't take his gaze from the woods. "There's a Sefry out there," he said.

"The tracks we saw earlier?" Ehawk asked.

"Most likely. Are you okay?" Aspar asked.

"Yes, I'm fine, thanks," Stephen said. "A little bruised, that's all."

"The boy?" Winna asked.

Stephen's voice sobered. "He died."

No one said anything at that. There wasn't much to say.

The forest was still, its normal sounds returning.

"You two stay with her," Aspar said. "I'm going to see what became of our friend's companion."

"Aspar, wait," Winna said. "What if it is Fend? What if he's leading you into another trap?"

He touched her hand. "I think the one trap was all he had planned. If we hadn't had the praifec's arrow, it would have worked well enough."

"You used the arrow?" Stephen said.

"It had Winna," Aspar said. "It was in the trees. There was nothing else I could do."

Stephen frowned, but then nodded. He walked over to the utin, knelt near the corpse, and gingerly removed the dart.

"I see what you mean," he said. "The other arrows didn't even penetrate a fingerbreadth." He shot them a wry grin. "At least we know it works."

"Yah. On utins," Aspar allowed. "I'll be back." He squeezed Winna's hand. "And I'll be careful."

He followed the tracks for a few hundred yards, which was as far as he dared alone. He'd told Winna the truth—he didn't fear a trap—but he did fear that the Sefry was working his way back to Stephen and Winna, to catch them while he was away. Fend would like nothing more than to kill someone else Aspar loved, and he'd just come as close to losing Winna as he ever wanted to.

"It still looks like he's alone," Aspar said.

They had been following the Sefry trail for the better part of a day.

"Traveling fast," Ehawk said. "But he wants to be followed."

"Yah, I reckon that, too," Aspar said.

"What do you mean?" Stephen asked.

"The trail is obvious—sloppy even. He's making no effort to lose us."

"Ehawk just said he seems to be in a hurry."

"That's not enough to account for it. He hasn't even tried the simplest tricks to throw us off. He crossed three broohs, and never even waded up or down the stream. Werlic, Ehawk is right—he wants us to follow him for some reason."

"If its Fend, he's likely leading us somewhere unpleasant," Winna said.

Aspar scratched the stubble on his chin. "I'm not sure it *is* Fend. I didn't get a very clear look, but I didn't see an eye patch. And the prints look too small."

"But whoever it was, he was traveling with the utin, just as Fend and Brother Desmond traveled with the greffyn. So it's probably one of Fend's bunch, right?"

"Well, so far as I know, Fend's outlaws are the only Sefry left in the forest," Aspar agreed. "The rest left months ago."

The trail had pulled them deep into the forest. Here there was no sign of the black thorns. Huge chestnut trees rose around them, and the ground was littered with their stickery issue. Somewhere near, a woodpecker drummed away, and now and then they heard the honking of geese, far overhead.

"What could they be up to?" Winna wondered aloud.

"I reckon we'll find out," Aspar said.

Evening came, and they made camp. Winna and Stephen rubbed down the horses while Ehawk started a fire. Aspar scouted, memorizing the land so he might know it in the dark.

They decamped at the first light of dawn and continued on. The tracks were fresher now—their quarry wasn't mounted, while they were. Despite his speed, they were catching up.

Midday, Aspar noticed something through the trees ahead and waved the others to a halt. He glanced at Stephen.

"I don't hear anything unusual," Stephen said. "But the smell—it reeks of death."

"Keep ready," Aspar said.

"Holy saints," Stephen breathed as they got near enough to see.

A small stone building sat on a rounded tumulus of earth. Around the base of the mound lay a perimeter of human corpses, reduced mostly to bone. Stephen was right, though—the stink was still there. To his saint-blessed senses it had to be overwhelming, Aspar supposed.

Stephen confirmed that by doubling over and retching. Aspar waited until he was done, then moved closer.

"It's like before," Aspar said. "Like the sacrifices your renegade monks were making. This is a sedos, yah?"

"It's a sedos," Stephen confirmed. "But this isn't like before. They're doing it correctly, this time."

"What do you mean?" Winna asked.

Stephen sagged against a tree, looking pale and weak.

"Do you understand about the sedoi?" he asked her.

"You mentioned something about them to the queen's interrogators, but at the time I wasn't paying much attention. Aspar was hurt, and since then—"

"Yes, we haven't discussed it much since then." He sighed. "You know how priests receive the blessing of the saints?"

"A little. They visit fanes and pray."

"Yes. But not just any fanes." He waved at the mound. "That's a sedos. It's a place where a saint once stood and left some bit of his presence. Visiting one sedos doesn't confer a blessing, though, or at least not usually. You have to find a trail of them, a series of places visited by the same saint, or by aspects of that saint. The fanes—like that building there—have no power themselves. The power comes from the sedos—the fane is just a reminder, a place to help us focus our attention in the saint's presence.

"I walked the faneway of Saint Decmanis, and he gifted me with the heightened senses I have now. I can remember things a month after as clearly as if they just happened. Decmanis is a saint of knowledge; monks who walk other faneways receive other blessings. The faneway of Mamres, for instance, conveys martial gifts on those who travel it. Great strength, alacrity, an instinct for killing, those sorts of things."

"Like Desmond Spendlove."

"Yes. He followed the faneway of Mamres."

"So this is part of a faneway?" Winna asked. "But the bodies . . ."

"It's new," Stephen said. "Look at the stone. There's no moss or lichen, no weather stains. This might have been built yesterday. The renegade monks and Sefry who were following the greffyn were using the creature to find old sedoi in the forest. I think it had the power to scent them out, and made a circuit of those which still had some latent power. Then Desmond and his bunch performed sacrifices, I think to try to find out what saint the sedoi belonged to. I don't think they were doing it right, though—they lacked certain information. Whoever did this did it correctly."

He passed his palm over his eyes. "And it's my fault. When I was at d'Ef, I translated ancient, forbidden scrifts concerning these things. I gave them the information they needed to do what you see here." He shook, looking paler than ever. "They're building a faneway, you see?"

"Who?" Aspar said. "Spendlove and his renegades are dead."

"Not all of them, it would seem," Stephen said. "This was built after we killed Spendlove."

"But what saint left his mark here?" Winna whispered.

Stephen retched again, rubbed his forehead, and stood straight. "It's my place to find that out," he said. "All of you, wait here—please."

Stephen nearly vomited again when he reached the circle of corpses. Not from the smell this time, but from the horror of details. Bits of clothing, the ribbon in the hair of one of the smaller ones, juxtaposed with her lopsided, not-quite-fleshless grin. A stained green cloak with a brass broach worked in the shape of a swan. Little signs that these had once been human beings. Where had the little girl got the ribbon? She was probably the daughter of a woodcutter—it might have been the grandest present she'd ever recieved in her life. Her father had brought it when he drove the hogs to market in Tulhaem, and she'd kissed him on the cheek. He'd called her "my little duckling," and he'd had to watch her be eviscerated, before he himself felt the knife, just below where a swan brooch pinned his cloak . . .

Stephen shuddered, closed his eyes to step over her, and felt—

—a hum, a soft tickling in his belly, a sort of crackling in his head. He turned to look back at Aspar and the rest, and they seemed far away, tiny. Their mouths were moving, but he could not hear them speak. For a moment, he forgot what he was about, just stood there, wondering who they were.

At the same time, he felt wonderful. His aches and pains were all gone, and he felt as if he could run ten leagues without stopping. He frowned at the bones and rotting flesh around the mound, vaguely remembering that the sight of them had bothered him for some reason, though he wondered why they should upset him any more than the branches and leaves that also littered the ground.

Musing at that, he turned slowly to regard the building behind him. It was built as many Church fanes were—a simple stone cube with a roof of slate and a perpetually open doorway. The lintel was carved with a single word, and with interest he noticed it wasn't Vitellian, the usual language of the Church—but rather old Vadhiian, the language of the Warlock Kingdoms. MARHIRHEBEN, it said.

Inside, a small, slender statue carved of bone overlooked a stone altar. It depicted a beautiful woman with an unsettling smile. On either side of her stood a greffyn, and her hands dropped down as if to stroke their manes.

He looked around, but saw nothing else of note. Shrugging, he left the fane.

As he stepped across the line of corpses again, something terrible tore loose and leapt from his throat. The world shattered like glass, and he fell into the night before the world was born.

CHAPTER SIX

THE HOUNDS OF ARTUMO

W HILE THE ARROW WAS still quivering, two men stepped into the road, and Neil guessed there were at least four in the bushes by the side. A faint scuff told him there was one behind him.

The two in front were dressed in faded leathers, and each bore a long-hafted spear. They also had kerchiefs pulled up to conceal their faces.

"Bandits?" Neil asked.

"No, clergymen," Vaseto responded sarcastically.

One of the men called something out.

"Of what saint?" Neil asked.

"Lord Turmo, I would think, patron of thieves. They've just asked you to dismount and strip off your armor."

"Did they?" Neil asked. "What do you advise?"

"Depends on whether you want to keep your things or not."

"I'd like to, thanks."

"Well, then," Vaseto said, and gave a clear, high whistle.

The man shouted something again. This time Vaseto shouted back.

"What was that all about?"

"I've offered them a chance to surrender."

"Good thing," Neil replied. "Try to keep low." He reached for his spear.

At that moment, furious motion erupted on the side of the road. Neil wheeled Hurricane and caught a glimpse of something very large and brown in the undergrowth. Leaves were flying, and someone shouted in anguish.

Confused, he turned back to the men on the road, just in time to see them go down beneath the paws of two huge mastiffs.

"*Oro!*" one of them screamed. "*Oro, pertument! Pacha Satos, Pacha sachero satos! Pacha misercarda!*"

Neil looked around. There were at least eight of the huge beasts.

Vaseto whistled again. The dogs backed up a pace or so from their victims, but kept their teeth bare.

Neil glanced at Vaseto, who was dismounting.

"Why don't you keep that big sword out," she said, "while I take the weapons from these fellows?"

"Have pity!" one of the men in the road said, in the king's tongue. "See how I speak your language? Perhaps a kinsman am I!"

"What sort of pity would you have from me?" Neil asked, keeping one eye on the dog that was guarding the fellow as he took his spear and two knives. "You meant to steal from me, yes? Perhaps even kill me?"

"No, no, of course not," the man said. "But it is so hard to live, these days. Work is scarce, food scarcer. I have a wife, ten little ones—please, spare me, master!"

"Hush," Vaseto said. "You said it yourself. Food is scarce. If my dogs eat a sheep or goat, I'll get in trouble. If they eat you, I'll only get thanks. So be quiet now, thank the lords and ladies you'll feed such noble creatures."

The man looked up. Tears were rolling from his eyes. "Lady Artuma! Spare me from your children!"

Vaseto squatted by him and tousled his hair. "That's disingenuous," she said. "First you molest a servant of Artuma, then you ask forgiveness of her?"

"Priestess, I did not know."

She kissed his forehead. "And how is that an excuse?" she asked.

"It's not, it's not, I understand that."

She searched at his belt, came up with a pouch. "Well," she said. "Perhaps a donation at the next shrine will help your cause."

"Yes," the man sniffled. "It might. I pray it might. Great lord, great lady—"

"I'm tired of your talking now," Vaseto said. "Another word, and your throat will be cut."

They disarmed the rest of the bandits and remounted.

"Shouldn't we take them somewhere?" Neil asked.

She shrugged. "Not unless you've got time to waste. You'd have to stay and wait for a judge. Without weapons, they'll be harmless for a while."

"Harmless as a lamb!" the man on the ground seconded; then he screamed when the dog lunged at him.

"No more talk, I told you," Vaseto said. "Lie there quietly. I leave my brothers and sisters to dispose of you as they see fit."

She trotted her mare down the road. After a moment, Neil followed.

"You might have told me about the dogs," Neil said after a few moments.

"I might have," she agreed. "It amused me not to. Are you angry?"

"No. But I'm learning not to be surprised."

"Oh? That would be a shame. It fits you so well."

"Will they kill them?"

"Hmm? No. They'll stay long enough to give them a good scare, then follow us."

"Who are you, Vaseto?" Neil asked.

"That's hardly a fair question," Vaseto said. "I don't know *your* name."

"My name is Neil MeqVren," he said.

"That's not the name you gave the countess," she observed.

"No, it isn't. But it is my real name."

She smiled. "And Vaseto is mine. I'm a friend of the countess Orchaevia. That's all you need to know."

"Those men seemed to think you are some sort of priestess."

"What's the harm in that?"

"Are you?"

"Not by vocation."

Which was all she would say in the matter.

Midday the next day, Neil smelled the sea, and soon after heard the tolling of bells in z'Espino.

As they rode over the top of a hill, towers came into view, slender spires of red or dark yellow stone rising above domes and rooftops that seemed to crowd together for leagues. Nearer, fields of darker olive green contrasted sharply with golden wheatland and delicate copses of knife-shaped cedars. Beyond, the blue sliver of the sea gleamed beneath a pile of white clouds.

To the west of the city stood another jumble of buildings, this one more somber, with no towers and no wall. That would be z'Espino-of-Shadows, he reckoned.

"It's big," Neil said.

"Big enough," Vaseto replied. "And too big for my taste."

"How can we ever find two women in all that?"

"Well, I supposed we'd have to think," Vaseto replied. "If you were them, what would you do?"

Hard to say, with Anne, Neil reflected. She might do almost anything. Would she even know what had happened to her family?

But even if she didn't, she was lost in a foreign country, pursued by enemies. If she had any sense, she'd be trying to get home.

"She would try to reach Crotheny," he said.

Vaseto nodded. "Two ways to do that. By sea or by land. Does she have money, this girl?"

"Probably not."

"Then I should think it would be easier to go by land. You ought to know—you just came that way."

"Yes, but the roads are dangerous, especially if those men are still hunting her." He shifted in his saddle. "The countess said something about a man who had his head cut off, and was yet still alive."

"She told you about that, did she? And you've waited this long to ask me about it?"

"I want to know what I'm up against."

"I would tell you if I knew," Vaseto said. "Not the usual sort of knight, but that's obvious. As the countess said, the fellow was still alive, after a fashion, but not exactly in a condition to speak." She wrinkled her brow. "Don't you object to this at all? You seem all too eager to accept a most absurd notion."

"I have seen shinecraft and encrotacnia enough this past year," Neil said. "I've no reason to doubt the countess and every reason to believe her. If she told me they were the *eschasl* themselves come back from the grave, I would credit it."

"Eschasl?" Vaseto said. "You mean the Skasloi? You Lierish can certainly mangle up words, I'll give you that. In any event, the men we're talking about are human, or started that way. We did find the more ordinary sort of corpse, as well. If I had to guess, they're from your country, or some other northern place, for several had yellow hair like yours, and light-colored eyes. They were not Vitellian."

"Which leads me to wonder how they came so deep into your country on a mission of murder."

Vaseto grinned. "But you already know the answer to that, or at least you have some suspicion. Someone here is helping them."

"The Church?"

"Not the Church, but maybe someone in the Church. Or it might be the merchant guilds, given your Sir Quinte's attentions. Or it could be any random prince, who knows? But they have aid here, of that you can be sure."

"And have they aid in z'Espino?"

"That's likely enough. A copper minser could corrupt most any official in this wicked town."

Neil nodded, looking with fresh eyes at the landscape that lay between him and city.

"What's that down there?" he asked, pointing to where the road they were on joined a larger way. Along it, numerous tents and stalls had been set up. Just past the joining, the road crossed a stone bridge over a canal, and there was a gate on the city side.

"That's where the merchant guilds take their taxes," Vaseto replied. "Why do you ask?"

"Because if I were looking for someone entering or leaving z'Espino, that's where I might place myself."

Vaseto nodded. "Good. I'll make you a suspicious man yet."

"They might be looking for me, too," Neil said.

"Good boy."

He felt she might have been talking to one of her dogs. He glanced at her, but she was staring intently at the travelers who were cueing up to cross the bridge.

"I have an idea," she said.

Neil pressed his eye to the crack in the wagon wall. Through the narrow slit, he saw mostly color—silks and satin and brightly dyed cotton swirling like a thousand flower petals in the wind. Faces were nearly lost in it, but he caught them now and then.

The wain jounced to a stop. He tried to find the view he was after, by half crouching and gazing through a knothole.

A group of men in orange surcoats was talking to the drivers of wagons and those on foot or with pack animals. They examined cargo sometimes, sometimes let the travelers pass with little comment. A few arguments erupted, ending when coins changed hands. Beyond all that, at the gate, were more men, these armed, and he could see the archers in the towers above the gate.

He kept looking, cursing the knothole for affording such a small field of vision. The guildsmen were moving toward the wagon he sheltered in. Soon, he would have to—

It wasn't his eyes that gave him the clue, but his ears. The cloud of unintelligible Vitellian surrounding him had become transparent. Now, through that clearness, he heard a language he recognized. A language he loathed.

Hanzish.

He couldn't make out what they were saying, but he knew the cadence of it, the long vowel glides and throat-catching gutturals. His hands clenched involuntarily into fists.

He moved to another crack, bumping his head in the process.

"*Hiss*, back there," a voice whispered furiously. "There's no bargain if you don't lie still, as you were told."

"A moment," Neil replied.

"No moment. Get in your place, *now*."

A face pushed through the curtain, and light flooded in. Neil saw only the silhouette of a broad-brimmed hat and the faint glint of leaf-green eyes.

"Do you see anyone with light hair out there?"

"The two Hanzish with the guildsmen? Yes. Now lie down!"

"You see them?"

"Of course I see them. They're watching people, watching the guildsmen do their work. Looking for you, I'd guess, and they'll find you if you don't lie still!"

Another face pushed through, this one Vaseto's. "Do it, you great idiot. I'm your eyes here! I've marked them. Now play your part."

Neil hesitated for a moment, but realized he had no choice now. He couldn't fight all of the guildsmen and the Hanzish, too . . .

He lay back, pulled the cloth up over his mouth, just as someone thumped on the back of the wagon. He tried to slow his breathing, but with a start realized he'd forgotten something. The coins! He found them and placed them on his eyes, just as the back wagon flap rustled.

He held his breath.

"*Pis'es ecic egmo?*" someone asked sharply.

"*Uno viro morto,*" A heavily ironic voice said. Neil recognized it as that of the Sefry man who spoke for the rest of them.

"*Ol Viedo! Pis?*"

Neil felt fingers grab his arm. He fought the instinct to leap up.

Then he felt fingers brush his forehead. His breath was going stale, and his lungs began to hurt.

"*Chiano Vechioda daz'Ofina,*" the Sefry replied. "*Mortat daca crussa.*"

The fingers jerked away. "*Diuvo!*" the guildsman shouted, and the flap closed. There followed an argument he could not make out. Finally, after long moments, the wagon started moving again. After an eternity of wooden wheels grinding and stopping on stone, someone tapped his boot.

"You can get up now," Vaseto said.

Neil took the coins from his eyes and sat up. "We're through the gate?"

"Yes, no thanks to you," Vaseto grumbled. "Didn't I tell you it would work?"

"He *felt* of me. In another instant he would have reckoned I was still warm."

"Probably. I didn't say it was without risk. But the Sefry played their parts well."

"What did they tell him?"

"That you died of the bloody-pus plague." She smiled. "The makeup helped."

Neil nodded, scratching at the counterfeit welts the Sefry had made of flour and pig's blood.

"He's probably off praying right now," she added. She jerked her head. "Come on."

He poked his head out the back of the wain. They were in some sort of square surrounded by tall buildings. One, with a high dome, was likely a temple. People bustled everywhere, as strangely and colorfully dressed as the caravaners at the bridge.

They went around to the front of the wagon, where three Sefry sat under an awning, swaddled thickly against the sun.

"Thank you," Neil said.

One of the Sefry, an old woman, snorted. The other two ignored him.

"How did you get them to help?" Neil asked Vaseto as she led him across the square.

"I told them I would reveal the hidden space in their wagon where they were carrying their contraband."

"How did you know about that?"

"I didn't," she said. "Not for certain. But I know a thing or two about Sefry, and that clan almost always carries contraband."

"That's good to know."

"They also owe me a few favors. Or did. We just used up most of them. So don't waste this chance. Keep that wig on. Don't let your straw mat show."

Neil plucked at the horsehair mummer's wig that had been

pulled over his own close-cropped hair. "I don't care for it," he muttered.

"You're a true beauty with it on," Vaseto told him. "Now, try not to talk too much, especially if someone speaks to you in Hansan or Crothanic. You're a traveler from Ilsepeq, here to visit the shrine of Vanth."

"Where's Ilsepeq?"

"I've no idea. Neither will anyone you tell. But Espinitos pride themselves on their knowledge of the world, so no one will admit that. Just practice this: 'Edio dat Ilsepeq. Ne fatio Vitellian.'"

"Edio dat Islepeq," Neil tried experimentally. "Ne fatio Vitellian."

"Very good," Vaseto said. "You sound exactly as if you don't speak a word of Vitellian."

"I don't," Neil said.

"Well, that explains it. Now come, let's find your girls."

CHAPTER SEVEN

AMBRIA

"I LIKE THAT ONE," Mery said absently. She was lying stomach down on a rug, her legs kicking up behind her.

"Do you?" Leoff asked, continuing to play the hammarharp. "I'm pleased that you like it."

She made fists and rested her chin on them. "It's sad, but not in the way that makes you cry. Like autumn coming."

"Melancholy?" Leoff said.

She pinched her mouth thoughtfully. "I guess so."

"Like autumn coming," Leoff mused. He smiled faintly, stopped, dipped his quill in ink, and made a notation on the music.

"What did you write?" Mery said.

"I wrote, 'like autumn coming,'" he said. "So the musicians will know how to play it." He turned in his seat. "Are you ready for your lesson?"

She brightened a bit. "Yes."

"Come sit beside me, then."

She got up, brushed the front of her dress, and then scooted onto the bench.

"Let's see, we were working on the third mode, weren't we?"

"Uh-huh." She tapped the freshly noted music. "Can I try this?"

He glanced at her. "You can try," he said.

Mery placed her fingers on the keyboard, and a look of intense concentration came over her face. She bit her lip and played the first chord, walked the melody up, and on the third bar stopped, a look of sudden consternation on her features.

"What's wrong?" he asked.

"I can't reach," she said.

"That's right," he said. "Do you know why?"

"My hands aren't big enough."

He smiled. "No one's hands are big enough. This isn't really written for hammarharp. That bottom line would be played by a bass croth."

"But you just played it."

"I cheated," he said. "I transposed the notes up an octave. I just wanted an idea how it all sounded together. To really know, we'll have to have an ensemble play it."

"Oh." She pointed. "What's that line, then?"

"That's the hautboy."

"And this?"

"That's the tenor voice."

"Someone singing?"

"Exactly."

She played the single line. "Are there words?" she asked.

"Yes."

"I don't see them."

He tapped his head. "They're still in here, with the rest of it."

She blinked at him. "You're making it up?"

"I'm making it up," he confirmed.

"What are the words?"

"The first word is *ih*," Leoff said solemnly.

"Ih? That's the servants' word for *I*."

"Yes," he said. "It's a very important word. It's the first time it's been used like this."

"I don't understand."

"I'm not sure I do myself."

"But why the servants' language? Why not the king's tongue?"

"Because most people in Crotheny speak Almannish, not the king's tongue."

"They do?"

He nodded.

"Is that because they're all servants?"

He laughed. "In a way, I suppose so."

"We all of us are servants," a feminine voice said from the doorway. "It's only a matter of whom we serve."

Leoff turned in his seat. A woman stood there. At first he noticed only her eyes, cut gems of topaz that glittered with a deep green fire. They held him mercilessly, and kept his throat tight for too long.

He broke the gaze finally.

"Lady," he managed, "I have not had the pleasure." He reached for his crutches and managed to stand and make a little bow.

The woman smiled. She had ash-blond hair that hung in curls and a pleasantly dimpled face that was beginning to show some age. He reckoned her to be in her mid-thirties.

"I am Ambria Gramme," she told him.

Leoff felt his mouth drop open, and closed it. "You're Mery's mother?" he said. "I'm very pleased to meet you. I must say, she is a delight, and a most promising student."

"Student?" Gramme asked sweetly. "Who are you? And what do you teach, exactly?"

"Oh, my apologies. I am Leovigild Ackenzal, the court composer. I thought Mery would have mentioned me." He glanced at the girl, who looked innocently away.

The smile widened. "Oh, yes, I've heard of you. Quite the hero, yes? For your part in the business at Broogh."

Leoff felt his face warming. "If I did anything commendable, it was by sheerest accident, I assure you."

"Humility isn't particularly fashionable in the court at the moment, but you *do* wear it well," Lady Gramme said. Her eyes drifted down his frame. "You are cut from good cloth, just as I've heard."

"I . . ." He stopped. He had nothing to say to that, and he tried to gather his composure. "I'm sorry, milady, I thought you knew I was giving Mery music lessons. I mean her no harm, I assure you."

"The fault isn't yours," Gramme replied. "Mery simply forgot to tell me. Didn't you, Mery?"

"I'm sorry, Mama."

"As you should be. Fralet Ackenzal is an important man. I'm sure he doesn't have time for you."

"Oh, no," Leoff replied. "As I said, she's a wonderful student."

"I'm sure she is. But at present my funds do not allow for the cost of tutoring."

"I ask for no compensation," Leoff said. "My expenses at the court are taken care of." He waved his hands helplessly. "I would hate to see her talent go to waste."

"She has talent, you think?"

"I assure you. Would you like to hear her play something?"

"Oh, no," Gramme said, still smiling. "I've no ear at all, I'm told. I trust your judgment."

"Then you won't mind?"

"How could I refuse such a kind gesture?" Her lips pursed. "But still, it puts me in your debt. You must let me make it up to you somehow."

"That's not necessary," he said, trying very hard to keep his voice from breaking.

"No, I know just the thing. I'm having a small fete on Saint Bright's Eve. You're new here, and could do with some introductions, I'm sure. I insist you attend."

"That's very kind, lady."

"Not at all. It's the least I can do for someone who indulges my little Mery. There, it's settled." Her gaze shifted. "Mery, when you've finished your lessons, come to my apartments, will you?"

"Yes, Mama," the girl replied.

"Good day to you, then," Gramme said.

"Good day to you, Lady Gramme."

"You might call me Ambria," she replied. "Most of my friends do."

* o o

Mery left a bell later, and Leoff returned to his work, a tense excitement growing in his belly. It felt right, it felt perfect, the way his composition was growing. It felt important, too, but that consideration he
tried to keep at a distance. If he thought about *that* too much, the
task grew daunting.

Toward vespers, he heard footsteps and a small rap at his door.
He found Artwair standing there, dressed much as when he had first
met him, in traveling clothes.

"My lord!" he said, reaching for his crutches.

"No, no, keep your seat," Artwair said. "Surely we've no need for
that."

Leoff smiled, realizing just how good it was to see the duke again.

"How are you getting along, Leoff?" Artwair asked, taking a seat
on a stool.

"The queen came to see me," he said. "She's commissioned a
work, and it's going—well, very well. I'm very hopeful for it."

Artwair looked a bit surprised. "What sort of a work? Not a requiem, I hope."

"No, something much more exciting. I tell you, it's something
that has never been done before."

Artwair raised an eyebrow. "So? Well, have a care, my friend.
Sometimes the new isn't always the best thing for the moment. The
local clergy is already muttering about you."

Leoff waved that away. "The queen has confidence in me. That's
all I care about."

"The queen is not the only power to be reckoned with in this
court."

"It can hardly be worse than Broogh," Leoff said.

"It most certainly can," Artwair said, his voice suddenly as serious
as Leoff had ever heard it. "These days, it most certainly can."

Leoff forced a chuckle. "Well, I'll try to keep that in mind. But it
is a commission, you know, and from the queen." He paused, again
taking in Artwair's clothing. In the court he had dressed in brocades
and linens. "Are you traveling soon?" he asked.

"Yes, actually, I've just stopped in to tell you good-bye. There's a bit of trouble in the east I've been asked to handle."

"More wayward musicians?"

Artwair shook his head. "No, something a little more demanding, I'm afraid. The queen has asked me take an army there."

Leoff's heart stuttered a beat. "Are we at war? Is it Hansa?"

"I'm not sure it's war, and I don't think its Hansa. Some of the locals have turned into man-eaters, it seems."

"What?"

"Sounds ridiculous, doesn't it? People running around naked, rending their neighbors limb from limb. At first it was hard to credit, even when the praifec said it was true. Now—well, several villages have been destroyed, but last nineday they killed everyone in Slifhaem."

"Slifhaem? I've been there. It's a town of some size, with a fortress." He paused. "Did you say *naked*?"

"That's how we hear it, and more of them every day. The praifec says it's some sort of witchery. All I know is, I'm to go and put a stop to it before they go pouring into the Midenlands."

Leoff shook his head. "And you're warning *me* to have a care."

"Well, I'd rather take the field any day and see my death coming on the edge of a sword than die from the nick of a pin or a goblet of poisoned wine here in Eslen," he said. "Besides, I'll be strapped in armor with a good sword in my hand and have five hundred excellent men around me. I don't reckon a bunch of naked madmen will have much chance to do me in."

"What if they have creatures with them, like the basil-nix? What if it's the Briar King himself driving them on, making them mad?"

"Well, I'll kill him, too, for good measure," Artwair said. "Meantime—ho, what's this?"

Leoff watched as Artwair picked up a shawl from the carpet.

"You've been making a few acquaintances, auy?" Artwair said, winking. "The sort that gets comfortable enough to leave things lying about?"

Leoff smiled. "Not of the sort you mean, I'm afraid. Mery must have left that."

"Mery?"

"One of my students. Lady Gramme's daughter."

Artwair stared at him, then gave a low whistle. "That *is* interesting company," Artwair commented.

"Yes, I got that reaction from the queen, as well," Leoff said.

"I should think so."

"But she's a delightful child," Leoff said, "and an excellent student."

Artwair's eyes widened. "You don't know who she is?"

"Yes, I just told you—Ambria Gramme's daughter."

"Auy, but do you know who *she* is?"

Leoff had a sudden sinking feeling. "Well—no, not exactly," he said.

"You are pleasantly naïve, Leovigild Ackenzal," the duke said.

"A role I'm growing tired of."

"Then you might ask a few questions, now and then. The lady Gramme is the girl's mother, yes. I might better say, she is the daughter of Ambria Gramme and the late King William the Second."

Leoff was silent for a moment. *"Oh,"* he finally said.

"Yes. You've made friends with one of the king's bastards—not a popular person with the queen, right now."

"The poor girl can't help her birth."

"No, of course not. But Lady Gramme is one of many who have visions of a crown in her future, and she isn't afraid to try anything that might bring that vision to pass. She's the queen's bitter enemy. Mery's lucky she hasn't met with some sort of . . . accident."

Leoff straightened indignantly. "I can't believe the queen would imagine doing such a thing."

"A year ago, I might have agreed with you," Artwair replied. "Now—well, I wouldn't get too attached to little Mery."

Leoff glanced off down the hall, hoping the girl wasn't within earshot.

"Ah," Artwair said. "It's too late for that, I see." He walked over and rested his hand on Leoff's shoulder. "The court is a dangerous place, just now," he said. "You've got to watch what sort of friends you make. If the queen ever suspected you had been drawn into Gramme's snares—well, then I'd be worried about *you* experiencing a bad fall." He lifted his hand. "Take me seriously," he said. "Keep away from Gramme. Don't attract her attention." He showed his teeth. "And wish me luck. If things go well, I'll be back before Yule."

"Best of luck, Artwair," Leoff said. "I'll ask the saints to keep you safe."

"Auy. But if they don't, no bloody requiems, please? They're damn depressing."

Leoff watched the duke leave, his heart sinking further. Artwair was the only adult he really knew in Eslen, certainly the only one he might call a friend. After him, there was only Mery.

And as for that, and Ambria Gramme—Artwair's warning had come a few hours too late. He had already attracted her attention.

CHAPTER EIGHT

TRUST

WHEN CAZIO BURST INTO the courtyard, Anne was huddled near the cookfire, patching a shawl. The nights had grown
cooler, and she had no money for a new wrap.

She smiled thinly at Cazio, who seemed—as usual—very pleased
with himself.

"I've got a present for you," he announced.

"What sort of present?"

"Ask me nicely, and I'll tell you."

"What sort of present, *please*?" she said impatiently.

He frowned. "Is that as nicely as you can manage? I was hoping
for something more in the way of a kiss."

"Yes, well, without hope, we'd have little to drive us on, would
we? If I gave you that kiss, what would you have left to hope for?"

"Oh, I can imagine a thing or two," he leered.

"Yes, but you could never truly *hope* for them," she said. Then
she sniffed. "Never mind. Unless your present is a new shawl, or a
warmer suit of clothes, I doubt that I've any need of it."

"Oh, no? How does passage on a ship sound?"

Anne dropped her darning needle. Then she frowned and picked
it back up. "Don't tease," she said irritably.

"A fine one you are to talk," he said.

"I've *never*—"

"I'm kidding," Cazio said. Then, quickly—"Not about the ship. It's all arranged. Passage for the four of us."

"To where?"

"Paldh. That's near Eslen, is it not?"

"Very near," Anne said. "Near enough. Is this true? You're not baiting me?"

"Casnara, I am not. I've just spoken to the captain."

"And it's safe?"

"As safe as we'll find."

Anne blinked at Cazio. After all this time, she'd begun to stop thinking about home, tried to live in the present, to get from one day to the next. But now—

Her room. Decent clothes. A crackling hearth. Warm baths. Real food.

Safety.

She got up and very deliberately planted a kiss right on Cazio's lips.

"For this one instant," she said, "I adore you."

"Well," Cazio said, his voice suddenly a little strained. "How about another, then?"

She considered. "No," she said at last, "the moment's gone. But I'm still grateful, Cazio."

"Ah, you're a fickle one," Cazio said. "All I've done for love of you, and so little in return."

Anne laughed and was startled that it felt genuine. "You love me, you love Austra, you love any young thing in a skirt."

"There is love, and there is true love," Cazio replied.

"Indeed. And I wonder if you will ever know the difference." She plucked at his sleeve. "I do appreciate your help, though I suspect that the fact that my father will pay—" She stopped suddenly.

She had forgotten.

Cazio noticed the change in her features. "Never mind thoughts of pay," he said. "I'm already the best swordsman in all of Vitellio. I've a mind to see if I have a match anywhere else, and your country is as good a place to start as any."

Anne nodded, but she was unable to return to the banter.

"In any event, you should pack your things," he continued. "This ship leaves in the morning, assuming you still want to take it."

"You're *sure* it's safe?"

"I know the captain. I don't like him very much, but he's a man of his word, and utterly trustworthy in a dull sort of way."

"Then we have to go," she said. "We must."

At the moment, a cry went up on the street. Anne looked past Cazio and found Ospero standing in the doorway. Outside, she saw men gathered.

"What's happening? she asked.

"They've found you again," Ospero replied. He had a dagger in his hand.

Neil breathed deeply of the sea air, and for the first time in a long while he felt at home. The language was unfamiliar, the clothing of those around him was strange, and even the scent of the sea was different from the cold, clean spray of Skern or Lier, but it was still the sea.

"Sit down," Vaseto said. "You'll attract attention."

Neil looked down at the woman, who sat cross-legged on the stone steps of the sea-guild hall, eating a greasy handful of fried sardines she'd bought from a vendor.

"In all of this?" he asked, tilting his jaw to indicate the streams and eddies of merchants, sailors, vendors, and vagabonds that surrounded them. He was still wearing his disguise. "I scarcely think we stand out."

"There are others here watching these boats. The reward for your friends is substantial."

"I haven't seen anyone else watching."

"That's because they know what they're doing," she replied. "If you *appear* to be watching the ships, someone will notice that."

"I suppose," he sighed. "I tire of this game of disguise, this tactic of hiding."

"Your friends are hiding, with good reason, and they seem to

have found a rather good place to hide. There is little more than un-
reliable rumor on the street as to where they might be."

"Maybe they've already gone."

"I don't think so," she replied. "There is *some* word that they have
been seen, and not long ago. If they're trying to book passage on a
ship, here is our best chance. The other watchers are probably working by description. You *know* the girls and might spot them even if
they are disguised. I know Cazio and z'Acatto. That is our advantage."

"It still rankles. And we've been at it for four days already."

"They've been here much longer than that."

"Yes, but why?"

"Looking for a ship going the right direction, at a price they can
afford. The girls have been seen working."

"Working? Both of them?" The princess of Crotheny, working?
Anne, working?

"Yes. As washerwomen, scullery maids, and the like."

"Unbelievable."

"Passage on a ship costs money. Coming from the coven, they
wouldn't have much, would they? Perhaps nothing. From what I know
of Cazio, he would have none at all, and if he did, z'Acatto would
drink it up in short order. It could take them another month or two to
earn the fare."

"There must be some other way to find them. I can't wait so
long."

She licked her finger and gave him a disgusted look. "Take a walk.
Pretend to look at the fish, or something. You're starting to annoy
me."

"I don't mean—"

"Go!" She waved the back of her hand.

"I'll check the other ships," he muttered.

He walked down the quay, trying to contain his frustration, trying
to think of some strategy that Vaseto had not. But he knew little of
cities, especially foreign ones and ones of this size. He had never
imagined so many people would crowd into one place. Eslen had

seemed unimaginably huge to him when he'd first seen it, but z'Espino was so vast, he had trouble comprehending it even when he was in the midst of it.

He pretended, as Vaseto suggested, to examine the wares of merchants and the cargo being unloaded from ships, but his attention drifted always to the ships themselves, and his desire to have one beneath his feet again. He hadn't felt the sea road under him since arriving at Eslen with Sir Fail. He hadn't realized how much he'd missed it.

Far down on his right, he saw the sky-spearing masts of a Saltmark brimwulf, and decided to walk the other way—the brimwolves were the favorite man-o'-war of the Hansan navy.

Walking left, his eyes traced a three-masted galley from Ter-na-Fath, from whose bow stared the carved wooden face of Saint Fronvin, the sea-queen, her hair carved to resemble churning waves. Moored just beyond was a langzkef of Herilanz, so like the galleys of the weihand raiders Neil had grown up fighting, with single sail, fifty oars, and an iron head for ramming. A battered, gallean shrimper was just putting in, its crew casting lines onto the dock.

Past the shrimper was a neat little boat, sleek of line as a porpoise, not too big, but with five masts in all. She would be quick in the turn, a wave-dancer. The cut of her looked northern, but nothing identified her origin immediately to his eye. She flew no standard, and she had no name painted on her. He stopped, scrutinizing the craft, challenged by its anonymity. A few men were working on board, light of skin and hair, which said northern, also. He couldn't hear if they were saying anything.

A little shock ran through him, as he realized someone was watching him from the porthole in the fo'c'sle. Someone with intense blue eyes, and a face so young, beautiful, and sad it made his heart tremor. For a long moment, their gazes were locked. Then she turned away, retreated into the darkness of the ship.

Embarrassed, he looked away. He'd done just the thing Vaseto told him to avoid—he'd been noticed.

He moved away from the dock, and his heart lifted a bit when he

saw an achingly familiar sight—the mast-shaped spire of a chapel of
Saint Lier. Without hesitation, he entered.

It had been too long since he had prayed. When he emerged a
short time later, his step felt lighter. As he walked back to where he
had left Vaseto, he studiously avoided looking at the strange ship.

"There you are," Vaseto said when he arrived. "I knew it would
be good luck to send you away."

"What do you mean?"

"Cazio. He just boarded that ship." She waved at a four-masted
merchantman.

"That's a Vitellian ship," he said.

"Yes. Bound for Paldh. Don't watch too closely."

"Were Anne and Austra with him?"

"No. Look at me."

With some difficulty, he tore his gaze from the ship and looked
into Vaseto's brown eyes.

"There," she said. "Pretend you're interested in me, not the
ship."

"I—" the image of another pair of eyes flickered through his
memory—those of the woman he'd seen on the ship. And then, with
a guilty start, Fastia's.

Vaseto must have seen something in his face, for the taut lines of
her own softened, and she reached a gentle hand to stroke his cheek.
"You call out a name in your sleep sometimes. Did you know that?"

"No," he said.

"Is she dead?"

"Yes," he said.

"You saw her die."

This time he only nodded.

"The pain will pass," she said. "Like any hangover."

He managed a humorless chuckle. "That's a strange comparison,"
he said.

She quirked her shoulders. "Perhaps an unfair one. I have only
observation to go by, not experience."

"You've never lost anyone you loved?"

She cocked her head, and a strange look came into her eyes. "I have never loved," she said. "I never will."

"How can you possibly know that?"

"It's part of who I am. I will never know the touch of a man."

"That's not the same thing as love," he pointed out.

"No, I suppose not. Yet I feel certain that I will never love."

"I hope that is not true."

"You can say that, when it has brought you such pain?"

"Oh, yes," he said.

"When she died—could you have said it then?"

"No," he replied. "I wanted to die myself."

She smiled and tousled his hair. "And that is why I shall never love. Now, don't look, but our friend has left the boat."

He started to rise, but she grabbed his hand. "Be still," she said.

"But we must speak to him."

"If we do, any others who are watching will see."

"Let's follow him, then."

"I'm not sure that's a good idea, either."

"But what if he did *not* take passage on that ship? What if we don't see him again? No. Right now he is my only link to Anne, and I cannot let him leave my sight."

She considered that, and then sighed. "You may be right," she said. "I may be too careful in this matter. But Anne—" She stopped abruptly, and for the first time Neil realized that Vaseto was somehow uncertain. And that she had said something she shouldn't.

"What about Anne?" he said.

"I cannot tell you. But she is important for more reasons than you know." She rose. "Come. Put your arm around me. Walk with me as you might a lover, and we'll follow Cazio."

He did as she said, slipping his arm around her waist. She was very slight, and it felt very awkward.

"That's him, there," she said. "In the plumed hat."

"I see him," Neil said.

They followed him through winding streets to a dim and dilapidated part of town, where rough-seeming men watched them pass with blandly hostile faces. At last Cazio went up the steps to a building and entered it.

Neil quickened his pace, but Vaseto dragged at him.

"Wait," she said, then gave a cluck. "No, never mind. It's too late."

Neil saw what she meant. Men seemed to have appeared in the street, all around them, armed with knives and clubs. Neil reached beneath his cloak and felt for the pommel of Crow, but it wasn't there. Like his armor, it was back in their lodgings.

Vaseto began speaking sharply in Vitellian, but the men continued to close in.

"Stay back," Ospero advised.

Ignoring him, Anne pushed past, trying to see. Ospero's men had surrounded a man and a boy. The man drew a knife, turning slowly. The boy was shouting something about how they were friends of Cazio's.

She looked at Cazio, who had a look of concentration on his face.

"You know him?" she asked.

"I think so," he replied. "I think he was a guest of Orchaevia's, from time to time. I don't know the other fellow."

"Wait," Anne shouted. "See what they want."

At the sound of her voice, the stranger's head snapped toward her. "Anne!" he shouted. "I'm sent by your mother!"

He was speaking the king's tongue, with an island accent. Anne's heart spun like a top.

"Ospero, tell your men to leave him alone, please," she said. "I think I know him."

"Let him come closer," Ospero said.

The boy said something low to the man, whose gaze had not left Anne. He nodded and walked to the door. As he did, he removed a wig, revealing the blond hair beneath.

"Sir Neil?" She gasped.

"Yes," he said, going down on one knee.

"No, no, get up," she said quickly.

He quickly obeyed.

"Mother sent you?" she asked. "How did you find me?"

"That's a long tale," the knight answered. "I went to the coven, and found it destroyed. The countess Orchaevia directed me here."

"I—" something seemed to explode in Anne then, like a glass bottle in a fire. Tears burst from her eyes, and though she barely knew him, she threw her arms around Sir Neil and wept.

Neil held Anne awkwardly in his arms, not knowing exactly what to do. He felt her tremble, and closed his eyes. And the sounds of the world dimmed.

Though sisters, Anne and Fastia did not look much alike. But Anne *felt* like Fastia. The scent of her neck was the same. Anne trembled, and Neil felt Fastia's dying shudder. His own tears suddenly threatened.

"Sir Neil?" Anne said, her voice muffled in his shoulder. "Sir Neil, that's—that's quite tight enough."

He released her and stepped quickly back. "I'm sorry, Pr— I'm sorry," he said. "I've just been searching for so long, and your mother—"

He felt a joy at saying that that nearly eased the swell of grief. He hadn't failed this time. He'd found Anne. Now he had only to get her home, and he could return to the queen's side, where he belonged.

"My mother? Is she still well?"

"Your mother is well," he affirmed. "She grieves, but she is well."

She lifted her chin. She didn't wipe at her tears, though, but left them to crawl down her face. "You were there, Sir Neil?"

He nodded, feeling his throat clutch. "I was there," he said. "I was there with your sisters. Your father was in another place."

Cazio coughed quietly and said something in Vitellian. One of the words sounded like *Roderick*. Anne rolled her eyes briefly and shook her head. Neil stood impatiently while the two conferred, with Vaseto putting in something now and then.

When they were done, Anne nodded at Cazio. "Sir Neil, this is Cazio da Pachiomadio da Chiovattio. He has proved himself a friend to me. Without his aid, Austra and I would never have escaped the coven."

Neil bowed. "I am honored to meet you," he said.

Cazio bowed, as well, and then Anne introduced Neil to the Vitellian. Neil presented Vaseto to both of them. When that was all done, Anne turned back to Neil.

"Cazio knows that I am a noble of Crotheny," she said. "He does not know my family name."

"You do not trust him?"

"I trust him. But I am cautious."

Neil nodded, trying to get Anne's measure. He hadn't known her long or well in Eslen, but she seemed very different from the willful brat he had heard described. She had certainly learned Vitellian quickly enough, and the roughness of her hands was proof that she had indeed been engaged in labor that few of royal birth could begin to imagine. That did not suggest a spoiled brat, but rather a woman who was learning to do things for herself. Learning to do the things that had to be done.

"I'm going to get your gear," Vaseto told him. "The ship Cazio has found passage on leaves in a few hours. You will be on it with them— the countess sent funds for your passage, and Cazio believes the captain will take on another passenger."

"You aren't going?"

Vaseto's face scrunched almost comically. "Go on the water? No, I don't think so. My task was to bring you this far. No more."

Neil bowed. "I am forever grateful, lady. I hope it was not too onerous a task."

"Not too. But remember your gratitude when we meet again."

"I hope we shall."

Vaseto smiled slyly. "No, there is no doubt. It has already been seen. Now, stay here, and I'll return with your things."

"I can come."

Vaseto shook her head. "You may be needed here, especially if others have followed."

Neil nodded at the sense of that. "Very well," he said.

Cazio plucked at Anne's sleeve. "A word with you alone, please, casnara?" he said.

Anne started to wave him off impatiently. She needed to talk to Sir Neil. She had so many questions—but then she saw the genuine concern reflected in Cazio's eyes, and stepped aside with him into the courtyard. Besides, Neil was talking to the strange little woman.

"Quickly," she said.

Cazio folded his arms. "Who is this man?" he asked.

"I've already told you, it's not Roderick. He is a servant of my mother's."

"And you trust him completely? He has something of the look of those knights who attacked you at the coven."

"He was my mother's most trusted servant," Anne assured him.

"And is he still?"

Anne paused at that. Sir Neil said that he had come from her mother. But she had no proof of it. From what she remembered he had come to court only a short time before she'd been sent away. True, he had saved her mother's life at Elseny's party, but what if that had been a ruse? The murderers of her father and sisters had not been named in the cuveitur dispatches. What if Sir Neil had been one of them?

With a cold shock, she suddenly understood how well it all fit. Only her mother and Erren had known that she had been sent to the coven Saint Cer. And perhaps, as her mother's bodyguard, Sir Neil. That would mean Roderick wasn't her betrayer. Not that she had ever really believed that, but . . .

Cazio observed the change in her eyes and nodded soberly. "Yes, you see? It is all too suspicious. Just as I finally find us passage on a ship, along he comes."

"It— Mother trusted him."

"But you don't," he said. "Not now that you've thought about it."

"Not now that you've put the idea in my head," she said miserably.

She noticed that the little woman was gone. Neil now stood by himself, trying to appear uninterested in their conversation.

For all she knew, he was fluent in Vitellian.

"Go find Austra," she whispered. "And z'Acatto. All of you go to the ship. I will follow in a short while."

"Why not go with me?"

"Because he'll insist on going. Even if he is who he says he is, and he is true to my mother's service, he won't let me that far from his sight now that he's found me."

"But he may murder you the moment I am gone."

That was true.

"Ospero," she said. "Do you think he will help?"

Cazio nodded. "He's still just outside. I'll tell him to watch you," he said.

She nodded. Then they returned to the street.

"Cazio's going to get the others," Anne told Neil. "I'm going up-stairs to pack my things. Would you keep watch here?"

"I will," Neil said. He looked wary. "Is there something I should know?"

"Not at the moment."

He nodded. When she went up the stairs, she was relieved that he did not follow.

She did feel a pang of guilt. If he was telling the truth, Sir Neil had come a long, hard way to find her, and she was betraying him.

But she could not take the risk, not when she knew him so little. If she was wrong, he could return home the way he had come, and she would apologize.

She would apologize a great deal.

CHAPTER NINE

LIFE OR DEATH

Aspar regarded Stephen's still face in the fire-glow.

"How did you meet him?" Ehawk asked, reaching to turn a spit, which speared the sizzling body of a sizable hedgehog.

Aspar grinned wryly and stared at a twig he'd been worrying with his fingers. He tossed it into the fire. "Up on the King's Road," he said, "about two days west of the Owl Tomb Bridge. He'd set out for Virgenya to study at the monastery d'Ef. Alone, because he thought it would be the sort of adventure he'd read about in books. When I ran across him, he'd been kidnapped by bandits." Aspar shook his head. "Didn't think much of him, then. He was always saying stupid things, carrying thousand-year-old maps as if they might do him some good."

"But he was your friend."

"Yah. Saved my life more than once, if you can believe it." He poked at the fire with a stick, and sparks gyred up toward the sky.

"He's not dead," Winna said anxiously. "Will you two stop talking about him as if he were dead?"

"Winna," Aspar said softly, "he has no pulse that I can find. There's no breath."

"*He's not dead,*" Winna insisted stubbornly. "He's never gone stiff, has he? It's been four days, and he still hasn't started to stink."

"Those the greffyn killed didn't rot, either," Aspar pointed out.

"Aspar White—" Winna broke off, turning to hide the tears in her eyes. Aspar stood and turned away, too, for he felt dangerously near tears himself.

He remembered Stephen's last, terrible scream. Then the boy had dropped as if all his tendons had been cut. He hadn't drawn breath since.

"Why haven't you buried him, then?" Winna exploded behind him. "Answer me that? If you're so sure he's dead, why haven't you given him one of your holter's burials?"

Aspar turned slowly to face her across the fire. "Because I want him there when we find the Briar King," he said softly. "I want him there when I kill the bastard." He reached down to touch the arrow case he'd thrust through his belt.

Winna quieted at that, but he couldn't tell what she was thinking. She just shook her head and closed her eyes.

"How will you find him?" Ehawk asked.

"The trail of thorns will lead us to him."

"How can you be sure?"

"I feel it," Aspar said, realizing how ridiculous it sounded, how he would scoff at anyone else who said such a thing.

"What about the Sefry's trail?"

"What about it?" Aspar asked. "We haven't come to find the Sefry."

"Asp," Winna said, "you said the Sefry was letting us follow him. Why would he do that?"

Aspar nodded at Stephen's body. "You have to ask that question?"

"Yes, I do. What if the Sefry just wanted us to *see* the fane? What if he wanted us to know that someone is building an evil faneway?"

"We don't know what kind of faneway they're building," Aspar said. "We don't even know if that's what they're doing."

"But Stephen said—"

"Yah. Do you think Stephen would have walked into the fane if he reckoned this was going to happen to him? He was wrong about something, for once, yah?"

"Maybe. Or maybe there was someone—or something—inside the fane we couldn't see."

"He looked fine when he went into the fane, and he didn't look hurt when he walked out. Wasn't until he left the mound that he collapsed."

"Still—"

"Winna." He tried to keep his voice gentle, but he felt the harshness creeping into it, like a burr caught in his throat.

He sighed. "Winna, I'm a holter. I know nothing of fanes or saints or shinecraft. That was Stephen. All I know is how to track things, find things, and kill things. That's what I'm supposed to do. That's what I will do."

"That's what the praifec ordered you to do," Winna said. "But it's not like you to be so obedient."

"He's destroying my forest, Winn. And I'll tell you, if I do know anything about greffyns and utins and evil fanes and what's happened to Stephen, it's this—things like this didn't happen before the Briar King stopped being a boygshin story and started walkin' around. When I stop him walkin' around, I reckon everything will go back to the way it was."

"And if it doesn't?"

"Then I'll find whoever built that shrine and kill them, too."

"I know you, Asp," Winna said. "You aren't made of death."

"Maybe not," he said, "but she follows me close." He put his head down then raised it back up. "Winna, here's what we'll do. You and Ehawk, you go back to Eslen. Tell the praifec what we saw here, and what Stephen said about it. I'm going on."

Winna snorted. "Not likely. You're going to drag poor Stephen around this forest by yourself?"

"He'll stay on Angel. Maunt this—I almost lost you to the utin. I've had Black Marys about it ever since. I can't think straight, not really, not with you in danger.

"There's only one arrow, you know. When we meet him, there's nothing anyone can do but me, and I'll do that best without any distractions. And you're right—Stephen thought there was something about that fane that needed dealing with. None of us kann enough to know what to do, and if we all find our ends out here, the praifec will never know what we've learned."

Winna's lips compressed. "No," she said. "That doesn't make nearly the sense you think it does. You think you can do everything by your-self? You think the rest of us do nothing but drag you down? Well, you were by yourself when you came stumbling down to the mon-astery d'Ef, weren't you? If Stephen hadn't found you, you'd have died. If he hadn't stood for you against the other monks, you'd have died. How are you going to feed yourself? If you leave Stephen to hunt, something will come gnaw on him."

"Winn—"

"*Stop it.* I made the same promise to the praifec that you did. You think I have no stake in this? My father lives in the King's Forest, Asp—at least I pray saints he still lives. Ehawk's people live out here, too. So you're just going to have to live with your fear for me. I can't fight like you, and I don't have Stephen's knowledge, but if there's one thing I'm good for, it's to make you more cautious than you would be normally. That's how I've saved your life, and don't deny it, you big stupid banf."

Aspar regarded her for a moment. "I'm the leader of the expedi-tion. You'll do what I say."

Her face went cold. "Is that how it is?"

"Yah. This is the last time you go against me, Winn. Someone has to be in charge, and that's me. I can't spend every moment arguing with you."

Her face relaxed a bit. "But we're all staying together."

"For now. If I change my mind again, that's the way it will be, understand?"

Her face hardened again, and he felt a little wind suck out of him. "Yah," she said at last.

The next morning the sky pulled on a gray hood of clouds, and the air was as wintry as Winna's mood. They moved almost silently, save for the snorting of the horses and wet plod of their hooves on the leaves. More than ever, Aspar felt the sickness of the forest, down in his bones.

Or maybe it was arthritis.

They found the trail of black thorns and followed it into the Foxing Marshes, where the ancient yellow stone of the Lean Gable Hills broke into steps for a giant to walk down to the Warlock. For normal-size folks like Aspar and his companions, the steps were a little more difficult to negotiate—they had to hunt for the places where rinns had cut their way and then gone dry. Where the thorns hadn't choked everything, the land was still green with ferns and horsetails that grew almost as high as the heads of the horses. Leaves from hickory and whitaec drifted as constantly as a soft rain.

And it was quiet as if the earth were holding its breath, which kept Aspar's spine crawling.

As always, he felt bad for being hard with Winna, which irritated him in its own turn. He'd spent most of his years doing exactly what he wanted, the way he wanted, without any leave from much of anyone. Now a smooth-handed praifec and a girl half his age had him dancing like a trained bear.

Sceat, Winna thought he was tame now, didn't she? But how could she understand what he was, at her age? She couldn't, despite the fact that she somehow seemed to.

"The Sefry came this way," Ehawk said softly, interrupting Aspar's quiet fume. He looked down to where the Watau's chin was pointing.

"That's awfully clear sign," he muttered. "Is that the first you've seen of 'im?"

"Yah," Ehawk allowed.

"Me, too." Of course he'd been so busy thinking about Winna, he'd missed even that.

"Looks like he's trying to lead us off again," Ehawk said. "South."

Aspar nodded. "He figured we'd come this way, following the thorns, and now he's left a roadsign." He scratched his chin. Then he glanced at Winna. "Well?" he asked.

"Well, what?" she retorted. "You're the leader of this expedition, remember?"

"Just checking to see that you do," he grumbled back. He studied the lay of the land. South was upcountry again, a stretch of ground he knew pretty well, and he had a feeling he knew where the Sefry was going.

"You two backtrack to the clearing we passed at noon," he said.

"I'm going to follow this trail a bit. If I'm not back by morning, then I'm probably not coming back."

"What is that supposed to mean?" Winna asked.

Aspar shrugged.

"What do we do if you don't come back?"

"What we discussed earlier. Head back to Eslen. And before you start thinking it, the reason I'm going alone is because I can move more quietly that way, and not for any other reason."

"I wasn't arguing," Winna said.

His heart dropped a little, but at the same time, he felt a bit of satisfaction. "Well, then. That's good," he said.

If Ogre resented climbing back up the hills he'd just come down, he didn't let on, ascending without the slightest whicker to the high-canopied forest of oak. By the time they came to the relatively flat tableland, Aspar was certain where the trail was headed and quit following it, in case some unpleasant surprise had been left in his path. Instead he circled around so as to approach the place from another direction.

The sun was slanting hard and orange through the trees when he heard voices. He dismounted, left Ogre near a stream, and crept closer on foot.

What he found wasn't really a surprise, but he still wasn't fully prepared for it.

The place was called Albraeth by those few who still called it anything. It was a cone-shaped mound of earth, bare save for a few struggling, yellowish weeds and a single gnarled tree, a naubagm with bark like black scales and leaves like drooping, serrated knives.

Some of the branches dipped low, and the rotting remains of rope still clung to some, though it had been years since the king's law had forbidden their use. It was here that criminals had once been hanged in sacrifice to Grim the Raver. It was here that Aspar had been born, on that sickly grass, below a fresh noose. Here his mother had died.

The Church had worked to end those sacrifices. Now they were busy with their own.

A perimeter of wooden beams had been planted in the ground around the mound, each about four kingsyards high, and to each beam a man or woman had been nailed, with their hands above their heads and their feet pulled straight down. Aspar could see the blood leaking from the holes in their wrists and ankles, but there was plenty more blood to see.

They had been cut open, each of them, and their entrails pulled out and arranged in deliberate designs. Some were still being arranged, and those who were doing so wore the robes of the Church. He wasn't certain what order. Stephen would know.

He counted six of them. He had twice that many arrows. Mouth tight, he pulled out the first, considering how to go about what had to be done.

He was still working that out when a greffyn paced out from behind the mound.

It was smaller than the one that had almost killed him, its scales darker and sheened with green, but there was no mistaking its hawklike beak and the sinuous, catlike play of its muscles. He could feel its presence, even at this distance, like heat on his face, and he felt a wave of dizziness.

The touch of the beast—even its glance—was deadly poison. That he knew from hard experience, and from the corpses of its cousin's victims. So poisonous, in fact, that even those who touched the corpses contracted gangrene, and most died. Even maggots and carrion-eaters would not touch a Greffyn's kills.

But the monks weren't dying. They didn't even seem concerned. And to his astonishment, one even reached out to stroke it as it walked by.

He took a deep breath, trying to sort that out, wishing Stephen were with him. He would recall some ancient tome or legend that would force this all to make sense.

Six monks would be hard to kill, especially if they were of the order of Mamres. Six monks and a greffyn would be impossible—unless he used the arrow again.

But that one was meant for the Briar King.

First one, and then all the monks suddenly straightened from their tasks and looked to the east, as if they had all heard the same secret call. Their hands went to their swords, and Aspar tensed, realizing that he would have to run from this and find help.

But then he understood that they hadn't found him out at all, that something else had their attention. He could hear it now, a distant howling, like dogs yet unlike dogs, terribly familiar and utterly alien.

Grim.

He remembered when he'd first met Stephen, they'd been on the King's Road when they'd heard howling off in the distance. Aspar had recognized them as the hounds of Sir Symon Rookswald, but he'd fed the boy's fear, told him it was Grim and his host, the hounds that carried off the damned souls who haunted the King's Forest. He'd put a good scare in the lad.

Now he found his own heart beating faster. Had they summoned Haergrim? Had they summoned the Raver?

The howling grew louder, and there was a rushing through the leaves. He realized his hand was shaking, and felt a momentary anger at his own weakness. But if the hidden world was waking, why not Grim? Grim the heafroa, the one-eyed god, the lord of the birsirks, the bloody wrath, as mad as any ancient, pagan god could be.

The greffyn had turned at the sound, too, and the sparse hairs along its spine stood straight. He heard it snarl.

And behind him he heard a voice, whispering soft in the Sefry tongue.

"Life or death, holter," it said. "You have a choice to make."

CHAPTER TEN

BETRAYAL

N EIL WAS STILL WAITING for Anne when the sun began to dim and Vaseto returned, leading Hurricane. On the horse was a pack carrying his armor and other few personal possessions. He walked out into the street and patted the stallion's muzzle, noting with amusement and concern the stares with which those in the neighborhood regarded them both.

Vaseto noticed, too. "I don't think they see horses in this part of town very much," she said, "much less warsteeds."

"I suppose they don't," Neil said, remembering he hadn't seen anyone mounted since they passed through the large square at the city gate.

Hurricane tossed his head restlessly.

"There, lad," Neil whispered. "Soon we'll be back where we belong. I promise you a good leg-stretching in Newland. You'll need it after passage on the ship."

"If they'll let you take her on," Vaseto pointed out. "Berth for a man is one thing. Berth for a horse is something else again." She shrugged. "But with what the countess passed along to you, you should be able to afford the room if they have it." She flashed him a smile. "In any event, it's now your problem. I have to get back to my dogs."

Neil bowed. "I still don't know who you really are, but thank you again."

"You know more about me than most," Vaseto said. "But if I were you, I would worry more about who *you* are. That's likely to be more useful to you."

With that cryptic comment, she walked up the street and vanished around a corner.

After a bit of reflection, Neil decided to put on his armor. If the men searching for Anne had had the same luck as he had, he might need it.

A bell later it occurred to him that not only hadn't Anne come back down, but that he hadn't seen Austra or Cazio, either. Cazio had talked as if there was something of a hurry, and yet where were they all?

He glanced at the old man they had called Ospero. He'd been watching Neil, not too pointedly, but without trying to hide it either. He'd been doing that since Anne had spoken to Cazio and had slipped upstairs.

"Can you tell me where Anne's room is?" he asked.

"Ne comperumo," the old man said, shrugging.

Neil looked around, hoping to spot someone who might speak the king's tongue. Still, Cazio wasn't back yet, and he had presumably gone to make the final arrangements.

Unless . . .

His heart fell like the bottom of a great storm swell.

Why? Why would Anne try to escape him? Were her Vitellian friends in league with the enemy?

No, there was a better explanation. What an idiot he was for not having seen it sooner. Anne had heard her father and sisters had been killed, but it was unlikely that she knew much more than that. Why should she trust a knight she barely knew, just because he claimed to have been sent to protect her?

It doesn't matter now, he told himself, trying to stave off panic. His duty was still his duty, whether Anne believed him or not. One way or another he would bring her home, safe.

He knew where the ship was—and Anne wouldn't be aware of that. He could still catch her, as long as they hadn't set sail already.

He nodded to Ospero and swung himself up into the saddle.

Ospero grinned faintly and raised his hand to wave.

Neil saw the flash of steel at the last instant. He twisted in the saddle and ducked, and felt something graze along his arm, which was where his heart had been a moment or two before.

Grimly he whirled Hurricane and drew out Crow.

As if on cue, men were bunching into either side of the street. In just a few moments there would be more, but Neil wasn't going to give them those moments. They were armed with knives and clubs, but one had a spear. If they managed to injure or immobilize Hurricane, his chances weren't good.

Ospero was shouting, and Neil cursed himself again for not knowing Vitellian.

He pointed Hurricane at the man with the spear and charged.

To his credit, the fellow seemed to know what to do. He knelt and braced the butt of the pole arm against the cobbles and aimed the point at the spot beneath Hurricane's breastbone.

Neil's breath was coming cool now, slow, in and out. He saw the men's faces, their scars, whether they had shaved or not.

At the last possible moment, he turned Hurricane to the side, avoiding the spear altogether. Using the cut known as reaper, he sent one of his attackers down to the street, where the stone drank blood from his headless corpse. Hurricane reared savagely and kicked down at another. Neil felt a blow to his leg, but then he was free of them, clattering down the darkening streets.

He felt down to his leg, but the armor had turned away the blow. Hurricane seemed unhurt, and so he kept the pace, watching pedestrians scatter, listening to their unintelligible remonstrations, and beginning to hate the whole adventure. The novelty of foreign places was definitely wearing off.

She should have given me a token, he thought angrily. *Something to convince Anne she really had sent me.*

His anger at the queen was a shock followed by shame. Who was he to question her?

He urged Hurricane on, hoping he still had time.

❊   ❊   ❊

Anne had recovered from her pangs of conscience by the time they reached the docks. When she saw the ships, she finally understood that she was really going home. Home, where she didn't scrub clothes or make cheese or get invited to become a whore.

In the back of her mind, she still knew it was going to hurt, too, to enter the castle and find that her father and sisters were really gone, but that moment was still far away. For now, she could cling to the good part.

"But why are we leaving Sir Neil?" Austra whispered near her ear. Cazio had found her washing the dirty plates at a *carachio* near the great square. Anne had worked there before, her mouth watering at the smell of the lamb roasted with fennel and garlic. Austra smelled like that now.

"Cazio didn't explain?"

"Yes, but Cazio does not know Sir Neil," Austra said.

"I can't believe it," Anne said. "You're questioning Cazio's judgment?"

Austra flushed a bit. "He knows more about Vitellio than we do," she said. "And he is very clever. But how can he know Sir Neil's heart? It seems wrong. He always seemed very honest to me."

"Austra, *we* don't know Sir Neil. For all we know, he killed my sisters and now he's come after me."

"He wasn't with the knights who attacked the coven."

"How do you know? We didn't see them all." She took Austra's hand. "The point is, we can't know. And if I'm wrong—why, he'll be fine. He made it to Vitellia, he'll make it back."

Austra frowned doubtfully.

"Not to interrupt," Cazio said, "but there's our ship just ahead."

Z'Acatto, who had been entirely silent since he had joined Anne in the alley behind their building, suddenly grunted. "I know that standard," he said. "Had you told me, I would never have agreed to this."

"Hush, old man," Cazio said in a low voice. "I did what I had to."

"You don't surprise me very often, boy," the fencing master muttered. "But today you've managed it."

"What's he talking about?" Anne asked.

"Nothing," Cazio replied quickly.

She turned to z'Acatto and saw that his eyes were very strange, as if he were angry, even furious. And then she realized his sword was already in his hand, its tip just clearing the scabbard. She wasn't afraid yet, just very curious as to why the old man was going to kill her. But she could feel the fear arriving as he grabbed her.

Z'Acatto pushed, and she stumbled to the cobbles, one knee striking the stone. She gasped at the pain and looked up, trying to understand what was happening.

A man—a man she did not know—was staring at z'Acatto's blade, which vanished somehow into the fellow's throat.

Cazio shouted then and drew his own sword, and suddenly men were everywhere, some in armor.

"Run!" Cazio shouted. "Run onto the ship!"

Anne scrambled that way, trying to regain her feet, but suddenly armored boots were there, and she looked up to see a steel visage staring down at her. The knight raised a sword that seemed to be only half there, a blur like the wings of a hummingbird, but moving through the colors of the rainbow with each heartbeat.

She stared up, frozen, as the blade cocked above her.

Cazio's blade drove over her head and took the knight in the gorget, and Cazio came flying behind it.

"Z'ostato en pert!" he shouted.

The knight stumbled back beneath the force of the blow, but Cazio was still airborne, and crashed into him, punching the man's visor with the guard of his weapon. The knight toppled and slammed to the ground. Anne scrambled up, helped by Austra, who took her hand, and both ran for the gangplank.

She could see a crowd of faces on the ship, watching in astonishment. Among them was one that seemed a little familiar, a dark, lean mustachioed face.

"Help us!" she shouted.

None of the sailors moved.

Two more men suddenly appeared between her and the ship, and everything seemed to slow to a stop. In the corner of her eye, she saw that the knight with the glowing sword was already up on one knee, dealing Cazio a thunderous backhand with his mailed glove. Z'Acatto was holding off at least four men, but two were starting to push around him. She and Austra were trapped.

Something snarled up in her, and she yanked out the dagger Sister Secula had given her, determined to give at least one cut. The men between her and the ship were more lightly armored than the knight, in chain and leather. They wore no helmets at all.

They laughed when she raised the weapon. Then, oddly, one suddenly toppled, his head grotesquely changing shape somehow as a long pole of some sort struck it. And then something huge exploded into the other man, knocking him away as if he were made of rags and straw.

Even as she realized it was a horse, she also realized it was falling. Another armored figure slammed to the dock a kingsyard away from her with a clang, but for a moment the way to the ship was clear. She bolted for it, tugging Austra behind her.

She hadn't gone more than halfway up the gangplank when she remembered Cazio and z'Acatto, and she turned to see what was happening.

The horse had regained its feet and was galloping madly about the dock. The knight who had fallen from it had risen, as well, and she suddenly understood by the rose on his helm that it was Sir Neil. As she watched, he cut savagely at the knight with the glowing sword, hitting him so hard, he actually left the ground. Then he turned on the men pushing past z'Acatto and decapitated one.

Cazio hesitated, but z'Acatto didn't. He quickly disengaged from his foes and charged toward the ship. After the slightest of hesitations, Cazio joined them.

Anne suddenly felt movement beneath her feet and realized the gangplank was being withdrawn. She was turning when two of the sailors grabbed her and yanked her the rest of the way up onto the ship. Not quite knowing why, she screamed and kicked, noticing as she did so that they had Austra, too. Z'Acatto leapt with an agility that belied his years, landing on the retreating ramp and bounding onto the boat, followed closely by a whooping Cazio.

On the dock, Sir Neil was a blade storm, beating the enemy away from the ship. There were at least eight against him, not counting the knight with the glowing sword, who was—against all things natural—rising again.

"Sir Neil!" she shrieked. "Come on!"

The sailors all around her were frantically cutting lines and pushing at the dock with long poles.

"He'll never make the jump," z'Acatto said. "Not in that armor."

"Go back for him!" she shouted. "Go back this instant." She slapped at the nearest sailor, the one who had looked familiar. "You can't leave him there!"

He caught her hand and glared down at her. "I am Captain Malconio, and this ship is leaving port. If you strike me again, I will have you hanged."

"But he'll die!"

"I see no reason to care about that," he said.

Through a red haze, Neil cut left, then right, hit a man in chain and breastplate at the shoulder joint and saw it cleave, the blood spurting as he yanked the edge back out. Grasping the blade of his weapon with his mailed left hand, he rammed the pommel into the face of the next opponent, then reversed the weapon and, still gripping it like a staff, plunged the tip down between the lip of the breastplate and chest. He felt the breastbone crack, and the man fell away.

He shifted both hands to the grip and struck at the next enemy, who managed to stumble out of the way, and Neil felt a cut from his left thud against his shoulder. He couldn't see where the blow came from, but he set his legs wide and sliced that way, waist level. As he felt his blow land, he turned so the fellow was in his field of vision. He was another of the lightly armored ones, and his eyes went wide as blood started from his mouth, and he fell clutching a crushed rib cage.

That turn also brought him back to the knight with the glowing sword who—instead of being dead as he should have been—was stepping up to make a cut at him.

Behind the knight, Neil was vaguely aware that the ship was farther from the dock than it had been. He could see Anne's red hair, and so knew she had made it aboard.

The oncoming knight chopped down, left to right, and Neil stepped in and thrust upward into the blow with the thickest part of his blade. The jolt of the impact went all the way to his feet—his opponent was strong, very strong, and his blade was moving much faster than it ought. Crow felt strange, too, lighter, and Neil suddenly understood that half his weapon had been sheared away. The glowing sword was coming back up from its downswing. Neil plunged his left arm down and caught the man's gauntlet, then hammered what was left of Crow into the enemy's visor.

An armored elbow came up under his jaw, and he lost his hold on the man, stumbling back. The cut came again, this time from the side, and he was too far away to grab the man's arm again, too slow even to interpose his hand. The witch-weapon sheared into his armor, cutting though it as it had Crow.

Desperately, Neil threw himself in the direction of the blow, even as the pain of the world sheeted through him. He lost the ground, saw the sky, then hit something that yielded strangely, and understood that he had thrown himself off the dock into the water. He twisted to try to see if Anne's ship was safely far away, but the water closed over his head, and the sounds of tumult vanished.

PART III

STRANGE RELATIONS

The Year 2,223 of Everon
The Month of Decmen

Tertiu, the third mode, invokes Saint Michael, Saint Mamres, Saint Bright, Saint Fienve. It evokes the sword, the spear, the clash of battle, the drums of war. It provokes fiery courage, anger, rage.

Ponto, the fourth mode, invokes Saint Chistai, Saint Oimo, Saint Satire, Saint Loh. It evokes the flattering courtier, the sharp-tongued jester, the knife thrust from behind. It provokes jealousy, hatred, deception, and betrayal.

—FROM *THE CODEX HARMONIUM OF ELGIN WIDSEL*

CHAPTER ONE

ASSASSIN

Breathing softly as she might, Muriele felt along the wall until she found the small metal plate she was searching for. She slid it up and latched it, revealing a faintly glowing circle the size of a fingertip. Leaning forward, she brushed her hair from her face, placed her eye against the peephole, and peered into the room beyond.

The Warhearth was empty, but a few flickering tapers illuminated it, giving just enough light to show the statue of Saint Fienve on a small table near William's old armchair, and suggesting but not quite revealing the paintings of battle and victory that covered the garish walls of the place.

The room still seemed unoccupied.

She sighed and consigned herself to patience. Erren had shown her the passages within the walls of the castle years ago, not long after she had become queen. The corridors were very narrow and very old. Erren claimed that her order of coven-trained assassins had manipulated the choice of architects when the palace was built, convinced him to include their covert additions, and then made certain that neither he nor the workman who built them would ever tell anyone. Thus the dark hallways were a secret kept only by the sisters of Cer, and a few of their charges.

Muriele had often wondered if such secrecy was truly possible, over the course of centuries. If other queens had been shown the passages as she had, surely a few of them would have told their husbands, daughters, friends.

And yet, in her time, she had never met anyone other than Erren in the recondite halls, which suggested her old friend had known what she was talking about.

They *were* well and cleverly hidden, the peepholes disguised and clotted with glass to keep them from being easily discovered. The doors were marvels, showing no seam when closed.

She had used them often since Erren's death. They seemed safer than her own rooms, and without Erren or a trustworthy replacement, she had to do her own spying, if she was to have the faintest idea what was being plotted around her. But tonight she wasn't merely browsing, trying to catch Praifec Hespero or some member of the Comven in secret conversation; tonight she had a particular business.

It had come to her in the form of a note, folded and slipped beneath her door, written in a clean, simple style.

Your Majesty,

You are in danger. So am I. I have information that can save your life and your son's throne, but I in turn need your protection. Until I have your pledge, I cannot reveal my identity. If you agree, please leave a note beneath the statue on the table in the Warhearth saying "agreed."

Well, there was her reply, safely hidden from sight—and here she was playing this childish game—but in five hours, no one had come to collect the note. She had signed the note "agreed," of course, but she was determined that she would know who the messenger was— the entire affair could be an elaborate ruse of some sort.

Perhaps whoever it was had come earlier, before she had been able to excuse herself from her duties. They might have read the note and then returned it to its hiding place. But the Warhearth was located in the central part of the castle, and while quiet at night, during the day any visitor would attract attention. Besides, why leave the note?

Darkness was just falling, and she had formally retired. She had until morning, and no use for sleep and the dreams it brought.

And so another bell passed before a sound caught her attention, a faint scuff of leather against stone. She squinted through the small hole, trying to see who or what had made the sound, and noticed a shadow edging from the west end of the room. That was peculiar, as the entrance to the Warhearth was on the east end. She waited impatiently for the figure to step into the light, and in due time was rewarded.

It was a woman; she saw that first, with curly chestnut locks, wearing a pale blue dressing gown. Her "friend" was clever, then. He'd sent a serving girl to fetch the note. *Perhaps I will recognize her,* she thought, *and thus know her master.* But she had little real hope of that. There were many servants in Eslen Castle, and she knew no more than a tenth of them on sight.

Then the woman turned, and the light caught her face, and Muriele blinked in utter astonishment. She did, indeed, know the girl, but she was no maid or serving girl. No, that youthful face belonged to Alis Berrye, the youngest of her late husband's mistresses.

Alis Berrye.

Anger, jealous and reflexive, began heating in Muriele, but she fought to cool it, because something wasn't right here. Alis Berrye had the brains of a leek. She was the younger daughter of Lord Berrye of Virgenya, who oversaw one of the poorest cantons in the country. William had taken a liking to her sapphire eyes and girlish curves when her family had visited two years earlier. Since William's death, she'd been all but invisible, and though it had crossed Muriele's mind several times to have her ejected from her old rooms, the truth was that she had far more important things to do than satisfy a pitiable and now irrelevant resentment.

Until now. Now Alis Berrye was once more very much her concern. Even Erren had thought the girl too stupid and frivolous to harbor political motives beyond keeping the king's favor. Gramme had always been the dangerous one. Berrye didn't even have issue, and had apparently never tried to conceive any.

That meant her first guess had been right, and Berrye was someone's servant in this. But whose? Besides William, she'd never shown obvious ties to anyone in the court. Still, there had been plenty of time for that to change, and in the present climate, with everyone scrambling for whatever position and advantage they could, someone had clearly found a use for the girl.

Berrye retrieved the message, read it, nodded to herself, and then turned again toward the west end of the room. A moment later there was a very soft sound, but it lifted the hairs on Muriele's neck.

The only exit from the west end of the room was a secret one that let into the very corridors Muriele now occupied. Alis Berrye knew about it.

She knew the girl used to meet with William in the Warhearth, at times. But William hadn't known about the passages at all.

Or maybe he had, and Muriele hadn't known her husband as well as she had supposed.

She felt a pang of loss so sudden and deep, it was shocking. She and William hadn't married for love, but they had found it, at least for a time. And even though she had always resented his mistresses, she'd always felt that one day, somehow, they would settle into their love again.

And she missed him—his laugh, the smell of his clothes, the silly names he called her in private.

All gone. And now it seemed he had known about the passages all along, and never told her, never trusted her with that information. That wouldn't be so bad—after all, she hadn't told *him*—but that he had told Alis Berrye of all people, the silliest, most irrelevant of his whores—that hurt.

It also worried Muriele. What if he had told Gramme, too?

She waited a bit, both hoping and fearing that the girl would come down her passage, so she could strangle her and hide the body where it would never be found, but after several minutes, when no one appeared, Muriele padded back along the long, winding way to her own chambers, feeling for the raised signs on the wall that gave the directions.

When she opened the secret door that led to her bedchamber just a crack, she knew something was wrong. She had left a lamp burning in her room, but no light greeted her. The room was utterly dark. Had her maid Unna come in and put out the light? Why would she do that?

She stood frozen for an instant, her eye pressing through the crack at the darkness. Maybe the lamp had gone out on its own.

Someone said something. A single word, too low to hear. She gasped and shut the panel, backing away, knowing whoever it was must have heard her, but her mind was cluttered with spidering fear-webs, and she couldn't do anything but gape at the blackness in front of her.

She could only think how wrong she had been. Berrye knew about the passages of Cer, so others did, too. Did the man in her room know? Was it a man?

Something bumped against the wall, and she heard the faint hiss of breath. Her hand dropped to the dagger she wore next to her chatelaine, but it gave her small comfort.

The bump was followed by a muffled tap, and then another, and another, moving along the wall. The chill in her grew so deep, she began to shake. Someone was searching for the door. But that meant that they didn't know where it was. It would be hard to find, from the other side. Still, she had given away its approximate location.

The tapping grew a little duller as it moved away from her, then began moving back. She could hear his breath now, and suddenly, another whispered word, though still she could not make out what it was.

She backed farther away, trembling, realizing that she was growing light-headed because she hadn't breathed. She kept her hands against the walls, guiding by them, and when she thought she had gone far enough, she quickened her pace, feeling more panicked than ever, because she didn't know if he was still in the room, or in the tunnels with her.

She found the doorway to the Hall of Doves, looked in, confirmed that no one was there, and burst into it, then pushed the panel closed behind her, and ran.

After a few moments she slowed to a walk, but being in the common halls didn't make her feel any safer, even where they were well-lit and populated by servants. Her enemy had an unknown face, and anyone in the castle might wear it. Worse—and this was just starting to sink in—if the person in her room had really come to kill her, this was no mere attempt at murder. It was an attempt at a coup. Which meant she needed help, now, and help she could trust.

She was still considering who might be trusted when she nearly collided with Leovigild Ackenzal. She yelped and jumped back. For his part, the composer looked extremely flustered and then tried to get down on one knee. He was having trouble doing so, and she remembered the last time she had seen him he had been on crutches.

The hero of Broogh.

"Never mind that," she said, calming her own anxiousness. "What are you doing in the halls at this hour, Fralet Ackenzal?"

"Majesty? I was just exercising my leg."

His face showed no signs of deceit, so she made a quick decision.

"Come with me," she commanded. "Are you armed?"

"A-armed?" he stuttered.

"No, I suppose you aren't. Ah, well. Come along anyway."

"Yes, Majesty."

She moved away quickly, then had to slow her pace so he could keep up with her, and she wondered why she wanted him with her. He was all but a stranger—why should she trust him? But she remembered the day he had played for her, the absolute earnestness of it, and somehow felt he could do her no harm. She rarely trusted her feelings, but at this point she had no choice but to do so.

He hobbled silently after her, clearly puzzled but unwilling to ask any questions.

"How is my commission coming along?" she asked, largely to break the strained silence.

"Very well, Majesty." A note of excitement entered his voice, which even under these circumstances was charming. She was struck by how much he resembled Neil MeqVren—Neil was passionate and excitable, a true knight with nothing cynical in him. This composer was like that, too, though his passion was of an entirely different nature. But they were both—authentic.

She desperately wished Neil were here now, but she had been right to send him after Anne. He was the only one she could trust with Anne's location.

"You will be done with it soon, I hope," she said. "I've already arranged for a performance and an accompanying banquet in the Candle Grove, about three weeks hence."

"Three weeks? Well, yes, it's nearly done. But I'll need to start rehearsing immediately."

"Just let me know what you need."

"I've wanted to talk to you about something, actually," he said.

"In regards to what?"

"The size of the ensemble, Majesty."

"Make it whatever size you wish," she replied.

"What I'm hoping for is a bit unusual," he said, a little uncertainly. "I—the composition I'm working on—I think it would be best done by thirty pieces."

She stopped and glanced curiously at him. "That's rather large, isn't it?" she asked.

"There has never been an ensemble of its size," he said.

He made it sound very important, and all of a sudden she was struck by the ridiculousness of the whole situation. Here she was in fear of her life and her kingdom, and she somehow found herself discussing how many musicians she ought to engage.

But her heart had slowed to its normal pace, and she felt almost eerily calm.

"Then why should ours be so large?" she asked.

"Because there has never been a piece written like this," he replied.

She stopped for a moment to study him, to see if there was any pride or haughtiness to be found in that statement. If it was there, it did not show.

"I've no objection to a large ensemble," she said finally. "Even the largest."

"The Church might, Majesty."

"On what grounds?"

He grinned, looking suddenly very boyish. "On the grounds that it's never been done before, Majesty."

She felt a wry smile twitch her lips. "Make it as large as you want," she said. "Larger, even."

"Thank you, Majesty."

She nodded.

"Majesty?" he asked.

"Yes?"

"Is something wrong?"

She closed her eyes, then opened them and began walking again. "Yes, Fralet Ackenzal, something is very wrong. There is someone in my suite, someone I did not invite there."

"You think— I mean, Majesty, do you believe it was an assassin?"

"I can't think what else it might be."

He paled. "That's— Well, shouldn't we call a guard, Majesty?"

"Unfortunately," she replied, "I don't trust most of the guards."

"How can that be? How can a queen not trust her guards?"

"Are you that naïve, Fralet Ackenzal? Do you know how many kings and queens have died at the hands of their own servants?"

"But I've heard the royal guards of Eslen—the Craftsmen?—that they are incorruptible."

"In the past few months, on different occasions, two of them have tried to kill me."

"Oh."

"They were bewitched, as it turns out, by some sort of encrotacnia, and they are now supposed to be protected against such shinecrafting. Nevertheless, I find it hard to put faith in them, since they killed two of my daughters."

"I can understand that, Your Majesty. I'm sorry."

"Beyond that there is the fact that one of them was stationed outside my door. It follows that he either let the assassin in, he is the assassin, or he's dead."

"Oh, saints."

"Precisely."

"And so—ah—I'm your bodyguard at the moment?"

She smiled at him. "Indeed you are."

"Majesty, I wouldn't be much use to you if you were attacked."

"But you are the hero of Broogh, Fralet Ackenzal. Surely the mere sight of you would frighten off most attackers."

"I think that rather unlikely," Ackenzal opined. "But I will protect you as best I can, Majesty. It's just—if you think there is a coup in progress, you ought to find better help and more of it."

"I know," she said. "And that's what we're going to do. But I don't like it."

"Why is that?"

"Because I'm going to have to apologize."

Fail de Liery waved her apology away.

"You were right," he said. "I went beyond my bounds, and more to the point, beyond my heart. Sometimes when more than one duty calls, it's difficult to decide which to follow. Glorien de Liery is my liege, but William was my emperor and you are my empress—and my beloved niece. It is I who owe you an apology—and my allegiance, if you will still have it."

She wanted to hug him right then and there, but at the moment they were queen and subject, and she did not want to spoil that moment.

"Now, tell me why you're here, Majesty," Fail said. "You look as if the dead are calling your name."

He listened as she explained.

When she was done, he nodded grimly.

"You'll have to come with us," he said at last. "Even if the Craftsmen are loyal, they won't let a party of armed men into the royal suites."

"I'm aware of that."

Fail nodded. "When you are ready, Majesty."

"I'm ready." She turned to Ackenzal. "You are excused," she said. "And I thank you for your company."

He bowed, less clumsily this time. "Thank you, Your Majesty. I am always pleased to be of service."

"When will my commission be ready?"

"It is more than half done already," he replied. "By the end of the month, I should think."

"I look forward to it."

"Thank you, Majesty. Saints be with you."

She watched him limp off, as Sir Fail roused his men.

They left Sir Fail's chambers with eight men-at-arms, and though the party encountered a number of puzzled looks, they met with no resistance.

They found two Craftsmen standing guard at the entrance hall of the royal residence. As they approached, one stepped forward, eying the men from Liery with evident suspicion.

"Stand aside, Sir Moris," Muriele commanded. "These men are accompanying me to my chambers."

Moris, a round-faced man with a blond mustache, reddened. "Majesty, I cannot allow that," he said. "No one but the royal family and the Craftsmen are allowed to bear arms beyond this point."

Muriele drew herself a bit higher. "Sir Moris, someone has invaded my chambers, apparently underneath your nose. You will let us pass, do you understand?"

"Invaded your quarters?" Sir Moris said. "That simply isn't possible."

"Yes, one would think," Muriele said dryly, "and yet I assure you it is so."

Moris chewed that for a moment. "If Your Majesty will permit us to look into the matter—"

She shook her head and brushed past him. "Strike any of these men with me, and I'll have your head," she said.

"Majesty, this—at least let me come with you."

"As you wish."

They found a Craftsman crumpled outside the door to her suites. His eyes were open, and blue, and very dead.

With a bellow, Sir Fail burst through the door, his men behind him.

On the other side of the door lay Unna's body, her little nightshirt a mess of blood. She would not see her twelfth year.

Muriele sat staring at Unna's body as Fail's men searched her apartments, but they found no one, and no sign of anyone other than the rather obvious corpses.

When it was certain, Sir Fail placed his hand on her shoulder. "I'm sorry," he said.

She shook her head and looked up into her uncle's eyes.

"No more of this," she said. "Sir Fail, I wish to induct you and your men as my personal guard."

"Done, Majesty."

She turned to Sir Moris. "Discover how this happened," she said, "or the head of every single Craftsman will roll. Do you understand?"

"I understand, Majesty," Moris said stiffly. "But if I may speak, every man among us is loyal to you."

"I'm afraid you're going to have to prove that, Sir Moris. Start with this: Bring me Alis Berrye, and bring her to me now. Alive and in secret."

She turned back to Sir Fail. Through her eyes he must have seen what was burning in her.

"Are you all right, Majesty?" he asked.

"No," she said. "I am sick. Sick to death of being a target."

She went to the window and threw it open, looking out over the few lights still twinkling in the dark city below.

"I believe," she said, "that I will start finding targets of my own."

CHAPTER TWO

A GAME OF FIEDCHESE

As Neil sank through the emerald waters, he heard the draugs begin to sing. It was a far-off song with no words, but he could still hear the bitter loneliness of it, the avarice. They sang from Breu-nt-Toine, the land beneath waves, where the only things of light and love were those that sank there to be devoured.

Now they sang of Neil MeqVren and his coming.

Neil beat against his slow fall, kicking with his legs and rowing up with his arms, but his armor took him down like an anchor, and he had little experience with swimming anyway, having grown up around seas far too frigid for such exercise. He couldn't even tell which direction was up anymore, so mirk was the water. He reached for the catches of his armor, knowing he would never get it off in time, wondering why he hadn't thought of it earlier.

He held on to his last breath, but it was gone, turning black inside him. The sea wanted in, and the sea could never be long denied.

You have me, foam-father, he thought. *I have always been yours. But there is more I need to do here.*

Yet Lier did not answer, and the dirge of the draugs grew nearer, until they were all around him. Still, he could see nothing of their cold eyes and shark's teeth through the lightless depths.

His lungs opened and the sea rushed in. At first it hurt, like nothing he had ever felt, but the pain was brief, and he felt a peace settle. He had failed the queen for the last time.

He was done.

His fingers had gone numb, and he could no longer feel the fastenings of his armor, but strangely, it felt as if it were falling away, as if someone else were taking it off for him, and a pale light rose around him. He felt himself settle upon a surface as soft as a down mattress, but as cold as winter breakers. Fingers traced across his bare back and down his arm, and though they had no more warmth than the sea, he knew the touch.

"Fastia," he groaned, and found it strange that he could speak when he was full of water.

"You have forgotten me," she whispered. It was her voice, but brittle and somehow distant, though she spoke in his ear.

"I have not," he said. "My love, I have not."

"Have. Will. It is the same."

The light was stronger. He grasped her hand and pulled, determined that now, at least, he should see her.

"Do not," she said. But it was too late. When he saw her, he screamed, and could not stop screaming.

He was still screaming when yellow light struck, and a face before him appeared as if in a sunrise. It was a woman's face, but it was not Fastia.

At first he saw only her paradoxical eyes. They were so dark a blue that her pupils were lost. She seemed both blind and capable of seeing to the heart of anything. There was a nearly unbearable sadness there, and at the same time an uncontainable excitement. They were the eyes of a newborn and of a tired old woman.

"Be calm," she said. Her voice had a faint husk to it. She was holding his arm, but suddenly she let go and stepped away from him, as if he had done something to make her fearful. Her eyes became shadows beneath her brows, and now he saw her face was strong, with high, broad cheekbones carved of ivory and hair like spider silk, cut very short, just beneath her ears. She glowed like a brand in the light of the lantern she held in one pale hand, but her gown was of black or some other dark color, and seemed not to be there at all.

Confusion gripped him. He was in a bed, and dry. It was air in his lungs, not brine, but he was still in the belly of the sea, for he could feel it all around him and hear the creak of timbers. He darted his gaze about the bulkheads of dark lacquered wood and understood that he was in a ship's cabin.

"Be calm," the woman repeated. "You are alive, if not entirely well. You only dream of death." Her free hand went to her throat and fingered a small amulet there.

He knew he was alive. His heart was thundering, his head ached, and his side felt as if it had been split open.

Which, if he remembered correctly, it had.

"Who are you?" he managed.

The question seemed to perplex her for a moment.

"Call me Swanmay," she said at last.

"Where—?" He tried to sit up, but something in his head whirled, and the pain in his side became overwhelming agony. He swallowed a howl so that it came out only as a grunt.

"Be *still*," Swanmay said, starting forward, then stopping again. "You've had many injuries. Don't you remember?"

"Yes," Neil murmured, closing his eyes, trying to keep his stomach from heaving. "Yes, I remember." He remembered her now, as well. This was the face he'd seen on the docks, the woman peering from the strange ship.

Which ship he was now likely on.

"We're at sea," he said. His thoughts were unschooled boys refusing to be brought to task. Fastia's dead touch still lingered on his shoulder.

"Yes," she said. "We put to sea two days ago."

"Two days ago?"

"Yes. You've been unconscious that whole time. I was starting to fear you would not wake."

Neil tried to think. Two days. What had happened to Anne?

Swanmay moved nearer again. "Do not think to harm me," she said. "If I call, my men will come in and kill you."

"I have no reason to harm you, lady," he said. "Or none that I know of. And I would not even if I knew a reason."

"That's very sensible," she said. "But in your sleep you made most violent sounds and motions. You fought whole battles, I think. Do you remember those dreams?"

"Nothing of battle," Neil said.

"A pity. I'm sure your dreams would be interesting." She paused. "I'm going to trust you. I'm going to sit here a moment, for I'm sure you have questions. I know if I awoke in a strange place, to a strange person, I would. I would be terrified."

She sat down on a small stool.

"I'll tell you this first," she said, "in case you're afraid to ask. The people you were fighting for—the people you were protecting—they escaped."

Neil sighed, and felt something in him relax a bit.

"You were right," he said. "I was afraid to ask that."

She smiled tentatively. "They cast off safely. One was calling after you and tried to leave the ship, but the others would not let her."

"They escaped," Neil repeated, relief coming like an eastern breeze.

"Yes," she said, and her tone became inquiring. "I wondered if I was aiding in some crime."

"I am no criminal, lady, I promise you that."

She shrugged. "Vitellio is not my home and I hardly care if you violated some law of their country. But I admire the way you fought. I admire the way you went to your doom singing. I've read stories about men like you, but never thought to meet one. I could not leave you to the depths."

"So you—how did you—?"

"Some of my men can swim. They dived with a stout rope and pulled you up, but by then you were senseless."

"I owe you and your men my life."

"Yes, I suppose you do, but I shouldn't feel too uncomfortable about it." She cocked her head. "Who was she?"

"Who?"

"The girl with the red hair. She was the one you fought for, yes?"

Neil didn't know quite how to answer that, and he suddenly realized he shouldn't. From the moment his body struck the sea, he had no certain idea of what had happened. Perhaps everything Swanmay said was true. Perhaps none of it was. Perhaps he was captive of the very people who had attacked him. They were, after all, from Hansa, or at least some of them were. Swanmay had a Hanzish look about her, though she could as easily be from Crotheny or Herilanz. Her flawless king's tongue told him nothing.

Her ship, he recalled, was unmarked.

"Lady," he said, reluctantly, "please forgive me, but I can tell you nothing of why I fought."

"Ah," Swanmay said, and this time her smile seemed stronger. "You're not stupid, then. You've no reason to believe anything I say, do you?"

"No, milady," Neil allowed, "none whatsoever."

"Never mind, then. I just wondered if your battle was a matter of love or duty. I see now that it is somehow both. But your love isn't for the girl on the boat."

He could see her eyes again, and this time they did not seem blind at all.

"I'm tired," he said.

She nodded. "You need time to think. I'll leave you for now, but please don't try to move. My physician says you will start to leak like a broken boat if you do, and you interest me. I'd rather you lived long enough to find a little trust in me."

"May I ask where we are bound?"

She clasped her hands on her knees. "You may, and I will answer, but how will you know I do not lie?"

"I suppose I don't."

"We're sailing west, at the moment, to the Straits of Rusimi, and from there to Safnia. After that, I cannot say."

She stood. "Fair rest, for now," she said. "If you need anything, pull that rope on the other side of the bed."

Neil remembered Hurricane then.

"Lady? What of my horse?"

Her face saddened. "I last saw him watching us depart. We have no berth or provisions for beasts aboard. I am sorry. I am certain so fine a beast will find a good master."

That was just another dull ache for Neil. Crow was destroyed, his armor damaged probably beyond repair, and Hurricane was lost. What more could he lose, except his life?

"Thank you, lady," he murmured.

He watched her leave. For a moment, before she closed the door behind her, he caught a glimpse of a ship's deck in moonlight.

He tried to pull his thoughts back together. He still had his duty.

Swanmay had said they were sailing west. Anne was supposed to be sailing east, toward Paldh.

If she was sailing anywhere.

Neil inspected his wounds as best he could, and discovered that Swanmay had told the truth about them, at least. The glowing sword had cut through his armor and two of his ribs. It hadn't gone into his vitals, but it had been a near thing.

So he wouldn't be walking, much less fighting, for a while. For the time being, whether she was lying or telling the truth, he was at Swanmay's mercy.

In fact, he was already worn-out, and though he tried to remain awake to ponder the situation, the sea—the one familiar thing around him—soon lulled him back to sleep.

When he woke again, it was to the soft strains of music. Swanmay sat nearby on a stool, strumming a small cherrywood harp with golden tuning pegs. The cabin window was draped, but daylight leaked through, and without the glow of fire she was like a creature from a children's story, a woman made from snow.

"Lady," he murmured.

"Ah. I did not mean to wake you."

"The sound of a harp is not the worst thing to wake to, especially one played so beautifully."

To his surprise she seemed to color a bit at that. "I was only passing the time," she said. "How do you feel?"

"Better, I think. Milady—I wonder if it is proper that you watch over me, so. I promise you, I will lie quiet. I have little choice."

She cast her eyes down a bit. "Well, it is my cabin," she said. "And I tire sometimes of being on deck. When it's bright like this, the sun hurts my eyes and burns my skin."

"You aren't Sefry, are you?" he joked.

"No. Just unused to daylight." She looked back at him. "But you've met Sefry, haven't you?"

"I have. It's not difficult to do."

"I've not seen one yet. I hope to, soon."

"I should not be in your cabin, lady," Neil persisted. "Surely there are more suitable quarters for me."

"There are none more suitable to someone in your condition," she replied.

"But this is not appropriate. Your men—"

She lifted her chin. "My men wished you left to the sharks. My men do not command here. I do. And I think I am in no danger from you. Do you disagree?"

"No, milady, but still—"

"I can change my clothes there, behind that screen, and wash, as well. There is a cot for me to sleep on."

"I should sleep on the cot."

"When you are better, you will. When you are better yet, you will sleep with the men."

"I wish—"

"What is your name?" she asked suddenly. "You have not told me your name."

"I—" He fumbled for a moment. "My name is Neil," he said finally. He was sick of lying.

"Neil," she repeated. "That's a good name. A Lierish name. Or perhaps you are from Skern. Do you—do you know the game of fied-chese?"

Neil raised his brow in surprise. "I know it, lady. My father taught me how to play when I was a boy."

"I wonder—would you like to play it? No one on the ship knows how, and they're too busy to learn. But you . . ."

"Well, it's something I can do from my back," Neil said. "If you have a board."

Swanmay smiled a little shyly and crossed to a small cupboard built into the cabin. From it she produced a fiedchese board and a leather bag full of playing pieces. The board was beautiful, its squares made of inlaid wood, one set red-brown and the other bone white. The throne in the center of the board was black.

The pieces were of matching beauty. The king was carved of the dark wood, and he wore a sharply peaked helm for his crown. His men were figured with shield and sword, and they were tall and slender like their king.

The raiders were of all sorts, no two pieces alike, and they were a bit grotesque. Some had human bodies and the heads of birds, dogs, or pigs. Others had wide bodies and short legs or no legs at all, just long arms that served the function. Neil had never seen a set like it.

"Which would you like me to play, lady?" Neil asked. "The king or raiders?"

"I have played the king far too often," Swanmay mused. "But perhaps I should play it again, to see if there is an omen in it."

And with that opaque statement she began setting up the board. The king went in the center, surrounded by his knights in the form of a cross. The raiders—Neil's men—were placed around the edge of the board. There were four gates, at each corner of the board. If the king reached any of the gates, Swanmay would win. Neil would win if he captured the king.

She took the first move, sending one of her knights east, but not so far as to strike one of his men. He studied the board a bit and countered by capturing the man.

"I thought a warrior might take that bait," she said. She sent another knight across the board, this one to block one of his pieces.

Five moves later, her king crossed through the north gate and Neil was left wondering what exactly had happened.

"Well," he said, "if it was an omen you were seeking, you found a good one."

"Yes," she replied. "In fact, I am nearly to my own gate. I hope to pass through it soon." She began placing the pieces back on the board.

"Have you been to Safnia?" she asked.

"No, milady, I haven't. I haven't been much of anywhere."

"More than I," she replied. "The only place I have ever been—besides the place where I was born—is this ship. And you're the only person . . ." She stopped, turning that faint shade of rose again. "I shouldn't talk about it. You were right to keep your own secrets. But I wish . . . no, tell me about some place, please."

Neil considered what he could tell her without revealing too much, though he was beginning to feel silly for his caution. If she were his enemy—in league with those who had attacked Anne—then surely she knew who Anne was, and surely she knew that he must be a vassal of Crotheny.

Well, she had at least guessed where he was from.

"I can tell you about Skern," he said.

"It's in the Lier Sea, yes? Part of Liery now?"

"Once it was Hansan," he said, watching for a reaction and finding none. "But now it is a Lierish protectorate."

"I know these things from books," she said. "But tell me what it is to be there."

Neil lay back and mused with his eyes closed, watching the colors of his childhood. "You're never far from the sea," he murmured. "You can smell it everywhere you go, even in the Keels."

"Keels?"

"It's a range of great stony mountains that cuts the island in two, not much more than stone and grass, really. I used to go up there with my fah to see my aunt Nieme. She kept sheep and lived in a sod house. It was nearly always raining, and in the winter the snow fell deep, but on a rare clear day you could see the coast of Saltmark, and the mountains on Skiepey—that's the next island over. It was like being at the top of the sky."

"You lived on the coast?"

"I was born in a village called Frouc, just on the coast, but I did most of my growing up on boats."

"Fishing?"

"When I was very young. After that, it was mostly fighting."

"Oh. How old were you when you became a warrior?"

"I went with my fah into battle the first time when I was nine, to carry his spears."

"Nine?"

"It's not an unusual age," Neil said. "Men are scarce."

"I suppose they would be, if they go to war at nine."

"Our enemies couldn't be convinced to wait until we had grown up," Neil replied.

"I'm sorry," Swanmay said. "I didn't mean to bring bad memories."

"Memories and scars tell who we are," Neil said. "I'm not ashamed or afraid of either."

"No, but some of them hurt, don't they?" she said softly. "I never went to war, but I know that." She glanced at the board. "You play the king this time."

"Are you in trouble, milady?" Neil asked. "Are you running from something?"

She didn't answer him right away. She waited until he had made his move, and chosen one of her own.

"If you could go anywhere you've been, or anywhere you've never been, where would you go?"

"At this moment I would go to Paldh," he said.

"That's where she's going, isn't it? Paldh?"

A sort of shock ran up Neil's spine, and he realized he'd let himself be lulled by the conversation. He'd managed—despite everything—to help Anne escape, to put her back on the road toward home.

Now he'd helped her enemies follow her again.

He looked at Swanmay's lovely white throat and wondered if he had the strength to throttle her before she called out and brought his doom upon him.

CHAPTER THREE

LESHYA

AREN'T MANY WHO CAN sneak up on me," Aspar muttered to the Sefry behind him. He hadn't turned, but he knew two things about the Sefry now that he didn't know before. The first was that it certainly wasn't Fend. He knew Fend's voice as well as he knew his own.

The other was that she was a woman.

"I wouldn't guess so," she answered. "But it's no matter. I mean you no harm if you mean me none."

"That will depend on a few things," Aspar said, turning slowly. He no longer feared that the monks or the greffyn might have spotted him. Whatever was coming from the east had attracted all of their attention. His immediate problem was the one behind him.

She was slight, even for a Sefry, with violet eyes and black bangs that dropped almost to her eyelashes. She had loosened her cowl so she could speak unmuffled, and he could just make out the sardonic bow of her lips. She looked young, but he guessed by the set of her eyes she wasn't. She might be as old as he was, or older, but Sefry aged young in the skin and lived longer than Mannish folk.

He wondered how he could have ever thought she was Fend, even at a distance.

"What things would those be?" she asked.

He could see both her hands, and they were empty. He relaxed slightly.

"You've been leading me around," he told her. "Playing with me. I don't like that."

"No? You didn't have to follow."

"I thought you were someone else."

She nodded thoughtfully. "Ah. You thought I was Fend."

The name jabbed him like a prickle. "Who the sceat are you?" Aspar hissed.

She put a finger to her lips. "I can explain that later," she said. "You'll want to watch what's about to happen."

"You know what's coming? You've seen it?"

She nodded. "It's the slinders. See—there they are."

"Slinders?" He looked back, and at first all he saw was forest. But the trees seemed to be shivering oddly, as if a wind was blowing through them in just one place. Blackbirds swirled up in clouds against the silvery sky. The monks stood like statues, frozen by the moment.

Then something came from the trees, creatures loping sometimes on four legs, sometimes on two. There were ten of them, and their baying became more frantic as their feet hit the clearing and they saw the monks.

At first Aspar thought they might be smaller versions of the utin or some other ugly thing from boygshin stories, but when he understood what they actually were, the shock went cold through him.

They were men and women. Naked, scuffed, dirty, bleeding, utterly mad—but Mannish, just as Ehawk had described.

As the leaves began to rustle in a strong autumn wind, the main pack of them came behind the leaders—twenty, fifty—more than he could count. He guessed at least a hundred. They moved strangely, and it wasn't just that they sometimes dropped to their hands. They ran jerkily, frantically—like insects, in a way. A few carried rocks or branches, but most were empty-handed.

The majority looked to be relatively young, but some were stoop-shouldered and gray-haired. Some were little more than children, but he didn't see any that looked as if they had seen fewer than fifteen winters.

They spread to encircle the monks, and their cacophonic yowling settled into a hair-prickling sort of song. The words were slurred and broken, just sounds really, but he knew the tune. It was a children's song, about the Briar King, sung in Almannish.

Dillying Dallying
Farthing go
The Briar King walks to and fro

"Those are the slinders?" he asked.

"It's what the Oostish have taken to calling them," the Sefry said. "At least those who haven't joined them."

As she spoke, the slinders began to fall, quilled black by arrows. The monks were firing with inhuman speed and precision. But it hardly slowed the wave of bodies. They poured around the fallen like a river around rocks. The monks drew swords and formed themselves into a ring fortress—only two kept their bows out, and they were in the center.

Almost without thinking, Aspar reached for his own bow.

"You're not that foolish," she said. "Why would you fight for them? You've seen what they do."

Aspar nodded. "Werlic." The monks deserved what they got. But what they were facing was so weird and dread, he'd almost forgotten that.

What was more, he *had* forgotten the greffyn. He remembered it now as it let out a low unearthly growl. It stood pawing the ground, the spines on its back stiff. Then, as if reaching a sudden decision, it turned and bounded into the forest.

Straight toward him.

"Sceat," Aspar mouthed, raising his bow. He already felt the sickness burning in the thing's eyes. He let fly.

The arrow skipped off the bony scales above its nostrils. The greffyn glanced his way, and with blinding speed changed direction, bounded off into the forest and was gone.

Aspar had tracked one greffyn over half of Crotheny. He'd never seen it run from anything.

If the greffyn had fought alongside them, the monks might have stood a chance. He had seen how their kind could fight, and even a poor fighter with a sword was more than a match for any number of naked, unarmed attackers.

But these attackers didn't care if they died, and that in itself was a potent weapon.

So he watched as the slinders hurled into the monks glittering blades like meat into a grinder, with much the same results. In instants the clearing was bathed in gore, viscera, severed heads and limbs. But the attackers kept coming without hesitation, without fear, like Grim's birsirks—though birsirks usually carried at least a spear. He saw one who had lost a leg dragging himself toward the monks. Another impaled himself on a sword, locking his hands around his foe's throat.

There was fighting against that, but there was no winning. One by one the monks were dragged down by sheer force of numbers and had their throats bitten out or their bellies clawed open. Then, with his stomach lurching, Aspar watched the slinders feed, tearing into the bodies like wolves.

He glanced aside at the Sefry, but she wasn't watching the slinders. Her eye was on the forest edge from which they had emerged. He followed her gaze and saw that the trees were still trembling, swaying even, and he felt as if the sun were rising, but there was no light. Just the feel of radiance on his face and the sense of change.

Something new stepped from the forest, then, not as tall as the trees but twice the height of a big man. Black antlers branched from its head, but its face was that of a man with birch-bark pale skin and a beard like thick brown moss. He was as naked as the slinders, though thick hair or moss covered much of him. Where his feet struck the ground, black briars spurted up like slow fountains.

"He didn't look like that before," Aspar muttered.

"He's the Briar King," the Sefry replied. "He's always different, always the same."

A crowd of slinders followed him, and when the briars sprouted, they hurled themselves upon them, trying to tear them from the ground. Their bodies were flushed with blood, for the thorns cut deep, but like the monks, the thorns were no match for determination and numbers. The slinders bled and died, but the thorns were ripped apart as surely as their human foes.

The Briar King, seemingly unconcerned with any of that, strode up to the fallen monks, and the forest at his back seemed to strain to follow him.

Grimly, Aspar reached for the black arrow. He knew his best chance when he saw it.

"And here is where your choice lies, holter," the Sefry whispered.

"No choice," Aspar said. "He's killing the forest."

"Is he? Are your eyes truly open, holter?"

For answer, Aspar fitted the arrow to the sinew of his bow.

The wind dropped, and then the Briar King turned. Even at that distance, Aspar could see the green glint of his eyes.

The slinders looked up, too, and started toward Aspar, but the horned monarch lifted one hand, and they stopped in their tracks.

"Think, holter," the Sefry said. "I only ask you to think."

"What do you know, Sefry?"

"Little more than you do. I only know what my heart tells me. Now ask yours what it tells you. I brought you here because no one knows this forest better than you—no Sefry, no Mannwight. Who is the enemy here? Who gave you that arrow?"

The wind was nothing now. He could make the shot almost without thinking.

He could end it.

"Those things that follow him," Aspar said, "they used to be people. Villagers."

"Yes," she agreed. "I've seen the empty villages."

"Then . . ."

But the Briar King had saved his life. He'd been poisoned by the greffyn, and the king had stooped upon him. He remembered only a dream of the roots, sinking deep, of treetops drinking in the sun, of the great wheel of seasons, of birth and death and decay.

He'd told himself it was a lie.

The Briar King turned very slowly and walked back toward the forest. Aspar pulled the bow to its full draw, and suddenly noticed that his fingers trembled.

The Briar King's gaze lingered. In the eyes of the greffyn, he'd seen only sickness. In the eyes of the Briar King, he saw life.

Cursing softly, he lowered the bow as the creature and its entourage faded into the trees.

The howling stopped, and the forest was quiet.

"I cannot say for certain that was the right choice, holter," the Sefry said, breaking the silence. "But it is the one I would have made."

Aspar returned the arrow to its case. "And now suppose you just tell me who you are?" he muttered.

"My clan is Sern," she replied. "My talking name is Liel, but I prefer the name I was given in Nazhgave—Leshya."

"You're lying. No one from clan Sern has left the Halafolk rewns in a thousand generations."

"Did you find any of my clan at Rewn Aluth? You've seen for yourself that we have. And I broke that prohibition long ago, before any of my folk."

"Sceat," he snarled. "How do you know so much about me, when I've never heard of you?"

She smiled grimly. "You think you know everything about the Sefry, Aspar White? You do not, and far less about me. As I said, I've been away. Thirty winters I spent in the north. I only came back when I felt him wakening."

"You didn't answer my question. How do you know so much about me?"

"I've taken an interest in you, Aspar White," she said.

"That's still no answer," he said. "I don't have much patience with Sefry two-talk." He narrowed his eyes. "Every Sefry in the forest left months ago. Why are you still here?"

"The others flee from their duty," she said sternly. "I do not."

"What duty is that? I've never heard of any Sefry having a duty to any beyond themselves."

"And I'm afraid that for the time being you'll remain unenlightened," she said. "Will you attack me for my silence?"

"I might. You got a friend of mine killed."

"The mannwight? I had no way of knowing that would happen—I only wanted you to see what the Church was doing. He must be somehow sensitive to the fanes. Was he a priest?"

"So you don't know everything either."

"No, of course not. But if he was a priest, and has walked another faneway, perhaps one related to this one, it might explain—"

"Wait," Aspar said, as memory suddenly struck him. "This sedos—is it part of the same faneway as the first one you led us to?"

She raised an eyebrow. "It seems most likely. Those monks built that fane first, then came here."

"And were they finished here? Did they complete their rites?"

She glanced at the messy corpses around the mound. "I think so," she said, "but I am certainly no expert on these matters."

"Then I'll bring the one who is," Aspar replied. He turned to leave.

"Stay a moment, holter. We still need to talk. We are, it seems, working toward the same purpose."

"I have only one purpose right now," Aspar replied, "and I doubt very much that it's the same as yours."

"I'm going with you, then."

Aspar didn't answer. He found Ogre, mounted, and rode toward where he had left the others.

But still the Sefry followed.

He found Ehawk, Winna, and Stephen not far from where he'd left them, except they had somehow gotten Stephen's body up into an ironoak, safely wedged in the crotch of two branches. Ehawk had his bow out.

"That's them," he said, when he saw Aspar. "That's what attacked us in the Duth ag Paé. Hear them?"

The song of the slinders had begun again, albeit very distantly. "Yah," Aspar said. "But I don't think they're coming this way."

"You saw them?" Winna asked, starting to clamber down.

"Yah. I saw 'em."

Winna's feet hit the ground, and she ran to throw herself into his arms. "We thought they had you," she whispered, pressing her face into his neck. He felt dampness.

"It's fine, Winna," he said. "I'm fine." But it felt good, after the days of tension and argument.

But then she stiffened in his arms. "He's here," she said. "Behind you."

"Yah. It's not Fend." Nonetheless, he shot Ehawk a cautioning glance. The boy nodded and stayed in the tree with his weapon ready.

"No?" she pulled away from him, and they watched the Sefry walk into the camp.

Leshya glanced at Winna, then bemusedly at Ehawk. "The squirrels run large here," she said.

"And dangerous," Aspar replied.

"Who is she?" Winna asked.

"Just a Sefry," Aspar grunted. "As full of lies and trouble as any of them."

"And she can speak for herself," Leshya said. She sat on a log and pulled off one of her buskins, spilling a rock from it and massaging her foot.

Winna stood watching her for a few moments, trying to absorb the new situation.

"Our friend was hurt because of you," Winna finally said, angrily. "You led us—"

"I heard he was dead," Leshya interrupted. "Was that opinion somewhat exaggerated?"

"Maybe," Aspar allowed.

"What?" Winna said. "You've changed your mind?"

Aspar held his hands out, cautioning. "Don't get your hopes up," he said. "But something like this happened to him before, to hear him tell it. When he walked the faneway of Saint whoever."

"Decmanis."

"Yah. He said he lost all feeling in his body, forgot who he was, that even his heart stopped beating. Maybe something like that's happened now. Maybe he just needs to finish the faneway."

Winna's eyes lit with hope, then dulled again. "We don't know about these things, Aspar. Last time he managed it alone, because the saints intended it. This time—" She nodded up at the still body.

"You said yourself he hasn't started to rot."

"But— No, you're right. We can't just do nothing. We have to try. But we don't even know where the rest of the faneway is."

"We know where part of it is," Aspar said. "That's a start."

"Consider carefully," Leshya interposed, "whether anyone—even your friend—should walk a faneway such as the Church is creating."

"The Church?" Winna looked at Aspar.

"Yah," he said. "There were priests at the sedos. They cut people up and hung them about, like we've seen before."

"But that was Spendlove and his renegades," Winna said. "Stephen said the Church didn't know anything about them."

Leshya snorted. "Then your friend was wrong," she said. "This is no small band of renegades. You think Spendlove and Fend were working alone? They are but a finger of stone on a mountain."

"Yah," Aspar said. "And what do you know of that? Where would I find Fend?" He cocked his head. "For that matter, you knew about the arrow. How *could* you know that?"

She rolled her eyes. "I saw you shoot the utin. I examined its body. The rest I either heard from you when I was following you or guessed. Someone from the Church gave it to you, didn't they? And asked you to kill the Briar King."

"Fend," Aspar insisted, not to be sidetracked. "Where is he?"

"I don't know where to find him," she said. "I heard he was in the Bairghs when I came through there on my way south. One rumor was that he was going to the Sarnwood Witch, but who knows if that's true?"

"Then how did you find us? How did you know who we were?" Winna demanded.

"You? Luvilih, I've no idea who you are, or who that boy in the tree is. But Aspar White is well known throughout the King's Forest."

"Not thirty years ago, I wasn't," Aspar said. "If you haven't been here in that long, then it's a fair question."

"No, it's still a stupid question. I was searching for the king's holter, so I started asking who he was and how I might find him. Among other things, I heard about your fight with the greffyn, and that you were the one who first saw the Briar King. They said you'd gone to Eslen, so I was on my way there to find you. I was in Fellenbeth a few ninedays ago and heard you'd come through heading this way. So I followed."

"But didn't bother to introduce yourself."

"No. I've heard of you, but I don't know you. I wanted you to see the things I had seen, and I wanted to see what you would do."

"And now you're our best friend," Winna said acidly. "And after all your help with the utin and leading poor Stephen straight to his doom, you reckon we're yours."

Leshya smiled. "You like them young, don't you, holter?"

"That's enough," Aspar said. "More than enough. What's the Church got to do with this?"

"Everything," Leshya replied. "You saw the monks."

"Not the praifec," Winna blurted angrily. "If he knew about this, why would he—?"

"—send you to kill the only enemy strong enough to interfere with his designs?" Leshya finished rather smugly. "Saints know."

"What makes you think the Briar King is against the Church and not with it?"

"Ask your lover."

Aspar nearly jumped at the word, and when he looked back at Winna found an odd expression on her face.

"What, Aspar?" she asked.

"We saw him," he told her. "The slinders—the things Ehawk saw, the things you heard—they were at his command. They killed the priests, and could have killed us, but he held them back."

"Then the Briar King is good?"

"Good? No. But he's fighting for the forest. The thorns that follow him—they're trying to destroy him, pull him down like they're doing the trees. The greffyn wasn't his servant—it was his foe."

"Then he *is* good," Winna insisted.

"He fights for the forest, Winna. But he's no friend of us, no friend of people."

"Still, you didn't kill him," she said. "You said you didn't even try."

"No. I don't know what's going on exactly. I can use this arrow only once more—as long as the praifec wasn't lying about that—and I don't want to use it on the wrong thing, if you catch my meaning."

Winna shot a sharp glance at Leshya. "We've no idea whom we can trust, then."

"Werlic."

"So what do we do? The praifec sent us out here to kill the Briar King. You didn't do it. So what do we do now?"

"We take Stephen to the sedos and see what happens. That's where we start. After that, we figure out who's lying to us, the praifec—" He looked straight at Leshya. "—or you."

The Sefry just smiled and pulled her boot back on.

CHAPTER FOUR

THE THIRD FAITH

A NNE MANAGED TO CRAWL out onto the deck before being sick again. She even made it to the steerboard rail, and there
her whole body spasmed and she vomited until she thought her
breast would tear apart. Then she slid trembling to the deck and pud-
dled there, weeping.

It was night, and if the ship wasn't still, the wind was. She heard a
sailor laugh briefly and another hush him. She didn't care. She didn't
care about anything.

She wished she could just die and have it over with. She deserved it.

She had killed Sir Neil, as certainly as if she had pushed him into
the ocean herself. He had traveled across half the world and saved
her—saved all of them—and all she had been able to do was watch
the sea close over his head.

If she lived forever, she would never forget the look of betrayal in
his eyes.

She took a deep, shuddering breath. It was better out here in the
air. When she went below to the tiny cabin she shared with Austra,
everything spun around. Two days now like that. She couldn't keep
any food down at all, and wine just made it worse, even when it was
mixed with water.

She rolled over onto her back and looked up at the stars.

The stars stared back at her. So did an orange half-moon that seemed somehow far too bright.

She was starting to feel sick again.

She fixed her eye on the moon, trying to make the motion go away, to focus beyond it. She picked out features from the dark splotches, remembered maps, and noticed strange patterns that signified nothing she had ever seen, but nevertheless seemed to have meaning.

The motion of the ship gradually faded, and the light of the Moon went from orange to yellow to—as she hung directly overhead—shining silver.

With a soft movement, the ship was gone altogether. Anne looked around, only half surprised this time to find herself in a forest still bathed in moonlight.

She gathered her feet under her and stood up shakily. "Hello?" she said.

There was no answer.

She had twice been to this place. The first time she had been forced—drawn from her sister's birthday party by a strange masked woman. The second, she had come herself, somehow, trying to escape the darkness of the cave where she had been confined by the sisters of the coven Saint Cer.

This time she wasn't sure if she had been called or come or something in between. But it was nighttime, where before it had always been bright. And there was no one here—no strange masked women making obscure statements about how she had to be queen, or the whole world was going to end.

Maybe they didn't *know* she was here.

A cloud passed across the moon, and the shadows in the trees deepened, seemed to slink toward her.

That was when she remembered that there were no shadows in this place, not under the sun, at least. Then why should they be here when it was night?

She was starting to think she wasn't in the same place at all.

And it dawned upon her that she had been wrong about another thing. There *was* someone there, someone her eye kept avoiding, would not let her stare straight at. She tried harder, but each time she turned one way, she found herself looking another, so the tall shadow was always at the corner of her eye.

A soft laugh touched her ears. A man. "What is this," a voice said. "Is this a queen, come to see me?"

Anne realized she was trembling. He moved, and she gritted her teeth as her head turned in response, so as not to see him. "I'm not a queen," she said.

"Not a queen?" he asked. "Nonsense. I see the crown on your head and the scepter in your hand. Didn't the Faiths tell you?"

"I don't know who you're talking about," Anne said. "I don't know any Faiths." But she knew she was lying. The women she had met here before had never named themselves, but that name seemed very right, somehow.

He knew, too. "Perhaps you do not know them by name," the voice purred, echoing her thoughts. The shadows drew closer. "They are known by many. Hagautsin, Vhateis, Suesori, Hedgewights—the Shadowless. It doesn't matter what they're called. They are meddlesome witches with not nearly the wisdom or power they pretend to."

"And you? Who are you?" Anne tried to sound confident.

"Someone they fear. Someone they think you can protect them from. But you cannot."

"I don't understand," Anne said. "I just want to go home."

"So you can be crowned? So you can become what the Faiths predicted?"

"I don't want to be queen," Anne replied truthfully, continuing to edge away. Her fear was a bright cord around her heart, but she reached for the power she had unleashed in z'Espino. She felt it quivering there, ready, but when she reached toward the shadow, there was no flesh, no blood, no beating heart. Nothing to work upon.

And yet there was something, and that something came suddenly, racing across the green from not one direction, but from all of them, a noose of darkness yanking tight. She balled her fists, trembling, and turned her face to the moon, the only place her flesh would let her look.

Light flashed through her, then, and the thing in her turned altogether different and she felt like marble, like luminescent stone, and the darkness was a wave of chill water that passed around her and was gone.

"Ah," the voice said, fading. "You continue to learn. But so do I. Do not hold your life too dear, Anne Dare. It will not belong to you for long."

Then the shadows were gone, and the glade was filled with perfect moonlight.

"He's right," a woman's voice said. "You do learn. There are more diverse powers in the moon than darkness."

Anne turned, but it wasn't one of the women she had seen before. This one had hair as silvery as the lunar light and skin as pale. She wore a black gown that flashed here and there with jewels and a mask of black ivory that left her mouth uncovered.

"How many of you are there?" Anne asked.

"There are four," the woman replied. "You have met two of my sisters."

"The Faiths."

"He named to you but a few of our names."

"I've never heard of you by any names until now."

"It has been long since we moved in the world. Most have forgotten us."

"Who was that? Who was he?"

"He is the enemy," she said.

"The Briar King?"

She shook her head. "The Briar King is not the enemy, though many of you will die by his hand. The Briar King is a part of the way things were and the way things are. The one you just spoke to is not."

"Then who was he?"

"A mortal, still. A thing of flesh and blood, but becoming more. Like the world, he is changing. If he finishes changing, then everything we know will be swept aside."

"But who is he?" Anne persisted.

"We do not know his mortal name. But the possibility of him has been arriving for millennia."

Anne closed her eyes, anger welling in her breast. "You're as use-less as your sisters."

"We're trying to help, but by our nature we are restricted."

"Yes, your sister explained that, at least," Anne replied. "But I found it just as unhelpful as anything else any of you have told me."

"Everything has its seasons, Anne. The moon goes through its cycle each month, and each year brings spring, summer, autumn, winter. But the world has larger seasons, stronger tides. Flowers that bloom in Prismen are dormant in Novmen. It has been so since the world was young.

"And yet the last time this season came around, the cycle itself was nearly broken, a balance was lost. The wheel creaks on a splintered axle, and possibilities exist that never did before. One of those possibilities is *him*. Not a person, at first, just a place, a throne if you will, never sat before but waiting to be filled. And now someone has come along to fill it. But we do not yet know him—we see only what you saw, his shadow."

"Is he the one behind the murder of my sisters and father? Did he send the knights to the coven?"

"Ultimately, perhaps. He certainly wants you dead."

"But why?"

"He does not want you to be queen."

"Why?" Anne repeated. "What threat am I to him?"

"Because there are *two* new thrones," the Faith said, softly. "Two."

Anne woke on the deck of the ship. Someone had slipped a blanket over her. She lay there a moment, fearing that if she straightened, the wave-sickness would return, but after a moment she realized that she felt well.

She sat up and rubbed her eyes. It was morning, the sun just peeking over the marine horizon. Austra was at the railing a few yards away, conversing in low tones with Cazio. She was smiling, and when Cazio reached to touch her hand, she went all rosy.

Silly girl, Anne thought angrily. *Can't she see there's no sincere love in him? He's just a boy, playing games.*

But why should Austra's foolishness bother her? After all, if he was focused on Austra, perhaps he'd leave *her* alone. That certainly would be for the best.

Still, Austra was her friend, and she had to watch out for her.

So she pulled herself to her feet using the rail. There was no renewal of her nausea. She felt well, at least physically.

"Ah, she's alive after all," Cazio said, glancing in her direction.

Austra jumped guiltily, and her blush deepened. Anne suddenly wondered if things had gone farther than a bit of hand-touching. While she was sick and asleep, perhaps?

She wouldn't have to ask. Austra would volunteer any information eventually. Or—maybe not. There had been a time when they shared everything, but they had grown apart. Anne knew it was her own fault, for hiding things from Austra. Perhaps Austra was getting her revenge.

"Do you feel better?" Austra asked. "You were missing from your bed, and I couldn't find you at all. I thought you had fallen overboard. Finally I saw you sleeping here, and brought a blanket to keep you warm."

"That was kind of you," Anne said. "I felt less sick out here. And altogether better now."

"That's good," Cazio said. "You've been a bit of a bore."

"Which makes our company perfectly matched," Anne replied.

Cazio opened his mouth to answer, but something behind her got his attention, and his brow furrowed. She turned to see what it was.

When she saw it was Captain Malconio, her jaw tightened.

"Well," he said. "You seem to be feeling better. The dead have risen."

"Not all of them," Anne said coldly. "Some remain quite dead."

Malconio's eyes flashed something that might have been anger or chagrin, it was hard to tell.

"Casnara, I'm sorry that you lost a friend back there. But I was never hired to fight a battle, only to give you passage." He leveled his gaze at Cazio, and her uncertainty about his mood vanished. Malconio was angry, and he had been before she ever said anything.

"In fact," the captain went on, "I was never let in on the fact that there was danger of any sort involved."

"Of course not," Cazio retorted. "I know better than to rely upon either honor or bravery from you, Malconio."

Malconio snorted. "And I know as well not to rely on sense, judgment, or gratitude from you. Or from your friends, I see. If we had delayed casting off another instant, my ship would have been overrun. Even if we hadn't all been killed, we would have been trapped in dock for twice ninedays, settling the legalities. As far as I can see, I've saved all your lives, and now I'm wondering why I shouldn't throw you overboard."

"Because," Cazio said, "If you try, I will acquaint Caspator with your gullet."

"You're making my decision easier, Cazio."

"Ah, by Diuvo stop it, you two," z'Acatto rasped, limping around the base of the mainsail. "Neither of you could lay a hand on the other, and you know it, so spare us all your childish threats."

Malconio nodded his head toward the swordmaster. "How have you put up with him all of these years?"

"By staying drunk," z'Acatto grunted. "But if I'd had the both of you around, I'd have had to find stronger drink. Which reminds me—is there any of that Gallean stuff left?"

"You already know each other?" Austra asked, her gaze switching from z'Acatto to the captain to Cazio.

"Hardly," z'Acatto said. "But they are brothers."

"Brothers?" Austra gasped.

Austra's surprise mirrored Anne's own, but she could see the resemblance now.

"No brother of mine would abandon the family honor," Cazio said evenly.

"In what way have I abandoned the family honor?" Malconio asked. "By leaving that rotting hulk of a house to you?"

"You sold off the country estate to buy a ship," Cazio said. "Land that's been in our family since the Hegemony held sway. You sold it for *this*." He flapped the back of his hand at the ship.

"There was no profit to be gained in the land, Cazio, nor had there been in a generation. I had no mind to laze around Avella and pick swordfights for a living, either—that role you most adequately filled. I've done well as a merchant. I own four vessels, and soon enough I'll have my own estates, built by my own hands. You cling to the Chiovattio past, brother. I represent our future."

"That's a pretty speech," Cazio allowed. "Do you practice it in front of a looking glass?"

Malconio started to reply, rolled his eyes, placed his hands on his hips, and smiled sardonically at Anne.

"Marry him and make his life miserable, won't you?" he said.

Anne drew herself up. "You presume far too much," she said, "even in jest. You are like your brother in that, if in nothing else."

"Thank Diuvo that's the extent of it."

"You should be so lucky as to be like your brother," Austra exploded. "He's a valiant fighter. We would be dead ten times over if it weren't for him."

"And if it weren't for *me*," Malconio said," you would be dead only one time, which, I think, would suffice."

Cazio lifted his finger and seemed about to add something, but his brother waved him off.

"Z'Acatto's right—this is useless. I should have known better than to take my brother on ship, much less his friends, but now I have. What's done is done, so, to the heart of the matter—who were those men that were pursuing you?"

"I thought your business with us was limited to our passage," Anne said. "Why this sudden curiosity about our enemies?"

"For two reasons, casnara. The first is that I am now connected in their minds with *you*. I have an enemy I never sought to offend. The second is that we are presently being followed by a rather fast ship, and I very much suspect that it contains your friends from the docks at z'Espino."

CHAPTER FIVE

ALIS BERRYE

"M AJESTY?"

Muriele looked up. It was the young man-at-arms whom Sir Fail had stationed in her antechamber.

"What is it?" she asked.

"Someone is knocking for admittance."

Muriele rubbed her eyes. She hadn't heard.

"See who it is."

"Yes, Majesty."

He vanished into her receiving room while she stared nervously at the concealed door. Though it seemed clear enough now that the assassin had entered through the front, she wasn't as sure he had left that way. The door was invisible, if one did not know it was there, but given sufficient time and the knowledge that it existed, the latch could certainly be found.

Until she could be sure he wasn't still there, hiding in the walls, she would never be comfortable being wholly alone.

The man-at-arms returned. "It is the praifec Hespero, Majesty," he announced.

"Is he alone?"

"Yes, Majesty."

"Very well." She sighed. "Admit him."

A moment later the dark-gowned praifec entered her chambers and bowed. "Majesty," he said.

Muriele had always felt there was something missing about the praifec, but she had never been able to say what it was. He was a man of intelligence, certainly, and even of passion when it came to matters of state and religion. He was well-spoken to the point of being glib. And yet somehow—even in his most impassioned argument—it seemed to her that he wasn't entirely present, that there was some basic quality that he was counterfeiting, that he didn't actually have. When she focused on any particular quality of his, however, it seemed genuine.

It could be, she decided, that she simply didn't like him, and what was missing was merely her acceptance of him.

"To what do I owe this visit, praifec?" she asked.

"To my natural concern for your well-being," he replied.

She lifted an eyebrow. "Please explain," she directed.

"I should think it should be evident," Hespero said. "Suddenly, in the middle of the night, Sir Fail and his guard sweep into the royal apartments. His Majesty, King Charles, is brought in, also under Lier-ish guard. The Craftsmen become agitated, and the entire castle is thrown into a state of disarray."

Muriele shrugged. "Someone tried to kill me, Praifec," she said. "Under such circumstances, disarray is only natural. What would you have me do?"

"Someone tried to kill you?" His surprise seemed as genuine as his concern.

"Unless their true intent was to slaughter my guard and then my young maid, I would have to conclude so," Muriele said.

"This is terrible. How was it done?"

She smiled grimly. "As when the churchmen killed my daughters, no one seems to know."

The praifec's mouth opened in a little *o*, then closed before he began speaking again. "Majesty, if you are implying that the Church had any hand in this, I forgive you. Clearly the stress has clouded your judgment."

"Nevertheless, this has the same stink about it," Muriele replied.

"Brother Desmond and his men were renegades," Hespero reminded her. "Worse, they were heretics practicing the forbidden arts."

"In afterthought, yes," Muriele agreed. "But I took the liberty of checking the roles of the monastery d'Ef and discovered that he—and his men—were trusted members of the Church until just before his death."

"Actually, I think he was probably considered less than sanctified when he murdered the fratrex of his order," Hespero said sarcastically. "The possibility of evil exists everywhere, even within the Church. I do not deny that. The murders of your children—and the methods used to accomplish them—have served to reawaken us to that simple but neglected truth. We have begun the most serious investigation of our various orders since the days of the Hegemony, a search which starts with the Fratrex Prismo himself and descends to the humblest frater and most rural sacritor. If you have any evidence at all that tonight's attempt on your life was connected with any man of the Church, I am compelled to ask you what it is."

"There is none," Muriele admitted.

"I see," the praifec returned. "Then what *is* known?"

"That someone killed the guard at my chamber door with a knife. That he then entered my apartments and slew my maid in the same fashion."

"But you escaped."

"I was not here," Muriele replied.

"That was very fortunate," the praifec said.

"Yes, it was," she said wearily. "Praifec, why are *you* here?"

Both eyebrows lifted in surprise. "To offer my support and my council."

"What council would that be?"

"Majesty, I must speak plainly. Though I now see your actions were spurred by fear and desperation—and were therefore perhaps in some way justified—they have created pandemonium. Rumors are abundant. Some say that this is some sort of Lierish coup, that you are being forced—or worse, have chosen—to take the kingdom by force."

"May I remind you, Praifec, that the kingdom is already mine?"

"It is not, Majesty," the praifec said, with what seemed excessive gentleness. "It is your son's, and he is a Dare, not a de Liery. You have no claim to the throne at all."

"Fair enough," Muriele replied. "Let me be candid, as well. Somehow, an assassin walked by or around the vaunted Craftsmen, entered my chambers, killed my maid, and would have killed me if I had had the bad fortune to be here. Since Cal Azroth, I have found it difficult to place full faith in the royal guard, and now I find it impossible. I trust Fail de Liery, and I trust his men. I do not trust anyone else in this castle, nor should I as you well may know. So I am protecting my life and the life of my son, and my son's throne as best I can. If you can think of a better way, please share it."

Hespero rubbed his forehead and sighed. "You are not a fool, Majesty. You must understand the repercussions of this. Whatever you are actually doing, if Hansa perceives that you are installing some sort of Lierish regency here, they will send armies. I and the praifec of Hansa have been working tirelessly to prevent this war. If you continue down this path, we will fail."

She spread her hands. "Then tell me what to do, Praifec."

He was silent for a moment. Then, hesitantly, he cleared his throat. "Well, there is a precedent here," he said at last.

"What precedent do you refer to?"

"Three hundred years ago, Liery ruled most of Crotheny, but controlled only the western part—the east was in relative chaos, until it was ceded to Virgenya."

"Yes. The lords of Liery hadn't the strength to control it, and considered it preferable to have it under Virgenyan control than Hansan."

"Yes," the praifec agreed, "the animosity between Liery and Hansa runs very deep, to the days of the Hegemony, perhaps to before, when they were warring tribes. In any event, while the Church recognized the legal cession and the marriage that concluded it—the first in the series of Lierish and Virgenyan alliances of which you are the most immediate example—Hansa was the stronger nation, and prepared to take eastern Crotheny by force. Or retake it, as they might put it, since it was originally tribes from Hansa that broke the hold of the Hegemony in this region."

"I see," Muriele said, stiffening. "You're suggesting I allow a *Pax Sacer*."

The praifec nodded. "As it was done then. His eminence the Fratrex Prismo could be persuaded to lend troops to secure the peace and allay suspicions that you are showing favoritism."

"And yet fifty years later, Hansa conquered all of Crotheny, east and west."

"True, but only after the *pax* was put aside."

"So your suggestion is that I allow the occupation of this city by troops from Vitellia."

"From z'Irbina," Hespero corrected. "The most holy Fratrex Prismo's own men. Only until the political situation here is peacefully resolved. It is the best way, Majesty. Hansa will never dare go against the Church. Peace will be preserved, countless lives saved."

Muriele closed her eyes. It was tempting. If she gave control to the Church, she could rest. She could concentrate on protecting the children she had left.

"The Church hasn't taken sides on the part of any country in three hundred years," she said. "Why now?"

"Surely you understand, Majesty, that this goes well beyond determining who will sit the throne of Crotheny a year hence. A great evil has risen in the world, one we do not understand, but one which we cannot ignore.

"You've read the latest reports from Duke Artwair, in the east? Half his men have been slain by what can only be described as hordes of naked madmen, by demons and monsters the likes of which the world has not seen since the Warlock Wars. Whole towns have been destroyed, and the east empties out. Eslen is near to bursting from the refugees, and we are still losing ground.

"But it isn't just on the frontiers—Broogh was in the heart of Newland, and destroyed by an unholy creature none of us suspected remained in the world. Now is the time for nations to unite, not for them to be divided. You must stand together against this dark rising of the tide, not fight amongst yourselves as it drowns you. That is what I am offering you—not merely the chance to save this earthly throne, but to make it possible for us all to combat the *real* foe— together."

"Under the leadership of z'Irbina."

Hespero fingered his beard. "The reason we do not take sides in the secular conflicts of nations, Majesty, is because we have a higher calling. Virgenya Dare cleansed our world of the first evil, of the Skasloi. And yet it seems that no matter how well and deeply evil is defeated, it always returns, in a different guise. It is the Church which took up Virgenya Dare's mantle and her mission. When the Black Jester rose, it was through the leadership of the Church that he was thrown down in defeat."

"Yes. And then the Church ruled most of the known world for six hundred years."

"It was a golden age," Hespero said, frowning at her tone. "The most perfect peace and prosperity Everon has ever known."

"You wish a return to that?"

"We could do worse, but I am suggesting no such outcome. What I am saying is that we must be unified, and not through war or con- quest. We need a cleansing, a *resacaratum*, that will prepare us for the great test to come. The *resacaratum* has already begun, Majesty, within the Church itself, but it must—it will—go further than that."

"You're asking me to let an army march through my gates and oc- cupy my country without a fight."

"By holy mandate, Majesty. To bring the peace and justice Crotheny so desperately needs."

"What if I refuse?" Muriele asked.

Hespero's face seemed to wither a little. "Then you deal us all a mortal blow," he said. "But we *will* be unified—we will fight this evil somehow. I am suggesting the best course of action, but not the only one."

"Suggest another," she challenged.

He shook his head, and his eyes glinted strangely. "It should not come to that. Please, Majesty—will you at least consider my words?"

"Of course, Praifec," she said. "They are wise words, and these are large matters, and I am tired. We will speak of this again soon. Be prepared to tell me in more specifics how your plan would be implemented."

"I pray the saints send you their best judgment, Majesty." He bowed and left, leaving Muriele with the distinct impression that she had been threatened.

Hespero seemed sincere, and he was correct—something terrible was happening in the world, and he probably knew more about it than she did. The Church's intention might be entirely pure, and it was entirely possible that Hespero was right, that allowing sacred troops in her city would be the best for everyone.

But she saw what the praifec had carefully hinted at, as well. Whatever the Church's ultimate motives and intentions, they needed a tool to accomplish them. A nation. If Crotheny would not be that nation, only Hansa remained.

She was still considering that when they brought in Alis Berrye, who was still wearing the dressing gown Muriele had last seen her in.

"Majesty," the girl murmured, bowing. She stood uncomfortably as Muriele appraised her. She was a pretty thing—there was no way around that, even with the dark circles under her sapphire eyes and her curly hair in absolute disarray.

"She has been searched?" she asked the man-at-arms.

"Yes, Majesty. She has no weapons."

"You searched her hair?"

"Ah—no, Majesty. But I shall."

He proceeded to do just that. Berrye took it with a tiny smile on her face.

"Do I seem so dangerous to you, Majesty?" she asked.

Muriele didn't answer, but nodded toward the man-at-arms. "Please leave us, sir," she said.

When the door was closed behind him, Muriele settled into an armchair.

"Lady Berrye," she said. "Much has happened in the past few bells. Doubtless you have heard some of the rumors."

"Some, Majesty," she allowed.

"Someone tried to kill me last night."

"That's terrible."

"Thank you. I know you've never wished me anything but the best of health."

Berrye looked puzzled. "I never have, Majesty. I have always admired you and wished you well."

"Even when you were in bed with my husband?"

"Of course."

"But it never occurred to you that it might bother me?"

Berrye shrugged. "That was a matter between you and His Majesty. If it bothered you, he was the one to tell. Unless I was the *only* one of his mistresses you took exception to."

"You are too bold, perhaps," Muriele said, "especially now, when you don't enjoy his protection."

"I have no one's protection, Majesty," Berrye said. "I am most acutely aware of that."

Something was wrong here, Muriele realized. Wasn't *anything* the way she thought it was?

"You *are* too bold," she repeated. "Where is the simpering, nervous girl who used to cower when I entered the room?"

Again, Berrye smiled faintly. "She died with William."

"You will refer to my late husband as his Majesty or as the king or not at all, Lady Berrye."

"Very well," she said easily.

"Enough of this," Muriele said. "My time is precious. You wrote to me claiming that I was in danger. Within a few bells of that correspondence, there was an attempt on my life. If you want that head of yours to stay where it is, you'll explain to me—this moment—precisely what you know."

If Berrye was surprised that Muriele knew she had left the note, she didn't show it. She stood straight, without any fidgeting, and met Muriele's gaze squarely. "I will tell you everything I know, Majesty, but I believe my letter also mentioned my own need for protection."

"At this moment, you need protection from me. And the only thing that will save you is the truth."

Berrye acknowledged that with a small nod of her head.

"Do you know *why* His Majesty was on the headland of Aenah that day?" she asked Muriele.

"You're going to tell me you know?"

"Prince Robert came to the king, in the Warhearth. He had been gone for some time, on a secret embassy to Saltmark. When he returned, he brought something with him—the severed finger of Princess Lesbeth."

"Lesbeth." Lesbeth was William's younger sister, Robert's twin. She had long been missing.

"Prince Robert claimed that Lesbeth's betrothed—Cheiso of Safnia—had betrayed her into the hands of the Duke of Austrobaurg, who was holding her hostage."

"For what ransom?"

"Saltmark, you remember, was pursuing a war against the Sorrow Isles. The ransom was that His Majesty arrange to secretly aid them in that war."

Muriele crossed her arms. "The Sorrows are a Lierish protectorate and thus under our protection, as well. He could not do that."

"His Majesty could and did," Berrye said. "You must know how much he loved Lesbeth."

"Everyone loved Lesbeth. But to aid our enemies in a war against our friends—William was rarely that poor in judgment."

"Prince Robert pushed him into it—he was very convincing, especially since he had Lesbeth's finger as proof. Ships from Crotheny, under assumed banners, attacked and sank twenty Sorrovian ships. His Majesty went to Aenah to collect the princess Lesbeth, and there he was betrayed."

"By whom? Austrobaurg was killed, as well." But a terrible sense was emerging, now. Perhaps the Lierish arrows that had slain her husband's guard had not been artificially planted after all. Perhaps it really had been the retribution of some Lierish lord who knew what William had done.

And if that were true, did Fail de Liery know? Had this entire attempt on her life been designed to lead her directly into his hands?

"I have a guess as to who the betrayer was," Berrye said, "but no certain proof."

"Well?"

The girl paced a few steps, hands clasped behind her back. Then she turned to face Muriele again. "Did you know that Ambria Gramme had another lover?" she asked.

Muriele snorted. "Whom *didn't* she spread her legs for—that's the question."

Berrye shook her head. "This was a very secret lover. A very important one."

"Do not tire me, Lady Berrye. Who was he?"

A small look of triumph spread across Berrye's face. "Prince Robert," she said.

Muriele took a moment to absorb that fact. After the initial shock, she realized that it wasn't really that surprising. Robert had always wanted what William possessed. He had even tried to seduce Muriele a time or two.

"What of it?"

"Prince Robert convinced His Majesty to pay the ransom. Prince Robert set the time and the place for both His Majesty and Austrobaurg to meet. Only the prince knew all the details."

"You believe Robert betrayed William to his death?"

"I believe it."

"Despite the fact that Robert was also killed in the ambush?"

Berrye blinked. "Robert was never found, Majesty."

"They only found part of William," Muriele said. "He was thrown into the sea. Presumably Robert . . ." She trailed off. Why had she so easily assumed Robert was dead? Because everyone else had?

"What has this to do with Gramme?" she demanded.

"I recently heard her speak of the prince as if she knew he was still alive. She intimated that she had seen him."

"She said this to you?"

"No," Berrye admitted, "but I heard it, nevertheless. And I think she knows it."

"You've made it your business to hear a great many things, it would seem," Muriele noticed.

"Yes, Majesty, I have."

"And *how* did you hear all of this?"

"I think you know, Majesty," Berrye said, pushing her disorderly curls away from her face, finally showing a bit of real nervousness. "The same way you knew who had left you the note."

"So. William knew about the passages."

To her surprise, Berrye laughed, a terse little giggle. "His Majesty? No, he knew nothing of them."

Muriele frowned. "Then how did you—?" It hit her then. "You're coven trained."

Berrye nodded infinitesimally.

Muriele sat back, trying to reform her picture of the girl, wondering if there was anything at all solid in her life.

"Did Erren know?" she asked, her voice sounding weak to her own ears.

"I do not think so, Majesty. We were not of the same order."

A chill tightened Muriele's spine. "There is only the order of Cer." But Erren herself had voiced the opinion that there were other, illicit orders.

"There is another," Berrye confirmed.

"And they sent you here."

"Yes, Majesty. To keep my eyes and ears open, to stay near the king."

Now it was Muriele's turn to laugh, though somewhat bitterly. "That you did most admirably well. Aren't you supposed to be celibate?"

Berrye looked down, shyly, and for the first time since the conversation had begun looked no older than her nineteen years. "My order has no such restrictions," she murmured.

"I see. And why come to me now with this knowledge?"

Berrye looked back up. Her eyes were round and threatening tears. "Because, Your Majesty, they are all dead—all my sisters. I am orphaned. And I believe their murderers were the same as those who killed William, Fastia, Elseny, and Lesbeth."

Muriele felt a sudden rush of sympathy, and her own grief threatened to surface, but she crushed it away. She would have time for that later, and she had already allowed herself to appear too weak in front of Berrye. Instead, she concentrated on the facts.

"Lesbeth? So Austrobaurg killed her?"

"I believe Austrobaurg never even saw her," Berrye said. "I think she died here, in Eslen."

"Then where did Robert get her finger?"

"From the author of all of this, of course. From the one who designed this entire tragedy."

"Gramme?"

"Or Robert. Or the both of them. I cannot say for sure."

"Robert loved Lesbeth better than anyone."

"Yes," Berrye said. "With a terrible love. I think an unnatural love that she did not share."

Muriele felt a sick twisting in her belly, and her mouth went dry. "And where is Robert now?"

"I don't know. But I think Ambria Gramme does."

"And where is she?"

"At her estates, preparing a fete of some sort."

"I've heard nothing of this," Muriele said.

"It was not widely advertised in Eslen."

"Then who attends it?"

"That I did not discover either," Berrye confessed.

Muriele sat back, her head whirling. She closed her eyes, hoping things would settle, but it was too much.

"If you have lied to me," she said at last, "you will not die quickly."

"I have not lied to you, Majesty," Berrye said. Her eyes were clear again, and her voice strong.

"Let us hope not," Muriele said. "Is there anything else you can tell me?"

"There is a good deal," Berrye said. "I can tell you which members of the Comven favor you and which do not. I can tell you who Gramme has on her side. And I can tell you she is planning to move against you soon."

"Have I cause to doubt Sir Fail and his men?"

"None that I know of."

Muriele sat up. "Lady Berrye, will you declare an oath to take me as your personal liege, swearing by whatever saints you swear by?"

"If you will protect me in turn, Majesty."

Muriele smiled. "You must know that I can barely protect myself."

"You have more power than you know," Berrye told her. "You just haven't learned how to use it. I can help you. I was trained for it."

"You would be my new Erren?" Muriele asked bitterly. "My new coven-trained bodyguard?"

"I would do that, Majesty. I swear it by the saints I swear by." She touched her forehead and breast with her thumb.

Muriele sighed. "I would be a great fool to trust you," she said.

"If I were already in your employ, I would tell you exactly that," Berrye said. "You have no reason to trust me. But I'm asking you to. You need me, and I need you. My entire order was slaughtered, women I loved. And believe me or not, but I cared for His Majesty. He was not a good king, but he was, for all his faults, a good man, and there are few such in the world. I would see those who brought him down go screaming to Mefitis, begging her mercy. And there is one more thing."

"What is that?" Muriele asked.

"Do not ask me to explain this. It is the one thing I cannot explain."

"Go on."

"Your daughter, Anne. She must live, and she must be queen."

A long shock ran through Muriele, starting at her feet and working up to the crown of her head.

"What do you know of Anne?" she demanded.

"That she is alive. That she was at Saint Cer. That the sisters of the coven Saint Cer, like those of my own order, were all murdered."

"But Anne escaped?"

"I have no proof, but I feel it in my heart. I see it in my dreams. But she has many enemies."

Muriele stared at the girl, wondering how she could have ever believed her to be the empty-headed pretty thing she had pretended to be. Even Erren had been fooled, which was remarkable. Alis Berrye was a very dangerous woman. She could also be a very useful ally.

Muriele rose and summoned the footman. "Give the lady Berrye an escort and instruct them to take her to her apartment, where she will retrieve her personal effects. Settle her in the small apartment down the hall. And please tell Sir Fail that I request his presence."

"You won't regret this, Majesty," Berrye said.

"See that I don't. Go along now, Lady Berrye."

She watched the girl go and then returned to her chair, ticking her finger against the wooden arm, waiting for Sir Fail.

It was time to pay a visit to her husband's other mistress. But she had another call to make first. One she had been avoiding.

She went to her dresser, and though she had made her decision, she hesitated before the small coffer, thinking of the Him, deep beneath the castle, where no light ever shone. His voice of silk and nightmare. She had not spoken to the Kept since that day she discovered the key in William's study, after his death.

But she had questions for him now. With no more faltering, she opened the wooden box.

The key was not there.

CHAPTER SIX

Observations on Diverse Things Such as Being Dead

By Stephen Darige

I had to learn to hear again once before. It was after I walked the faneway of Decmanis. Each stop along the way took something from me—the sensation in my hand first, then my hearing, then my sight—until there was nothing left of me but a body, not even a mind. Somehow I finished the path, and it all came back to me, but different, better.

That's how it is to be dead. I heard a lot at first, but it made no sense. It was just noise, like the wailing of ghosts in the halls of the damned. Then the noises began to make sense, and eventually to become familiar.

I can hear Aspar, Winna, and Ehawk, but my body is lost to me. I cannot speak to them or move a finger or an eyelid.

I remember I used to care for them.

I do still, in many ways. When Winna is near I can smell her, feel her, almost taste her. When she touches me, it sends shivers through me that somehow are not revealed on my dead flesh.

I heard her and Aspar last night. She smells different when they do that, sharper. So does Aspar.

Observations of the quaint and curious holter-beast—in the act of procreation, this ordinarily closemouthed creature vocalizes extraordinarily, though only in low tones. He makes rhymes of his lover's name—mina-Winna, fenna-Winna, and the inevitable winna-Winna. He calls her by other silly appellations of his own invention, notwithstanding that Winna is already a rather silly name.

There's someone new, a Sefry. Winna doesn't like her because Aspar does, though he denies it every way he can. I wonder if she looks like his wife, the dead one?

They're taking me to the next faneway, which for them is clever. I wonder what will happen there? The first was very strange, and I am hard put to explain why it affected me the way it did. It was consecrated to one of the damned saints, she who was known as the queen of demons. Perhaps Decmanis is punishing me for stepping on her faneway, and yet somehow that doesn't feel right. The only other possibility that occurs is that she is somehow also an aspect of Saint Decmanis, which would be very interesting indeed, not to mention heretical.

Can saints be heretics?

We're approaching the fane. I can feel it like a fire.

A SPAR SURVEYED THE CLEARING and the mound. The bodies were still there, and none of them were moving. Of the Briar King and his hunt there was no sign, save the dead bodies of slinders and the monks they had killed.

"Oh, saints," Winna said when she saw the carnage.

"Weak stomach?" Leshya asked.

"I've seen bodies like this before," Winna said. "But I don't have to pretend I like it."

"No, you don't," the Sefry agreed.

"So what do we do now?" Winna asked.

Aspar shrugged and dismounted. "Take Stephen up on the mound, I reckon. See what happens."

"Are you quite certain this is the wise thing to do?" Leshya asked.

"No," Aspar answered shortly.

Stepping carefully, they picked their way around where the bodies were thickest and up to the top of the sedos. Aspar laid Stephen out in the very middle.

As he'd more or less expected, nothing happened.

"Well, it was worth a try," he muttered. "You three watch him. I'm going to have a better look around."

Aspar walked back down through the carnage, feeling tired, angry at himself for having nursed such a forlorn hope. People died. He knew that by now, didn't he? He used to be easy about it.

The slinders looked like people now, their faces relaxed in death. They could have come from any village around the King's Forest. He was thankful that he didn't see anyone he knew.

After a time he wandered to the edge of the forest, and before he realized it found himself standing beneath the gnarled branches of the naubagm and the strands of rotted rope that hung from them. The earth had drunk a lot of blood in this place. It had drunk his mother's blood.

He'd never been told what brought her here. His father and foster mother rarely spoke of her, and when they did it was in hushed tones, and they made the sign against evil. Then they had died, and he'd ended up with Jesp.

A raven landed on the uppermost branch of the tree. Farther above, he saw the black silhouette of an eagle against the clouds. He took a deep breath and felt the land roll away from him, getting bigger, stretching out its bones of stone and sinews of root. He smelled the age and the life of it, and for the first time in a long while felt a kind of peaceful determination.

I'll fix this, he silently promised the trees.

"*I'll fix this.*" It was the first thing Jesp had said when she found him. He'd been running and bleeding for a day, the forest turned to shadow around him. When he finally fell, he'd dreamed he was still running, but now and then he woke and knew he was lying in the reeds of some marsh, half covered in water. He'd been awake when he heard her coming, and tried to reach for his knife, but he didn't have the strength to move. Seven winters old, he'd been. He still re-membered the way his breath whistled, because he'd kept forgetting that's what it was, kept thinking it was some sort of bird he'd never heard of.

Then he'd seen Jesp's face, that ancient, pale Sefry face. She stood there for what seemed a long time, while he tried to talk, and then she knelt down and touched his face with her bony fingers.

"I'll fix this," she said. "I'll fix you up, child-of-the-Naubagm."

How she knew that about him, she never said. But she raised him, and filled him with Sefry nonsense, and she died.

He missed her. And now that he knew that Sefry stories weren't all nonsense, he desperately wished he could talk to her again. He wished he'd paid more attention when she was alive. And maybe he wished that he'd thanked her, at least once.

But that was done.

He sighed and cracked his neck.

A few kingsyards north, something ran out of the forest, moving faster than a deer.

It was a man, dressed in the habit of one of the monks. He had a bow, and he was making straight for the sedos, where Aspar could still see the others.

With a silent curse, Aspar pulled a shaft from his quiver, set it to the string, and let it go.

The monk must have seen the motion from the corner of his eye—even as the arrow arced toward him, he dropped into a sudden crouch and whirled, firing at Aspar.

Aspar's shot missed by a thumb's breath; the monk's missed Aspar by just twice that.

Aspar stepped behind the Naubagm as the monk fitted and fired another arrow. It struck quivering into the ancient tree.

The monk turned again and sprinted toward the mound and out of range. Cursing—and at a much slower pace than his adversary—Aspar ran after him.

The monk did a strange, twisting dance, and Aspar realized that Ehawk and Leshya were firing at him now. Both missed, and before either could draw new arrows, the churchman shot back. Aspar watched in throat-choking helplessness as Ehawk jerked weirdly and fell. Winna was crouching, but still far too large a target.

Leshya fired again and again without success.

The monk's dodging gave Aspar a chance to get back in range, and he drew back to shoot, still running.

His bowstring snapped with a hollow thud.

He drew his ax, snarling.

Leshya drew and shot. This time the monk had to dodge so violently that he stumbled, but he rolled and came back up, facing Aspar.

Aspar threw the ax and sidestepped. The churchman's shaft sang through empty air, but the ax also missed.

The monk suddenly jogged to the right, and Aspar grimly understood he had no intention of closing for close combat. He'd just keep running and shooting until they were all dead or he was out of arrows.

He reached into his haversack, found his extra sinew, pulled it out to restring the bow. An arrow struck his boiled leather cuirass with a thump, and he cursed and dropped to the ground. He finished stringing his bow. Another arrow plowed the soil right in front of his nose, and now the monk was hurtling toward him again, ignoring Leshya.

Aspar nocked the arrow to his string, the bow turned flat to the ground. It was an awkward pull, and he knew the other man would have one more shot before he got his.

But the monk stumbled, an arrow suddenly standing in his thigh. He shouted, turned, and loosed his dart toward the mound, but another arrow hit him in the center of the chest, and he sat down, hard. Aspar fired, hitting him in the right collarbone, and the fellow pitched over, howling.

Leshya was on him almost immediately, kicking the bow from his hands.

"Don't kill him," a familiar voice shouted.

Aspar looked toward the mound. Stephen stood there, holding Ehawk's bow. Winna was running toward him, and nearly barreled him over with a hug.

Aspar couldn't stop the smile from raising his lips. It felt too good, seeing Stephen standing there.

"Sceat," he murmured. "It worked."

"Keep him alive," he told Leshya, waving at the monk.

She was already binding the man's hand with cords. "If it can be done," she said. "I've a few questions to ask him myself."

Aspar hesitated. She had helped in the fight. She had probably saved his life when the Briar King came. But trusting her—trusting any Sefry—was a foolish proposition.

She looked back up, as if he had shouted his thoughts. Her violet gaze held his for an instant, and then she shook her head in disgust and returned to her task.

Aspar took another good look around the clearing, then started toward Stephen and Winna, his step feeling lighter.

It grew heavier again when he saw Ehawk. The boy was sprawled on the grass, pawing weakly at an arrow in his thigh. The ground around him was slick with blood. Winna and Stephen were already ministering to him.

"Hello, Aspar," Stephen said without looking.

"It's good to see you up and—ah—alive," Aspar said.

"Yes, it's good to be that way," Stephen replied, not looking up from his task. "Winna, put something in his mouth so he doesn't bite his tongue off."

"I can deal with that, if you're not up to it," Aspar offered.

"No," Stephen said. "I trained for this. I'll do it. But I could use some foolhag for this wound, to stop the bleeding."

Aspar blinked. The last time Stephen had confronted a bleeding wound, he'd collapsed in a fit of vomiting and been useless. Now he bent over Ehawk, his hands slick with blood, working quick, sure, and steady. The boy had certainly changed in the few months he had known him.

"I'll find some," he said. "Ehawk, how are you, boy?"

"I've f-felt better," he gasped.

"I'll bring *saelic* for the pain," Aspar promised. "You just breathe deep and slow. Stephen knows what he's doin'."

He went after the herbs, hoping that was true.

As soon as Ehawk's bleeding was staunched and his leg bandaged, they put him on his horse, loaded the still-unconscious monk on Angel, and set off to get as far from the sedos as possible before nightfall.

"We're going the wrong way," Leshya said.

"I picked it, I'm in charge, it can't be the wrong way," Aspar pointed out.

"We should be following the monk's trail."

"What trail? The Briar King's hunt missed him, that's all."

"I doubt that," she said. "I think he came to bring them a message." She held up a document with some sort of seal on it.

"That's a Church seal," Stephen said from where he was riding by Ehawk, some ten yards away.

"Well, your eyes are still good," Aspar said.

"Yes." Stephen smiled.

"How are you?"

"A little confused. I don't know what's happened since—well, whatever it was happened."

"You don't remember?" Winna asked.

Stephen trotted nearer. "Not really. I remember going into the sedos and feeling strange. Or, rather, not feeling much of anything. The bodies made me sick—I was going to *be* sick—and then suddenly I didn't care. They might as well have been stones."

"The letter?" Leshya interrupted.

"Stephen is our friend," Winna snapped. "We thought he was dead. You're going to have to tend your own beehive for a breath or two."

Leshya shrugged and pretended interest in the forest.

"Was when you came down you fell," Aspar said.

Stephen shook his head. "I don't remember that, or anything else until I woke up on the sedos and saw you fighting the monk."

"That was a nice shot you made. Didn't know you could handle a bow so well."

"I can't," Stephen said.

"Then—?"

"You remember how I hit Desmond Spendlove with his knife? Sometimes I can see something done and—well, *do* it. It doesn't always work, and never with anything complicated. I can't watch someone fight with a sword and learn how to do it, though I might be able to make some of the strokes. But to know when to do them—that's different."

Shooting a bow isn't that simple either, Aspar thought. *You have to know the weapon, allow for the wind . . .*

Something was different about Stephen, but he couldn't say what.

"That was one of the, ah, saint gifts you got?" he asked.

"From walking the faneway of Saint Decmanis, yes."

"And do you have anything new like that? From this sedos?"

Stephen laughed. "Not that I know of. I don't feel any different. Anyway, I didn't walk the whole faneway, just two sedoi, if I understand what happened."

"But something happened," Aspar persisted. "The first killed you; the second brought you back to life."

"What would the next one do, I wonder?" Leshya asked.

"I've no intention of finding out," Stephen replied. "I'm alive, walking, breathing, I feel good—and I don't want to have anything more to do with the saint that faneway belongs to."

"You know the saint?" Leshya asked.

"There was a statue in the first one," Stephen said, "with a name: Marhirehben."

"I've never heard of him," Winna said.

"Her," Stephen corrected, "at least in that aspect, the saint is female. If the word *saint* really applies."

"What do you mean?"

"Marhirehben was one of the damned saints, whose worship was forbidden by the Church. Her name means 'Queen of Demons.' "

"How can a saint be completely forgotten?"

"She wasn't. You've heard of her—Nautha, Corpse Mother, the Gallows Witch—those are some of her names that survive."

"Nautha isn't a saint," Winna protested. "She's a monster from children's stories."

"So was the Briar King," Stephen said.

"Anyway, *somebody* remembers her old name." He frowned. "Or was reminded. She was mentioned in several of the texts I deciphered. Another of her aspects was 'mother devouring.' She who eats life and gives birth to death." He looked down. "They couldn't have done this without me, without my research."

"Stephen, this isn't your fault," Winna said.

"No," Stephen said. "It isn't. But I was an instrument of whoever's fault it is, and that doesn't please me."

"Then we should follow the monk's trail," Leshya said.

"Let me see the letter," Stephen said. "Then we can decide what to do. We were sent to find the Briar King, not to chase my corrupt brethren all over the King's Forest. It may be that one of us ought to take word back to the praifec."

"We already found the Briar King," Aspar said.

"What?" Stephen turned in his saddle.

"It was the Briar King and his creatures killed the rest of those monks back there," Aspar explained.

"You said something about the Briar King's hunt," Stephen said, "but I didn't realize you had seen *him* again. Then the arrow must not have worked."

"I didn't use it," Aspar said.

"Didn't use it?"

"The Briar King isn't the enemy," Leshya replied. "He attacked the monks and let us be."

"He is the enemy," Ehawk's voice came weakly. "He turns villagers into animals and makes them kill other villagers. He may hate the monks, but he hates all men."

"He's cleansing his forest," Leshya said.

"My people have lived in the mountains since the day the Skasloi fell," Ehawk said. "It is our right to live there."

Leshya shrugged. "Consider," she said. "He wakes, and discovers his forest is diseased, and from the rot monsters are springing which will only hasten its end. Utins, greffyns—the black thorns. It is the disease he is fighting, and so far as he is concerned, the people who live in this forest and cut its trees are part of that disease."

"He didn't kill us," Aspar pointed out.

"Because," she said, "like him, we are part of the cure."

"You don't know that," Stephen said.

Again she shrugged. "Not for certain, I suppose, but it makes sense. Can you think of another explanation?"

"Yes," Stephen said. "Something is wrong with the forest, yes, and terrible creatures are waking or being born. The Briar King is one of them, and like them he is mad, old, senile, and terribly powerful. He is no more our friend or our enemy than a storm or bolt of lightning."

"That's not so different from what I just said," Leshya replied.

Stephen turned to Aspar. "What do you think, holter?"

Aspar blew out a breath. "You may both be right. But whatever is wrong with the forest, the Briar King isn't the cause of it. And I think he is trying to fix it."

"But that could mean killing every man, woman, and child within its boundaries," Stephen pointed out.

"Yah."

Stephen's eyes widened. "You don't *care*! You care more about the trees than you do about the people."

"Don't talk for me, Stephen," Aspar cautioned.

"You talk, then. You tell me."

"Read the letter," Aspar said, to change a topic he wasn't sure about himself. "Then we'll reckon where to go from here. It may be that we should have another talk with the praifec."

Stephen frowned at him, but took the letter from Leshya's hand. When he examined the seal, he smiled grimly.

"Indeed," he said. "We may well want to have another conversation with Praifec Hespero. This is his seal."

CHAPTER SEVEN

AT THE BALL

"FRALET ACKENZAL?"

Leoff looked up at the young man who stood at his door. He had blue eyes and wispy yellow hair. His nose bent to one side, and he seemed a bit distracted by it.

"Yes?"

"If it please you, I've been sent to conduct you to the lady Gramme's affair."

"I . . . I'm quite busy," Leoff said, tapping the music notation on his desk. "I've a commission . . ."

The man frowned. "You *did* accept the lady's invitation."

"Well, yes, actually, but—"

The fellow wagged his finger as if Leoff were a naughty child. "Milady made it quite clear that she would be most insulted if you did not attend. She's had a new hammarharp brought in just for you."

"I see." Leoff cast his gaze desperately around the room in the vague hope that he would see something that would get him out of this predicament.

"I've not much to wear," he attempted.

The man smiled and beckoned to someone unseen. A round-faced girl dressed in servant's garb appeared, bearing a bundle of neatly folded clothes.

"I think these will fit you," the man said. "My name is Alvreic. I'm your footman for the night."

Seeing no escape, Leoff took the clothes and went to his bed-chamber.

Leoff watched the slowly turning saglwics of a malend on the side of the canal and shivered, both from the cold and the memory of that night near Broogh. A full moon, pale in the daylight, rose just behind it, and in the clear air he heard the distant barking of dogs. The autumn smell of hay was gone, replaced by the scent of ash.

"I had rather thought the ball was to be held in the castle," Leoff ventured.

"Is the coat not warm enough?"

"It's a beautiful coat," Leoff said. It was, for it was quilted and embroidered with leaves on the high collar and wide cuffs. He just wished it were as warm as it was pretty.

"The lady has excellent taste."

"Where *are* we going, may I ask?"

"Why, Grammeshugh, of course," Alvreic replied. "Milady's estate."

"I thought the lady Gramme lived in the castle."

"She does, most of the time, but she does have the estate, of course."

"Of course," Leoff repeated, feeling stupid.

He felt as if he were in one of those dreams where one kept getting farther and farther from one's goal, gradually forgetting altogether what that goal was.

He still remembered his intention had been to avoid the party. After Artwair's warning and the strange night with the queen, any connection to the lady Gramme seemed foolish.

So he'd decided to pretend he'd forgotten her invitation. That had clearly failed, so his next-best hope had been to make a brief appearance and then quietly excuse himself. Now somehow he'd left the castle, passed down through the gates of the city, and onto a narrowboat headed back out across Newland. It would be night soon, and the city gates would close—it would be tomorrow before he could get back to his rooms.

He should simply have refused to go, but it was too late for that. Now he could only hope the queen didn't find out.

The world darkened, and Leoff huddled against it. For him, there was no longer anything innocent about the night. It hid things, but unfairly it did not hide him. On the contrary, it seemed as if he were prey for everything out there, and he felt hunted. He even slept with a lamp lit, these nights.

Presently he noticed a line of cheerful lights ahead, and as they drew nearer saw lanterns strung along the side of the canal. They led up to a quayside pavilion, where twice a score or more canal boats were docked.

Music was in the air. He first heard the high, sweet voice that sounded like a flageolet, but with a more haunting timber and odd glissando passages between certain notes. The rhythm was odd, too, first in two, then in three, to two, broadening to four. The unpredictability of it made him grin.

So did the underlying play of the croth and the bright comments of a push-pull. The tune seemed light and cheerful, but overall it felt melancholy, because the foundation was a slow, deep movement of a bass vithul, played with a bow.

It wasn't exactly like any music he had ever heard, which was both exciting and strange.

They were near enough to dock before the lantern light showed him the faces of the players—four Sefry men, their broad hats set aside for night, faces like silver sculptures in the moonlight.

Two normal men came to take the bowline and tie the boat up. Ignoring his guide, Leoff stepped off onto the quay and approached the Sefry, hoping to speak with one of them. The flageolet, he saw, had no windcap; the musician was blowing directly onto the diagonal cut made into the bone—ivory?—instrument. The other instruments were standard, so far as he could see.

"Come, come," Alvreic said. "Make haste. You're late already."

The musicians showed no sign that they noticed his attentions, and the song did not seem near its end.

The lanterns continued up a low hill, limning a road that led to the looming shadow of a manse. As Leoff and Alvreic made their way silently up to the estate, a voice joined the music, and everything about the piece snapped into place in a way that brought a sigh to his lips. He strained to hear the words, but they weren't in the king's tongue. He had a sudden, vivid image of the cottage by the sea where he had grown up. He saw his sister Glinna playing in his mother's garden, her blond hair muddy, her face huge with smile, his father on a stool, playing a little croth.

A pile of stones, that house now. Ghosts, his father and sister.

And it suddenly seemed he *did* understand the words, if only for an instant.

Then the din from the manse trod over the Sefry melody. There was music in that, too, a familiar country dance that seemed heavy and vulgar after what he'd just heard. But by the laughter and shouts he made out along with it, he guessed it was pleasing to most of its audience.

Presently they reached a pair of immense iron-bound doors, which—at a sign from Alvreic to someone unseen—slowly creaked open. A doorman in bright green hose and brown tunic greeted them.

"Leovigild Ackenzal," Alvreic said. "He's to be announced."

Leoff held back a sigh. So much for avoiding notice.

They followed the doorman down a long, candlelit hall to another pair of doors, which also swung open, this time to reveal a hall ablaze with lamp- and candlelight. Sounds came pouring out, music mixed with the chatter of the crowd. The musicians were at the far end, a quartet, now playing a pavane. Perhaps twenty couples were dancing to it, and easily twice as many standing about in conversation.

But as he entered the room, all that stopped, and more than a hundred people turned to regard him. The music fell silent.

"I present Leovigild Ackenzal," the doorman announced in a clear, carrying voice. "Composer to the court and hero of Broogh."

Leoff wasn't sure what he had been expecting, but the sudden roar of applause took him utterly by surprise. He'd performed before the public before, of course, and had received praise for his composi- tions. But this—this was something different. He felt his face red- dening.

The lady Gramme appeared suddenly on his arm, coming from nowhere. She leaned in to peck his cheek, then turned back to the crowd. Leoff noticed someone else stepping up on his other side, a young man. He put a hand on Leoff's shoulder. Leoff could only stand there, feeling more and more uncomfortable.

When the crowd finally quieted, Lady Gramme curtsied to them. Then she smiled at Leoff.

"I suppose I might have told you that you were the guest of honor," she said.

"I beg your pardon?" Leoff blurted.

But Gramme already had turned back to the crowd. "Fralet Ackenzal is nothing if not modest, my friends, and it won't do to em- barrass him too much, nor would it do for me to keep him to myself, when so many of you wish to visit with him. But this *is* my house, af- ter all, and I'm allowed a few liberties."

She smiled through the chorus of laughter that followed her state- ment. Then, when she spoke again, her voice was suddenly serious.

"This hall is full of light," she said. "But do not be fooled. Outside there is darkness, whether the sun is shining or no. These are hard days, terrible days, and what makes it worse is that our own courage seems to have deserted us. Adversity crowns heroes, isn't that the old saying? And yet who has been crowned here? Who has stepped forth from the shadows of our tragedies and taken a strong hand against the rising evil? I—like you—have despaired that such men no longer seem to be born in this world. And yet this man, a stranger to our country, not even trained as a warrior, has been our savior, and I hereby crown him our hero! From hence, let him carry the title of *Cavaor!*"

Something settled on Leoff's head as the crowd began cheering again. He felt it and realized it was a metal circlet.

The crowd suddenly stilled again, and Leoff waited nervously to see what would happen next.

"I think they'd like a word from you," the lady said.

Leoff blinked, surveying the waiting faces.

He cleared his throat.

"Ah, thank you," he said. "It is most unexpected. Most. I, umm—but you haven't got it quite right."

He glanced at Gramme nervously, and his tension increased when he saw the small wrinkle that appeared between her eyes.

"You were at Broogh, weren't you?" someone shouted.

"I was there," Leoff said. "I was, but I wasn't alone. That is, no credit goes to me. Duke Artwair and Gilmer Oercsun, they deserve the credit. But lady, I have to disagree with you. I haven't been here long, but this country has many heroes. A townful of them. They died for you at Broogh."

"Hear, hear," a few shouted.

"There is no doubt of that," Gramme said. "And we thank you for helping us to honor them." She shook her finger at him as if scolding a child. "But I was present when Duke Artwair gave his report, and if there is one man in this kingdom who does have the courage and sense of his ancestors, it is the duke. Indeed, I wished to have the duke here tonight, but it seems he has been ordered to the eastern marches, far from the court and Eslen. Still, in his absence, I will not dispute his word, Cavaor Ackenzal, and should hope you would not either."

"I would never do that," Leoff said.

"I did not think so. Well, enough of my talking. Be at home here, Leoff Ackenzal—you are among friends. And should the mood strike you, I hope you will try my new hammarharp, and tell me if it is as well-tuned as I am assured it is."

"Thank you, milady," Leoff said. "I'm really quite overwhelmed. I'll examine it right away."

"I don't imagine you will," she said, "but you are welcome to try."

She was right. He's gone only a few steps before a young woman of perhaps sixteen had taken his arm.

"Won't you dance with me, cavaor?"

"Ah . . ." He blinked stupidly at her. She was pretty, with a friendly, oval face, dark brown eyes, and red-gold hair hanging in ringlets.

The music had started again, a whervel in triple meter.

He glanced around. "I don't know this dance," he said. "It seems a bit lively."

"You'll pick it up," she assured him, taking his hands. "My name is Areana."

"It's my pleasure to meet you," Leoff said, fumbling at the steps. As she said, it wasn't difficult—very much like the country rounds of his youth—soon he had it.

"I'm fortunate to be the first to dance with you," Areana said. "It's good luck."

"Really," Leoff said, feeling his neck burn. "Too much has been made of this. Tell me of yourself, rather. What family are you?"

"I'm a Wistbirm," she replied.

"Wistbirm?" He shook his head. "I'm new to this country."

"There's no reason you should have heard of us," she said.

"Well, it must be a good family to have produced such a charming daughter," he said, feeling suddenly bold.

She smiled at that. It felt good, dancing with her. His leg was still stiff, and occasionally moved awkwardly, so their bodies bumped. It had been a long time since he'd been this close to a woman, and he found himself enjoying it.

"What's the court like?" she asked.

"Haven't you been there?"

She stared at him and then giggled. "You think I'm nobility?"

Leoff blinked. "I suppose I did."

"No, we're just lowly landwaerds, my family—though my father is the Aethil of Wistbirm. Do you find me less charming now?"

"No less," he replied, though now he realized that she had the accent he'd heard in the countryside—not as thick as Gilmer's but still marked—and very different from the lilt of the court speech he'd come to know. "It's not as if I have noble blood myself."

"And yet there is such nobility in you."

"Nonsense. I was terrified. I barely remember what happened, and it's a miracle I wasn't killed."

"I think it was a miracle that brought you to us," Areana said.

The song ended with a sort of bumping bang, and Areana stepped back from him.

"I shan't hog you," she said. "The other ladies will never forgive me."

"Thank you very much for the dance," he replied.

"Next time you will have to ask me," she said. "A girl in my position can only be so bold."

There was no shortage of bold girls, however, all of whom, as it turned out, were from the landwaerd families. After the fourth dance, he begged a break, and made toward where the servers were dispensing wine.

"Eh, cavaor," a rough voice said. "How about a dance for me?"

Leoff spun on the voice, delighted. "Gilmer!" He shouted, and caught the little man up in a hug.

"Hey, now," the man grumbled. "I was just joking. I'm not hopping about with you."

"But where were you earlier, when Her Ladyship was giving the honors? This ball should be for you, not me."

Gilmer laughed and clapped his shoulder, then whispered, "I snuck in with a crowd. But never fear—this party aens't for neither of us."

"What do you mean?"

"Weren't you listening to the lady's pretty speech? Haven't you noticed the quality of the guests?"

"Well, they seem to be mostly landwaerden."

"Auy. Oh, there's nobility about—there's Her Ladyship, of course, and the Greft of Nithergaerd over there in the blue, the Duke of Shale, Lord Fallow, Lord Fram Dagen, and their ladies, but most here are landwaerden or fraleten. Country- and townfolk."

"It seems an odd sort of party for a lady of the court to throw," Leoff admitted.

Gilmer reached for a passing tray and snagged them two cups of wine.

"Let's walk a bit," he said. "Have a look at your hammarharp."

They moved toward the instrument, which was still across the room.

"These families here are the backbone of Newland," Gilmer said. "They may not have noble blood, but they have money, and they have

militias, and they have the loyalty of those who work the land. They
haven't been happy with the noble families for a generation, but things
are worse now, especially since what happened at Broogh. There's a
deep canal between the royals and the people out here, and it's getting deeper and wider every day."

"But Duke Artwair—"

"He's a different sort, and as the lady Gramme said, he's been
sent away, hasn't he? And the emperor don't turn his eye here. He
don't hear us or see us, and he don't help us."

"The emperor—," Leoff began.

"I know about the emperor," he said. "But his mother, the
queen—where is she? We've heard nothing from her."

"But she—" He stopped, unsure if he was allowed to mention his
commission.

He sipped his wine. "What is this, then?" he asked. "Why am I
here?"

"I don't know," Gilmer replied. "But it's something dangerous.
I only slipped in to warn you. I'll be leaving as soon as I see my
chance."

"Wait. What do you mean, something dangerous?"

"When the nobles court the landwaerds like this, it's not usually
just to be friendly. Especially when no one seems to know who is
really in control of this country. The lady Gramme has a son, you
know—he was standing just next to you. I suppose you know who his
father was."

"Oh," Leoff said.

"Auy. Take my advice—play something on that hammarharp and
then get out of here."

Leoff nodded, wondering if Alvreic would take him back if he
asked.

They had reached the instrument. It was beautiful, maple lacquered a deep red with black-and-yellow keys.

"What are you doing, now that your malend is burned?"

"Duke Artwair arranged a new position," Gilmer said. "One of the
malends on Saint Thon's Graf, near Meolwis. Not too far from here."

"I'm glad to hear that."

He settled on the stool and glanced back up. Gilmer was gone. With a sigh he touched the keyboard and started playing.

It was an old composition of his, one that had pleased the Duke of Glastir very well. He'd once been pleased with it, too, but now it felt clumsy and childish. He pushed on to the end, adding variations in hopes of making it more interesting, but when he was done, it felt hollow.

To his surprise, the final notes were greeted by applause, and he realized a small crowd had gathered, Lady Gramme among them.

"Enchanting," she said. "Please play something else."

"Whatever you would like, milady."

"I wonder if I could commission a piece from you."

"I would be pleased to do so, though I've already agreed to one commission I must complete first."

"I was rather thinking you could invent something for this occasion," she said. "I'm told you can do such things, and I've made a wager with the Duke of Shale that you can make an impromptu that pleases."

"I could try," he agreed reluctantly.

"But see here," said the duke, a puffy man in a jacket that looked too tight, "how shall we know if he is inventing and not playing some obscure older piece?"

"I think we can trust to his honor," Gramme replied.

"Not where my purse is concerned," the duke huffed.

Leoff cleared his throat. "If it please you, Duke, hum a snatch of some favorite tune of yours."

"Well . . ." He considered for a moment, then whistled a few notes. The crowd murmured laughter, and Leoff wondered exactly what sort of tune it was.

Leoff spied Areana in the crowd. "And you, my dear," he said. "Give me another melody."

Areana blushed. She looked around nervously, then sang:

Waey cunnad min loof, min goth moder?
Waey cunnad min werlic loof?

Thus cunnad in at, is paed thin loof
That ne nethal Niwhuan Coonth

She had a sweet soprano voice.

"Very well," Leoff said, "that's a start."

He began with Areana's tune, because it began with a question: "How will I know my lover, good mother? How will I know my true love?" He put it in a plaintive key, with a very light bass line, and now the mother answered, in fuller, more colorful chords, "You'll know him by his coat, which has never known a needle."

He separated the two halves of the melody now, and began weaving them through each other, and as counterpoint added in the duke's whistle near the top of the hammarharp's range. When they heard that, almost everyone laughed, and Leoff himself smiled. He'd guessed the juxtaposition of the lover's riddle song against the other, probably vulgar tune, would amuse, and now he made it a dialogue: the girl asking how she would know her lover, the leering lecher who overheard her, and the stern mother warning the fellow away, bringing it all to a head with a sort of bang as the mother threw a crock at the man and he ran off, his melody quickly fading, until only the girl remained.

Waey cunnad min loof? . . .

Raucous applause followed, and Leoff suddenly felt as if he'd been playing in a tavern, but unlike the polite and often insincere acknowledgment he'd had in the various courts he had entertained, this felt sincere to the bone.

"That's really quite remarkable," Lady Gramme said. "You have a rare talent."

"My talent," Leoff said, "such as it is, belongs to the saints. But I'm glad I pleased you."

The lady smiled and began to say something else, but then a sudden commotion at the door made everyone turn. Leoff heard a clash of steel and a howl of pain, and grim-faced men in armor bearing swords burst into the hall, followed by archers. The room seemed to explode into chaos; Leoff tried to get up, but someone bumped into him from behind and he tumbled to the floor.

"By order of the emperor," a heavy voice thundered above the general din, "you are all arrested for collaboration against the throne."

Leoff tried to rise, but a boot struck him in the head.

CHAPTER EIGHT

SWANMAY

NEIL TENSED HIMSELF AND saw all his roads go black. If he killed Swanmay, he would protect Anne's destination and serve the queen in the only way he now could. But to kill a woman he had promised not to harm would be the end of any honor he could claim.

Either way, he was certainly dead.

He stared at Swanmay's white throat, willing her closer, wondering how he could have been so wrong about her.

She bowed her head slightly, and wisps of her short hair fell across her face. "I wish I could grant you your wish, Sir Neil," she said. "But I cannot take you to Paldh. I am nearly free, do you understand? If I help you more than I have, I jeopardize everything. And you would probably be killed, which I would not see."

He let his head relax on the pillow. Bright spots danced in his vision, and for a moment he wondered if she had enchanted him somehow.

But he recognized the onset of the battle rage. It was leaving him now, but his blood was still moving too fast, and he was beginning to shake.

"Are you well?" she asked.

"I was dizzy for a moment," he said. "Please. What did you mean—about me being killed?"

"I told you that your friends' ship escaped the harbor, and that much was true. But they were followed—I saw the ship sail after them. If they are not caught at sea, they will be caught at Paldh. I imagine there will be a fight then, and you are in no condition to fight."

"I beg you, lady. Take me to Paldh. Whatever your trouble— whatever it is you are fleeing—I will protect you from it. But I must reach Paldh."

"I believe you would try to protect me," Swanmay said. "But you would fail. Don't you understand? The people who attacked your friends—I flee them also. Your enemy is my enemy. I took a greater risk than you can know saving your life. If they had noticed me, recognized my ship, all would have been done. If I follow them, they cannot fail to know me."

"But—"

"You know you would not be able to protect me," she said softly. "The *nauschalk* cannot be slain. He beat you when you were hale and whole—do you think you could do better now?"

"Nauschalk? You knew him? Know what he is?"

"Only from the old tales. Such things are no longer supposed to exist, and until a short time ago, they did not. But now the law of death has been broken."

Her voice had gone a little eerie, as if she spoke to him from a great distance. Her eyes were mirrors.

Neil tried to sit up. "Who are you, lady, to speak of such things? Are you a shinecrafter?"

She smiled weakly. "I know something of those arts, and others you will not have heard of."

"I cannot believe that," Neil said, feeling cold. "You are too kind, lady. You cannot be evil."

Her brow dropped in a frown, but her mouth bent up at one side. She steepled her fingers together. "Thank you," she said. "I don't think I'm evil. But why would you think I am?"

"Shinecrafters are evil, milady. They practice forbidden arts, abhorred by the Church."

"Do they?" she asked.

"So I have always been told. So I have always believed."

"Then perhaps you have been wrong. Or perhaps I *am* evil, and we merely disagree on what evil is."

"There can be no disagreement there, milady," Neil said. "Evil is what it is."

"You live in a simple world, Sir Neil. I do not begrudge you that. In truth, I envy you. But I believe things to be more complicated."

He was about to retort, when he remembered the choice he had been facing only moments before. Maybe it *was* more complicated. He was no churchman, to debate such things.

The law of death has been broken. Fastia had said that, in Eslen-of-Shadows.

"Lady, my apologies. You speak of things I don't understand. What is the law of death?"

She chuckled. "Simply that things that die stay dead."

"Are you saying that the man I fought was dead?"

"No, not exactly. But he exists because someone who should be dead is not. Someone has passed beyond the lands of fate and returned. That changes the world, Sir Neil, breaks something in it. It allows things to happen that could not before, creates magicks that have never existed. It is what allowed me to escape."

"Escape from where, lady? Who pursues you?"

She shook her head. "It is an old story, yes? The woman locked in the tower, awaiting a prince who would rescue her? And yet I waited, and did my duty, and no man came. So I had to escape myself."

"What tower?"

She combed her fingers through her hair and then dropped her head down, the first motion he had seen from her that resembled defeat. "No," she whispered, "I cannot trust you that much. I cannot trust anyone that much."

"Your crew? What about them?"

"With them I have no choice—and I believe they love me. If I were wrong about them, you and I would not be speaking now. Still, in a day or a month or a year, one of them will betray me. It is the way of men."

"You have seen this in some vision?"

"No. But it is most likely."

Neil sighed. "You are nothing if not a mystery, Lady Swanmay."

"Then perhaps I am nothing."

"I do not think so."

She smiled wistfully. "I would help you if I could, Sir Neil. I cannot."

"Then put me off at the next port," he urged. "Let me make my own way. I won't tell anyone about you."

"Is my company so tiresome?" she asked.

"No. But my duty—"

"Sir Neil, believe me when I say that the pain of leaving behind your obligations will fade."

"Never. And you cannot think so, either. You are too good for that."

"A moment ago you called me evil."

"I didn't. I said you couldn't be."

She considered that. "I suppose you did, in a roundabout way." She shrugged. "But whether you are right or not, I must believe that there is more to life than duty."

"There is," Neil said. "But without duty, the rest of it is meaningless."

She stood and paced away from the lamplight, then turned to regard him with a slightly feral glint in her eye. "When you fell in the water," she said, her words measured carefully, "you were still conscious. Yet you didn't try to take off your armor. Not a single catch was unfastened."

"I didn't think to take it off, at least not until it was too late," Neil replied.

"Why? You are not stupid. Armor is not new to you. Any man who was drowning would have tried to take it off, and instantly unless—"

"What, lady?"

"Unless he thought of his armor as so much a part of himself that he believed he could *not* take it off. Unless he would rather die than take it off. As if, perhaps, he wished to die."

He felt a moment's disorientation. How could she—? "I have no wish to die, Swanmay," Neil insisted.

She stepped back into the light. "Who was she? Was it Fastia?"

Now it felt as if he had been struck by a spinning bolt. He opened his mouth before his sense overtook him.

"I don't know that name," he lied.

"You spoke it many times as you slept. She is the one you love, yes, not the girl on the ship?" She lowered her voice further. "The King of Crotheny had a daughter by that name. They say she was slain at Cal Azroth."

"Who are you, lady?" Neil demanded.

"No one," she replied. "Your secret is safe with me, Neil MeqVren. The only reason I ask these questions is to satisfy my own curiosity."

"I cannot trust you about that."

"I know. Did you really want to die?"

Neil sighed and laid his head back. "You change targets so frequently, lady."

"No. This is the one I have aimed at all along."

"I did not seek to die," Neil said. "But I was—I think I was relieved. Relieved that there was nothing I could do."

"And then I spoiled it all."

"You saved my life, and I am grateful."

Swanmay regarded her nails. "There was a time, Sir Neil," she said, "when I stood with a razor in my hand and contemplated my wrists. There was another when I held a goblet of poison, fingers away from my lips. Of anyone I have ever known, I think you might understand why, how the unstoppable crush of duty can extinguish the flames in us."

"Duty *is* the flame in me."

"Yes. And when you fail it, or worse, when it fails you, there is nothing left."

"No."

"I shed my armor, Sir Neil. I did not drown. I will find better things to fill my life with, better reasons to rise one day to the next."

"But you haven't found them yet."

"Now you shoot at my target."

"It seems only fair."

"You've missed," she said. "I've no longer any target to shoot at." She came and sat by him again.

"I do not care who you are, Sir Neil. I do not care whom you have served. But I would like you to serve me. I need someone like you, someone I can trust."

Neil smiled faintly. "If I betray one master, how could you ever trust me not to betray you?"

She nodded. "I suppose you have a point. I was hoping you wouldn't make it."

"But you'd already thought of it."

"Of course. But it seems to me you have been the one betrayed, not the other way around."

"The one I serve has never betrayed me."

"That isn't what you mumble in your sleep," Swanmay said. "I will go now. Think about what I've said."

"I do not think I will change my mind. I beg you once more—let me off at the next port."

"If you decline my offer, I will put you off when you are well enough to travel, though not before," she said.

He watched her leave, and through the open door heard the squeal of gulls. He waited a moment, then, ignoring the pain in his side, he went to the porthole.

The sapphire sea danced beneath the sun, and less than a league away, he made out a coast.

Then it wasn't a trick. If their course had been set for Paldh, they would be in deep water. No island in the southern Lier Sea was as big as that.

He sank back down onto the bed, wondering what he mumbled in his sleep. Or had that been a guess? The queen hadn't betrayed him, but . . . he did feel betrayed. She had sent him away from her, and she was surrounded by a dangerous court. If she were attacked, there would be nothing he could do. He had begged her to keep him near.

But he had been relieved when she finally did send him away, because part of him felt her death would be on her own head, that he wouldn't be responsible. In Vitellia, he had felt truly alive again, actually competent, facing foes he could see and fight, even if they didn't die when he cut them. Even that was easier than the knife-bladed shadows of the court.

Serving Swanmay had its appeals, and part of him yearned for it. *You have forgotten me*, Fastia had told him.

I haven't.

Have, will. It is all the same.

There were tears on his face, and a hundred yards of pain knotted beneath his chest began to loosen and uncoil, as he turned his face to the bedclothes and cried.

She came back six bells later, when the sun had gone into the wood beyond the world. He pretended he was asleep, and she did not try to wake him. He listened to her settle on the cot beyond the screen, heard her shift and toss for a while before her breathing softened and become shallow and regular. Then he rose, holding his bandaged side, and shuffled across the wooden deck.

The hatch was latched but not locked, and he cracked it and peered out. The deck was mostly quiet and only faintly lit by a moon he could not see. Two men were standing by the wheel, speaking in soft accents. Another stood against the steerboard rail a few kingsyards away. There was no one to backboard, however.

Keeping low, he pushed the door a little wider.

He nearly hit a man with it. He sat just beyond the hatch, a spear across his knees.

She was right. She needed better guardians. But Neil couldn't be one of them.

No one called out as he approached the side of the boat. He strained in the moonlight, trying to make out whether or not the land he had seen earlier was still close. He thought he saw distant lights, though it could have been sparks from the fire in his side.

With no further hesitation, he slipped over the rail.

He hit the water with a splash. The cold shocked him, but he managed to turn onto his back and begin stroking and kicking with his feet, hoping the wound in his side didn't come open again. He had no plan for what he would do when he got to shore, but every day on the ship took him farther from where he had to go.

"*Hwas ist thata?*" someone shouted. "*Hwas fol? Airic?*"

"*Ne, ni mih.*"

Neil grimly kept stroking with dogged determination. He knew the language—it was Hanzish, the tongue of the enemy.

The sound of voices receded. Once he thought he heard Swanmay's voice, but he wasn't certain. Then there was only his own struggle with the waves.

His arms became leaden all too quickly, and despite the fire in his ribs, he felt the warmth draining from his body. If shore was not near, then he would complete the death Swanmay had saved him from.

Was she right? Did he want to die?

He summoned an image of the queen, her pale face and dark hair, and hands reaching for her from every direction, but he could not hold it. Instead, in the half-face of the moon, he saw Swanmay's blue eyes. A strange despair seized him, and more questions, always questions. If she was Hanzish—and he was now certain of that—then why had she helped him? Whom was she fleeing?

The ocean swelled beneath him, and his face went under. He sputtered the water from his mouth and nose and turned to swim on his belly. He heard a faint shushing that might be surf and might be the dying beat of his heart.

He swam on. It was all he could do.

He woke to a blue sky and the warm crackle of a fire. For a moment he thought he'd been dreaming, but then Swanmay's voice broke through it. He felt immensely better, as if he had slept for ten days. The pain in his side was only a dull ache now, and for a moment he thought that perhaps everything that had happened since he had left Eslen was merely a dream.

But then he heard the chatter all around him, in Hanzish, and reached for his sword.

"You are a very stupid man," Swanmay's voice informed him.

He opened his eyes and sat up. He lay on a blanket. The fire was nearby, and beyond it there was a sandy shingle and the sea. Two langschips were pulled up on the beach, and Swanmay's ship was anchored a hundred kingsyards offshore.

In the other direction was a plain covered in short, wiry grass. Swanmay sat beside the fire, on a small stool. Her men seemed to have set up camp. Nearby, two of them were dressing a small, odd-looking deer.

Swanmay wore a broad-brimmed hat, as if she really were a Sefry, but her face looked drawn and weary. The blue in her eyes had dulled, as if something vital had left her.

"I'm sorry," he said. "I had to try."

"I understand that now," she replied. "It makes you no less stupid."

He conceded that with a nod.

She shrugged. "We weren't able to fully provision at z'Espino. My men are remedying that now." She cocked her head. "How do you feel?"

"Wonderful," he replied.

"Good. Do you remember anything?"

"The last thing I remember was hearing the sound of the surf."

"We found you on the strand. Your wounds were open, and your breath was faint. You were very cold."

"But now—what happened?"

"As I told you, I know some arts. I hesitate to use them, because there is a price." She smiled fiercely. "You are fortunate that the walls between life and death are so thin."

A sick dread fluttered in Neil. "Was I dead? Did you—?"

"You were not dead. The life in you was a flickering candle, but it was not extinguished."

"Lady, whatever sorcery you used, you should not have. Tell me its price, and I will pay it."

"It isn't yours to pay," she said softly. "And it is already done." Her voice grew firmer. "And I make my own decisions. Have no fear, you are not cursed or possessed of spirits unhultha. You will not walk the night and do evil at my bidding."

"I could never imagine you doing me harm," Neil replied.

"No? Yet you spurned my company when you owed me your life." Her voice rose. "Do you understand? You threw your life away in z'Espino, and with it any duty or obligation you ever had. You threw it away and I picked it up. Can you not concede that it is mine now? Do you feel no duty toward me?"

"Of course I do," Neil blurted, "and *that* is the problem. And now I owe you twice, but I cannot repay you. That is agony to me, lady. Do you understand? You have put me between the rising tide and the cliff—"

"And can think of nothing better to do than drown yourself again." She snorted. "Enough. I am done with this."

"Done?"

"You will never enter my service, I see that now. But you do owe me twice, and I do not expect you to forget that. One day I will ask you a favor and you will answer. Do you understand?"

"If I can."

"No. If you feel obligation toward me, then take it as a geis. I will not call on you soon."

He sighed and bowed his head. "Are you saying you will release me now if I accept this geis?"

"Hush. By noon we leave here, and I will take you to Paldh, no matter what you say now. But if you have any of the fabled integrity of Skern, you will take my geis."

"I swear by the saints my fathers swore by, and take this geis," Neil said. "When you have need of me, I will come, so long as it does not bring harm to those it is my charge to protect."

"Very well," she said. She stood and looked off across the distant fields. "I never went ashore in z'Espino," she said softly. "This is the only strange land I have ever set foot on. It is fair."

"Lady—"

"Make the ship ready," she called to her men in Hanzish. Then she strode away from him without even a backwards glance.

CHAPTER NINE

THE WIND AND THE SEA

"WILL THEY CATCH US?" Anne asked, watching intently as the masts of the pursuing ship appeared and disappeared behind the high swells. The sky was a turquoise gem, flawed only with a few streaks of white cloud. There was no land in sight.

Captain Malconio put his callused hands on the rail and leaned forward. Perversely, she noticed that he exuded the same faintly almond scent Cazio had when he sweated.

"Lord Netuno knows," he said. "That's a fast ship, a brimwulf built in Saltmark. And they've got a strong wind behind them."

"Are they faster than us?" Anne asked.

"Much faster," Malconio said.

"Then they *will* catch us."

Malconio scratched his beard. "Ah, well—there's more to it than speed, della. We can run against the wind a little better than she can, and we've got a shallower keel. If we can reach the shoals around Terna-Fath before nightfall, I give us a chance."

"Only a chance?" Cazio sneered.

Malconio regarded his brother with narrowed eyes. "It's not often I have the need to outrun a man-o'-war," he said acidly. "In fact— why, that's *never* happened to me before. It took you to come along and present me this delightful opportunity, *frater mio*. Indeed, it occurs to me our pursuers might be satisfied if I just gave up my cargo."

"You won't do that," Anne said.

Malconio's eyebrows shot up, and he looked at her as if she had just asked to cut off his foot. "Pardon me? I wonder how you formed that opinion?"

"These men came after me when I was in the coven Saint Cer. They killed every sister there. What makes you think they would spare you?"

"There's also the maritime guild to consider," z'Acatto added a bit drunkenly. He waved the narrow-necked bottle of wine he'd found somewhere. "You know they would never stand for it if one of their ships had been accosted, for any reason. The captain of the ship behind us won't take that risk—he'll never give you the chance to report him. So don't be a *collone*."

"Easy, old man," Malconio said. "You know I was just talking—it's the family curse. But if we can't slip them, we'll never be able to fight them. A ship like that will carry three or four arbalests, probably armed with sea fire. My brother will never even get to use his sword, unless they want the girl alive, for some reason." He looked back at Anne. "Is that likely to be the case?"

"I don't think so," Anne said. "I think they just want to see me dead."

"And you still won't tell me why?"

"I still don't know why," Anne said helplessly.

"Well," Malconio said. "So we run, and hope the breeze favors us."

They tacked hard to the north, and at first the larger ship seemed to drop back a bit, but then it started picking up speed again. It wasn't even noon yet.

"Unless we get some luck, they'll have us long before we reach the shoals," Malconio finally admitted.

"Well, then, they're in for a fight," Cazio told his brother, resting his hand on the hilt of his rapier.

"I told you before," Malconio said, "they've no reason to come close when they can sink us from a distance." He put his hands on his hips. "But suppose they did try to board us—that fellow with the glowing sword—how do you intend to fight him? Your friend back at the docks dealt him a blow that should have had him buried in two places. But he was walking fine, last I saw him."

"I've fought his kind before," Cazio said with that overabundance of confidence that Anne found so infuriating. "I'll cut off his head and send him to the bottom of the sea."

"Last time you had me to drop bricks on him," z'Acatto reminded him. "What shall I drop on this one?"

Cazio shrugged. "Perhaps an anchor? Surely we can find something."

Malconio folded his hands. "What? No single combat this time? What of your honor?"

"It's hardly honorable to fight with the aide of hell," Cazio replied. "I've sworn to protect these ladies. I'll do that even if I have to fight with less than perfect honor."

Malconio rolled his eyes. "It doesn't matter anyway," he said. "They've twice our numbers without taking Casnar z'Estrigo into account. Drop an anchor on him if you wish, though I have only so many anchors." He nodded at the approaching ship. "But it won't come to that. See those arbalests? What did I tell you?"

Anne could see some sort of ungainly devices mounted on the other ship's deck, but couldn't make out what they were supposed to do. Austra saved her the embarrassment of asking what an arbalest was, by asking herself.

"It's a huge mechanical bow," Malconio replied. "Hurls stones, lead balls, pots of flame—things like that."

"Don't you have any sort of war engines, Captain?" Anne asked. "Some way to fight back? Surely you've had to fend off pirates before."

Malconio shook his head. "We've got one small arbalest. It's all we ever needed against the few pirates that dare the wrath of the guild."

"I suggest you set it up, then," z'Acatto said.

"I suppose you're right, old man. A little fight is better than none at all. And perhaps Netuno will smile on me. He has before."

◦ ◦ ◦

Five bells later, their pursuer lobbed a few experimental stones at them. They fell short, but not far short, and Malconio's sailors stood nervously with their bows and set up their arbalest—which did indeed resemble a large crossbow. Anne could hear the sailors on the other ship now and see them scuttling about on the deck and in the rigging.

"We'll be within their range long before they're in ours," Malconio said. "Ladies, I suggest you go below." He glanced off toward the horizon, where black clouds were piling up. "It's not often I wish for a storm, but you might pray to whatever saints you revere that that one catches us before they do. In a blow, we might be able to lose them."

"I'll stay up here," Anne said.

"And do what?" Cazio asked. "Can you shoot a bow?"

"I could try."

"We don't have enough arrows to waste them," Malconio said. "Go below. It's my ship, and that's an order."

Anne prepared another objection, but let it fade behind her lips. Sir Neil had died because of her last poor decision. Malconio knew his business far better than she did.

"Come on, Austra," Anne said.

"Take this," Cazio said. He held out the hilt of a dagger.

"I have one," she said.

"I don't," Austra said.

"You take it, then," Cazio replied.

Austra took the weapon, but her face puckered. "I want to stay up here with you," she said.

Cazio smiled and took Austra's hand. "My brother is right this time," he said. "Up here you would only be a distraction. With you safe below I can fight the way the saints intend me to."

Austra lowered her eyes, then suddenly reached up and kissed Cazio on the lips.

"Don't die," she said.

"I won't," he assured her. "I'm not meant to die at sea. Go on, and be brave."

She nodded and turned away, stumbling toward their cabin, trying vainly to hide her tears.

Cazio glanced at Anne then, and for a moment she couldn't take her gaze away from his. She felt as if she had been caught doing something she shouldn't have, but couldn't form the words of an excuse.

Cazio broke the spell.

"Well, that's one kiss for luck," he said. "How about another?"

"That wasn't a kiss for luck," Anne said softly. "And you're still a fool."

Then she followed Austra.

"She's right," Malconio said, once the two women were out of sight. "You're a fool, and playing at a fool's game."

"What could you possibly mean?" Cazio asked, irritated.

"Two girls. The one you've set your hopes on is the *rofola*—Diuvo knows why—but you're cozying up to her friend."

"I've no interest in Anne," Cazio lied, "though if I did, it would be none of your business."

"Your very apparent interest in her is about to get me killed, so it's entirely my business," Malconio said, "but I'll let that pass. Still, it's cruel to play with a girl's heart."

"Anne doesn't have a heart."

"I'm talking about the other one now."

"Ah, but you just said we were about to be killed, so there's no time for that to happen."

"Yes, well, that's your best hope." To Cazio's surprise, Malconio clapped him on the shoulder. "Stay under cover. You won't be of any use until they actually board us, if they do."

He started off.

"Wait a moment," Cazio said.

His brother paused. "Only a moment."

"What do you know about z'Acatto?"

Malconio shrugged. "Less than you, I should think. What do you mean?"

"A man in z'Espino—a man who knew him—called him Emrature."

"That's odd," Malconio conceded.

"So I thought."

"He did fight in the wars," Malconio said. "Almost everyone did, even father."

"Yes, but as a commander? Then why would he—?"

"Why would he dedicate his life to teaching the ill-behaved brats of a nearly destitute nobleman how to swing a sword around? I don't know. Maybe you should ask him."

"Have you ever tried asking him anything personal?"

Malconio smiled. "Once or twice, when I was too young to know better. But he's always loved you, Cazio. You were different to him. It was you he stayed for."

"Who killed our father, Malconio?"

His older brother's features softened a bit. "Cazio, I've never understood you. Maybe when we were boys—we had a little fun, didn't we? You were so serious and sober, like a little priest. Then after father died—"

"I don't want to talk about this. And you don't have time."

"This may be the only time," Malconio said. "After father died, you took to the sword as if you had no other life. Like any little boy, you were sworn to avenge his death. We wouldn't tell you anything about the duel because we were afraid you would run away and try to find the man."

"I would have."

"But when you were older and—do not doubt this—the best dessrator in Avella, maybe in the whole Tero Mefio—you never asked, never tried to find out."

"Because I didn't care anymore," Cazio replied. "Father was a fool. He frittered away our estates and got himself killed."

"You fight duels every day," Malconio said. "How can you fault father for fighting one? Especially when you know nothing of the circumstances?"

"I know he was hit in the back," Cazio said softly. "I saw the body, Malconio. What kind of duelist gets hit in the back?"

Malconio's face worked silently for a moment. "I didn't see the fight, and neither did you," he finally said. "Why do you suddenly care about this again?"

"I don't know," Cazio said. "It just popped into my head."

"Z'Acatto saw the fight. He's the one you need to talk to. But— father wasn't so bad, Cazio. When our mother was still alive, he was a better man. A lot of him left with her."

Another uncomfortable silence followed.

"Have you seen Chesco lately?" Cazio asked.

"Two months ago. He's well. He's got three ships of his own. You know, you've always been welcome to join us."

"I can't abandon our name and our home," Cazio said. "I can't."

Malconio rolled his eyes. "Look around you," he said. "You *have*— you just don't know it yet."

Cazio sighed and looked off at the distant storm. "It won't get here in time to help us, will it?"

Malconio shook his head. "It's not even coming this way."

Anne felt a little queasy again as she sat on the edge of her cot. Austra was peering out through the thick panes of the window.

"They're coming from backboard," Anne said, "the other way."

"I know," Austra said stiffly. "It's just—we should be up there."

"They're right," Anne said. "We'd just be in the way."

"We might be able to help," Austra protested. "It's not like we haven't been in danger before."

"Yes, but we don't know anything about sailing or arbalests. And I think Captain Malconio hopes that if our enemies don't see us there's some small chance they'll think they're chasing the wrong boat."

Austra shook her head. "Those men are guided by devils. They'll never stop until we're dead."

"Until *I'm* dead," Anne corrected. "It's me they're after, not the rest of you."

Austra's brow bunched. "You're not thinking of running off again? You promised me you wouldn't. Or are your promises to me no good now?"

"What's that supposed to mean?" Anne demanded.

"Nothing."

"Look, you're the one spending all the time with Cazio. You're the one who has no time for me, anymore," Anne said.

Austra turned away and said something under her breath.

"What was that?" Anne asked.

"Nothing."

"Tell me!"

Austra spun then, her face red. "You've been lying to me! Lying! Who *are* you?"

Anne stepped back from her sheer fury. "What on earth are you talking about?"

"I mean you *know* why they're after you. You *know*, and yet you won't tell me. And like you said, I'm going to get killed as dead as you, and so is Cazio, and z'Acatto—as dead as Neil MeqVren!"

"Don't mention him!" Anne said.

"Why? Because it's your fault he got killed?"

Anne's growing anger collapsed into a lump in her throat, congealed fury and sorrow and frustration. She couldn't say anything.

Which was fine. Austra had plenty more to say.

"Something happened to you at the coven. You see things other people don't. You can do things other people can't. I've been waiting for you to explain, but you aren't going to, are you?"

"Austra—"

"You don't trust me, do you? When was I ever anything but your loyal friend, even when it was dangerous for me?"

"You don't understand, Austra. *I* don't understand."

Something struck the ship, hard, and they heard men yelling above deck.

"Well that's not good enough!" Austra shrieked.

The sails of the *Della Puchia* began to drop as their pursuer threw a wind shadow over them, and moments later the first of the arbalest stones struck their bow with a hollow thud and bounced off into the water.

"That didn't do much," Cazio observed.

"They were just finding their range," Malconio said grimly. "It will get worse."

"They aren't coming any closer."

"Yes. They're right in assuming my weapon doesn't have that kind of range. They've got us in their wind shadow, so we can't move. They'll stay there and pound us until we sink."

"Then why did you even set up the arbalest?"

"In case they were stupid. They aren't."

While Cazio watched, a pair of the enemy war engines fired, nearly at the same time. Two flaming balls leapt skyward, leaving tails of thick black smoke.

"I see what you mean about it getting worse," Cazio said.

One of the balls plunged harmlessly into the sea, but the other hit squarely in the middle deck, blossoming in a tulip of flame. One of Malconio's sailors caught fire, too, and fell screaming and thrashing to the deck as his comrades tried to smother the fire with a wet canvas.

Cazio gripped Caspator's hilt until his knuckles went white. Malconio was right—he would never even get a chance to kill one of them. He'd never felt so helpless in his life.

He glanced at his brother, intending to ask him if there was anything he could do, but noticed Malconio wasn't watching the other ship, but was staring out across the sea. And he was smiling.

"What?" Cazio asked.

"Look there," he said. "At the water."

Cazio followed his gaze but didn't see anything remarkable.

Malconio put his hand on the steersman's shoulder. "Prepare to come about," he said. "You see where?"

"Aye, I see it," the fellow said. "It'll be close."

"What's going on?" Cazio asked.

"Watch their sails," he replied.

Cazio tried, but it was difficult, as about that time another volley of flaming pots came hurtling toward them. One struck the mainsail.

"Put that out!" Malconio hollered. "We're about to need it."

At that moment, the sails of the other ship went suddenly slack.

"Come about, *now!*" Malconio thundered.

Sailors leapt to their tasks, pulling yards. The boom swung around and the still-flaming sail filled with a faint puff of air. It hardly seemed enough to move the ship, but then the men all cheered.

"What happened?" Cazio asked.

"Netuno took their wind and sent us one from another direction," Malconio said.

"It's not much of a wind," Cazio observed.

"No, which makes it perfect for us. We can run straight before it, and we'll start out faster than her."

"I thought *she* was faster," Cazio said.

"Aye, in full wind. But we'll make the speed faster, because we're smaller. By the time they turn and start again, we'll have two leagues on them."

Once again, his brother was right. Even though they barely seemed to be moving, the big ship wasn't moving at all. The arbalests kept up the rain of fire, however. Cazio joined the crew putting out the fires as they slowly, painfully tacked out of range. When the arbalest rounds started at last falling short, another cheer went up.

They ran straight with the wind, then—no more tacking—and with a sluggishness Cazio found maddening they began to outpace their pursuer.

But by dusk the big ship was gaining again.

The sounds of bombardment waxed and then gradually waned away. Since her outburst, Austra had huddled on her cot, unspeaking.

"They're cheering," Anne noticed. "It must be good news."

Austra nodded vaguely but still wouldn't meet her gaze.

"I'll go see what's happening," Anne said. "Do you want to come along?"

Austra shook her head and closed her eyes. "It's too much," she said.

Anne regarded the younger girl for a moment, wishing there were something she could say. "You were right before," she said finally.

"About what?"

"Back when I tried to run away. When I thought I could dress as a man and make my own way in the world. When I wanted adventure. You told me that I was being stupid, that I would starve or be killed or kidnapped within a nineday."

"Oh, right," Austra said. "I did say that."

"At the time I only agreed to stay because you asked me to, because I worried about what would happen to you if I left. Now I know you were right about everything. I didn't know anything at all about how the world works. I barely do now. But if there is one thing I do know, it's that I don't want any more adventure. I want to be back in Eslen. I want the worst thing that could happen to me to be a scolding from Fastia or mother. And I want you there with me."

"I'm glad you finally admit that I can be right about something," Austra said.

"A lot of people have died for me," Anne said. "The sisters at the coven. Sir Neil. I'm afraid to go abovedecks, because I'm afraid to find out who else. I don't want anyone else to die for me, Austra. I'm sick of this whole thing."

"Well, why not try telling them that?" Austra said. "The next time those men catch up with us, just tell them you don't want to play anymore, and that you'll be good, and please leave us alone."

Anne smiled, thinking Austra was joking and the mood was finally starting to lighten. But then she saw her friend's face.

"It doesn't matter what you're sick of," Austra said. "It's all going to happen anyway."

Anne felt her heart slacken. "Please, Austra—"

"You still aren't going to tell me what's going on."

Anne felt herself near tears, and even nearer to begging. "I think if I tell you anything, it will only make things worse for you. I'm afraid it will get you killed."

"I'm going to get killed anyway," Austra said. "Can't you feel it? Don't you know?"

"What on earth are you talking about?"

"Nothing. Nothing."

"Austra—"

"I'm tired now."

Austra rolled over so her back was to Anne.

Anne watched, helpless, her eyes wet. How could she tell Austra about her visions? How could she burden her best friend with trying to decide whether Anne had gone mad, or whether she was so important to the world that if she did not become queen it would end? How could she tell anyone about the man in the woods?

She didn't believe it herself, after the visions had faded.

Anyway, it would make breaking her promise harder to do, and Austra would try to come with her. She hadn't lied just now when she told Austra that she'd been right about running away the first time. But things were different now. Now Austra had Cazio to protect her. This time she wasn't running from her duty, she was running toward it, and if the Faiths were so insistent that she must be queen, *they* could bloody well protect her until she was.

She wouldn't have her friends dying for her anymore.

Because Austra was right. They wouldn't stop. They would never stop. And though it would hurt Austra when she left again, Austra would live, and she would be protected.

Resolved to that, she went back up abovedecks to see whom else she had killed, and to find out whether any of them would live through the night.

She found the ship still following, and getting closer. As night fell, clouds rolled in, and the dark that followed was complete. Malconio put the ship through a series of turns as the wind quickened. There was no cheering now, because the only thing their enemies might have to follow was sound.

Anne returned to her cabin to try and sleep, but was awakened a few bells later by an explosion. Throwing on her dressing gown, she ran back up on the deck, fearing the ship had somehow found them.

But the ship hadn't found them—a storm had.

CHAPTER TEN

CANALS

LEOFF AWOKE TO A splitting headache and a small voice in his ear.

"Get up sir," it said. "Please don't be dead."

The voice was nearly drowned out by a background cacophony of shouting and stamping feet. With an effort, Leoff opened his eyes. At first he saw only a blur, which, as it sharpened, became Mery's small face.

"What's happening?" he groaned.

"You aren't dead!" she exclaimed.

"No," he agreed, "though I might be soon." He felt the side of his head, and his fingers came away sticky with blood. That didn't seem like a good sign.

"Hurry," Mery urged, "before the soldiers get here." He realized she was tugging at his hand.

He tried to rise, but a wave of dizziness went through him.

"No, don't stand up," she said. "Just follow me."

He crawled on hands and knees, following Mery through the pandemonium. He figured that he must have been unconscious for only a few seconds.

Mery vanished behind a tapestry and he followed, wondering what he was doing and why.

When he got behind the tapestry, he saw the blue fringe of Mery's dress as it vanished through a narrow slit in the wall. The slit went for about a kingsyard and then opened into a larger, torch-lit corridor.

"Wait," Mery cautioned, waving him back. "Not yet."

He waited, his head feeling huge, swollen with pain.

"Now, quickly."

She stood and darted across the hall, to an open doorway there. He followed, making it somewhat shakily to his feet, and saw, down the hall, several men in the king's colors standing in front of a much larger door, brandishing swords and spears at those in the ballroom. They seemed far to busy to notice him.

"Good," Mery said. "I don't think they saw us."

"What's happening?"

"I don't know," she said. "Come on."

His head felt a little better, but he sincerely hoped Mery knew what she was doing, because after a few moments in the darkened maze of the manse he knew he would never find his way back. Mery never hesitated, however, taking turn after turn, leading him through huge rooms and tiny compartments. It was as if the entire building were a sort of magic chest, with ever smaller and cleverer boxes nested within. The din of the ballroom was well behind them.

He concluded by touch that the cut on his head wasn't serious. He only hoped the bone hadn't broken.

Finally, Leoff felt fresh air. The room was utterly dark, but Mery led him to what felt like a shaft that was angling down and away from him.

"In there," she said. "We have to go through there."

"What is it?"

"This is the kitchen," she explained. "They dump the garbage in here."

"Maybe we should just wait here until things calm down," Leoff said.

"The bad men will find us," she said. "We have to get outside."

"The bad men may be outside, too," he said.

"Yes, but there are secret ways out there," she said. "Don't you want to go back to Eslen?"

"Wait," he sighed. He was trying to sort it out. The "bad men" were the queen's men. Those in the corridor wore the same colors as the knight—Fail de Liery—to whom he had escorted the queen only two nights before.

Someone had tried to kill the queen, and two nights later her men were attacking Ambria Gramme's ball.

Had Gramme planned the assassination?

Saints, what had he gotten himself into?

"Yes," he told her. "I think we had better get back there." Otherwise, he was going to be implicated in this whole affair, and he suspected that would lead to a loss of more than simple employment.

But the queen might find out anyway. Running would only make him look guilty.

Still, there was also Mery to consider, wasn't there?

Hoping he would fit, he pulled himself down the shaft, which reeked of pork grease, rotten vegetables, and less wholesome things.

The pile he landed on was worse. He was glad it was too dark to see exactly what it was.

Another night lost in Newland. He was really beginning to hate this place.

He caught Mery when she came out, sparing her the same messy stop he'd found.

"Which way now?" he asked.

"We'll go get a boat on the canal."

"I think the bad men came on the canal," Leoff said. "I think there will be a lot of them there."

"Not that canal," she said, "there's another one. Come on. This way."

They mazed through dark gardens of hedges trimmed fantastic, around still marble basins that glimmed faintly in the moonlight. The grass crunched with frost, and two owls were making ghostly conversation. Not too far away, he could hear men's voices, but they were growing fainter.

He stopped suddenly.

"What is it?" she asked.

"Gilmer. My friend Gilmer was in there."

"The little man? No, he left when you started playing the hammarharp."

"Oh. Good." Or maybe not. How long had the soldiers been outside? They might have caught him as he left.

But there was nothing he could do about it right now, not with Mery. She was probably in more danger than he was.

"How did you know to run, Mery?" he asked, suddenly suspicious. "It was like you had the whole thing planned out."

"Yes," she said, after a silence.

"Why?"

"I always have a way planned out."

"But why?"

"Mother says they may come to kill me one day."

"Did she say why?"

"No. Only that they might come one day, the king's men, and kill me and my brother. So I figured out ways to run and places to hide. It's how I found the music room."

"You're a very clever girl, Mery."

"Are you going to marry my mother?" she asked.

"What?" For a moment his dizziness returned. "Did she say something like that?"

"No," Mery replied.

"Then why do you ask?"

"Because I like you."

He took her hand. "I like you, too, Mery. Come on, let's find someplace warm."

They found the canal easily enough, and several small narrowboats. They were approaching them when Mery suddenly grabbed him by the arm.

"Shh," she said.

There were voices in the darkness, and straining, Leoff made out several indistinct figures near the canal. He and Mery crouched behind a bush.

"They captured the lady Gramme and her son," one of the men said in a husky baritone.

"That's of no concern," a second man said. Something about that voice sent a chill through Leoff. It wasn't the voice itself, which was perfectly normal, tenor, cultured. But just as any note played on a lute had numerous smaller tones hidden within it, there was something hidden in that voice—something somehow *wrong*.

"How can you say that?" the baritone asked. "Our plans are ruined."

"Hardly. I'm amazed that Muriele discovered this, much less acted on the information, but once our spies reported them coming, I did my best to encourage them."

"What do you mean?"

"Some of my men met them at the docks with bow and arrow and killed one or two, then fled into the darkness. After that, the queen's men didn't ask questions—they stormed through the front door, where the guards naturally reacted to them before they understood who they were fighting. What was probably meant to be a peaceful interrogation ended up in bloodshed. Do you know how many were killed?"

"I'm not sure, my lord—but more than a few."

"I feel foolish for not having planted the evidence of this meeting myself," the tenor said. "Still, it's all worked out quite well."

"I really don't see how."

"He's right," a third voice said. This one sounded familiar to Leoff, but he couldn't place it. "If one of us had been found there, things might be different. As it is, Muriele's men will find little of substance—little to justify this attack. It will seem as if they burst into an innocent gathering and began slaughtering landwaerden."

"Indeed," the tenor agreed. "Even the few loyal members of the Comven won't be able to support this action. I believe this moves us well ahead of our schedule."

"I urge caution, my lord," the third man said. "Give the kingdom time to absorb this before you move."

"No, I don't think so," the second man said. "The time to strike is now."

"You mean tonight?" the baritone asked incredulously.

"Not tonight. But soon. Go to the camp. Tell them to be ready to cross the water."

"Yes, my lord."

One of the figures moved to the narrowboats, and soon he was rowing away on the canal.

"I'll take my leave now, as well," the familiar voice said. "But heed my advice—moving too quickly could be a mistake."

"No, this is the perfect time."

"There are many who still sympathize with the queen, and many more who will not care for you, milord. The situation does favor you, but there might be ways to sweeten it."

"Well, your advice is always welcome," the tenor said.

"After tonight, the landwaerden will be incensed," the familiar voice went on. "Through Gramme, you can be certain of their support. The nobility, however, will not care much about a few dead waerds. In fact, this might actually draw a few of them back to the queen."

"She's worried them enough by forming her own Lierish guard."

"Yes. But what if she began truncating all lines of succession other than Charles and Anne?"

"You mean by killing Gramme and her bastards?"

"Precisely."

"But we need Gramme, I think, and her son could prove useful. He is, after all, William's."

"Yes. The assassinations of Gramme and the boy might be seen as bungled. But the girl is of no use to us."

"Mery? No, I suppose she isn't. And she's probably in the queen's custody right now. I suppose it couldn't hurt matters. Can you arrange this?"

"It wouldn't be hard," the familiar voice said.

"Before tomorrow?"

"Are you in that much of a hurry?"

"Three days. No more."

"That's sufficient time, I suppose," the familiar voice sighed. "I hope you know what you're doing."

"Just be ready to play your part, and all will go perfectly."

"That's just it. My men won't arrive for another month."

"We don't need your men, Praifec. Only your word. Do I have it?"

"You have it."

They left then, the praifec on foot, the other man in a narrowboat. Leoff held Mery still, shivering to the bone, only partially from the cold.

"I told you," Mery said softly.

"It's not going to happen, Mery," Leoff promised. "They aren't going to kill you. Come on."

"If we go to the castle, they'll find me."

"I know. We're not going to the castle."

They took one of the narrowboats and went the direction the other man had not. By morning, they had reached a small, cheerful-looking town called Plinse. There Leoff carefully obtained directions to the vicinity of Meolwis. He also bought a cloak to hide Mery's dress, and from there the two of them followed Leokwigh Road north. They reached Meolwis near sundown and stayed in an abandoned house. The next day, they went west along the dike of Saint Thon's Graf, and within a bell had come upon a malend.

Hiding Mery below the birm, Leoff went to the door and rapped on it.

To his great relief, Gilmer was the one who answered it, his eyes bugging in gnomish surprise.

"It's good to see you well," the little man said, after they'd embraced. "I heard about the trouble at Her Ladyship's. Almost caught some of it myself. I guess you must have heeded my advice."

"I was still there," Leoff said. "Someone helped me escape."

"One of the young ladies, eh?"

Leoff smiled. "I need a favor, Gilmer."

"You've just to ask."

"This isn't an easy favor, and it's dangerous. Let me explain it before you say yes."

He called Mery in and related everything that had happened, including what the two of them had heard that night.

"Who do you think it was?" Gilmer asked. "Besides the praifec? Who were the other two?"

"I've no idea."

"One of them was Prince Robert," Mery said.

Gilmer looked at her. "Prince Robert's dead, lass."

"It was him," the girl insisted.

Gilmer made a long, low whistle. "This aens't good. Not one bit good." He slapped his knees. "But you've done the right thing. There's nothing you can do back there. The royals will settle that mess and that's that. But the praifec—well, they go that way sometimes."

"I can't let anything happen to Mery," Leoff said.

"No, of course you can't," Gilmer replied. He tousled the girl's hair. "I don't care if the fratrex Prismo himself has come up from z'Irbina, there's no little girl getting killed while I'm around. No, you two will stay here. When this all blows over, we can reckon what to do."

"Gilmer, I need you to keep Mery safe—that much is true. But I've got to go back."

Gilmer shook a finger at him. "That's crazy," he said. "You think you'll stop a palace coup all by yourself? Or that anyone would be grateful to you even if you did? You were the guest of honor at that party. Even if the queen wins, she's going to think you a traitor. Learn your lesson, son—stay away."

"I can't. The queen needs to be warned." He squared his shoulders. "Besides, I have a commission to finish and a concert to perform."

PART **IV**

ROADMARKS

The Year 2,223 of Everon
The Month of Decmen

Ponto, the fifth mode, invokes Saint Diuvo, Saint Flenz, Saint Thunor, Saint Rooster. It evokes the passionate new love, the raucous banquet, the freely flowing wine. It provokes delight, giddy joy, lust.

Sesto, the sixth mode, invokes Saint Erren, Saint Anne, Saint Fiendeseve, Saint Adlainn. It evokes the ache one will not wish away, the quiet sadness after physical love, unrequited longing. It provokes erotic sadness.

—FROM *THE CODEX HARMONIUM OF ELGIN WIDSEL*

CHAPTER ONE

FRIENDSHIPS

A NNE PULLED A COMB through her salt-knotted hair and watched the gulls on the strand fight over the scraps of fish and more dubious once-living things. The birds weren't the only scavengers; twenty or thirty people—mostly children—were also searching the sand for treasure from the waves.

Farther down the shore, the battered hulk of the *Della Puchia* was dry-docked in scaffolding, and beyond that lay the huddle of whitewashed cottages that was the Gallean village of Duvré.

It was hard to remember any particulars about the storm. The bells of vicious thunder, snapping spars, and plunging waves all blurred together into a single long terror. It had left them adrift and sinking with only a single makeshift sail and the good fortune to be within sight of shore. They had followed the coast for nearly a day before finding the fishing village and the anchorage it offered.

A cold wind was coming off the sea, but the clouds were gone. The only remaining signs of the storm were its wreckage.

The comb snagged, and she yanked at her hair in frustration, wishing for a bath, but the village didn't have an inn, as such, just a small tavern. Besides, their money was all but gone. Cazio had the last of it and was trying to buy horses and supplies. Captain Malconio had figured it would be a week before the ship was ready to sail again, and she had no intention of waiting that long.

According to its inhabitants—at least as best as any of Malconio's men could understand them—Duvré was about ten leagues south of Paldh. They had planned to go by land to Eslen anyway, so they had decided that they might as well get started.

With a sigh, she rose and started back toward the village, to make sure Cazio was doing what he was supposed to be doing, and not playing nip with Austra someplace. The brief solitude had been nice, but it was time to get going.

She found him in the tavern, of course, along with z'Acatto, Malconio, Austra, and a crowd of locals. It was close and smoky inside and smelled overwhelmingly of the dried cod that hung everywhere from the rafters. The two long tables were pitted and polished by use, and the floor—like the walls—was built of a sort of plaster made of ground-up seashells.

Malconio was speaking—something about the wonders of a city named Shavan—and a wizened little man with no more than three or four teeth was making a running translation in Gallean. Children in red and umber tunics of rough wool and women with their hair wrapped up in black cotton scarves all leaned in, laughing sometimes and commenting among themselves. They glanced at her when she entered, but quickly returned their attention to Malconio.

Anne put her hands on her hips and tried to catch Cazio's eye, but he either hadn't seen her or was ignoring her in favor of Austra, who—with him—was quaffing wine from a ceramic jug.

Z'Acatto was slumped with his head on the table.

Impatiently, Anne pushed through the crowd and got Cazio's attention by patting his shoulder.

"Yes, casnara?" he asked, looking up at her. Austra turned her head away, feigning interest in Malconio's story, which just rolled right along.

"I thought you were buying supplies and horses."

Cazio nodded. "That's exactly what I'm doing," he said. He patted the shoulder of a stout, middle-aged man with a sunburnt face and startling green eyes. "This is Tungale MapeGovan. I'm doing business with him."

The man—who seemed well on his way to being thoroughly drunk—smiled up at Anne.

"*Hinne allan,*" he commented, scratching his belly.

"Well, can't you hurry it up?" she asked, ignoring the disgusting fellow.

"They don't seem to do things in a hurry here," Cazio remarked. "My kind of people, really."

"Cazio."

"Also, we don't have enough money," he said.

"You've money for wine, it seems."

Cazio took another swig. "No," he said, "we're earning that with stories."

"Well, how much do we need?" she asked, exasperated.

He set the jug back on the table. "He wants twice what we have for an ass and four days' provisions."

"An ass?"

"No one around here has a horse—even if they did, we could never afford it."

"Well, one ass hardly seems worth the trouble," Anne said. "Just buy the food."

"If you want to carry it on your back," Cazio remarked, "I'll settle that right now."

"If I have to, I will. We can't wait here any longer."

Someone tugged lightly on her hair. She gasped and discovered Tungale fondling it.

"Stop that," she said, brushing his hand away.

"*Ol panné?*" he asked.

Cazio glanced at the translator, but he was still busy with Malconio's tale.

"She's not for sale," Cazio answered, shaking his head.

That was a little too much.

"*For sale?*" she shouted.

Malconio stopped in midsentence, and the table erupted in laughter.

"*Ne, ne,*" Tungale said. "*Sé venné se panné?*"

"What's he saying?" Anne demanded.

The translator smiled broadly, emphasizing his mostly toothless condition. "He wants to know how much your *hair* costs."

"My hair?"

"*Sé venné se?*" he asked Tungale.

"*Té,*" Tungale replied.

"Yes," the translator said. "Your hair. How much?"

Anne felt her face burning.

"Her hair isn't—," Cazio began, but Anne put a hand on his arm.

"The ass and food for a nineday," she said.

Austra turned at that. "Anne, no."

"It's only hair, Austra," Anne replied. She nodded at the translator. "Tell him."

Despite her brave words, she had to work hard to keep from crying when they sheared it off, with everyone in the room whooping and laughing as if they were watching a troupe perform its antics. She kept the tears in, though, and resisted the temptation to rub the stubble that remained on her scalp.

"There," she said, got up from her chair, and nearly bolted outside. There she did tear up a bit, not so much from the loss of her hair as from the humiliation.

She heard footsteps behind her.

"Leave me alone," she said without turning.

"I just thought you might want this."

She looked back, a little surprised to find that it was Malconio. He was holding one of the black scarves the women of the village wore. She stared at it for a moment.

"You know," he said, "you could have asked me for the money. I'll have to sell off some goods here anyway to get the ship repaired. Cazio's too proud, but *you* could have asked."

She shook her head. "I can't ask you for anything, Captain. Some of your men died because of me, and your ship was wrecked. I owe you too much already."

"That's true, in its way," Malconio said. "But sailors die and ships are wrecked. There is such a thing as fate, and it's a waste of time to wish you hadn't done something. Better to learn from your mistakes and move on. I don't hold any grudge against you, Anne. I took you as a passenger because my brother asked me to, and despite what I said earlier, I do have some idea what to expect from my brother and his—situations.

"Do you know how hard it must have been for him to come to me? But he did, which tells me something about you. That you dragged him away from the Tero Mefio says even more. The Cazio I knew never did much for anyone but himself. If he's improved, how can I let him show me up?"

Anne managed a little smile at that. "You do love him, don't you?"

Malconio smiled. "He's my brother."

He proffered the scarf, and she took it. "Thank you," she said. "One day I will be able to repay you."

"The only payment I ask is that you watch out for my little brother," Malconio said.

"I'll do my best."

Malconio smiled, but the smile quickly vanished as he lifted his head and his eyes focused behind her. "There they are," he sighed. "I should have known they wouldn't sink."

Anne followed his gaze. There, where sea and sky met, she saw sails.

"Oh, no," she whispered.

"They aren't coming this way," Malconio said after a moment. "They're probably looking for a deeper port—she's missing a mast, you see?"

Anne didn't, but she nodded. Malconio was right, though—the ship wasn't sailing toward land, but parallel to it.

"If they see your ship—," she began, but Malconio shook his head.

"It's not likely at that range, not with the *Della Puchia* in dry-dock and without masts. But even if she did, she couldn't come in—not through those reefs we passed. Her keel's too deep." He turned to Anne. "Still, I would go if I were you, and quickly. If they have seen the *Puchia*, they'll send men back over land as soon as they find a harbor with deeper water. You could have all the time in the world, but on the other hand, you might have only a day."

"What if they do come here?" Anne asked. "They'll kill you."

"No," Malconio said. "I'm not fated to die on land. Get the others and make a start. You've still got a few bells before sundown."

Cazio found his brother with his ship.

Malconio scowled when he saw him. "Are you still here? Didn't Anne tell you we saw the ship?"

"Yes," Cazio said. "I just—" He fumbled off, suddenly unsure what he wanted to say.

"Good-byes are bad luck," Malconio grumbled. "Implies that you don't expect to see each other again. And I'm sure to see you again, right, little brother?"

Cazio felt something bitter suck in his lungs. "I'm sorry about your ship," he said.

"Well, we'll talk about that again when you've made your fortune," Malconio said. "Meanwhile, you let me worry about it. It is my ship, after all."

"You're making fun of me," Cazio said.

"No," Malconio replied. "No, I'm not. You have a destiny, *fratrillo*, I can feel it in my bones. And it's your own—not mine, not our father's, not our revered forefathers'. It's yours. I'm just glad somebody finally got you out looking for it. And when you've found it, I expect you to come to my house in Turanate and tell me about it."

"I'd like to see it," Cazio said.

Malconio smiled. "Go on," he said. "*Azdei,* until I see you next."

Cazio clasped his brother's hand, then trudged back up from the strand to where the others waited.

There was only one road out of Duvré, and it was really no more than a narrow track. Cazio led the way, leading their newly purchased donkey, sparing one glance back at his brother's ship before they entered the trees above the village. He saw Malconio, a tiny figure, working with his men.

Then he turned his eyes to the road ahead of him.

The forest soon gave way to rolling fields of wheat. They saw a few distant houses, but no village even the size of Duvré. Dusk found him building a campfire beneath an apple tree so ancient its lower limbs had drooped to the ground.

Anne hadn't said much since she lost her hair. Cazio had never seen a woman without hair and he didn't like the look. It was better when she wrapped the scarf on her head.

He tried to start a conversation with her once or twice, but her answers were terse and didn't go anywhere.

Austra was quiet, too. He gathered the two girls had had some sort of fight on the ship, and both were still sulking about it. He wondered if the fight had been over him. Austra was taking very well to his attentions; if Anne was jealous, she wasn't showing him, but she could be taking it out on Austra.

Which left z'Acatto, who had grumbled drunkenly at having been roused from his stupor, but who by the time they started setting up camp was getting pretty garrulous. When Cazio drew Caspator and began a few exercises, the old man grunted, came to his feet, and drew his own blade.

"I saw you attack with the *z'ostato* the other day," he said.

"I did," Cazio said.

"That's a foolish attack," z'Acatto said. "I never taught you that."

"No," Cazio agreed. "It was something one of Estenio's students tried on me."

"Uh-huh. Did it work?"

Cazio grinned. "No. I replied with the *pero perfo* and let him impale himself."

"Of course. Once your feet leave the ground, you can no longer change direction. You sacrifice all your maneuverability."

"Yes."

Z'Acatto made a few passes in the air. "Then why did you do it?" he asked.

Cazio thought back, trying to remember. "The knight almost had Anne," he said, after a moment. "I might have reached him with a lunge, but my point would not have pierced his armor and the force of the blow wouldn't have been enough to stop him. But with the whole weight of my body behind my tip, I was able to topple him. I think I crushed his windpipe through his gorget, too, but since he was a devil of some sort, that didn't matter."

Z'Acatto nodded. "I never taught you the *z'ostato*, because it is a foolish move when fencing with rapiers. It is not so foolish when fighting an armored man with a heavy sword."

Cazio tried to hide his astonishment. "Are you saying I was right to use it?"

"You were right to use it, but you did not use it correctly. Your form was poor."

"It worked," Cazio protested.

Z'Acatto wagged a finger at him. "What was the first thing I told you about the art of dessrata?"

Cazio sighed and leaned on his sword. "That dessrata isn't about speed or strength, but about doing things correctly," he said.

"Exactly!" z'Acatto cried, flourishing his weapon. "Sometimes speed and strength may allow you to succeed *despite* poor form, don't get me wrong. But one day you will not have that speed and strength, either because you are wounded, or sick—or old, like me. Better to prepare for it."

"Very well," Cazio conceded. "What did I do wrong?"

Z'Acatto set his guard stance. "It begins *thus*, with the back foot," he began. "It must explode forward, and your arm must already be rigid and in line. You should make the attack to the outside line, not the inside, because it's closer. After you strike, you pass, perhaps to thrust again from behind, perhaps merely to run away. Try it."

Under the old man's guidance, Cazio practiced the motion a few times.

"Better," z'Acatto said. "But the leap should be more forward— you shouldn't leave the ground so far behind. The more you go up, the slower it is, and above all this must be quick."

"What is my target, on an armored man?" Cazio inquired.

"The gorget was a fair choice. If the arm is lifted, that's good, too, right in the pit of it. If you're behind, up under the helm. The back of the knee. The eye-slits, if you can hit them."

Cazio grinned. "Didn't you once teach me that one doesn't fight a knight?" Cazio asked.

"One doesn't *fence* with them," Cazio replied. "That doesn't mean you can't kill them."

"Except, apparently, in the case of our present enemies," Cazio reminded him.

"Most of them are flesh and blood," z'Acatto scoffed. "The others we merely need to decapitate. We know it can be done."

He raised his rapier and held it above his head, hilt up and the tip pointed more or less at Cazio's face. "If the broadsword is held like this, and he thrusts, don't parry. Counterattack along his blade and void to the side. Never meet a broadsword with a simple parry. Use your feet—wait for the cut, then thrust, watch for the backswing."

For the next two hours, by firelight, they played at rapier and broadsword, and for the first time in a long time, Cazio felt a return of the sheer joy of dessrata, of learning and practicing with his mestro.

Finally, panting, the old man retired his weapon to its scabbard. "Enough," he sighed. "I'm getting too old for this."

"A few more?" Cazio begged. "What if the blow comes from beneath, but—?"

"No, no. Tomorrow." z'Acatto sagged down onto a rock, wiping a sheen of sweat from his brow.

"When did you fight knights, z'Acatto?" Cazio asked.

Z'Acatto just grunted and looked at the fire.

"Ospero called you Emrature. What did he mean by that?"

"That was a long time ago," z'Acatto murmured. "Times I don't like thinking of when I don't have to."

"You've never said anything about being a commander."

Z'Acatto shook his head. "I just said I don't like to talk about it, didn't I?"

"Yes."

"Well." He got up, stretched out on his blanket, and closed his eyes.

Cazio watched him for a long while. The girls were already asleep. It looked like he had the watch.

* * *

The next day was cool and clear. The fields continued, and after a bell of traveling, they saw a castle on a distant hill. Cazio could make out the white walls and yellow roofs of a small town that lay beneath it.

Presently they reached a fork in the road. One path led toward the castle; the other continued straight.

"Straight on is our direction," Cazio said.

"You're awfully cheerful this morning," Austra noticed. The two of them and the ass were somewhat ahead of the others. Anne was lagging back a bit, and seemed deep in thought. Z'Acatto was limping.

"I suppose I am," Cazio replied. "Why wouldn't I be? I'm in the company of a beautiful casnara, the sun is shining, and we've escaped danger, at least for the moment. Best of all, we're not on a ship."

"There is that," Austra said.

"And all of this," Cazio said, waving his arm about. "It's a change. It's certainly not Vitellio. Is Crotheny like this?"

Austra shook her head. "This is more like Vitellio, really," she said. "Crotheny is wetter. There are more trees and the fields are greener, even this time of year. It's colder there, too."

"Well, I'm looking forward to seeing it. You must be. You must be ready to go home."

Austra lifted her shoulders diffidently. "I'm not sure what home is now," she said. "Everything's changed. I don't know if there will be a place for me anymore."

"What do you mean?"

"I mean I don't know if Anne will still want me as her maid."

"Maid?"

She looked surprised. "Didn't you know?"

"I didn't. I thought you were cousins or friends."

"Well, we *were* friends."

He glanced back at Anne and lowered his voice. "I've noticed you two haven't been very friendly lately."

"We had a fight on the ship," Austra admitted. "I said some things I shouldn't have."

"Well, you've known her for longer than I have," Cazio said, "but she isn't the easiest person in the world to get along with."

"She used to be, to me," Austra said.

"But something's changed."

"Yes. She's changed. Something's happened to her, and she won't tell me what."

Cazio tugged at the mule, who seemed interested in something on the side of the road. "Well," he said, "you tell me her father and sisters were killed, and someone's making a pretty good effort to kill her, too. That's probably had a bit of an effect."

"Of course. But it's more than that."

"Well, I'm sure you two will make up soon," Cazio said. "Or at least I hope so. I hate to see such long faces."

They went another few steps in silence. "I'm glad you're here, Cazio," she said. "Anne is the only friend I ever really had."

"I hope I'm your friend," he said.

"You feel like a friend," Austra replied. "But not like Anne."

"No? What sort of friend am I, then?"

"The sort I rarely even dared to imagine," she replied.

Feeling strange and oddly guilty, he slipped his hand into hers.

Malconio was right. His interest had always been in Anne, though what drove him crazy about that was that he couldn't exactly say why. But Anne was difficult. She still thought she was in love with this Roderick fellow. He'd thought by showing Austra some attention, he might get Anne to look his way—a lot of women were like that. At times he thought he might be succeeding. At others he felt he was wasting his time.

But meanwhile he had succeeded all too well with Austra. There was no mistaking her affection.

To his surprise, he realized he was genuinely starting to return it. She was kind and intelligent, and in her own way every bit as pretty as Anne. Oddly, every time he looked at her, she seemed prettier. Austra was the sort of girl you wanted to hold and comfort, and tell everything would be all right.

But he still wanted Anne.

A little after noon, they reached the great Vitellian way which was, finally, a real road, wide enough for carriages. One passed them, and

Anne watched it go by longingly. She and Austra had traveled to Vitellio in such a carriage, with all the luxuries she had grown up expecting.

Now she was returning home with an ass.

There was one way the two journeys were similar—Austra hadn't been talking to her much in the carriage, either. She had been punishing her for trying to run away. That argument had been fixed with a promise. She didn't think this silence could be so easily broken.

Austra had Cazio now, anyway. The two of them had been holding hands all day.

They stayed that night in a barn just outside of Pacre. The farmer spoke a little king's tongue, and told them they would be crossing into Hornladh soon. Her heart quickened a little at that, and she asked him if he knew where Dunmrogh was. He said it was in the east, but wasn't sure of the way.

That night she lay awake, feeling guilty for not thinking of Roderick more. She knew she loved him, but so much had been happening.

Deep down, she knew it was more. Cazio had planted doubts about Roderick, and though she knew he was wrong, she couldn't get them completely out of her mind. She needed to see him again. Was he in Eslen or back home in Dunmrogh?

Perhaps when they reached Paldh, she could find a courier to carry word to Dunmrogh that she was coming home.

The next day, the fields gave way to expansive vineyards that ran over the hills all the way to the horizon. Anne remembered them from their trip in the carriage—she remembered that she had never imagined there were so many grapes in the entire world.

She glanced over at Austra, who for once wasn't walking twenty yards ahead of her.

"The Teremené River must be up ahead," Anne ventured. "If I remember from your journal."

"I think you're right," Austra said.

"That was clever of you," Anne went on, "keeping that journal. At least we know where we are. How many days do you think we are from Eslen?"

"It was five days by carriage," Austra said. "But we didn't travel all day, and we spent two nights in Paldh."

"Six days, then, or seven do you think, if we press hard?"

"That might be right," Austra allowed.

Anne bit her lip. "Are we going to continue like this?" she asked. "Not talking?"

"We're talking," Austra said.

"You know what I mean."

Austra sighed and nodded. "It's just—I still love you, Anne, but sometimes I think you can't love me."

"That's nonsense," Anne said. "You're my best friend. You've always been my best friend. And I still need you."

"It just hurts, the way you keep shutting me out."

"I know," Anne said.

"But you aren't going to stop."

Anne sighed. "Let me think about it. But can we call a truce for the time being?"

"We aren't at war."

"Well, I'm glad to hear that," Anne said, trying to sound bright.

They chatted after that, speculating about how things would be in Eslen. It wasn't as comfortable as it once had been, but it was better than the silence.

After about a bell, Austra asked for a break so she could answer the call of nature.

"I'll join you," Anne said. "The morning wine's gone straight through me."

Cazio and z'Acatto took the opportunity to sit. "Take your time," Cazio said. "The ass needs a rest."

The two girls strolled up a hill through long rows of grapevines, until they couldn't see the men anymore. Anne wished it was the season for grapes—the dried fish and hard bread they'd purchased with her hair hadn't been good to start with, and she was really sick of it now.

"What's that down there?" Austra asked, when they'd finished what they climbed the hill to do.

Anne peered in the direction the other girl was pointing. The hill sloped down away from where they had left the men, to form a little valley between it and the next hill. A line of willows marked a stream, but before the stream there was what first appeared to be an irregular wall of red brick. Then she saw there was more to it.

"It looks like some sort of ruin," Anne said.

"Can we get a closer look?" Austra asked.

Anne didn't really feel like it—she had had enough of explorations and adventures to last a lifetime. But Austra was talking to her again.

"A small look," she granted. "We shouldn't delay too long."

They made their way down the hill. The formal vines ended halfway down and picked up on the next hill, but the valley was unruly, grown up with wild vines, brush, and bushes. The ground was littered with bricks.

"It must have been a castle, or a mansion," Austra said, when they drew nearer.

Anne nodded in agreement. Grapevines concealed most of the structure. One wall still stood higher than their heads—the rest had crumbled almost to the foundations. Still, they could see the outlines of the rooms that had been there, and it had been a house of considerable size.

Now that they were down here, it was also apparent that there were more buildings, or what had once been buildings. Yet there was something odd about them. Even in ruin, there was something familiar.

Curious, Anne stepped over the remains of a wall and into the nearest ruin. There was a sort of mound not far in, which on closer inspection turned out to be a broken stone box. Something dull and white caught her eye, and she bent to pick it up. It was thin but heavy, and with a start she realized it was a small piece of lead foil. She felt the slight raising of letters on it, and with a gasp dropped it.

"What's wrong?" Austra asked.

"This is a city of the dead," Anne whispered. "Like Eslen-of-Shadows." She backed away from the box, which could only be the remains of a sarcophagus.

"Saints!" Austra murmured, looking around. "But where is the living city? We're too far from Pacre, and I don't think we're to Tere-mené yet."

"No one has kept this up," Anne said. "The city-of-the-quick must be gone, too. Maybe it was farther down the valley."

"A whole town, gone?" Austra wondered aloud. "How could that happen?"

"It happens," Anne said. "It might have been a plague, or war—" A shiver went down her back. "Let's get out of here. These aren't our ancestors. They might not like having us here."

"Wait," Austra said. "Look over there."

Anne reluctantly followed Austra around another pile of rubble. Beyond it stood a construction that was more or less intact, square, four-walled, though with no roof. The arch of the doorway had fallen in, but the opening was still there. Inside, trees and vines grew so thickly, they seemed nearly impenetrable.

"It's a horz," Austra said. "It looks almost like the one back home—where we found Virgenya's tomb."

A strange sensation settled on Anne as she realized Austra was right. She felt something turn behind her eyes and the faint whisper of a voice in a language she did not know.

"We have to leave, Austra," she said urgently. "We have to leave now."

Austra turned, and her eyes widened. "Your face," she said, sounding concerned. "Are you all right?"

"I just have to leave."

The feeling faded as they put the horz behind them.

"What was it?" Austra asked.

"I don't know," Anne replied. Then, seeing the skeptical look on Austra's face, she said, "I really *don't* know. But I'm feeling better now."

Austra suddenly frowned. "Did you hear that?" she asked. "Was that Cazio?"

"I didn't hear anything."

Austra started running up the hill, but Anne caught her by the hand. "Wait," she whispered. "Slowly. Quietly."

"Why? It sounded like he was shouting."

"All the more reason," Anne said. "What if he was trying to warn us?"

"Warn us?" Austra's voice sounded a little panicky.

They hurried to the top of the hill, crouching low, and peered down through the grapevines.

Cazio and z'Acatto were there, along with some twenty riders. Cazio was down on his knees, his sword several yards away, and one of the men was binding his hands behind his back. Z'Acatto was standing and already bound.

It was the knights and soldiers from the docks.

"They've found us," Anne whispered.

"Cazio," Austra gasped. Then she opened her mouth to shout it, and Anne had to clap a hand over it.

"No," Anne barely sighed. "We have to run."

Austra closed her eyes and nodded. Anne removed her hand.

"We can't leave them," Austra said anxiously.

"They didn't kill them," Anne said. "They won't unless they catch us, do you see? But if they do catch us, we'll all die."

"I—"

"They'll come up here," Anne said. "We're lucky they haven't already, but they recognized Cazio and z'Acatto, so they know we must be somewhere. The only way we can help them is by staying free."

"I suppose so," Austra relented.

They started back down the hill, toward the ruins, creeping at first, but when they heard horses' hooves coming up behind them, they began to run.

CHAPTER TWO

THE BLIND, THE DEAF, AND THE DARKNESS

WHEN ALIS BERRYE ENTERED, Muriele waved her to a seat.

"Tell me what is happening," she said. "Tell me how I might die today."

Berrye frowned and clutched her hands together. "Majesty," she said, "first I'd like to discuss the matter of the attack on Lady Gramme's manse."

"Go on," Muriele said, reaching for her cup of tea.

"You ordered that because of my suggestion that Prince Robert was there, and that the lady Gramme was plotting against you. I fear I have failed you."

"Because we did not find Robert?" Muriele took a sip of the tea. "That's hardly a surprise. That matter went very poorly, but it was not your fault. There should not have been an attack, for one thing. My orders were to surround the place so no one could sneak away. Sir Fail was then to enter with my authority and conduct a peaceful search. Instead, his men were set upon and they reacted like the warriors they are. But Robert aside, it's fairly clear that Gramme was conspiring to win over the support of the Newland landwaerden. That in itself was worth knowing."

Berrye continued to look troubled. "Majesty, I could have discovered that myself, without bloodshed."

"You have the presumption to tell me that sending my men to Gramme's was a mistake?"

"It is my duty to tell you such things, Majesty," Berrye replied. "It is in the nature of what you have asked me to do."

Muriele raised an eyebrow, but Berrye was right. Erren had never shied from telling her when she had been a fool. Of course, Erren had been older, and her friend of many years. Having this *girl* remonstrate with her was—annoying.

"Very well, I accept that," she said reluctantly. "I know that it was an unpopular move, particularly in certain quarters. But I felt I had to make some show of force, make some statement that I will not sit passive and be a target."

"Maybe so," Berrye agreed, "but you might have picked another battle. The landwaerden are no longer disaffected with the throne—they are furious at it. Your support in the Comven is weaker than ever, and the rumor in the streets is that you have gone mad. Worst of all, the praifec has begun to speak against you."

"Really," Muriele said. "What does the praifec say?"

"He suggests pointedly that you have wrested power from your son."

"He knows very well Charles isn't capable of making decisions."

Berrye nodded. "That is, I believe, his point. His further point being that your son should be removed from your council and placed under his."

Muriele smiled bitterly. "Only a few days ago, he suggested that I allow troops from z'Irbina to camp in this city. Did you know that?"

"No, but I could have guessed it. The Church is in motion, Majesty. I do not know the exact nature of their agenda, but I think it certain they are ending their long recusion from direct interference in secular affairs."

Muriele settled her cup on the arm of her chair. "Hespero said something like that, too," she said. "Very well—kill him for me."

"Majesty?" Berrye's eyes widened fractionally.

"I'm joking, Lady Berrye."

"I . . . Oh, good."

"Unless you think I've gone mad, as well."

"I don't think that at all, Majesty," Berrye assured her.

"Well, good," she said sarcastically. "You've told me what I did wrong—I'm open to your suggestions of what to do right."

"It's of the greatest importance that you win the landwaerden and merchants back to your cause, Majesty," the girl replied. "I cannot stress that enough."

"Believe it or not," Muriele said, "I had entertained thoughts along those lines some weeks ago. I commissioned a piece of music to be composed for them and for the common people of the city. The performance was to be some three weeks hence, with a banquet to accompany it. I didn't know that Lady Gramme had beaten me to it. Now I suppose there's little point. It will only seem like an apology."

"Which is precisely why you should go ahead with it," Berrye said. "But you must go farther, I think, and consider what laws you might reform to pacify them. I would suggest a formal hearing where they may present their demands."

"I'll do so tomorrow. What else?"

"Whether you've thrown in with Liery or not, everyone thinks you have. You have two choices: either disprove that notion by marrying Berimund, or make it true in every sense by marrying one of the Lierish lords."

"No," Muriele said. "What else?"

"Free Gramme immediately," Berrye urged. "You haven't proved she's done anything wrong, and if something happens to her while she is in your custody, it will only make you look worse."

"I was rather hoping something *would* happen to her while she was in my custody," Muriele replied.

"I hope that's another joke, Majesty."

"It is, Lady Berrye, but just barely. I'll have her freed within the hour. Is there anything else?"

"Yes. Make some appearances outside this hall. And get some sleep—you're getting circles beneath your eyes."

Muriele chuckled. "Erren used to comb my hair. Are you going to start that, too?"

"If you wish, Majesty," Berrye said cautiously.

"No, thank you. I think I would find it a trifle too familiar, having my husband's mistress running a comb through my hair."

"That's understandable."

"Did you comb his hair?"

"I— Now and then," Berrye confessed.

"Did that strange snuffling noise he made in his sleep annoy you?"

"I found it endearing, Majesty."

"Well. Thank you, Lady Berrye. We'll speak again when you have more to report."

Berrye got up to leave.

"One moment, Lady Berrye," Muriele murmured, reaching a reluctant decision.

"Yes, Majesty."

"The assassin who invaded my chambers took something. A key."

"A key to what, Majesty?"

"I'm about to show you."

Berrye paused at the edge of the light.

"Come along," Muriele said.

"But majesty, there are no more torches. Perhaps we should return for a lantern."

"One shall be provided," Muriele said. But she turned to the younger woman. "It's good to know you don't know all my secrets."

"I know nothing of this place, except that once—not long before he died—His Majesty went someplace in the dungeons, and when he returned he was pale, and would not speak of it."

"I did not know this place existed until after William died. I found a key in his room, and the questions it brought up led me here. But no one would admit to knowing what was down here."

She stepped into the darkness, and Berrye followed. Muriele felt for the wooden door she knew was there and found its handle.

"There is no music," she whispered.

"Should there be?" Berrye asked.

"The Keeper sometimes amuses himself by playing the theorbo," Muriele said.

"Keeper?"

Instead of answering the implicit question, Muriele rapped on the door. When no immediate answer came, she rapped again, harder.

"Perhaps he is asleep," Berrye said.

"I do not think so," Muriele replied. "Come, let us take one of the torches—"

She was interrupted by the nearly soundless opening of the door.

The Keeper's face appeared ruddy in the faint light from up the hall. It was an ancient, beautiful face, not obviously male or female. His filmed, blind eyes seemed to search for them.

"It is the queen," Muriele said. "I need to speak to you."

The Keeper didn't answer, but searched toward her with a shaking hand, and Muriele understood that something was terribly wrong.

"Keeper," she said. "Answer me."

His only response was to open his mouth, as if to scream.

She saw than that he had no tongue.

"Saints," she gasped, backing away, and then with an astounding violence, she retched and stumbled against the wall. She felt as if there were maggots writhing in her belly.

Berrye was suddenly there, supporting her with surprising strength.

"I'll be fine—," Muriele began, and vomited again, and again.

When at last the sickness passed, she straightened herself on wobbly legs.

"I take it he used to have the power of speech," Berrye said.

"Yes," Muriele answered weakly.

The Keeper was still standing there, impassive. Berrye circled him, peering closely.

"I think his eardrums have been punched out," she said. "He cannot hear us, either."

Shaking, Muriele approached the aged Sefry. "Who did this," she whispered. "Who did this?"

"Whoever took your key, I presume," Berrye said.

Muriele felt strange tears on her face. She did not know the Keeper—she had met him only once, and then she had threatened him with the loss of his hearing. She had not meant it, of course, but she had been distraught.

"His whole life is spent here," Muriele said, "in the darkness, without sight. Serving. But he had his music and conversation when someone came. Now what does he have?"

"His ears may heal," Berrye said. "It has been known to happen."

"I will send my physician down." She reached toward the groping hand and took it in her own. It gripped back with a sort of desperation, and the Keeper's face contorted briefly. Then he dropped his fingers away, stepped back, and closed his door.

"What does he keep, my queen?" Berrye asked.

Muriele strode back up the hallway and wrested a torch from the socket. Then, with Berrye following, they descended a stair carved in living rock.

"There are bones in the rock," Berrye observed as they padded down the damp steps.

"Yes," Muriele replied. "The Keeper told me they are older than the stone itself."

Beyond the foot of the stair stood an iron door scrived with strange characters. The air smelled like burning pitch and cinnamon, and the echo of their voices seemed to stir other, fainter utterances.

"Over two thousand years ago," Muriele began, "a fortress stood where Eslen now stands, the last fortress of the Skasloi lords who kept our ancestors as slaves. Here Virgenya Dare and her army pulled down the walls and slew the final members of that demon race. They slew all but one—him they kept crippled but alive."

She approached the door and placed the tips of her fingers against it.

"This door requires two keys—the one that was taken from my room, and the Keeper's. Beyond that door is another, through which no light may be brought. And there he is."

"The last of the Skasloi," Berrye said softly. "Still alive after all this time. I could never have imagined."

"The Skasloi did not die natural deaths," Muriele said. "They did not age as we do."

"But why? Why keep such a thing alive?"

"Because it has knowledge," Muriele said, "and sight beyond that of mortal men. For two thousand years, the kings of Crotheny have wrested advice from him."

"Even the sisters of the coven don't know about this," Berrye said. "Surely the Church must not, or they would have had him killed." Her eyebrows lifted a little. "You have spoken to it?"

Muriele nodded. "After William and my children were slain. I asked him how I could revenge myself on the murderers."

"And he told you."

"Yes."

"Did it work?"

Muriele smiled bitterly. "I don't know. I cursed whoever was behind the murders, but I do not know who he was. Therefore I do not know whether my curse succeeded. But I felt as if it worked. I felt something move, like a tumbler in a lock."

"Curses are dangerous," Berrye cautioned. "They send out ripples like a stone striking water. You can never know what your intent will result in."

"*Queeeeeen,*" a voice scratched in Muriele's head.

"He's speaking to me," Muriele murmured. "Can you hear him?"

"I don't hear anything, Majesty," Berrye said.

"*Queeeen, stink of woman, stink of motherhood. Doors stand between us. Will you not come to me?*"

"I cannot," she said. "I do not have the key."

Something like black laughter rattled in her skull. "*No. He has it. The one you made.*"

Muriele's heart clenched like a fist in her chest.

"The one I made? What do you mean?"

"*I sing of him, I sing and sing. When the world itself cracks, perhaps I will die.*"

"Tell me," she demanded. "Tell me who it is. You cannot lie to me."

"*You don't have the key . . .*" The voice soughed away, like a wind dying. Muriele's last impression was of glee.

"Answer me," she shrieked. "Quexqaneh, answer me!"

But the voice did not return, and by degrees, Muriele calmed herself.

"We have to find out who came here," Muriele told Berrye. "We must know what he spoke to the Kept about, and I must have my key back."

"I will do my best," Berrye said. She sounded a little shaken, and looked very young. Muriele suddenly regretted sharing the secret of the Kept with her, but who else could help her? Sir Fail and his men would be of no help in matters of espionage. Berrye had proved that she had some facility in that area. Constrained as her choices were, telling Berrye was the only thing she could do.

And it was already done, now.

They left the dungeons. She returned to her rooms, summoned her personal physician to attend the Keeper, signed the order for the release of Gramme and her son, and retired early to bed.

Dreams of spiders and serpents and eyeless old men woke her every few hours.

The next day she prepared to hold court, as Berrye suggested. She had avoided it since the attempt on her life, but she couldn't avoid it forever. So she had Charles dressed, and when Berrye was late, began dressing herself. She chose a gown of purple safnite with a stiff fan of lace around the collar and began working herself into it, though she knew she couldn't do up the back. It occurred to her that she needed a new maid, but her grief over Unna was still fresh enough that she couldn't bear the thought of choosing one. She thought she might assign Berrye to the task, and realized just how much she was already relying on the young woman.

She isn't Erren, she reminded herself. *She was your husband's whore.*

But there was something about her so like Erren, a certain confidence that could only come from coven training, that Muriele found herself slipping into old habits.

Old habits could be fatal. She still had no proof that Berrye's intentions were honest. And she was *late*.

She was just getting really irritated when the girl finally arrived. She was opening her mouth to complain when she saw Berrye's expression.

"What?" Muriele asked.

"He's here, Majesty," she said, sounding out of breath. "Prince Robert is here. I have seen him."

So it was true. Muriele closed her eyes. "He's in the castle?"

"In the throne room, Majesty, waiting for you."

"Do you know what he intends?" She lifted her eyelids.

Berrye sat and put her palms to her forehead. Muriele had never seen her so upset.

"He has his guard with him, Your Majesty, forty men. The Duke of Shale and Lord Fram Dagen have at least twenty men each. Every other member of the Comven has his guard with him, and there is word of landwaerden militia in the city."

The room seemed to pulse, expanding and shrinking with Muriele's heartbeat. She sat heavily in her armchair, unmindful of her half-finished job of dressing.

"He's here to take the throne," she said. Her mouth was dry.

"That is my best guess, Your Majesty."

"It is the *only* guess."

"I should have seen this coming," Berrye said bitterly.

"You did see it coming," Muriele muttered.

"But not so soon," Berrye disagreed. "Not nearly this soon. I thought we had time to act, to blunt the blow."

"Well, we haven't." She closed her eyes, trying to think. "Sir Fail has thirty men. There are twenty Craftsmen—if I can trust them—and their men-at-arms, altogether another hundred men I'm not sure I can count on. Indeed, they might well choose Robert as their king."

"They cannot, by law," Berrye said. "Not while Charles and Anne live."

"No one knows Anne is alive, and Charles—they might make exception for Charles due to his nature. Robert might go farther. If he slew the father, he might well slay the son."

She stood and turned her back to Berrye. "Lady Berrye, would you do my fastenings?"

"You still intend to attend court?"

"I'm still thinking," Muriele said.

Berrye began latching the fastenings. Muriele could feel the girl's breath on her hair. Her heartbeat seemed to slow, and an odd calm settled as a plan began sorting itself out.

"You know the passages," Muriele said, as Berrye latched the third hook. "Do you know the way out of the city?"

"The long passage that goes under the wall? The one that can be filled with water?"

"That is the only one I know," Muriele replied.

"I know where it is," Berrye said. "I've never been there."

"But you're certain you can find it."

"I studied the plans of this castle at my coven. So far I've found no error in them." She fastened the last catch and the collar.

"Good."

Muriele strode to her antechamber and summoned the guard outside the door.

"Bring Sir Fail here immediately," she said.

The knight had taken up residence in Elseny's chambers, which were just down the hall. He arrived a few moments later.

"Sir Fail," she said. "I need another favor of you."

"Whatever you require, Majesty."

"I need you to take Charles to Liery."

The old man's mouth dropped open, and he stared at her for a moment. "What?" He finally managed.

Muriele crossed her arms and regarded her uncle. "Prince Robert, as fate would have it, is not dead at all. He has returned, and I believe today he will seize the throne. I want my son kept safe, Sir Fail."

"I—surely we can stop him. He has no right—"

"I will not risk that," Muriele replied. She nodded at Alis Berrye. "You know this lady?"

"Lady Berrye, yes." He looked puzzled.

"There is a safe way out of the castle, a secret way. She knows it, and will lead you out. You are to collect Charles and leave immediately. Leave me two escorts, and take the rest of your men in case there are enemies at your ship."

"But of course you're going with us," Fail said.

"No, I'm not," Muriele replied. "That is the favor I am asking, and there is no time to discuss it beyond a simple yes or no."

"Muriele—"

"Please, Sir Fail. I've lost two of my daughters."

He straightened. "Then yes. But I will return for you."

"And you will have the rightful king behind you when you do," Muriele told him. "Do you understand?"

"I understand." Fail's eyes misted, and his head sagged. Sighing, she stepped forward and hugged him.

"Thank you, Uncle Fail," she said.

He squeezed her arms. "Saints be with you, Meur," he murmured.

Berrye caught her arm. "I'll be back, after I've shown them the way."

"No," Muriele said. "Stay with them. Watch my son."

When they were gone, she returned to her armchair for half a bell, to give them time to get started. Then, taking a deep breath, she rose and left her rooms and marched down the corridor to where Sir Moris Lucas, captain of the Craftsmen, was housed.

He answered her knock with a look of vast surprise.

"Majesty," he said. "To what do I owe this honor?"

"Sir Moris," Muriele began, "I have not treated you and your men well, these past months."

"If you say so, Majesty," he replied, sounding uncertain.

"That being said, I must ask you to bear a few direct and impertinent questions."

"I will answer any question Her Majesty puts to me," the knight assured her.

"Are the Craftsmen faithful to me and my son Charles?"

Moris stiffened. "We are faithful to Charles as king and to you as his mother," he replied.

"And do you recognize any other claim to the throne?"

Moris' frown deepened. "Princess Anne has a claim, but she is not, to my knowledge, present."

"You have heard that Prince Robert has returned?"

"There is a rumor to that effect," Moris said.

"What if I were to tell you that I think he slew my husband and the Craftsmen and Royal Horse who rode with him to the headland of Aenah?"

"I would call that a reasonable supposition, Majesty. And if you're asking if I would follow Prince Robert, the answer is no."

"And you trust your men?"

He hesitated. "Most of them," he finally admitted.

"Then I lay this geis on you, Sir Moris, and on your men. I want you to leave this castle and this city, even if you must fight your way out."

His eyes rounded like regaturs. "Majesty? We will stand by you."

"If you do, you will die. I need you alive, outside of the castle, outside of Eslen, where you can find the support you need to enforce my justice. I want you to take Hound Hat, and I want you to dress one of your men in a heavy cloak and hood, so that it appears you have Charles with you."

"But the king, Majesty—"

"Is still the king. He will be safe, I assure you."

Moris absorbed that for several breaths. "Do you want us to leave now, Majesty?"

"Now and as quietly as possible. I want no blood spilled unless it's absolutely necessary."

He bowed. "By your command, lady. Saints be with you."

"And with you, sir," she replied.

She returned to her quarters, thinking that at least now she would know—once and for all—if the Craftsmen could indeed be trusted. Actions proved better than words.

She put on her circlet, collected the two escorts Fail had left her, and went to court.

CHAPTER THREE

SWORDSMAN, PRIEST, AND CROWN

W HEN STEPHEN BROKE THE praifec's seal, he knew he had severed himself from the Church. The seal was sacrosanct, to be opened only by the intended recipient. Punishment for a novice or priest who broke that sacred trust began with expulsion from holy orders. After that, they were subject to temporal punishment—which could be anything from a whipping to death by drowning.

But to Stephen, that was nothing. For the Church to prosecute him for the crime, they would have to know he had committed it, and if he wished to hide that from them, he probably could. No, the reason he broke the seal was because he knew in his heart the rot he'd found in the monastery d'Ef wasn't just a bad spot on a pear—the whole fruit was rotten, through and through, along with the tree it grew on.

If the fathers of the Church were behind the waking of the Damned Saints, the implications were staggering. And if the Church itself was corrupt, he wanted no part of it—or, rather, no part larger than the one he had already played. He would serve the saints in his own way.

"Stephen?" Winna asked. "What does it say?"

He realized he'd been staring past the inked characters without reading them. He tried to clear his mind and concentrate.

Strange, he thought. Besides the signature and a verse that looked like Vadhiian, the letter was gibberish.

"Ah. It's some sort of encryption," he told them. "A cypher."

"A knot of words *you* can't untie?" Aspar said. "I doubt that."

Stephen nodded, concentrating. "Given time, I could read it. It's based on Church Vitellian, and an older liturgical language called Jhehdykhadh. But written as it is, it doesn't mean anything. There is this verse here, though . . ." He trailed off, studying it. It *was* Old Vadhiian, or some closely related dialect.

"There's a *canitu* here," he said, "in the language of the Warlock Lords, a *canitu subocaum*—ah, an 'incantation to invoke.' "

"Invoke whom?" Leshya asked.

"*Khrwbh Khrwkh*," he replied, shaking his head. "I've never heard of it, whatever that is. But not all the Damned Saints are commonly known. Actually, it sounds more like a place than a person—it means something like 'bent mound.' "

"Could it refer to a sedos?" Leshya asked.

"Easily," Stephen replied. "And given what we've seen so far, that makes the most sense. It's just that they've prefixed the name with *dhy,* which usually indicates that the name following will be that of a saint. It's quite puzzling."

"In any event," Leshya said, "it's pointless to go back to Eslen to alert your praifec, since it seems perfectly clear he's well aware of what's going on out here."

"Well, *I'm* not clear on it," Aspar said.

"Neither am I," Leshya shot back, "but we know now that the Church is waking an old faneway, and it seems just as certain that it's not a good idea to let them finish it."

"They may *have* finished it," Aspar said.

"I don't think so," Stephen said. "I believe these are the instructions for the consecration of this *Khrwbh Khrwkh,* whatever exactly it might be. And the canitu appears to be part of a longer piece—or more specifically, the *end* of a longer piece."

"You're saying that we have what they need to finish it."

"Yes, that's exactly what I'm saying. Listen, I'll try to translate for you." He cleared his throat.

And now to the Bent Mound
The Bloody Crescent
Blood for the Bent Mound
Blood of Seven
Blood of Three
Blood of One
Let the Seven be mortal in all ways
Let the Three be Swordsman, Priest, and Crown
Let the One be Deathless
Beat then the Heart of Bent Mound
Flow from the Spectral Eye
Flow from the Mother Devouring
Flow from Pel the Rage Giver
Flow from Huskwood
Flow from the Twins, Rot and Decay
Flow from the Not Dead.
Here it begins, the way is complete.

There was a moment of silence, and then Aspar grunted. "A drinking song it's not."

"I'm not sure about all of it," Stephen admitted. "That bit about swordsman, priest, and crown, for instance. The words here are *Pir Khabh*, *dhervhidh*, and *Thykher*. The first is very particular, a man who fights with a sword. *Dhervhidh* means 'someone who has walked a faneway,' but not necessarily in orders. The third, *Thykher*, could be anyone of noble blood or it might mean a king specifically. Without better resources, better reference materials, I've no way of knowing for sure."

"What was that about 'deathless'?" Winna asked.

"*Mhwrmakhy*," Stephen said. It really means 'servant of the *Mhwr*,' another name for the Black Jester, but they were also called 'anmhyry' or 'deathless.' " We don't know much about them except that they don't exist anymore."

"Didn't exist anymore, you mean," Leshya said. "That used to be true of a lot of things."

"Granted," Stephen agreed, a little diffidently. Something was gnawing at him about the list of "flowing froms."

Aspar noticed his inattention. "What is it?" he asked.

Stephen folded his arms across his chest.

"A faneway has to be walked in sequence, and the whole faneway has to be awake, so to speak, for its power to flow properly. That's why something strange happened when I set foot on one, probably because I already have a connection to the sedoi."

"And so?" Leshya asked.

"Well, if I understand this invocation, the last sedos in the faneway is *Khrwbh Khrwkh*," Stephen explained. "We don't know where that is, obviously, but according to this verse, the first one is the Spectral Eye . . ."

"You know where that is?" Aspar asked.

"In a minute," Stephen said absently. "I'm still thinking this through."

"No, please, take your time," Aspar muttered.

"The second one, 'Mother Devouring'—that's the fane I went in, I'm certain of it. The first one Leshya led us to. That's one of the titles of Marhirheben.

"Aspar, back when you were tracking the greffyn, after you sent me off to d'Ef, you said you found a sacrifice at a sedos. Where was that, exactly?"

"About five leagues east of here, on Taff Creek."

"Taff," Stephen considered. Then he reached into his saddle, back where his maps were rolled up. He selected the one he wanted, then sat down cross-legged and rolled it out on the ground.

"What map is that?" Leshya asked, peering down at it.

"Stephen is in the habit of carrying maps a thousand years out of date," Aspar said.

"Yes," Stephen said, "but it may have finally done some good. This is a copy of a map made during the time of the Hegemony. The place-names have been altered to make sense to the Vitellian ear and to be written in the old scrift. Where would the Taff be, Aspar?"

The holter bent over and studied the yellowed paper. "The forest is different," he said. "There's more of it. But the rivers are near the same." He thrust his finger at a small, squiggling line. "Thereabout," he said.

"See the name of the creek?" Stephen asked.

"Tavata," Winna read.

Stephen nodded. "It's a corruption of Alotersian *tadvat*, I'll wager—which means 'specter.' "

"That's it, then," Leshya said.

Aspar made a skeptical noise.

Stephen moved his finger over a bit. "So the one on the Taff is the first. The one I stepped into is the second, and about here. That last one was about here." He placed his finger on curved lines indicating hills. One, oddly, had a dead tree sketched on its summit.

"Does that mean anything to you, Aspar? Do you know anything about that place?"

Aspar frowned. "It used to be where the old people made sacrifice to Grim. They hung 'em on that Naubagm tree."

"Haergrim the Raver?"

Aspar nodded slowly, his face troubled.

"I've never heard of Pel," Stephen allowed, "but the fact that both he and Haergrim are connected to rage is interesting, isn't it?"

"I follow you now," Leshya said. "So far, the monks have been moving east, and we've seen the first three of them. So where is the fourth?"

"Huskwood. In Vadhiian, *Vhydhrabh*." He moved his finger east, until it came to rest on the d'Ef River. There was a town labeled Vitraf.

"Whitraff!" Winna exploded. "It's a village! It's still there!"

"Or so we hope," Stephen said grimly.

"Yah," Aspar said. "We'd best go see. And let me know when our prisoner wakes. He might be convinced to tell us more about this."

But when they checked him, the monk was dead.

They gave the monk a holter's funeral—which amounted to nothing more than laying him supine with his hands folded on his chest—and set off across the Brog-y-Stradh uplands. The forest often dissolved into heathered meadows and lush, ferny cloonys. Even with winter set to pounce, in these parts, the King's Forest seemed to teem with life.

Stephen could tell that Aspar and Leshya saw things he didn't. They rode at the front like dour siblings, guiding Ehawk's mount. Winna had ridden with them for a time, but now she dropped back.

"How are you feeling?" she asked.

"I feel fine," Stephen said. But it wasn't completely true—there was something nagging at him. He couldn't tell her, though, that when he had awakened on the mound and grabbed Ehawk's bow, he'd very nearly put an arrow into her instead of the monk.

Those first few heartbeats, he had felt a hatred that he couldn't have imagined before, and could not now truly recall. Not for Winna specifically, but for everything living. It had faded so suddenly that he almost doubted he'd truly felt it.

He'd remembered dreams of some sort on first waking, as well, but those were gone, too, leaving only a vague, unclean feeling.

"What about you?" he asked. "I've never seen you so subdued."

She grimaced slightly. "It's a lot to take in," she said. "I'm a hostler's daughter, remember? A few months ago my greatest worry was that Banf Thelason might get drunk and start a fight or Enry Flory might try and run off without paying for his ale. Even when I was with Aspar when he was tracking the greffyn, it was pretty simple. Now I don't know who we're supposed to be fighting. The Briar King? The praifec? Villagers gone mad? Who does that leave out? And what good am I?"

"Don't talk like that," Stephen said.

"Why not? It's what Aspar has been saying all along. I've denied it, come up with excuses, but down in the marrow, I know he's right. I can't fight or track, I don't know much of anything, and every time there's a brawl, I have to be protected."

"Not like Leshya, eh?" Stephen said.

Her eyes widened. "Don't be cruel," she whispered.

"But it's what you're thinking," he said, surprised to hear such bold words coming from his mouth. "She's beautiful, and more his age. She's Sefry and he was raised that way, she can track like a wolf and fight like a panther, and she seems to know more about this whole business than the rest of us put together. Why wouldn't he want her instead of you?"

"I—" She choked off. "Why are you talking this way?"

"Well, for one thing, I know how it feels to think you're useless," he said. "And no one can make you feel as perfectly useless as Aspar. It's not something he does on purpose—it's just that he's so good at what he does. He says he doesn't need anything or anyone, and sometimes you actually believe him."

"You, useless?" she said. "You've saint-given talents. You've knowledge of the small and the large and everything between, and without you we wouldn't have the faintest idea what to do."

"I wasn't saint-blessed when Aspar met me," he pointed out, remembering vividly the holter's undisguised contempt, "and Aspar certainly thought I was dead weight. By the time we parted, I thought he was right. But I was mistaken. So are you, and you know it."

"I don't—"

"Why did you follow Aspar, Winna? Why did you leave Colbaely and your father and everything you knew to chase after a holter?"

She bent her mouth to one side, a habit he found winsome. "Well, I never maunted to actually *leave* Colbaely," she said, "not for this long. I thought Asp was in danger and went to warn him, and then I reckoned I'd go back home."

"But you didn't. Why?"

"Because I'm in love with him," she said.

That pricked a peculiar feeling in Stephen, but he pressed on through it. "Still, you must have been in love with him for a while," Stephen said. "It didn't happen that fast, did it?"

"I've loved him since I was a little girl." She sighed.

"So why, suddenly, did you do something about it?"

"I didn't intend to," she said. "It's just—I found him all laid out on the ground. I thought he was dead, and I thought he would never know."

"Why did you imagine he would care?"

She shook her head and looked miserable. "I don't know."

"May I tell you what I think?" Stephen asked.

Winna tossed her hair out of her face. It had been cut short when he met her, but now it was getting pretty long. "Why not?" she said morosely. "You've been about as blunt as I can imagine already."

"I think you saw in that moment that Aspar was missing something. He's strong and determined and skillful, and he's smart, in his way. But he doesn't have a heart, not without you. Without you, he's just another part of the forest, wandering farther and farther from being human. You brought him back to us." He paused, retracing the words in his mind. "Does that make any sense?"

Winna's brow crinkled, but she didn't say anything.

"It's why the three of us work so well together," he went on. "He's the muscle and the knife and the arrow. I have the book knowledge he pretends to disdain, but knows he needs, and you're sovereign to us both, the thing that ties us all together."

She snorted. "Swordsman, priest, and crown?"

He blinked. She was referring to the Vadhiian incantation.

"Well, it is a very old trinity," he said. "Even the saints break out in threes, that way—Saint Nod, Saint Oimo, and Saint Loy, for instance."

"I'm not a queen," Winna said. "I'm just a girl from Colbaely who's gone off where she doesn't belong."

"That's not true," Stephen said.

"Well then where does *she* fit in?" she asked, jerking her nose toward Leshya.

"She doesn't," Stephen said. "She's another Aspar, that's what she is, and he won't get a heart from her, nor she from him."

"Aspar's never much wanted a heart," Winna said. "Maybe what he needs *is* a woman who's more like him."

"Doesn't matter what he wants," Stephen said. "Love doesn't care what's right, or good, or what anyone wants."

"I know that all too well," Winna said.

"Do you feel any better at all?"

"Maybe," she said. "If I don't, it's not for lack of trying. Thank you, Stephen."

They rode silently after that, and Stephen was glad, because he wasn't sure he could defend Aspar much longer without breaking faith. He hadn't lied—everything he'd said was true.

Including, unfortunately, the bit about love not caring what was right, or good, or what anyone wants.

Whitraff was there, but even at a distance it looked dead. The air was chill, yet not a single line of smoke traced the sky. No one was in the streets, and there was no sound that might come from man or woman.

Most of the villages and towns around the King's Forest weren't all that old—most, like Colbaely, had sprouted up in the last hundred years. The houses tended to be built of wood and the streets of dirt. Aspar remembered Whitraff as an old town—its narrow avenues were cobbles worn shiny by a hundred generations of boots and buskins. The heart of the town wasn't large—about thirty houses huddled around the bell-tower square—but there had once been outlying farms to the east and stilt houses along the riverfront that went on for some way. It had always been a pretty lively place, for all of its small size, because it was the only river port south of Ever, which was a good twenty winding leagues downriver.

Now the outliers were ash, but the stone town still stood. Looking down on it from the hill above, Aspar noticed that the bell tower was missing. It was simply gone. In its place—on the mound where the tower had once stood—was the now all-too-familiar sight. A ring of death.

"Sceat," he muttered.

"We're too late," Winna said.

"Far too late," Leshya said. "This was done months ago, to judge by the burned homesteads."

Aspar nodded. The dead scattered around the sedos looked to be mostly bone.

"Bad luck, that," he said, "to build your town on the footprint of a Damned Saint."

"I don't see how you can joke about it," Winna said. "All those people . . . I don't see how you can joke about it."

Aspar glanced at her. "I wasn't joking," he said softly. Lately it seemed impossible to say the right thing around Winna. "Anyway, maybe it's not so bad as it looks. Maybe the rest of the townsfolk got away." He turned to the Sefry. "This is a good position. You and Ehawk keep a watch from up here while we go down to have a look."

"Suits me," Leshya said.

They took the road in, and despite his words, it was as he'd feared. No one came out to greet them. The town was as quiet as its twin, Whitraff-of-Shadows, just upstream.

Of the people there was no sign.

Aspar dismounted in front of the River Cock, once the busiest tavern in the village.

"You two watch my back," he told Stephen and Winna. "I'm taking a look in here."

There wasn't anyone inside, and there were no bodies, which wasn't terribly surprising. But he did find that a roast on a spit had been allowed to burn to char, and one of the ale taps had been left open, so all the beer had drained out to form a still-sticky mass on the floor.

He went back out into the square.

"They left in a hurry," he said. "There's no blood, or signs of fighting."

"The monks might have thrown the bodies into the river," Winna suggested.

"They might have, or they might have gotten away. But here's what I'm wondering—this river isn't the busiest around, but someone would have noticed *this,* and as Leshya said, this must have happened a couple of months ago, maybe even before we fought Desmond Spendlove and his bunch. Why hasn't anyone cleaned up the bodies? Why hasn't anyone moved in, or at least sent word downriver?"

"Maybe they did," Stephen said, "and the praifec kept it to himself."

"Yah, but rivermen who saw this would talk it all up and down the river. *Someone* would have come to have a look."

"You're thinking the Church left it garrisoned?" Stephen asked.

"I don't see sign of that, either. Plenty of ale and stores left in the tavern—you'd think a garrison would have tucked into that. Besides, I didn't see any smoke coming in, and I don't smell it now. But if it isn't garrisoned, why hasn't some passing boatman robbed the tavern?"

"Because no one who's come here has left," Winna said.

"Werlic," Aspar agreed, scanning the buildings.

"Maybe there's a greffyn here," Stephen said.

"Maybe," he conceded. "There was one with the monks back at Grim's Gallows." He didn't mention that it had avoided him.

"I'm going down the waterfront," he decided. "You two follow and keep me in sight, but not too close. If a greffyn's been killing boatmen, we ought to find their boats and bodies."

His boots echoed hollowly as he made his way down the little street that sloped toward the river. Soon enough he made out the wooden docks. Still there. He didn't see any boats at all. Crouching in the shadow of the last house, he peered intently at the far bank of the river. The trees came right up to the water, and nothing obviously worrisome caught his eye. He glanced back and saw Winna and Stephen, watching him nervously.

He motioned that he was going closer.

A tattered yellow wind-banner fluttered in the breeze, producing nearly the only noise as he approached the planking of the docks. The only birds he heard were quite distant.

Which was odd. Even in an empty town, there ought to be pigeons and housecrows. On the river there should be kingfishers, whirr-plungers, and egrets, even this time of year.

Instead, nothing.

Something caught his eye, then, and he dropped back into a crouch, bow ready, but he couldn't identify what he'd seen. Something subtle, a weird play of light.

And the scent of autumn in his nostrils that always meant death was near.

Slowly, he began to back up, because he could feel something now, something hiding just beneath the skin of the world.

He saw it again, and understood. Not the world, but the *water*. Something huge was moving just under the surface.

He kept backing up, but he remembered that being far from the water hadn't helped the people of Whitraff.

The water mounded up suddenly, and something rose above it with the sluggishness of a monster in a dream that knows its victim can't outrun it. He had only an impression of it at first, of sinewy form and sleek fur or possibly scales, and of immensity.

And then it called in a voice so beautiful that he knew he'd been wrong, that this creature was no destroyer of life, but was the very essence of it. He'd come to the place where life and death changed, where hunter and hunted were one, and all was peace.

Relieved beyond words, Aspar lay down his bow, stood straight, and walked to meet it.

CHAPTER FOUR

BORDERLANDS

SOMEONE BEGAN SHOUTING JUST as Anne and Austra reentered the ruined city of the dead. Anne whipped her head around and saw two fully armored men on horseback charging down the hill.

"They've seen us!" she shouted unnecessarily.

She ducked behind the first building, practically dragging Austra with her, looking wildly around for somewhere to hide.

Death or capture lay in every direction—the orderly rows of grapes on either side of the valley offered no real protection; they might elude their pursuers for a little longer, but in the end they would be run down.

Hiding posed the same problem, of course, and there really wasn't anyplace to hide.

Except the horz. If it was as thickly grown as it looked, they might be able to squeeze into places where larger, armored men couldn't follow.

"This way," she told Austra. "Quickly, before they can see us."

It felt like forever, reaching the walled garden, but as they passed through the ruined arch, the knights still weren't in sight. Anne got down on her hands and knees and began pushing through the gnarled vegetation, which if anything grew more thickly than in the horz Austra and she used to haunt in Eslen-of-Shadows. The earth smelled rich, and slightly rotten.

"They're going to find us," Austra said. "They'll just come in after us, and we'll be trapped."

Anne wriggled between the close-spaced roots of an ancient olive tree. "They *can't* cut their way in," she said. "Saint Selfan will curse them."

"They murdered sisters of a holy order, Anne," Austra pointed out. "They don't care about curses."

"Still, it's our only choice."

"Can't you—can't you *do* something, like you did down by the river?"

"I don't know," Anne said. "It doesn't really work like that. It just happens."

But that wasn't really true. It was just that when she had blinded the knight outside the coven and hurt Erieso in z'Espino, she hadn't premeditated it, she'd just *done* it.

"I'm frightened of it," she admitted. "I don't understand it."

"Yes, Anne, but we're going to *die*, you see," Austra said.

"You've a point there," Anne admitted. They had gone as far into the horz as they could. They were already lying flat on their bellies, and from here on, the plants were woven too tightly.

"Just lie quiet," Anne said. "Not a sound. Remember when we used to pretend the Scaos was after us? Just like that."

"I don't want to die," Austra murmured.

Anne took Austra's hand and pulled her close, until she could feel the other girl's heartbeat. Somewhere near she could hear them talking.

"*Wlait in thizhaih hourshai,*" one of them said in a commanding voice.

"*Raish,*" the other replied.

Anne heard the squeak of saddle leather and then the sound of boots striking the ground. She wondered, bizarrely, if anything had happened to Faster, her horse, and had a painfully clear flash of riding him across the Sleeve in sunlight, with the perfumes of spring in the air. It seemed like centuries ago.

Austra's heart beat more frantically next to hers as the boot sounds came nearer and the vegetation began to rustle. Anne closed her eyes and tried to work past her fear to the dark place inside her.

Instead she touched sickness. Without warning it swept through her in a wave, a kind of fever that felt as if her blood had turned to hot sewage and her bones to rotting meat. She wanted to gag, but somehow couldn't find her throat, and her body felt as if it had somehow faded away.

"*Ik ni shaiwha iyo athan sa snori wanzyis thiku,*" someone said very near them.

"*Ita mait, thannuh,*" the other growled from farther away.

"*Maita?*" the near man said, his tone hesitant.

"Yah."

There was a pause, and then the sound of something slashing into the vegetation. Anne gasped as the sick feeling intensified.

Austra had been right. These men showed no fear of the sacred.

She pressed herself harder against the earth, and her head started to spin. The earth seemed to give way, and she began sinking down through the roots, feeling the little fibers on them tickle her face. At the same time, something seemed to be welling up from beneath her, like blood to the surface of a wound. Fury pulsed in her like a shivering lute string, and for a moment she wanted to catch hold of it, let it have her.

But then that, too, faded, as did the nausea and the sensation of sinking. Her cheek felt warm.

She opened her eyes.

She lay in a gently rolling spring-green meadow cupped in a forest palm of oak, beech, poplar, liquidambar, everic, and ten other sorts of trees she did not know. Over her left shoulder, a small rinn chuckled into a mere that was carpeted with water lilies and fringed by rushes, where a solitary crane moved carefully on stilt legs, searching for fish. Over her right shoulder, the white and tiny blue flowers of clover and wimpleweed that were her bed gave way to fern fronds and fiddleheads.

Austra lay next to her. The other girl sat up quickly, her eyes full of panic.

Anne still had her hand. She gripped it harder. "It's all right," she said. "I think we're safe, for a moment."

"I don't understand," Austra said. "What happened? Where are we? Are we dead?"

"No," Anne said. "We aren't dead."

"Where are we, then?"

"I'm not sure," Anne told her.

"Then how can you be certain—?" Austra's eyes showed sudden understanding. "You've been here before."

"Yes," Anne admitted.

Austra got up and began looking around. After a moment she gave a start. "We've got no shadows," she said.

"I know," Anne replied. "This is the place where you go if you walk widdershins."

"You mean like in the phay stories?"

"Yes. The first time I came here was during Elseny's party. Do you remember that?"

"You fainted. When you woke, you were asking about some woman in a mask. Then you decided you had been dreaming, and wouldn't talk about it anymore."

"I wasn't dreaming—or not exactly. I've been back here twice since then. Once when I was in the Womb of Mefitis, another time when I was sleeping on the deck of the ship." She gazed around the clearing. "It's always different," she went on, "but I know somehow it's always the same place."

"What do you mean?"

"The first time it was a hedge maze. The second time it was a forest clearing, and on the ship it was in the midst of the forest, and dark."

"But how? How did we come here, I mean?"

"The first time I was brought here by someone," Anne explained. "A woman in a mask. The other times I came myself."

Austra folded down into a cross-legged position, her brows knitted. "But—Anne," she said, "you didn't *go* anywhere, those other times. I wasn't there in the womb of Mefitis, but you were still on Tom Woth, that day. And you were still on the ship."

"I'm not sure of that," Anne said. "I might have gone and returned."

"I'm not certain about Tom Woth," Austra granted her, "but I *am* sure about the ship. I didn't take my eyes off you. That means, wherever we think we are—or wherever our shadows have gone—our bodies are still there for the knights to find and do with as they please."

Anne raised her hands helplessly. "That may be, but I don't know how to get back. It always just happens."

"Well, have you ever tried? You brought us here, after all."

"That's true," Anne conceded.

"Well, *try*."

Anne closed her eyes, trying to find that place again. It was there but quiet, and seemed in no mood to stir.

Austra gasped.

Anne opened her eyes, but didn't see anything immediately. "What is it?"

"Something's here," Austra said. "I can't see it, but it's here."

Anne shivered, remembering the shadow man, but there were no shadows now. A warm wind was picking up, almost summery, bending the tops of the trees and ruffling the grass. It had a scent of festering vegetation about it, not exactly unpleasant.

And it blew from every direction, toward them, forcing the trees, ferns, and grass to bow as if she and Austra were lords of Elphin. And at the edge of her hearing, Anne heard the faint, wild music of birds.

"What's happening?" she murmured.

Suddenly they came, over the treetops—swans and geese, fielies and swallows, brieches and red-Roberts, thousands of them, all swirling down into the clearing, clattering, cawing, and screeching toward Anne and Austra. Anne threw up her hands to cover her face, but a yard away the birds spiraled around them, a cyclone of feathers whirling up to cloud the sky.

After a moment, the fear faded, and Anne began to laugh. Austra looked at her as if she had lost her mind.

"What is it?" Austra asked. "Do you know what's happening?"

"I've no idea," Anne said. "But the wonder of it . . ." She needed a word she didn't have, so she stopped trying to find it.

It seemed to go on for a long time, but the winds finally subsided and went to their quarters, taking the birds with them, leaving only the crane, still fishing for his catch. The sound of the birds faded last.

"Anne, I'm sleepy." Austra sighed. Her panic seemed to have left her.

Anne found her own lids suddenly very heavy. The sun was warmer now, and after the rush of events, natural and otherwise, she felt as if she had been awake for days.

"Faiths, are you here?" she asked.

There was no answer, but the crane looked up and regarded her before going back to his task.

"Thank you," Anne said.

She wasn't sure whom she was speaking to, or what she was thanking them for.

She woke in the horz with Austra beside her, still clutching her hand. They were both covered in severed limbs and foliage. The knights had done it—they had defiled the sacred garden. She and Austra lay at the terminus of their destructive, sacrilegious path.

Well, she thought. *We're not dead. That's a start.* But if Austra was right, and the land of the Faiths was just a sort of dream, how could their assailants have missed them?

She listened quietly for a long time, but heard nothing except the drone of an occasional insect. After a time, she woke Austra.

Austra sat up, took in their return, then mumbled a faint prayer to Saint Selfan and Saint Rieyene. "They didn't see us," she said. "Though I can't imagine why not."

"Maybe you were wrong," Anne said. "Maybe we didn't leave our bodies behind after all."

"Maybe," Austra said dubiously.

"You stay here," Anne said. "I'll go out and have a look."

"No, let me go."

"If they catch you, they'll still come after me," Anne said. "If they catch me, they'll have no reason to come in after you."

Austra reluctantly consented to that logic, and Anne went back out of the horz, walking this time through the torn and trampled vegetation.

Near the entrance she found a pool of dark, sticky liquid which she recognized as blood. There was more outside, a trail of it that abruptly stopped.

She poked around a few of the ruins, but the horsemen seemed to be gone. They weren't on the road, either, when she climbed the hill and looked down.

Cazio, z'Acatto and the horsemen were gone.

"We have to find them," Austra insisted desperately. "We have to." Tears were streaming down her cheeks, and Anne couldn't blame her. She'd had her own cry before going back to the horz to collect her friend.

"We will," she said, trying to sound confident.

"But how?"

"They can't have gone far," Anne pointed out.

"No, no," Austra said. "We might have been in there for a year. Or ten years, or a hundred. We've just been in Elphin, haven't we? Things like that happen."

"In kinderspells," Anne reminded her. "And we don't know that it's Elphin, anyway. I've never been gone more than a bell or so. So we ought to be able to follow them."

"They might have already killed Cazio and z'Acatto."

"I don't see their bodies, do you?"

"They might have buried them."

"I don't think those men are the sort likely to do such a thing. If they don't fear the consequences of murdering an entire coven or cutting up a horz, they wouldn't pay much mind to leaving a couple of bodies on the road. Besides, the knights had them all bound up, remember? They're probably taking them back to their ship."

"Or Cazio told them some clever lie about where we'd gone," Austra suggested, sounding calmer now, "and they're waiting to see if he told the truth before they torture him."

"That's possible," Anne said, trying not to think about Cazio being tortured.

"So which way do we go?" Austra asked.

"Their ship sailed north past Duvé," Anne said. "So it seems reasonable that they came from farther up the road, the direction we're going."

"But Cazio would have sent them south, to keep us safe."

"True," Anne agreed, staring at the road in frustration, wishing she knew the tiniest thing about how to follow a trail. But even that many horsemen made little impression on such a well-traveled road, or at least none that her untrained eye could find.

But then she saw it, a small drop of blood. She walked a few paces north and found another, and another after that.

There were none to the south.

"North," she said. "One of them was bleeding by the horz, and I guess he still is. Anyhow, it's the only sign we've got."

In some distant age, the river Teremené had cut a gorge in the pale bones of the countryside, but he hardly seemed the sort of river to do that now. He appeared old and sluggish beneath a wintry sky, hardly troubling the coracles, barges, and sailboats on his back.

Nor did he seem resentful of the impressive stone bridge that spanned him at his narrows, or the massive granite pylons that thrust down into his waters to support it.

Anne switched her gaze to the village that rested beyond the stone span. She vaguely remembered that it was also called Teremené, and they hadn't stopped there during their last trip on the Vitellian Way.

"Austra," Anne asked, "when we crossed into Vitellio, there were border guards. Do you remember?"

"Yes. You flirted with one, as I recall."

"I did not, you jade," Anne protested. "I asked him to be more careful inspecting my things! And never mind that anyway. Were there border guards here? This is the border between Tero Gallé and Hornladh. Shouldn't there be guards?"

"We weren't stopped," Austra confirmed, after a moment of thought. "But we weren't stopped when we crossed into Hornladh from Crotheny, either."

"Right, but Hornladh is a part of father's—" She broke off as grief bit. She kept forgetting. "Hornladh is part of the Empire. Tero Gallé isn't. Anyway, it looks like there are guards there now."

Austra nodded. "I saw them inspecting the caravan."

"So why the sudden vigilance?"

"The caravan is going into Hornladh, and we were leaving it. Maybe the Empire cares who comes into its territory, and Tero Gallé doesn't."

"Maybe," Anne sighed. "I should know these things, shouldn't I? Why didn't I pay more attention to my tutors?"

"You're afraid it's the horsemen?"

"Yes—or they may have offered a reward for us, like they did in z'Espino."

"Then it doesn't matter if they're legitimate guards or not," Austra reasoned. "We can't take the risk."

"But we have to cross the bridge," Anne said. "And I was hoping, once in the Empire, we might find some help. Or at least ask if anyone has seen Cazio and z'Acatto."

"And get something to eat," Austra added. "The fish was tiresome, but it was better than nothing."

Anne's stomach was rumbling, too. For the moment it was just unpleasant, but in a day or two, it would be a real problem. They didn't have even a copper miser left, and she had already sold her hair. That only left a few things to sell, none of which she cared to think about.

"Maybe when it gets dark," Austra proposed dubiously.

Something moved behind them. A little rock went bouncing down the slope and past their hiding place. Gasping softly, Anne swung around to see what it was and discovered two young men with dark hair and olive complexions staring down at them. They wore leather jerkins and ticking pantaloons tucked into high boots. Both had short swords, and one of them had a bow.

"*Ishatité! Ishatité, né ech té nekeme!*" the man with the bow shouted.

"I don't understand you!" Anne snapped back in frustration.

The shouter cocked his head. "King's tongue, yes?" he said, coming down the slope, arrow pointed squarely at her. "Then you *are* the ones they look for, I bet me."

"There's one behind us now," Austra whispered.

Anne's heart sank, but as the two moved closer her fear began to turn to anger.

"Who are you?" she demanded. "What do you want?"

"Want you," the man said. "Outlanders come by yesterday, say, 'Find two girls, one with red hair, one with gold. Bring them or kill them, make no difference, but bring them and get much coin.' Here I see me girl with gold hair. I think under that rag, I see hair is red." He gestured with the weapon. "Take off."

Anne reached up and removed the scarf. The man's grin broadened. "Try to hide, eh? Doing not so good."

"You're a fool," Anne said. "They won't pay you. They'll kill you."

"You say," the man replied. "I think not to trust you." He stepped forward.

"Don't touch me," Anne snarled.

"Eshrije," the other man said.

"Yes, right," the bowman replied. "They say red-hair is witch. Better just to kill."

As he pulled back on the bow, Anne lifted her chin in defiance, reaching for her power, ready to see what it could really do. "You will die for this," she said.

A brief fear seemed to pass across his face, and he hesitated.

Then he gasped in pain and surprise, stumbling, and she saw an arrow standing from his shoulder. He dropped his bow, groaning loudly, and the other man started shouting.

"Stand away, Comarré, and the rest of you, too," a new voice said. Anne saw the owner, farther up the hill—a man in late middle age, with a seamed, sun-browned face and black hair gone half-silver. "These ladies don't seem to like you."

"Damn you, Artoré," the man with the arrow in his shoulder gritted. "This no business of yours. I saw first."

"My boys and I are making it our business," the older man replied.

Their attackers backed away. "Yes, fine," Comarré said. "But another day, Artoré."

At that, an arrow hit him in the throat, and he dropped like a sack of grain. The other two had time to cry out, and then Anne found herself staring at three corpses.

"No other day, Comarré," Artoré said, shaking his head.

Anne looked up at him.

"I'm sorry you had to see that, ladies," he said. "Are you well?" He stepped closer.

Anne grabbed Austra and hugged her tightly. "What do you want?" she asked. "Why did you kill them?"

"They've had it coming for a long time," the man said. "But just now I figure that if I let them go, they'll go tell that pack of Hansan knights, then they come looking for me, burn down my house—no good."

"You mean you aren't taking us to them?"

"Me? I hate knights and I hate Hansans. Why would I do anything for them? Come, it's dark soon, and I think you're hungry, no?"

Anne numbly followed the man named Artoré along a rutted road delimited by juniper and waxweed, into the hilly country that stretched beyond sight of the river. There they were quickly joined by four boys, all armed with bows. The setting sun lay behind them, and their shadows ran ahead in the subdued dusk. Swallows cut at the air with crescent wings, and Anne wondered once again exactly what had happened in the horz, why the knights hadn't seen them.

They strolled past empty fields and thatch-roofed houses built of brick. Artoré and his boys chatted amongst themselves and exchanged greetings with their neighbors as if nothing out of the ordinary had happened.

"This is Jarné," Artoré informed her, patting a spindly, tall young man on the shoulder. "He's the eldest, twenty-five. Then there's Cotomar, the one with the chicken nest in his hair. Locheté, he's the one with the big ears, and Senché is the youngest."

"I didn't thank you," Anne said guardedly.

"Why should you? Figured we were going to take you to town, just like Comarré planned. Eh?"

"Are the knights still in town?" Anne asked.

"Some of them. Some of them are out in the countryside, and three of them went east with a couple of fellows they had all tied up."

"Cazio!" Austra gasped.

"Friends of yours, I take it."

"Yes," Anne said. "We were following them, hoping for a chance at rescue."

Artoré laughed at that. "I wonder how you thought you were going to manage that."

"We have to try," Anne said. "They saved our lives, and as you said, they are our friends."

"But against men like that? You're braver than you are smart. Why do they want you?"

"They want to kill me, that is all I know," Anne said. "They've chased us all the way from Vitellio."

"Where are you trying to get to?"

Anne hesitated. "Eslen," she finally said.

He nodded. "That's what I figured. That's still a long way, though, and it's not the direction they're taking your friends. So which way will you go?"

Anne had been thinking about that a lot, since Cazio and z'Acatto had been captured. It was her duty to go back to Eslen, she knew that. But she also had a duty to her friends. As long as their captors had been headed north, she hadn't been forced to choose. Now she was, and she knew without a doubt which choice her mother—and the Faiths—would call the right one.

The thing was, whichever way she chose, she didn't have much chance of surviving, not with Austra as a companion.

"I don't know," she murmured.

"Anne!" Austra cried. "What are you saying?"

"I'll think of something," she promised. "I'll think of something."

Artoré's house was much like the others they had passed, but larger and more rambling. Chickens pecked in the yard and beyond, in a fence, she saw several horses. The sky was nearly dark now, and the light from inside was cheerful.

A woman of about Artoré's age met them at the door. Her blondish hair was caught up in a bun, and she wore an apron. Wonderful smells spilled through the doorway.

"There's my wife," Artoré said. "Osne."

"You found them, then," she said. "*Dajé Vespré* to you, girls."

"You were looking for us?" Anne said, the hair on her neck pricking up.

"Don't be frightened," the woman said. "I sent him."

"But why?"

"Come in, eat. We can talk after."

The house was as cheery inside as it looked from the outside. A great hearth stood at one end of the main room, with pots and pans, a worktable, ceramic jars of flour, sugar, and spices. Garlic hung in chains from the rafters, and a little girl was playing on the terra-cotta-tile floor.

Anne suddenly felt hungrier than she had in her life. The table was already set, and the woman ushered them to sit.

For the next half bell, Anne forgot almost everything but how to eat. Their trenchers were sliced from bread still hot from the baking. And there was butter—not olive oil, as it always was in Vitellio but *butter*. Osne ladled a stew of pork, leeks, and mussels onto the bread, which in itself should have been plenty, but then she brought out a sort of pie stuffed with melted cheese and hundreds of little strips of pastry and whole eggs. Added to that was a sort of paste made of chicken livers cooked in a crust, and all washed down with a strong red wine.

She felt like crying with joy—at the coven, they'd eaten frugally—bread and cheese and porridge. On the road and in z'Espino they had lived near starvation and eaten what they could find or buy with their meager monies. This was the first truly delicious meal she had eaten since leaving Eslen, all those months ago. It reminded her that there could be more to life than survival.

When it was done, Anne helped Osne, Austra, and the two youngest boys clear the table and clean up.

When they were finished, she and Osne were suddenly alone. She wasn't sure where Austra had got off to.

Osne turned to her and smiled. "And now, Anne Dare," she said, "heir to the throne of Crotheny—you and I must talk."

CHAPTER FIVE

THE PORT OF PALDH

SWANMAY WAS AS GOOD as her word. They reached the mouth of the Teremené River five days after she made her promise.

By that time Neil could stand, and even walk, though he tired quickly, so when he heard that land had been sighted, he pulled on the clothes that Swanmay had supplied for him and went up on deck.

A cloud cover was breaking up with the rising of the sun, painting the landscape with long brushes of light. Corcac Sound, Neil reflected, was what Newland would have been, without the canals and malends and the sheer force of human will to keep the water back—a thousand islands and hammocks, some of which vanished at high tide, and all green with marsh grass and ancient oaks. They sailed past villages of houses raised on stilts and men in skiffs hauling in cast-nets full of wriggling shrimp. Beyond the river channel, a maze of creeks and waterways wandered off to the flat horizon.

He found Swanmay near the bow.

"We're nearly there," she said. "I told you, you see."

"I did not doubt you, lady." He paused uncomfortably. "You said the men who attacked me are the same men you fear. Yet they did not recognize your ship in z'Espino. Why do you fear they will recognize it now, if they are in the port of Paldh?"

A hint of a smile touched her lips. "In z'Espino they didn't yet know they were looking for me. Another day or so there and the news would have reached them. For certain, it has reached Paldh by now."

"The news of your escape?"

"Yes."

"Then—if I may—I would propose not to hold you strictly to your word. Put me off here, before we reach port. I'm sure I can find the mainland."

She looked out over the marshes. "It's quite beautiful, isn't it?" She seemed to ignore his suggestion.

"Yes," he agreed.

"I've never seen anything like it." She turned to him. "It's kind of you to think of me, Sir Neil."

"It's nothing compared with what you've done for me, lady. I would not see you hurt."

She shrugged. "I'm in no physical danger. They will not kill me, if that is what worries you."

"I'm grateful for that," he said.

"I accept your offer," Swanmay decided. "There is only a small chance that I will escape the Lier Sea now, with my head start gone. But it is a chance, nonetheless. I may yet win my game of fiedchese."

"I pray you do, Lady Swanmay," he told her gravely.

"That isn't my real name, you know."

"I didn't," he replied. "I wish I knew your real name."

She shook her head. "I will provide you with a boat and some supplies."

"That isn't necessary," he said.

"It won't cost me anything, and it will make your life easier. Why shouldn't I do it?" She lifted her head. "But if you would repay me for the boat, I have a suggestion."

"Anything, if it is in my power."

"It is. A kiss—just one. It's all I ask."

In the light of the sun, her eyes were bluer than any sky. He suddenly remembered the words to a song he'd liked when he was a boy, *"Elveher qei Queryeven."*

If you'll not stay and share my bed,
The lady of the Queryen said
Then all I ask is for a kiss,
A single kiss instead.

But when Elveher bent to kiss the Queryen lady, she stabbed him in the heart with a knife she had concealed in her sleeve.

With her otherworldly beauty, Swanmay might as easily be Queryen as human.

"Why should you want that, lady?" he asked.

"Because I may never have another," she replied.

"I—" He suddenly realized she wasn't joking.

"Anything in your power, you said."

"I did." he admitted, and he bent toward her, held by those strange, beautiful eyes. She smelled faintly of roses.

Her lips were warm and somehow surprising, different from any lips he had ever kissed, and with their touch, everything seemed oddly changed. When he pulled away, her eyes were no longer so mysterious. They held something he thought he understood.

"My name is Brinna," she said. There was no knife in her hand.

Before the next bell he sat in a smallboat and watched her ship until he could no longer see the sails. Then he began to row upstream. Each time the oars dipped in the water, he seemed to hear Fastia telling him he would forget her.

The tide came in and eased his journey, but Paldh was several leagues upstream, and he was still very weak and had to rest frequently. Still, the exertion felt good, and the salt-marsh smell pleased him. Near sundown, he made dock at a fishing village, where a sandy-haired boy of about twelve took his bowline. He checked the wallet Brinna had given him and found coins in it. He selected a copper for the boy, but turned it in his fingers before giving it to him. It bore a sword on one side, but no inscription. He took a gold out and looked at that. It had the likeness of a man on it, and an inscription that read MARCOMIR ANTHAR THIUZAN MIKIL. Marcomir was the king of Hansa.

He sighed and returned the coin to his purse.

The boy said something in Hornish, which Neil knew only a few words of.

"Do you speak any king's tongue, lad, or Lierish?" he asked, in the best Hornish he could command.

"*Tho*, sure, I speak king's tongue," the boy said, in a slow, lilting accent. "Do you need a place to stay? The Moyr Muk has a room in it." He indicated a long building built of leather planks and a shingled roof.

"My thanks," Neil said. "Say, what's your name, lad?"

"Nel MaypPenmar," the boy told him.

Neil smiled. "That's almost the same as my name. I'm Neil Meq-Vren. Nel, do you know your ships?"

The boy swelled his chest out a little. "Tho, sir, I sure do."

"I wonder, have you seen a Vitellian merchantman come through here in the past few days, the *Della Puchia*?"

"I've seen that ship," the boy said, "but not lately."

"What about a big brimwulf with no name or standard?"

"That one I saw, three days ago. She caught that storm and was listing hard, needed a new mast."

"Storm?"

"Tho, a bad one. Some ships went down in that one—one of 'em out of here, the *Tunn Carvanth*."

"Maybe the *Della Puchia* came by and you didn't notice?"

"Maybe," Nel said dubiously. "You can ask around in the Moyr Muc. Why? You have kin on it?"

"Something like that," Neil replied. "Thanks." He got his things and started toward the inn.

Beside the door was hung a placard with a painting of a porpoise on it, confirming Neil's idle suspicion that "*Moyr Muc*" was the same as *meurmuc*, which was what they called dolphins on Skern. It meant "sea-pig," which he'd always thought was a poor name for such a beautiful creature. Of course *Neil* meant "champion," a name he didn't much deserve, either. He had lost his armor and his sword, and now it might be that the princess he had been sent by his queen to retrieve was at the bottom of the Lier.

None of the handful of people in the Sea Pig allowed that they had seen the *Della Puchia*, but they pointed out that the shallow-drafted Vitellian ship could have made port at half a dozen other places to weather the storm. That made Neil feel a little better, but the larger problem remained—if Anne was still alive, it was because the *Della Puchia* had done just that, which meant once again he had lost her trail.

Not too surprisingly, no one in the village of Torn-y-Llagh owned a sword, but he managed to buy a fishing spear and a knife, which was better than nothing. He ate a supper of boiled cod and bread, enjoying the simple familiarity of it. The next morning, feeling even stronger, he set out once more for Paldh.

Paldh was an old city. When the great harbors of Eslen were still marsh, before the building of the great Thornrath wall, it had been the only deepwater port of any size for a hundred leagues in either direction. In those days before the Crothanic Empire, Crotheny, Hornladh, and Tero Gallé had all relied upon Paldh for their shipping. They had battled over it with their navies, and before them the Hegemony and the Warlock Kingdoms.

How many thousands of ships lay rotting in the channel of the Teremené River, no one could know, but the oldest of them had not been built by human beings.

Nor had the oldest walls of the city, most of which appeared to stand on a regular gray cliff thirty yards above the highest tide. Neil had never before seen them, but now that he paddled alongside he saw that what he had heard was true; above the barnacled high-water mark, one could still discern the faint seams that stretched between the original blocks of stone. When he reached the harbor, the massive barrier swept in an enormous semicircle that was something over a league in length, and here an ancient quay of the same stone provided the anchor for the floating docks.

The quay was perhaps a hundred yards in width, and a sort of sailor's city had grown up on it—taverns, inns, gambling houses, and brothels all crowded against the artificial bluff. Even from afar Neil could see that the dock town was teeming with colorful life.

He made out the brimwulf almost immediately, because he passed the dry-docks on his way in, and there she was, up on scaffolding with workmen scurrying about, making a music of hammers and saws. There were a number of other ships there, none of them the one Anne had sailed on.

He thought back to his fight in z'Espino. The brimwulf had been far down the docks from the *Della Puchia.* The sailors on her wouldn't have seen the fight—and he'd been in armor anyway.

He paddled his boat over to the quay and tied her up near the ship, then climbed out onto the time-smoothed stone.

He waved at one of the nearer sailors.

"Hello, there," he attempted in Hornish.

"*Ik ni mathlya Haurnaraz,*" the sailor replied.

Neil forced a laugh, and switched to Hanzish. "Neither do I," he said. "It's good to hear you speak—I'm so tired of trying to understand the gibberish around here."

The sailor smiled and poked a rough finger at Neil's boat. "You come all the way here in that?"

Neil shook his head. "No, the ship I served on was beached in the storm the other night. I bought this from a fisherman."

"Bad storm, that," the sailor said. "We almost went down in it."

"Pretty good blow," Neil conceded.

"What ship was that you were on?" the man asked.

"The *Esecselur,* out of Hall." That seemed safe enough—Hall was one of the most remote and least visited islands in the Sorrow chain, and it was—last he'd heard—one of the few under Hanzish rule.

"Ah, explains your accent," the fellow said. "Well, what do you need?"

"I wondered if you might use another hand, at least until the ship is repaired. I'd work for a place to stay and a coin or two until I can get a berth on something headed home."

The sailor scratched his head. "Well, the captain did tell the *frumashipmanna* to hire some local help, but I'm sure he'd rather have someone who speaks the godstongue."

Neil hoped he didn't flinch at that. He'd spent most of his life fighting people who spoke Hanzish. The fact that they thought their language was the language of the saints was just a reminder of why.

He must have hidden his feelings well, for the sailor then introduced him to the firstshipman, who looked him up and down, asked him the same questions the other fellow had, and then shrugged.

"We'll give you a try," he said, "But I'm telling you now you won't pull a berth with us. The lord whose ship this is is peculiar about who he takes aboard. But if you're still interested, it's a schilling a day plus a middle meal, and you can sleep in the tents."

"That's fair enough," Neil said.

"And your name?" the man asked.

"Kniva," Neil improvised. "Kniva Berigsunu."

"You ever trim out a mast?"

"Before I was six," Neil answered.

"Over there, then. If I don't like your work, you don't get paid."

Working on the mast was a good place to be—it allowed him to see all who came and went. He didn't see anyone he recognized, though, and certainly none of the knights or their men-at-arms. That was a good sign, probably—it suggested that they were still looking for Anne and her companions.

It made him feel itchy, working side by side with his enemies, but after a time he relaxed. The other men toiling on the mast seemed to take him for who he said he was, and he managed to get friendly with a couple of them. They were both from Selhastranth, an island off Saltmark, and their language and bad blood aside, Neil's island boyhood had been much like theirs.

So at the end of the day, as they collected their schillings, he wasn't surprised when Jan and Vithig asked him along to the tavern.

The *curm valc* the inn served was bitter and thick, not that different from the ale they brewed on the islands—and Neil knew he ought not have much of it. He'd never been a big drinker, and it had been a long time since he had imbibed more than a little wine.

Jan and Vithig showed no such inhibitions, swaging it down as if it were water. By the time their portions of eel stew arrived, they were well on their way to Saint Leine's hall.

After a round of bragging about various exploits at sea, Neil leaned forward. "I've seen strange things lately," he said, in a low voice. "Uncanny things. I've heard the draugs singing and seen a dead man walk on Ter-na-Fath. My fah says the end of the world is coming."

Both of their faces scrunched up at that. Jan was a big, ruddy man with a bald crown and dark eyes, while Vithig's face was so angular, it looked as if he had swallowed an anvil and it had stuck in his head.

"You don't have to tell us things is weirding," Vithig said. "We've seen things—"

Jan put a hand on his arm. "No, don't do that," he said.

Vithig nodded sagely. "*Aiw*, I know. But it's not right. I've said His Lordship's men aren't men at all, some of 'em—and I'll say it again." He punched a finger at Neil. "Just you be glad they won't offer you a berth, is all I'm saying."

"Vith, keep it down," Jan growled.

"I didn't see anything strange aboard ship."

"Aiw—they've gone, thank *Ansu Hlera*, off south to chase—"

"*Vith!*" Jan pounded the table so hard, their bowls and mugs rattled.

Neil took another swallow of his ale. "No fighting lads," he said. "I didn't mean to stir up any trouble. How does the saying go? 'Wise is the man who guards his lord's Rune-hoard.'"

"Here, that's what I'm saying," Jan said.

"Well spoken," Vithig murmured. "I admit I'm not wise, not when *Ansu Woth*'s blood is in me." He raised his tankard. "May we die in warm seas," he toasted.

"To wisdom," Neil replied, and took his swallow. "Now, let me tell you about the great wurm we sighted in the Sorrows."

"You never saw any wurm," Jan protested.

"*Aiw*, but I did, and a great monster it was."

He launched into a story his grandfather used to tell, and by the end of it, Jan had calmed down and Vithig was threatening to sing. Bold as he felt, Neil didn't reckon to take any more risks by pressing—

it would be nice to know what lord owned the ship, but he already knew what he wanted to know, and with only a single day lost.

Much later, they staggered back to the tents, and Jan and Vithig fell straight into ale slumber. Neil considered killing them, but didn't for several reasons. A fair fight would draw attention, and slitting their throats while they slept would destroy what little honor he had left. He doubted the sailors would make any connection between their comments and his absence the next day, and if they did, they would just reckon they had scared him off.

Anyway, sailors didn't talk to their officers and lords any more than they had to, and killing them was much more likely to make people wonder where he had got off to. Finally, Jan and Vithig were decent fellows who didn't deserve a bad end at his hand just because they had said something they shouldn't have.

So before anyone woke, he gathered his things and left, climbing the ramp up into the city of Paldh. There, with the money Brinna had given him, he found a sword he could afford. The blacksmith balked at selling it to him, so Neil showed him the cut on the back of his hand and small silver rose pendant at his neck—the two things he still had that marked him as a knight.

"Anyone can cut themselves," the blacksmith pointed out, "and you might have taken the rose from a dead knight."

"That's true," Neil allowed. "But I gave you my word I'm a knight of Eslen."

"Carrying Hanzish coin," the blacksmith countered dubiously.

Neil added another gold coin to the five already on the table. "Why did you make this if you don't want to sell it?" he asked. "What knight commissioned it?"

"The city guard buys from me," he said. "I've license to sell to them."

"And surely to a knight who has lost his effects," Neil said. "Besides, I'm leaving Paldh, and not likely to return."

The blacksmith found a cloth and wrapped the sword up tightly. "Just keep it hidden until you're out of town, hey?"

"That I'll do," Neil said. He took the sword and left. At a stable on the road outside of town, he purchased a horse that seemed to have a bit of intelligence in its eyes, and some tack for it, leaving him only a few schillings for food. Thus mounted he set out south on the Great Vitellian Way.

The sword wasn't much of a sword—it was more of a steel club with an edge—and the horse wasn't much of a horse. But then, he wasn't much of a knight, though at last he felt something like one again. What he would do when he found the uncanny knight and his men he did not know, but he was ready to figure it out.

CHAPTER SIX

THE RETURN

THE COURT THAT GREETED Muriele and the two men of her bodyguard was absolutely still. This was, she reflected, a miracle, something that heretofore she would have thought impossible in a place so plenty with gabbling fools. After her guards took their positions at the door, the only sound was the tap of her heels upon the marble, and that ceased when she sat in the queen mother's throne.

"Well," she said, putting on her absolutely false smile, "the prime minister will not be attending court today, so I'll take the issues in the order they come to hand. Praifec Hespero, does the Church have any business with the throne today?"

Hespero frowned slightly. "Queen Mother, I wonder where is His Majesty Emperor Charles? He really should attend court."

"Yes," Muriele replied. "I told him that, but His Majesty can be quite stubborn when he has a mind. And I wonder, Your Grace, when you stopped addressing *me* as Majesty?"

"I *am* sorry, Queen Mother, but by all of our laws, it isn't proper to address you so. Only the king and queen are thus referred to, and you are neither at this time. The court has continued to address you so from respect and in deference to your grief."

"I see. And now it must be that you no longer respect or grieve with me. Such a shame." She was amazed at how calm she felt, as if the whole thing were a parlor game.

"Queen Mother," the Duke of Shale interrupted, trying to make his comically rounded face seem somehow stern, "the Comven has posed grave questions concerning the recent conduct of the throne— indeed, we question the very legitimacy of that conduct."

Muriele leaned back in the throne and feigned surprise. "Well, by all means, discover to me these questions, gentlemen. I am eager to hear them."

"It is more the question of legitimacy that is at issue," Shale explained, his blueberry eyes showing sudden wariness.

"Do you or do you not have questions for me?" Muriele wondered.

"No specific questions, Your Highness, only a general—"

"But my good Duke—you said that the Comven has raised grave questions concerning the conduct of the throne. Now you say you have no questions about that conduct. You are either a liar or a buffoon, Shale."

"See here—"

"No," Muriele interrupted, her voice growing louder. "*You* see *here*. By every law, Charles is king and emperor, and you are his subjects, you palavering, feckless miscreants. Do you honestly think I don't know what you are all about, today? Did you believe I had walked into your childish trap unawares?"

"Queen Mother—," the praifec began, but she cut him off.

"You, hold your tongue," she said. "Your place by absolute decree is limited to council, Praifec."

"It is all I have offered, Queen Mother."

"Oh, no," Muriele demurred. "You have gossiped like the meanest prostitute in a brothel. You have incited, you have conspired, and every person in this room knows that because they are the ones with whom you have done so. You have offered to occupy this kingdom with Church troops and you have threatened to lend them to Hansa if we won't have them. You have tendered me your goodwill with one hand and a knife with the other, and you are certainly the poorest excuse for a man I have ever seen, much less a man who pretends to holiness. So enough from you, and enough from your Comven puppets and your petty aspirations. Let *him* come before me. Let the murderer whom you fools would place on the sacrosanct throne of Crotheny stand before me, so I can see his face."

The crowd erupted, then, as if they were all hens and someone had just thrown a cat amongst them. The praifec alone was silent, gazing at her with a perfectly blank expression that was somehow the most threatening gaze she had ever met.

As the crowd began to quiet its frenzy, it parted, and there he came—Robert Dare, her husband's brother.

He wore a black doublet and black hose and held a broad-brimmed hat of the same dark hue in one hand. His face was paler than she remembered, but with the same handsome, sardonic cast, the same small goatee and mustache. He smiled, and his teeth were white. He swaggered from the crowd, his effetely narrow sword wagging like the tail of a braggart hound, and bent one knee to her.

"Greetings, Queen Mother."

"Rise," she said.

And there he was, when her eyes met his—there was her husband's murderer. Robert could not hide a thing like that, not from someone who knew him. His glee was too obvious.

"I am sorry to find you so distraught," he dissembled. "I had hoped this all might proceed more reasonably."

"Had you?" Muriele mused. "I would imagine that's why so many of your personal guard can be seen skulking about. Why landwaerden militias gather outside the city, and why your toadies on the Comven have brought so many swords. Because you think what you're about to do is reasonable?"

"What am I about to do?" Robert asked, showing a sudden anger. "Does the Queen Mother have the gift of reading the hearts and minds of others? Did a phay whisper in your ear? What is it you so impudently *presume* I am 'about to do,' Highness?

"Take the throne for yourself," she said.

"Oh," Robert said. "Oh, well, yes, I am going to do *that*." He turned to the crowd. "Does anyone object?"

No one did.

"You see, Queen Mother, much as we all love Charles, there is no doubt that if he had half a wit, it would be half again what he has now. And as Duke Shale was trying to explain in his more elegant fashion, the court does not like your decisions or, in fact, *you,* my arrogant sister-in-law. You have made alliance with Liery, slaughtered honest landwaerden, refused the peace with Hansa, and today we've seen you insult the praifec, the Church, and everyone in this room. And accuse me baselessly of murder.

"Meanwhile, our citizens are killed by basil-nix, we have an unde-clared war with the forces of Hell on our marchlands, and will soon have a quite certainly declared one with Hansa. And you would ob-ject to my leadership because you prefer to cling to power through your poor, saint-touched son? It really is too much, Queen Mother."

Muriele did not feel the slightest flinch at his words. "I object to your leadership," she said, "because you are a fratricide and worse." She leaned forward and spoke very deliberately. "You know what you are, Robert. *I* know what you are. You murdered William, or arranged it. Probably my daughters, as well—and I think Lesbeth. You will not have the opportunity to kill my son."

His eyes flared with a weird rage when she said that, but she was sure only she could see it. Then his expression changed to chagrin. "Where is Charles?"

"Safe from you."

He looked around. "Where is Sir Fail, and his guard? Where are the Craftsmen?"

"I sent them away," Muriele said. "They might otherwise have battled your usurpation, and I would not have blood spilled in these halls."

He glowered at her for a moment, then leaned in close.

"That was very clever of you, Muriele," he breathed. "I have un-derestimated you. Not that it will do you any good in the end."

He raised his voice and turned to the crowd. "Find His Majesty and take care not to harm him. Arrest his guard and arrest the Crafts-men. If they resist, kill them. As of now, I am assuming the regency of this kingdom and this empire. Tomorrow at this time we will hold court and discuss particulars."

Two of his guard had come up. "Take the Queen Mother to the Wolfcoat Tower. Make sure she is comfortable there."

As they led her away, Muriele wondered just how long she had left to live.

Not surprisingly, Muriele had never been in the Wolfcoat Tower— Eslen Castle had thirty towers, all told, if one were liberal with the definition. There was no need for semantic laxity with the Wolfcoat— or more properly The Wolf-Coat's. It leapt up sixty yards from the eastern side of the inner keep, tightening into a spire so sharp, it seemed a spear aimed at the heavens.

Maybe it had been—Thiuzwald fram Reiksbaurg, "the Wolf-Coat," had not been, as the histories recorded him, a humble or altogether sane man, and it had been commissioned by him. Later in the same year it was finished, the Wolf-Coat lay dying in the Hall of Doves, struck down by William I, the first of her husband's line to rule Crotheny.

Now she found herself imprisoned there. Robert probably thought he was being subtle.

He had meant what he had said about making her comfortable, however. Within a few bells the dusty stone apartments had been furnished with bed, armchair, stools, rugs, and the like, though it was notable that none were from her own quarters.

She had a view, as well. Her rooms were about three-quarters up the edifice and boasted two narrow windows. From one she could see the rooftops and plazas of the southern half of the city, a slice of Eslen-of-Shadows, and the marshy rinns. The other faced east, giving her a magnificent view of the confluence of the Warlock and Dew rivers.

Comfortable or not, view or not, she was trapped in a prison. The walls of the tower were sheer and smooth. Guards were stationed outside her door—Robert's guards—and the door was securely locked from the outside. From there it was perhaps two hundred steps down a narrow stairwell, past an entire garrison of guards, to reach the inner keep. She imagined it was time to start growing her hair out.

Deciding to ration a view that with time would grow wearisome, she sighed and settled into her armchair to think, but found there was little to think about. She had done what she could, and any further decisions had been removed from her, except perhaps the decision to end her own life, which she had no intention of making. If Robert wanted her dead, he would have to do it himself, or at least give the order.

She heard the outer anteroom door open, then close. There followed a gentle knock on her inner door.

"Enter," she said, wondering what new confrontation had come to her.

The door swung open, revealing a woman she knew.

"Alis Berrye at your service, Queen Mother," she said. "I'm to be your maid."

Fear thrilled through Muriele, and once again it felt as if the floor she had trusted was gone.

"You came back," Muriele said, her tongue feeling like the clapper of a lead ball. She was tired of this game. "Is my son captured? Is he dead?"

"No, Majesty," Berrye said in a lower voice. "All went as you planned."

"Don't torture me," Muriele entreated. "Robert has everything now. There cannot be anything he wants except my torture. Unless you hate me for some reason, just tell me the truth."

Berrye knelt before her, took her hand, and kissed it. "It is the truth. I don't blame you for doubting, but I saw the ship sail. You took the prince completely by surprise."

"Then how is it you are here?" Muriele asked.

"You needed a maid. Prince Robert picked me."

"Why would he do that?"

"I suggested it. After he sent you up here, I heard him wondering aloud what servant he could find for you that would most annoy. I chose that moment to wish him congratulations, and he laughed. A few moments later I was on my way here. He didn't know, you see."

"You were in the court?"

"I had reached it only just as you were removed—I missed your cataloguing of the praifec's offenses, though I wish I hadn't. There was much discussion of it."

"This is true, not some trick?"

"I am locked in here, just as Your Majesty is. I have no more freedom than you, for Robert would never risk even the possibility that we might grow friendly."

"If what you say is genuine," Muriele said, "if you really have determined to help me, then why are you here? You might have done me more good outside."

"I considered that, Your Majesty, but out there I can't protect you. If you are murdered, any intelligence I gather will be worthless. Here there are a thousand subtle ways they might kill you. I can detect and counteract at least some of them. And who knows, perhaps I will be granted some limited movement, if we act the part of raging hatred when the guards are within earshot."

"I asked you to protect my son," Muriele reminded her.

"He has protectors," Berrye explained. "You do not."

Muriele sighed. "You're as willful as Erren was," she half complained, "and it's done now. I don't suppose you know if there are any hidden passages in this tower?"

"I think there are not," Berrye said. "It shouldn't prevent us from searching, but I don't remember any from the diagrams." She paused. "By the by, I think it must have been Prince Robert himself in your chambers that night."

"From what do you conclude that?"

"Why didn't he just put you in your own chambers?" she asked. "He could just as easily have kept you guarded there, and it is the more usual way of the doing these things. Why put you all the way over here, farther from his sight and control?"

"It's a symbol," Muriele said. "The last Reiksbaurg to rule Crotheny built this place."

"I think he knows about the passages," Berrye disagreed. "I think he knows you could escape your own rooms. And that is very peculiar, Your Majesty. Very peculiar indeed."

"I don't see why," Muriele said. "It's a wonder everyone doesn't know about them by now."

Berrye laughed. "It *is* a wonder, Your Majesty, and more specifically a glamour. Men cannot *remember* the passages."

"What do you mean?"

"I mean they can be shown them, they can even walk in them—but a day later they will have forgotten them. Most women, too, for that matter. Only those with the mark of Saint Cer, or the lady I serve, can remember them for any length of time—we and those we choose to give the sight. Erren must have chosen you—but she could not have chosen a man."

"Then Sir Fail won't remember how he escaped the castle?" Muriele asked.

"No, he won't. Nor will his men, or Charles. It is a very old and very powerful charm."

"But you think Robert remembers?"

"It is one explanation for why he moved you. The only one I can presently discern."

"Robert is a highly suspicious man, as you recently pointed out," Muriele said. "He may have merely *feared* that I would have some way to escape."

Berrye shook her head. "There's more. The key—who else would want the key to the chamber of the Kept? And the cruelty done the Keeper very much suggests Robert."

"That's two good points," Muriele admitted. "But if you're right, then he's somehow immune to the spell."

Berrye nodded. Her face drew up almost with a look of pain, as if she had bitten her tongue.

"He isn't normal," Berrye said. "There's something unnatural about him."

"This I know," Muriele said. "I have known it for a long time."

"No," Berrye averred, "this is something new. Some quality about him that was not there before. My coven-sight aches when I look at him. And the smell—like something that is rotting."

"I didn't notice a smell," Muriele said, "and I was near him."

"The scent is there." She folded her hands together and gripped them into a fist. "You said the Kept gave you a curse—a curse against whomever killed your husband and children."

"Yes."

Berrye nodded. "And you carried it through."

"Yes. Do you think Robert is cursed?"

"Oh, certainly," Berrye responded. "That is part of what I sense, though not the whole of it. But what sort of curse was it? What was it supposed to do?"

"I'm not sure," Muriele admitted. "The Kept told me what to write, but the cantation was in a language I did not recognize. I wrote it on a lead sheet and put it in a sarcophagus below the horz in Eslen-of-Shadows."

"Below the horz?"

"Underneath it, actually. It was very peculiar—I don't think any-one knew it was there. The entrance to it was far in the back, where the growth is thickest. I was forced to crawl on hands and knees to find it."

Berrye leaned forward and spoke urgently. "Do you know whose tomb it was?"

"No, I've no idea," Muriele said.

"The cantation—do you remember any of the words? Do you know what saint they were addressed to?"

"The words themselves were too strange. The saint was one I've never heard of, Mary-something."

Berry's lips parted, and then she put one hand to her mouth.

"*Marhirheben?*" she said, and her voice quavered.

"That sounds right," Muriele said. "There were several *h*'s in the name, I remember. I remember wondering how it could be pro-nounced."

"Holy saints," Berrye said weakly.

"What did I do?"

"I—" she trailed off. She seemed terrified.

"What did I do?" Muriele insisted.

"I can't be sure," she said. "But nothing can prevent that curse, do you understand? Nothing at all."

"I don't understand," Muriele said. "You say Robert is cursed. From my point of view there's nothing wrong with that—it's precisely what I wanted."

"If you cursed a man in Her name, Majesty, nothing could save him from it, not even death. And if he was already dead when you cursed him . . ." She looked down at the floor.

"It would bring him back?" Muriele asked, unbelieving.

"It would bring him back," she confirmed. "And there is something about the prince that feels—dead."

Muriele put her forehead in her palms. "These things, they are not real," she said. "They cannot be."

"Oh, they are very real, Majesty," Berrye assured her.

Muriele looked back up at her. "But why do you suspect that Robert died? After all, it was his plan to assassinate William."

"Plans go wrong. William had faithful men with him, and there was a fight. In any case, there were plenty of people who hated Robert enough to kill him—and he was absent from the court for an awfully long time."

"This is still conjecture," Muriele said.

"It is," Berrye said. "But it would explain other things I have heard about. Terrible, unnatural things that ought not to be."

"I only cursed Robert—"

Berrye shook her head violently. "Majesty, if he came back from the dead, you have done more than curse one man. You have broken the law of death itself, and that is a very bad thing indeed."

CHAPTER SEVEN

A CHANGE OF PATRONS

P LEASE," LEOFF BEGGED THE soldier, "can't you tell me what's happened, what I'm supposed to have done?"

"Don't know," the soldier said. He was a short fellow with a puffy red face and an unpleasant nasal voice. "Word was left at the gate to grab you if you turned up—and you turned up. That's all I know. So just keep moving and don't make my life difficult with a lot of questions I can't answer."

Leoff swallowed, but resigned himself to waiting.

They were in a part of the castle he hadn't been in before—not that that was a surprise, because he hadn't seen most of the castle. They'd already passed the court, so they weren't going there. They went down a long hall with high arches and a red marble floor, then into a large room of alabaster. Light streamed in from broad windows trimmed with pale green and gold drapes. The rugs and tapestries were done in similar colors.

When he saw the men who waited in the room, he felt his scalp prickle, and his heart jerked erratically.

"Fralet Akenzal," one of the men said, "or shall I call you *cavaor*?"

Leoff did not know the face, but he knew the disharmonic voice instantly. It was the man from the dike; the one Mery had said was Prince Robert.

"I—I'm sorry, my lord," Leoff stuttered, bowing. "I don't know how to address you."

The other man, of course, was the praifec. "You would not know Prince Robert," he said, "but he is now your regent. You may refer to him as 'Your Highness' or 'my Prince.' "

Leoff bowed again, hoping the shaking in his legs wasn't visible. Did they know that he had heard them, somehow? Did they know?

"It is my great honor to meet you, Your Highness," he said.

"And mine to meet you, Fralet Ackenzal. I hear you performed a great service for our country in my absence."

"It was nothing, my Prince."

"And I've also heard that you're excessively modest, a trait I've little understanding of." He stood and put his hands behind his back. "I'm glad you're well, though I see you've been injured." He pointed at the bandage on Leoff's head. "You were at the lady Gramme's ball, were you not?"

"I was indeed, Your Highness."

"A tragic thing, that," the prince opined. "It won't happen again."

"My Prince, if I may ask, has something happened to His Majesty?"

The regent smiled an unpleasant little smile. "I did not have you brought here, Fralet Ackenzal, so that you could question *me*. You will understand the situation in due course. What I would like to know at the moment is where you have *been*."

"Wh-where I have been, Your Highness?" Leoff stammered.

"Indeed. You were nowhere to be found when the smoke cleared at Lady Gramme's and now, five days later, you suddenly reappear at the gates of the city."

Leoff nodded. "Yes, Sire. As you might expect, I was frightened and disoriented. My head injury made me dizzy, and I became quite lost in the dark. I wandered until I collapsed. A farmer found me and took care of me until I was able to travel."

"I see. And you were alone, when this farmer found you?"

"Yes, Sire."

The prince nodded. "You know the lady Gramme's daughter, Mery, I believe? You were instructing her in the playing of the hammarharp?"

"I was, my Prince."

"You did not see her at the ball?"

"No, Sire. I wasn't aware that she was there."

The prince smiled and scratched his goatee. "She was, and now no one can find her. An attempt was made to kill the lady Gramme and her son when they were in the queen mother's custody, so we fear the worst."

Leoff tried to look upset. It wasn't difficult. "I pray nothing has happened to her," he said. "She is a wonderful child and a gifted musician."

The prince nodded. "I had hoped you knew something of her whereabouts."

"I'm sorry, my Prince."

The regent shrugged. "How did you escape from the manse? The entrances were well guarded."

"I don't remember, Sire," Leoff said. "I was very confused."

"Ah," the prince said. "Ah." He crossed the room, settled into an armchair, and snapped his fingers. A steward immediately brought him a cup of wine.

"Suppose," the prince said, "I *tell* you what happened?"

"Your Highness?"

The regent took a sip of the wine and made a face. "You were taken prisoner," he said, "by the queen's Lierish guard, and kept in a dank cell for five days, until report reached me that you were there. I then had you freed."

Leoff frowned. "My Prince—"

"Because if that *isn't* what happened," the prince went on, examining the fingernails of his right hand, "I might have to accept the report from a nearby village of a man who looked like you and a girl who looked like Mery traveling together. I would then have to conclude that you had lied to me, which would be a capital offense, even if you did it to protect a little girl you rightly thought was in danger from the queen mother." He looked back up at Leoff. "I should think you would like my story better."

"I—yes, Your Highness," Leoff replied, feeling thoroughly miserable.

Robert smiled and clapped his hands together. "We have an understanding then," he said. "And if you happen to hear from Mery, or learn her whereabouts, her mother misses her, and she is no longer in danger from the queen mother, so let someone know, would you, please?"

"Yes, Your Highness."

"Very good. Now, I am given to understand that you were commissioned by the queen mother to produce a musical performance of some sort?"

"Yes, Your Highness. For the Yule celebration, in the Candle Grove. There was to be a feast and general invitation to the people of the city and countryside."

"A wonderful idea," the prince said. "Please submit the work to His Grace the praifec for review."

"Yes, Your Highness," Leoff said.

"Fine. I'm done with you now." He dismissed Leoff with a wave of his hand.

As soon as Leoff was alone, he leaned against a wall, his limbs feeling like water. What was he to do? If he told them where Mery was, what would happen to her? To him? Did they know or suspect that he and the girl had heard their plot? Were they still looking for her?

But he had to do something, and in this he could have only one ally.

He squared his shoulders and continued walking.

"Yes?" the footman said. "How can I help you, Fralet?"

"I must speak to Her Ladyship," Leoff said. "It is a matter of utmost importance."

The footman looked irritated, but he nodded and left. He returned a few moments later. "Follow me, please."

He led Leoff to a sitting room with an immense pastoral tapestry covering one wall. Shepherds and rustically dressed women picnicked beside a pool, entertained by a goat-legged man with a harp and three nymphs playing flute, lute, and sackbut.

Gramme looked drawn and disheveled, but rather than diminishing her beauty, disorder somehow augmented it.

She didn't waste any time on her usual pleasantries.

"Do you have news of my daughter, Fralet Ackenzal?" she barked.

"She is alive and well, my lady," Leoff assured her.

"Are you quite out of your mind?" she snapped. "Do you know the penalty for kidnapping?"

"Please, my lady," Leoff said. "I did not kidnap her—I was only trying to keep her safe. I was afraid for her life."

"Well," Gramme said, looking down and ticking her finger on her armchair. She took a deep breath and let it go before meeting his gaze again.

"You are not a father, are you, Fralet Ackenzal?" she asked.

"No, lady, I am not."

"Do not become one," she advised. "It is tremendously annoying. I never wished for a daughter, never once, you know. She has been nothing but a liability to me, and yet, despite all reason and very much against my will, I find I have feelings for her. I thought she was dead, Fralet Ackenzal, and you are to blame for that."

"Lady, forgive me for the worry I've caused, but I think if I had not acted as I did, she *would* be dead now."

Gramme sighed. "I am distraught, and you have a point. An attempt was made to poison my son and me when we were in the queen mother's 'protection.' No doubt she intended to kill Mery, as well." She took a deep breath. "Very well, let this be forgotten. The prince wants to tell a different story of you anyway, and I think it unwise to stand in his way on that matter. Just tell me where I can find my daughter."

"I would prefer to fetch her myself, Your Ladyship," Leoff said. "If you could provide me with a horse or carriage—"

Her brow furrowed again. "Why won't you tell me?"

"Because I left her in the care of someone, someone I would not want to see implicated in my actions. I hope you can understand that."

After a moment, she nodded brusquely. "That will do. I will arrange for my carriage to take you."

"Milady? I wonder if I might inquire as to—ah—what has happened in my absence. Things seem to have—changed."

"You haven't heard?"

"No, madam, I have not."

She smiled faintly and leaned back. "Prince Robert returned from the dead, as it were, and yesterday proclaimed himself regent."

"But what of His Majesty, Charles?"

"Muriele managed to spirit him away, somehow, along with her Lierish guard. The Craftsmen have also left the city."

"But the queen?"

"The queen *mother* remains in Eslen," Gramme said. "She has been placed under arrest." She pursed her lips. "Why do you think my daughter is still in danger?"

The sudden return to their earlier conversation left Leoff a bit breathless. "I don't think I made it clear that I thought she was still in danger," he said.

She nodded. "No, but you think it so."

"I—" He searched for some explanation that would not reveal what he had heard. If Mery somehow died before returning to Eslen, it would be just one more weapon to use against the queen. He had already allowed himself to become such a tool—he would not let Mery die to become one, as well.

"It's just a feeling I have," he murmured. "But I think once I have returned her to you, she will be safe."

"And she is safe where she is?"

He thought about that—the prince had received reports of the two of them together, but he didn't have Mery, which suggested he hadn't been able to follow their trail all the way to Gilmer's.

"I believe she is, milady."

"Then let her remain where she is for a time. I will contact you when I'm ready for you to fetch her."

"Thank you, Lady Gramme."

She looked at him frankly. "No—thank *you*, Fralet Ackenzal."

He returned to his quarters, hoping for rest and peace, and found the praifec instead, glancing through the sheets of music on his desk. He felt a surge of unaccustomed and blistering anger.

"Your Grace," he said, trying to keep any venom from showing in his voice.

"I hope you don't mind," the praifec said, "I let myself in."

"Your Grace is always welcome," Leoff lied.

"This is the piece the queen commissioned?"

"Most of it, Your Grace."

"I flatter myself that I know something of music," the praifec said. "Before I entered the clergy I studied in the Academy of Saint Omé. My course was Letters, but music was a requirement, of course."

"What instrument did you choose?" Leoff asked.

"The lute, primarily, and harp of course. I was born in Tero Gallé, where the harp is revered." He frowned slightly at the sheet music. "But I do not fully understand this. What are these words written below the staff?"

"They are meant to be sung, Your Grace."

"Along with the instruments?"

"Yes, Your Grace."

"Then how can this be considered a serious composition?" the praifec wondered aloud. "It seems very common, like something that might be performed in a tavern or in the street. The music that comes from this court should elevate the soul, even if it is to be performed for less-than-noble ears."

"I promise you, Praifec, it will elevate. This is something very new."

"The world is suddenly full of new things," the praifec reflected. "Few of them good. But go on, Fralet—explain this 'new thing' to me."

"It is a marriage, Your Grace, of drama and music."

"Like the lustspell one hears in the streets?" Hespero asked disdainfully.

"No, Your Grace—and yes. The lustspell are narrated by song, and the actors mime the parts. I propose to have the actors themselves sing, accompanied by the orchestra."

"That doesn't sound substantially different to me."

"But it is, Your Grace. Her M—the queen mother asked me to write something not for the nobility, not for the court, but for the people, to give them hope in these dark times. They are—as you say—familiar with the lustspell. But while the street performances I have seen are vulgar in content and poorly drawn, I intend to give them something that will stir their souls—as you say, uplift them."

"As you uplifted them in Glastir, by starting a riot?"

"That was an unfortunate event," Leoff said, "but it was not the fault of my music."

Hespero didn't say anything, but continued leafing through the pages.

"This triad is in the seventh mode," he noticed.

"Indeed, Your Grace has an excellent eye."

"Triads in the seventh mode are not to be used," the praifec said firmly. "They have a disharmonious influence on the humors."

"Yes, yes," Leoff said. "Precisely, Your Grace. This is a point in the piece where all seems lost, when it appears that evil will triumph. But if you turn the page here, you see—"

"The third mode," Hespero interrupted. "But these aren't mere triads, these— How many instruments is this written for?"

"Thirty, Your Grace."

"Thirty? Preposterous. Why do you need three bass Vithuls?"

"The Candle Grove is quite large. To project over the voices— but you see, also, here, where they each depart to different themes."

"I do. This is extraordinarily busy. In any event, to shift from seventh to third mode—"

"From despair to hope," Leoff murmured.

The praifec frowned and continued, "Is to excite first one passion and then another."

"But Your Grace, that is what music is meant to do."

"No, music is meant to edify the saints. It is meant to please. It is not meant to stimulate emotion."

"I think if you just heard it, Your Grace, you would find it—"

The praifec waved him to silence with his own sheet music. "What language is this?"

"Why, Your Grace, it is Almannish."

"Why Almannish, when Old Vitellian is perfectly suited to the human voice?"

"But, Your Grace, most of the people attending the concert do not understand Old Vitellian, and it is rather the point that they should understand what is being sung."

"What is the story, in brief?"

Leoff related the story Gilmer had told him, including the embellishments he had added.

"I see why you choose that tale, I suppose," the praifec said. "It has a sort of common appeal that will be popular with those for whom it is intended, and it promotes the idea of fealty to one's sovereign, even unto death. But where is the king in all of this? Where is he in his people's hour of need?" He paused, crooking a finger between his lips.

"How is this?" he suggested. "You'll add something. The king has died, poisoned by his wife. She rules through her daughter, who has— against all that is right and holy—been named his successor. The town is invaded, and the people send for help from her, but it is denied. After the girl sacrifices herself, the invaders, overcome with fury, swear to slaughter the entire populace, and it is then we learn that the king's son—whom all thought dead—is indeed alive. He saves the village and returns to take his rightful place as king."

"But, Your Grace, that isn't what—"

"And change the names of the countries," the praifec went on. "It would be too incendiary to name a Hansan as the villain, given the current climate. Let the countries be, let me see—ah, I have it. Tero Sacaro and Tero Ansacaro. You can guess which is which."

"Is there anything else, Your Grace?" Leoff asked, feeling himself wilt.

"Indeed. I will give you a list of triads you may *not* include in your piece, and you will not have chords larger than a triad. You may retain your thirty pieces, but only for the sake of volume—you will simplify the passages I mark. And this most of all—voice and instruments shall *not* be joined together."

"But Your Grace, that's the whole point."

"That is *your* whole point, but it is not one you will make. The instruments will play their passages, and then the players may recite their lines. They may even sing them, I suppose, but without accompaniment."

He rolled the papers up. "I'll borrow these. Write the new text, with my inclusions. Do it in Almannish if you must, but I will have a complete translation, and likely some amendments, so do not become too attached to it. I will return this to you in two days' time. You will have two days to alter it to my satisfaction, and you will begin rehearsals immediately after that. Is this all clear?"

"Yes, Your Grace."

"Cheer up, Fralet Ackenzal. Think of it this way—the patron who originally commissioned this piece is no longer in a position to reward you for it. You are fortunate you still have a position here at all. The regent is your new patron—mind you do not forget that."

He smiled thinly and turned to leave.

"Your Grace?" Leoff said.

"Yes?"

"If I am to start rehearsals so soon, I must retain the musicians. I have a few in mind."

"Make a list of them," the praifec said. "They will be sent for."

When the praifec was gone, Leoff closed the door and leaned against the hammarharp on balled fists.

And then, very slowly, he grinned. Not because he was happy, or because anything was funny, but because he wasn't worried or afraid anymore. That had been swept away by a clean, cold fury the like of which he had never felt before. This man, this fool who styled himself a praifec had just sowed a very large field, and soon enough he would reap it. If Leoff was a fighting man, he would take his sword and cut down the praifec, and Prince Robert, and whomever else he could reach.

He wasn't a fighting man. But when he was done, the praifec would wish Leoff's weapon was the sword. That he promised himself and every saint he knew.

CHAPTER EIGHT

THE NICWER

STEPHEN FIRST THOUGHT THE water itself had drawn up in a fist to smite at Aspar, but then the fist resolved itself into a wide, flat head with yellow-green eyes that glared like huge round lanterns, all arranged on a thick, long neck. It was a shade between olive and black, and looked weirdly horselike, somehow.

Horselike. That struck a bell instantly in his saint-blessed memory. He jammed his palms up to his ears.

"Winna, cover—," he began, but it was too late, as the beast started to sing.

The note cut through his hands like a hot knife through lard; sliced straight into his skull and began slashing about. It was beautiful, just as the old legends told, but to his oversensitive awareness it was a terrible beauty that stung like hornets and wouldn't let him think. Through a red shroud, he saw Aspar calmly put down his bow and begin walking toward the creature. Winna was starting toward it, too, tears streaming down her face.

He dropped his useless hands and picked up Ehawk's bow. It was only seconds before Aspar walked into the creature's gaping jaws.

He screamed as his shaking hands raised the weapon, trying to cancel the noise in his head, trying to remember the clean motion Aspar used when firing. He drew and released. The arrow skittered harmlessly off the monster's skull.

The note it sang changed in tenor, and he felt his taut muscles loosen and a strange joy surge through him, like being drunk, happy and warm. He dropped the bow and felt a silly grin spread across his face, then laughed as the nicwer—that's what it was, a nicwer—curved its muzzle down toward Aspar.

The neck suddenly snapped back like a whip, the wonderful song cut off by an anguished bellow. Something whispered by his ear, and his eyes caught the blur of an arrow in motion. It struck the nicwer beneath the jaw, and he saw there was already an arrow there, buried in a sort of sack or wattle he hadn't noticed before.

He turned in the direction the arrow had come from and saw Leshya running down the street toward them, still fifty yards away.

She was supposed to still be up on the hill, but he was glad she wasn't. He picked up the bow and ran toward Winna.

Aspar felt as if everything good in him had been ripped out— mornings waking in the ironoaks, the quiet of the deep forest, the feel of Winna's skin—everything wonderful was gone. All that was left was the ugliest beast he had ever seen about to take a bite out of him with sharp, gleaming, serrated black teeth. With a hoarse cry, he threw himself aside, suddenly noticing a stench like the bloated belly of a long-dead horse or the breath of a vulture.

He came back up with his dirk and ax out, feeling silly. He saw it better now, as it heaved itself up on the dock. Its head was otterlike, as wedge-shaped as a viper, and twice the size of the biggest horse skull he had ever seen. Like the greffyn and the utin, it was covered in scales, but also with oily green-black fur. At first he thought its body was that of a huge snake, but even as he reckoned that, it suddenly heaved up onto the dock with short thick forepaws. The feet were webbed and had talons the length of his arm. Silent now save for a sort of gurgling whistle, it lurched toward him, dragging the rest of its mass up from the river. He backed away, unsure what to do. If he let it sing again, then he would surely walk stupidly back into its jaws, as he had almost just done.

At least he knew what had happened to the people of Whitraff. They had walked smiling down to the river and been eaten. He remembered an Ingorn story about something like this, but he couldn't remember what it was called. He'd never much cared for stories about nonexistent creatures.

Another arrow appeared in the sack below its throat, but aside from being unable to croon its damning call, the beast seemed relatively untroubled. It was all out of the water now, except for its tail. Its rear legs were as squat as the front, and as far from them as the length of two horses, so that its belly dragged along the wooden planks. Although it *looked* clumsy, once on land it moved with a sudden speed Aspar wouldn't have guessed at. It lunged at him and he dodged aside, cleaving his ax at the back of its neck. To his surprise, the blade sheared a notch in the scales, albeit not a deep one.

He was still surprised when the head swung violently into him, knocking him off his feet. He rolled, feeling as if his ribs had been cracked, and came up to find the head darting toward him once more. From his crouch Aspar twisted away, cutting at the exposed throat with his knife and feeling the tissue part in a long, ragged slash. Blood sprayed his arm, and this time he dodged the counterattack and came to his feet running.

As soon as he was clear, arrows began pelting the beast. Most were bouncing off; for now it was tucking its head down to protect its vulnerable throat. Aspar saw that Leshya and Stephen were doing the shooting.

The monster was bleeding, but not as much as Aspar had hoped. Still, after a brief hesitation, it seemed to decide it had had enough. It sprinted back to the river, slid in, and vanished beneath the surface, leaving him panting and wondering if the thing was poisonous, like the greffyn. But though he felt a mild burning where the blood had touched his skin, it was nothing like the sick and immediate fever he'd felt confronting the other beast.

Leshya and Winna were a different story. Winna was on her hands and knees vomiting and Leshya was leaning on her bow, the blue veins of her face prominent beneath her skin.

Stephen seemed fine.

Aspar went to Winna and knelt by her. "Did it touch you?" he asked.

She shook her head. "No."

"It'll be fine, then," he murmured. He reached out to stroke her head.

"Don't," Leshya snapped. "The blood."

Aspar stopped inches short of touching Winna, then pulled his hand back and walked away. "Werlic," he acceded.

Leshya nodded. "The gaze of the *equudscioh* isn't fatal, not like some *sedhmhari*, but its blood would infect us." She cocked her head. "I wonder why it hasn't infected you. Or why our priest here wasn't as affected by its song as you two."

"You know what it is?" Aspar said.

"Only from stories," the Sefry replied.

"Do the stories explain how it could do that to us just by—by *braying*?" Aspar demanded. He still missed it, that sound, that perfect feeling. If he heard it again . . .

"There are certain musical notes and harmonies that can affect men so," Stephen said. "It's said the Black Jester created songs so powerful that entire armies ran on their own blades upon hearing them. He was inspired, they say, by a creature known as the *ekhukh*. In Almmanish the same beast is called a nicwer, in Lierish *eq odche*. I think in the king's tongue it's nix, if I remember my phay stories."

"Fine, I know what it's called in five languages now," Aspar grouched. "What *is* it?"

Leshya closed her eyes and swayed unsteadily. "It's one of the sedhmhari, as I told you. It isn't dead, you know, or likely even dying. We should retreat to the hill if we're to discuss this. And you need to clean the blood off you, for our sakes. Even if you have some sort of immunity, we do not."

"Werlic," Aspar said. "Let's do that."

❖ ❖ ❖

They found that despite his injury, Ehawk had crawled halfway down the hill.

"The song," the boy gasped. "What *was* that?"

Aspar left the others to explain while he went to wash.

He found a small brooh trickling down the hillside. He stripped off his leather cuirass and shirt and soaked them while he wiped his arm and face with a rag.

By the time he was done cleaning up, Winna and Leshya seemed to be feeling better.

When he approached, Leshya pointed down toward the river. "I saw it from up here, moving beneath the water. We should be able to see it if it emerges again."

"Yah," Aspar grunted. "That's why you left your post."

"I couldn't shoot it from up here," she argued. "Besides, Ehawk was still watching."

"I'm not chastising," Aspar said. "The three of us would be in its belly now if you hadn't come along."

"Why didn't its song affect you?" Winna asked, a bit sharply.

"I'm Sefry," Leshya rejoined. "Our ears are made differently." She quirked an amused smile at Stephen. "I don't care for Mannish music that much, either."

Winna raised an eyebrow at that, but didn't pursue the matter.

Stephen did, however. "Still," he remarked, "how could you have known it wouldn't lure you as it did us?"

"I didn't," she said, "but it's a good thing to know, isn't it?"

Winna regarded the Sefry. "Thank you," she said. "Thanks for saving our lives."

Leshya shrugged. "I told you we were in this together."

"So how do we kill it?" Aspar asked impatiently.

"I don't think we do," Stephen replied.

"How's that?"

"We might be able to prick it to death, given time, but time is what we don't have. This faneway must be nearly complete. Aspar, we have to stop them from finishing it."

"But *we* have the instructions for the last fane," Winna said.

"Yes," Stephen said, "which only means they need to send a rider to Eslen to see the praifec. That gives us a little more time, but not until next month. The nicwer has lost its voice, and that's its most dangerous weapon. We'll have to leave it to the riverboaters to kill it." He turned to Leshya. "You called it a sedhmhari. What did you mean by that? It's a Sefry word?"

"Mother Gastya called the greffyn that," Winna supplied.

Leshya's eyes went round. "You spoke to Mother Gastya?" she said, clearly surprised. "I thought she was dead."

Aspar remembered his last sight of the old woman, how she seemed to be nothing but bone. "Maybe she was," Aspar said. "But that's not far nor near."

Leshya acquiesced to that with a twist of her mouth. "There is no true Sefry language," she clarified. "We abandoned it long ago. Now we speak whatever the Mannish around us do, but we keep old words, too. *Sedhmhari* is an old word. It means 'demon of the sedos.' The greffyn, utin, and nicwer are all sedhmhari."

"They're connected to the sedoi?" Stephen asked.

"Surely you knew that," Leshya said. "The greffyn was walking the sedoi when you first saw it."

"Yah," Aspar said. "It's how the churchmen were finding them."

"But you're implying a deeper connection," Stephen persisted.

"Yes," Leshya said. "They are spawned by the power of the sedoi, nourished by them. In a sense, they are distillations of the sedos power."

Stephen shook his head. "That doesn't make sense. That would make them distillations of the saints themselves."

"No," Leshya said carefully, "that would make the *saints* distillations of the sedos power, just as the sedhmhari are."

Aspar almost laughed at the way Stephen's jaw dropped. For an instant he seemed the same naïve boy he had met on the King's Road, months ago.

"That's heresy," he finally said.

"Yes," Leshya said dryly. "And wouldn't it be terrible to contradict a church that's sacrificing children to feed the dark saints? I'm very ashamed."

"Yet—" Stephen didn't finish his thought, but his expression grew ever more furiously thoughtful.

"It seems to me most of this is moot, at the moment," Winna interrupted. "What matters is finding that last sedos, that Bent Hill."

"She's right," Aspar concurred. "If we don't have time to kill the nicwer, we don't have time for you two to stand here and go all bookish for a nineday."

Stephen reluctantly conceded that with a nod. "I've looked on my maps," he said, "but I don't see anything marked that looks at all like Khrwbh Khrwkh. Logic dictates that it has to be to the east." He knelt and flattened the map on the ground so they could all view it.

"Why?" Aspar asked.

"We know the order of the faneways from the invocation, and we know where the first one was. These others have been leading steadily east. Most faneways fall in lines or arcs that tend to be regular."

"Wait," Winna said. "What about the faneway they meant to sacrifice *me* at? That was near Cal Azroth, and so would be north."

Stephen shook his head. "They did a different ritual there, not the same thing at all. That wasn't part of this faneway, but a sedos used for the single purpose of possessing the queen's guards. No, this faneway goes east."

Aspar watched as Stephen's index finger traced a shallow curve, across what must be the Daw River and into the plains near where Dunmrogh was located now.

"That's the Daw there, and the Saint Sefodh River there?" Aspar asked.

"Yes," Stephen replied.

"The forest extended that far—all the way into Hornladh? It's no wonder the Briar King is angry. The forest is half the size it was."

"A lot of it was destroyed in the Warlock Wars," Stephen said. "The Briar King can hardly hold that against us."

Leshya snorted. "Of course he can. He doesn't care which particular Mannishen destroyed his forest, only that it was destroyed."

"There's still a stand of ironoaks in Hornladh," Aspar said. "I passed through there on my way to Paldh once. Had a funny name—Prethsorucaldh."

"Prethsorucaldh," Stephen repeated. "That *is* a strange name."

"I don't speak much Hornish," Aspar admitted.

"The ending, *caldh*, just means 'forest,'" Stephen said. "*Preth* means a 'copse,' like a copse of trees. *Soru*, I think, means a 'louse' or 'worm' or something like that."

"Copse-Worm-Wood?" Leshya said. "That doesn't make a lot of sense. Why would they call it a copse and a forest in the same name?"

Stephen nodded. "Doesn't make a lot of sense, which means it probably wasn't originally a Hornish name. It was something that sounded like *Prethsoru*, so over time they substituted words that made sense to them."

"What do you mean?" Leshya asked, sounding as lost as Aspar felt.

"Like this place, Whitraff," Stephen explained. "In Oostish, it means 'White Town,' but we know from this map that the original name was Vhydhrabh, which meant 'Huskwood,' corrupted through Vitellian to 'Vitraf.' When Oostish speakers settled here, they heard the name and thought it meant White Town, and so it stuck. You see?"

"This is hurting my head," Aspar said. "Is there any point to this?"

"Preth-whatever doesn't sound anything like Khrwbh Khrwkh," Winna tentatively pointed out. "At least not to me it doesn't."

"No, nothing like it at all," Stephen mused. "But it reminds me . . ." He paused. "The map is Vitellian, made just as the Hegemony was taking control of this territory. Most of the names on it were originally Allotersian or Vadhiian. But later on, there must have been Vitellian names for towns and landmarks."

"Do you have another map from later on?" Leshya asked.

"No, not of that region," Stephen told her. "And I still don't see how Khrwbh . . ." He stopped again and seemed to stare off into the weird. It worried Aspar, sometimes, how quickly and oddly Stephen's mind worked, ever since he walked the faneway of Decmanis. Not that it hadn't worked strangely to start with.

"That's it," Stephen murmured. "It has to be."

"What's what?" Aspar asked.

"They *translated* it."

"Translated what?"

"Names of places are funny," Stephen said, his voice growing more excited—as it always did when he'd figured something out. "Sometimes, when a new people with a new language come along, they just keep the old name, not knowing what it means. Sometimes they bend it so it does mean something, as with Whitraff. And sometimes, when they *do* know what the old name means, they translate it into their own tongue. Ehawk, what do your people call the King's Forest?"

"*Yonilhoamalho,*" the boy replied.

"Which means?" Stephen pressed.

"The King's Forest," Ehawk responded.

"Exactly. In the language of the Warlock kings, it was named Khadath Rekhuz. The Hegemony called it Lovs Regatureis, and during the Lierish Regency it was Cheldet de Rey. In Oostish it's Holt af sa Kongh, and when Virgenyan became the king's tongue we started calling it the King's Forest. But the meaning remains unbroken after a thousand years, you see?"

"All that to spell what?" Aspar asked, a little put off that he still didn't see where this was going, and knowing he was going to feel stupid when Stephen reached his conclusion.

"I think *Prethsoru* came from Vitellian *Persos Urus,*" Stephen replied triumphantly.

"Hurrah," Aspar said. "What the sceat does that mean?"

"Bent Hill," Stephen rejoined, too smugly. "Do you follow me now?"

"Sceat, no, I didn't follow any of that," Aspar shot back. "It's a bridge made of mist."

"Probably," Stephen admitted.

"And if I take your meaning, you're saying we should ride hell-bent for a forest in Hornladh based on nothing more than this silly wordplay?"

"Exactly," Stephen promptly replied.

"And—let's get this clear—even *you* don't think you're right about this?"

"A blind shot in the dark," Stephen allowed.

Aspar scratched his chin. "Let's get going, then," he said. "That's twenty leagues if it's a yard."

"Wait!" Leshya protested. "If he's wrong—"

"He's not wrong," Aspar said.

"What about the nicwer?" Ehawk asked. "We still have to cross the river."

"There's a ford a league downstream," Aspar told him. "If it follows us there, at least we'll be able to see it. After that we can double back to the Old King's Road. It goes straight to Dunmrogh." He nodded at Stephen and Winna. "You two help Ehawk get mounted. Leshya, you come with me and we'll get some supplies from the tavern."

He saw Winna's frown, and felt a flash of exasperation. Leshya was the only one of them immune to the song of the nicwer. Didn't Winna *know* it made more sense for the Sefry to go back to town with him? After all, there might be more than one of the beasts in the river.

He didn't say anything, though. He wasn't going to embarrass himself by explaining something that ought to be understood. Winna still had a lot of learning to do.

"Keep a close watch on the river," he said instead. "Yell if you see anything. And put something in your ears."

"You should do the same," Winna shot back.

"Then I couldn't hear you yell, could I?" he countered, starting off toward town, Leshya a pace behind him.

CHAPTER NINE

SORORITY

FOR A MOMENT, ANNE'S tongue was frozen by surprise. "I'm sorry?" she asked, finally. "Who do you mean? I think you've mistaken me for someone else."

"I haven't," Osne said. "Word came to me that you might pass this way. Do you think it coincidence that my husband found you?" She placed her hands on the table, palms up. "Sister Ivexa," she said softly. "One sister of the coven Saint Cer did not die in the attack, and the coven has many graduates and allies across the land. Word has spread quickly both of your plight and of your pursuers."

Anne felt as if all she had to walk upon was a sword's edge beneath her feet. The simple thought that someone actually knew who she was and wanted to help her instead of kill her was nearly too much to accept. It ran hard up against the fact that this could just be another betrayal in fair disguise.

She was far too tired to parse out which was more likely.

"If you wanted me dead, you could have had that," Anne said.

"I do not wish any harm to you, Anne," Osne assured her.

"It's been a long time since I've been able to easily trust words like that." She placed one hand flat on the table, feeling the solidity of the wood. "Who survived the massacre?" she asked.

"You did not know her as a sister," Osne said, "and in some ways she is not, but more."

Anne knew then, without thinking, as if she had always known. "The countess Orchaevia."

Osne nodded. "Unfortunately, you fled her estates before she was aware of what was happening. But now you are among friends again."

"What do you want from me?" Anne asked warily.

Osne reached across the table and took her hand. "Only to help you return to Eslen and your destiny."

Anne felt the callused hand in hers, as substantial and real as the table.

"You—you are a sister of the coven, Osne?"

"I attended," the older woman said. "I did not take my vows, but still when they call, I will answer. I would not risk all for the coven Saint Cer—not my life, or the life of my husband and sons—but I will risk them for you, Anne Dare. I have *seen*. The Faiths have sent me dreams."

"The Faiths!" Anne exclaimed. "You know of them? Who are they?"

"Some claim they are merely very powerful seers, others say they are as old as the world, goddesses of fate. Even the sisters of the coven argued over their nature. I think the truth lies somewhere between, myself. What cannot be denied is their wisdom. Whether they are centuries old or eons old, they have seen more of this world than we, and they know much more of its future." She paused. "You have seen them, spoken to them?"

"Three of them," Anne said.

Osne sighed. "I have never been so blessed as to be called. I have heard their voices in my dreams, caught glimpses of what they see, that is all. You are a lucky young woman."

"I don't feel lucky," Anne said. "I feel trapped."

"We are all trapped," Osne said, "if that's how you want to think of it."

"Is there another way?" Anne asked.

"Yes," Osne said. "We are all vital. Each of us may be just a thread, but without the threads, there is no tapestry."

"Then how can one thread be more important than the others?"

"Some threads are warp and some are weft," Osne said. "The warp must be there to weave the other threads through. The warp must be there first."

"You're as bad as the Faiths." Anne sighed.

Osne smiled and gripped her hand more tightly. "They've told you what you must do, haven't they? And given you at least some hint of why."

Anne conceded that with a nod. "It's not that I'm fighting it," she said. "I've been *trying* to return to Eslen."

"And now you shall," Osne vowed. "My husband and sons will take you across the river and past your enemies in town. They will escort you to Eslen."

"I can't go straight home," Anne told her. "Not yet."

"But you just said that was your goal," Osne said.

"The two men who rescued me at the coven, and have been protecting me since, were captured by the horsemen. I have to rescue them first."

Osne's brow bunched in worry. "I'm sorry about your friends," she said, "but they aren't your first duty."

"Maybe not," Anne said, "but I won't leave them to die. I have to do something."

Osne closed her eyes. "That's not the path you're supposed to walk."

"I can choose another path?"

Osne hesitated. "Yes. But then the future becomes cloudy."

"Let it. If I'm not true to my friends, whom can I be true to? What good am I to anyone?"

Osne closed her eyes for a moment. "How many horsemen are with your friends?"

"Artoré saw them. He said three."

"Then I will send Artoré and my sons after them, and find a safe place for you until they return."

"No," Anne said. "I want to go with them."

"They may not succeed," Osne said softly. "If one of the knights is a *marevasé*, they might not succeed."

"A what?" Anne asked.

"One who cannot die. They have other names."

"Oh," Anne said. "One of them is like that," she said. "Maybe more."

"Then you know the risk is great."

"You'd send your husband and sons to their deaths, just to get me to Eslen?"

"I'd rather not," Osne admitted. "I'd rather you let them escort you home. There would still be some risk in that, but not like sending them to battle a marevasé.

"You don't understand," Anne said. "These men—Cazio and z'Acatto—risked *everything* for us."

"And so would we, dear."

"I see that," Anne flared. "I'm tired of people dying for me, do you understand? I can't take any more of it."

"People die for their queens," Osne exclaimed. "That is a burden you *must* accept, or there is no point in you reaching Eslen. There are much harder decisions than this ahead of you, Anne."

"Cazio and z'Acatto know nothing about my supposed destiny," she said. "And I'm sure if I do nothing they will die. But how can I risk your family, too?"

"Because we *do* accept your destiny, and our role in it. If it is your decision to follow the horsemen, we will abide by your decision." Her eyes became more intense. "I could have drugged your wine," she said. "Artoré could have simply *taken* you home. But a queen who cannot make her own decisions is a poor queen indeed."

Anne rubbed her head. "I hate it," she snarled. "I hate it all."

"They may be dead already," Osne pointed out. "If the horsemen believe they have lost you, I can't think of any reason they would keep your friends alive—except perhaps as bait, in the hopes you will follow."

Anne felt tears on her face. She remembered Cazio, when she first met him, brash and teasing and full of life. To think of him dead hollowed her out.

But her father was dead. Elseny was dead. Fastia was dead.

"I will go to Eslen," she said, and a great sob tore from her chest. Osne came around the table and took her in her arms, and Anne let her hold her like that, even though she hardly knew the woman. She wept, and Osne rocked her as night eased through the window and into her heart.

Anne and Austra were given lodging in a windowless room. By lantern light, the plaster looked dark yellow. It was simply furnished with a bed, a basin of water and towel on a wooden stand, and a night pan beneath the bed. Away from the hearth it was cold, and Anne slipped quickly into the nightgown Osne had given her, then beneath the thick woolen comforters. Austra was already there, asleep, but she woke when Anne settled in beside her.

"That was a long talk," Austra said. "What was it about?"

Anne took a deep breath. Her chest ached from crying.

"Osne was at the coven Saint Cer, many years ago," she explained. "She knows who we are because the countess Orchaevia sent word along the roads to look for us and keep us safe."

"The countess? How odd."

"It's not odd," Anne said. "The countess was a member of the coven, too."

"That's even odder, in a way, but it makes some sense. The countess must have known who you were, to go to so much trouble."

"I'm supposed to be queen, Austra."

Austra started a laugh that never quite finished. "How do you mean?" she asked.

"Father, you remember. He had the Comven legitimize Fastia, Elseny, and me to succeed him. Fastia and Elseny are gone, and only I remain."

"But Charles is still alive," Austra said. "The cuveitur said nothing about his death."

"Our enemies don't care about Charles," Anne said. "They do not want a *queen* in Eslen. They fear a queen."

"Why?"

Anne explained then, about everything. About the Faiths, about the dark man in the forest, about her dreams. When she finished, Austra's eyes were round with wonder.

"Why couldn't you have told me all of this before?" she asked.

"Because I didn't believe it myself," Anne said. "Because I thought it might somehow put you in more danger. But now I know I have to tell you."

"Why? Because I've been to where the Faiths are?"

"No, because tomorrow Artoré and his sons are going to sneak us across the river and take us to Eslen."

"But that's wonderful," Austra said, then started, and her voice dropped in tone. "You mean *after* we rescue Cazio."

Anne shook her head. "No, Austra. We can't go after them. I'm sorry."

"I don't understand. With Artoré we can save them."

"Artoré and his boys are no match for those knights," Anne said.

"You don't know that, Anne, you—"

"I can't *risk* it, don't you understand?"

"No! How can you even imagine leaving them to die?"

"Austra, I know how you feel about Cazio, but—"

"No! No you don't—you can't." She was crying now. "We can't just give up."

"We've no choice," Anne replied.

"We do!"

"You have to listen to me," Anne said. "This is hard for me. Do you think I want to do this? But if we go after them, and it's a trap—which it probably is—then not only do Cazio and z'Acatto die anyway, but so do Artoré and his sons, and so do we."

"I never thought you a coward," Austra said.

"If it was just our lives I was risking, I would be following them this instant," Anne said. "If it was just these few men, I would still do it. But if I am to believe the Faiths, and Osne—and Sister Secula, for that matter—then I cannot risk my life here. I must return straight-away to Eslen."

"And why do you believe them? Why should I believe you? You, a queen who can save the world from destruction. Do you know how ridiculous that sounds?"

"I do. But I'm starting to believe it."

"Of course you do! You're to be queen and savior of all that's good. Your head is as swollen as a melon!"

"Austra—"

"Oh, no," Austra said. "Don't try. Don't talk to me. Don't ever talk to me again."

She turned her back, sobbing again, and Anne's own tears returned, albeit silently this time. She lay awake for a very long time before exhaustion finally claimed her.

When she woke the next morning, Austra was gone.

"It looks like she took a weather-cloak and some bread," Osne said. "But no one saw her leave."

"Austra is no thief," Anne said.

"I know that. I'm sure she feels as if her need outweighed everything, and equally sure she intends to return the cloak. It isn't of any consequence—I would have given her those things anyway."

"Well, she can't have gone far," Anne said. "If we hurry, we'll find her." She knew she was going against everything she had said the night before, but this was *Austra,* and besides, she wouldn't have caught up with the horsemen yet. It should be safe.

"We'll have to go that direction for a few leagues anyway," Artoré said. "And we'd best get started now."

"The horses are ready, Atté," Cotmar, the second eldest boy, said. "And Jarné has seen to the supplies."

"Osne, get the princess outfitted, and we'll be on our way."

Osne dressed her in one of the boys' clothes—riding breeches tucked into leather boots, a cotton shirt and heavy woolen overshirt, weather cloak and battered, broad-brimmed hat. They rode out before the next bell.

"That's her mark there, Atté," Cotmar said, pointing to something on the path that Anne couldn't see at all.

"Té, somebody told her about the upper crossing," Artoré mused. "She must have stopped and asked Vimsel. Smart girl."

"Well, we knew better than to try to cross the bridge at Teremené," Anne said. She patted her horse's mane. "What's his name?" she asked.

"*Tare,*" he told her.

"Tarry," Anne repeated. "I hope he's faster than his name."

Artoré gave her an odd look, but didn't say anything.

They continued along, with the road following close to the river, until they reached a rickety-looking rope bridge. The chasm was even deeper at this point than it had been at Teremené, and Anne tried hard not to look down as she swayed across its span. They picked up Austra's trail on the other side, where it intersected a way that was broad enough for wagons.

The chalky road led them higher into the hills, wandering along ridgetops when it could and reluctantly dipping into valleys when it couldn't. The hills themselves were slumped and worn, virtually tree-less. Gray and white sheep grazed on the slopes, along with the occa-sional goat or horse. They saw scatterings of houses built mostly of undressed stone with thatched roofs.

"Té, there's the horsemen, I'll wager," Artoré said, after a time.

"How can you tell?" Anne asked. This time she could see the marks of horses, at least.

"One dismounted here. See the scuff of his spurs? The horse-shoes have a funny shape, too, and there're three of them."

"And Austra?"

"She took a horse from that farm back there," he replied. "This is her." He pointed to a slurred sort of track. "Trotting him. She's in a hurry."

"How far ahead?"

"She's about an hour ahead, and they're more than half a day."

"Can we speed up?"

"Sure, but if she leaves the road, we might miss it."

"She can't track the way you can. She'll stick to the road, and hope the men who have Cazio do, too."

"Well, then," Artoré said. He urged his horse to a trot.

"Come on, Tarry," Anne said. At first she just matched the trot, but, just to see what he could do, she encouraged the horse to a run and then a hard-out gallop, and for an instant, despite it all, she found herself grinning. She loved riding, and while Tarry wasn't as quick as her own steed, Faster, he was a good runner, and she hadn't been on a horse in a long time. She'd almost forgotten what it was like.

She knew she couldn't push him like that for long, however, so she went back to a trot and they traveled like that, alternating. The leagues between them and Teremené lengthened as their shadows did, until at last night came, with the prints of her stolen horse the only sign of Austra.

They camped on a hill overlooking the road.

"We'll catch her tomorrow," Artoré promised. "She's wearing her horse out, and he'll be slower. That should put us near the Dunmrogh road, and we can take that west toward Eslen."

"Dunmrogh," Anne said. "We're near Dunmrogh?"

"About five leagues, I'd say. Why?"

"Just curious. I know someone from there." *Roderick*. He would help—his family had troops, surely. With his aid, they could go after Cazio and succeed.

But he was more than likely in Eslen. Still, if they were going to be so close, it wouldn't hurt to find out, would it?

But on the heels of that thought came Cazio's suspicions. What if her enemies were *going* to Dunmrogh? What if he really was in league with them?

She put speculation from her mind.

Tomorrow she would *know*.

The hills sloped gently down into a plain Artoré named *Magh y Herth,* the "Plain of Barrows." Anne didn't see any barrows, only leagues of yellowed grass and the occasional line of trees marking a stream. Geese streamed overhead and occasional herds of cattle cropped by the side of the road. Now and then side roads led off to small villages, made visible by their bell towers.

Around midday, a line of green appeared on the horizon, eventually resolving into a forest. The road led them beneath the huge, arching branches of ironoak, ash, everic, and hickory. The hoofbeats of their horses were muffled here by falling leaves. The forest felt old and clingy, like a decrepit man trying to hug her.

"Prethsorucaldh," Artoré said, gesturing at the trees. "You would call it 'Little Worm Wood.' "

"That's an odd name," Anne said. "Why is it called that?"

"I've heard some tale about a monster of some sort that lived in the ground, but I don't recall any details. They say it used to be a part of the King's Forest, but during the Warlock Wars an army of fire marched on either side of the Saint Sefodh and cut it off. Since then it's been shrinking. Now it's the Lord of Dunmrogh's hunting preserve."

"An army of fire *what*?"

"That's what the stories say—Sverfath of the Twenty Eyes summoned an army of fire and sent it against his enemy—oh, what was her name?—Sefhind the Windwitch. Some say it was an army of flaming demons, others that it was a living river of fire. But those are stories, you know? I've never read the sober histories. But if it was fire, it wasn't an ordinary one, because the trees never came back. You'll see when we get to the other side—not a tree between here and the river."

"Atté!" One of the boys shrieked, Anne wasn't sure which one, and in the space after his cry she heard a peculiar noise, almost like rain though the leaves, but with a peculiar whirring to it. Jarné—who was riding ahead—clutched at his heart and jerked weirdly, then fell off his horse. Everything came into focus then, as she understood that arrows where riving the air around them.

"Go!" Artoré shouted, and slapped at Tarry's tail. The horse started forward violently. Pulse racing, Anne lay close to the stallion's mane and gave him his head. A couple of arrows hissed by her, so close she could feel the wind, and she wondered what it would feel like when one hit her.

As it turned out, it felt like a hard sort of thump—she thought she'd hit a branch or something. But when she looked down, she saw a long feathered shaft in her thigh. Just as she was wondering why it didn't hurt, it began to, and her head went light.

Tarry screamed, and she guessed he'd been hit, too, though she couldn't see where.

"I'm sorry, I'm so sorry," Anne gasped. She wasn't sure who she was talking to. Everyone, she guessed.

Tarry kept running, and after a few long moments Anne realized the arrows had stopped. She looked back and didn't see anyone at all.

"Artoré!" she shouted. Her leg was throbbing now, and she felt feverish and weak.

When she turned back around she saw a horseman, coming from the other direction.

CHAPTER TEN

OVERTURES

MURIELE WOKE TO SOFT humming. Sleepily, she opened her eyes and looked for the source.

"Ah," a male voice said. "Good morning to you, Queen Mother."

She went rigid when she saw that it was Robert, seated lazily in her armchair. Alis Berrye was in his lap.

"Get out of my room," Muriele commanded.

"Well, it's not actually your room, you know," Robert countered. "It belongs to the Crown, and that belongs to me at the moment."

Muriele didn't answer, because there wasn't anything to say. She couldn't call for the guards, because they wouldn't come. She looked around, searching for something—anything—to use as a weapon, but there wasn't anything.

Berrye giggled.

"Come now, dear," Robert said to the girl. "Off we go. I've some things to discuss with your lady here."

"Oh, can't I stay?" Berrye pouted.

"This will be grown-up talk," Robert said. "Go into your room and shut the door."

"Well—I will. But she's been very rude to me. I think you should punish her." With that, she got up and vanished into her quarters. Robert stayed where he was, stroking his mustache.

"That was quite a surprise the other day," he said. "I commend you—I didn't think you had the resources to even know I was coming."

"Did you kill my daughters?" Muriele demanded. "I've no doubt about William."

"Well, I can't be two places at once, can I?" Robert challenged reasonably.

"No. But you can arrange for others to do your evil work. I imagine you wanted to kill William with your own hand."

He laughed. "You know me so well, Muriele. Yes, so I did want that satisfaction, and you know? It was harder than I thought it would be. William was—well, he was right brave there at the end. A credit to our name. Of course, if he hadn't been such an utter buffoon, it would never have happened. Even you have to admit, my dear, that he wasn't much of a king."

"He was a better king than you will ever be, and a far better man, you septic dement."

He sighed. "As to your daughters, I didn't order that, though I knew it would happen. William killed them, really, when he legitimized them to take the throne."

"The praifec was behind it?"

Robert wagged a finger. "Ah, no, that would be telling you more than you need to know. Anyway, the truth is so much larger than you can imagine. I don't wish to tax your powers of comprehension. Though, again, you are more canny than I thought you were." He put his hands on his knees and leaned forward. "Here's the thing. I need you to put an end to any hopes you might have of a countercoup. There really are problems facing us that require a united front. I know you're a bit angry at me right now, but you're a practical woman—"

"Really?" Muriele interrupted. "You think I'm a *bit* angry with you? Robert, you've lost what little sense you ever had. I would far sooner die than cooperate with you in the least fashion."

"Yes, you see? That's what I was talking about. You're angry. That's why I'm so disappointed Charles isn't here—then I would have a life dearer to you than your own to hold in balance. As it is, I must appeal to reason."

"Lesbeth," Muriele snapped. "Why did you kill Lesbeth? She could never have been queen."

His face pinkened. "Surely you know why," he said.

"How can you expect me to even begin to understand someone who would kill his own sister?"

"No one loved Lesbeth more than I," Robert asserted, starting to look truly angry. "*No* one. But some things can't be forgiven; some slights can't be taken back."

"What slights?"

"*That* you know!" Robert shouted, bounding to his feet. "Everyone knew! It was beyond belief."

"Pretend that I do not," Muriele said through gritted teeth.

He looked at her as if *she* were the one who had lost her mind. "You will really feign that you don't know?"

"I so feign," Muriele said.

"She—she didn't ask my permission to marry," he growled, his voice rising steadily in volume. "She asked William, oh yes, but she did not ask *me*." The last word reported from his lips like a cauldron exploding.

Frost seemed to settle on Muriele's spine. "You're quite mad, you know," she whispered, suddenly terrified, not so much of Robert as at things that must be in his head.

Some unidentifiable emotion worked across his face, and then he vented a bitter snicker. "Who wouldn't be?" he muttered. "But enough of that. Why do you continue to distract me with these questions? The Craftsmen are camped outside the city and refuse to see me. Why?"

"Perhaps they don't recognize the legitimacy of your claim, my lord."

"Well, then, they're going to die, which is a pity, because they will doubtless take many of the landwaerden forces with them. It's just going to make people like you less, you know, and weaken us as a nation that much more."

"You would set pikemen against knights? That is despicable."

"They forfeit their knighthood in opposing the Crown," Robert said. "I'm not going to wait for them to move against me. There are already reports that they are gathering their own footforces."

"And of course, there is Liery," Muriele said. "They will hardly stand still for what you've done."

Robert shook his head. "I've made it clear to the Hansan ambassador that we will not object if their fleet sails against Liery."

"The covenant between Crotheny and Liery is sacred," Muriele said. "You cannot break that."

"You broke it when you took a Lierish guard and used it against the landwaerden," he retorted.

"That's utter nonsense," Muriele said.

He shrugged and stood. "In any event, if I were you, I would not look to help from Liery."

"Nor can we look to their help when Hansa attacks us," Muriele said. "We can't be divided from them. Robert, this is insane."

"You keep using words like that," he said. "I wonder if you really know what they mean." He waved his hands, as if to fan her words out the window. "Look, look, you can *prevent* this, Muriele. Call back the Craftsmen, bring back Charles. I remain as sovereign with you by my side, and all will be happy."

"Are you actually suggesting that I marry my husband's murderer?"

"For the good of the nation, yes. It is the most elegant solution possible, I'm sure you agree." He crossed his arms and leaned against the window casement.

"Robert," Muriele said, "I'm sorely tempted to do exactly as you suggest in order to get the chance to drive a knife through your heart while you're sleeping, but I could never keep up the charade for that long." She crossed her arms, too. "How does *this* sound? You relinquish the throne, send your guard away, and disband the landwaerden army. I will bring Charles and the Craftsmen back, and then we will hang you. Does that suit you as elegant enough?"

Robert quirked a smile and walked toward the bed. "Muriele,

Muriele. Time has not blunted your tongue or your beauty. Your face is as lovely as ever. Of course, they say the face goes last, that age works from the toes up. I've a mind to discover if that is true." He grabbed the cover and yanked it from the bed.

"Robert, do not dare," she commanded.

"Oh, I should think I shall," he said, reaching for her breast. She put up her hands to stop him but he clamped her wrists in fingers like steel bands and pushed her roughly back. Very deliberately he flung one leg over her and pulled the other up until he was straddling her, then lowered himself until his body crushed against hers and his face hovered two hands above. Never taking his gaze from hers, he let go one of her hands and reached with the other down between her legs and began hiking up her nightgown. He planted one knee between her thighs and began prying them apart.

He seemed to grow heavier, pinning her to the bed, and his face was now so near hers, it was distorted, the face of a stranger. She remembered Robert as an infant, as a little boy, in the court, but she couldn't make any connection between that and what was happening to her, this *thing* with his hand in her privates. She felt her limbs go limp as he started to undo the fastenings of his breeches, and rolled her head to the side so she could not see his face. His hands moved on her like giant spiders, and he smelled like carrion, just as Berrye said.

She let her gaze slip along Robert and past him and saw Berrye creeping toward Robert's back, something held tightly in one hand. Muriele shook her head and mouthed the word *no*.

Then, lazily, feeling as if she had all the time in the world, she reached for the hilt of Robert's knife, drew it, and stabbed it into his side. It went in easily. She'd always imagined it would be something like cutting into a pumpkin, stabbing someone, but it wasn't like that at all.

Robert jerked, grunted, and sat up on her, and then she drove the blade into his heart. He fell back with a moan, and she squirmed from beneath him, still holding the knife. She was just starting to shake when Alis was suddenly there, supporting her, murmuring reassurances.

Robert picked himself up off the floor, his breath coming in harsh wheezes.

"First the husband, then the wife," he gasped. "I'm beginning to hate this family."

There wasn't any blood, Muriele noticed—or at least not very much. Something was oozing from Robert's wounds like syrup, but it wasn't red. She looked at the knife, still in her hand. It was coated with a sticky, clearish resin.

She flinched as Robert staggered across the room, but he seemed to ignore her and slouched once more into the armchair.

"It does still hurt, though," he said absently. "I wondered about that." He glanced up at her. "I suppose we won't marry after all."

"Robert, what have you done?" Muriele whispered.

Robert glanced down at the wound in his chest. "This? I didn't do this, love. I was minding my own business, dying—William managed to stab me, you know, against all reason. And then I did die, I think, and now—well, I'm as you see." He wagged a finger at her. "*You* did *this*, naughty girl. The Kept told me so."

"So it *was* you in my room, that night."

"Of course," he confessed, wiping his brow. "It's so strange that I didn't know about the passages. That's how you got Charles out, isn't it?"

Muriele didn't answer. She dropped the knife and clung to Alis.

"You two seem very friendly," Robert noticed. "Alis, were your attentions to me fraudulent? I mean, I *knew* they were, but I supposed they came from a desire to resume your place as a palace whore."

"Please leave her alone, Robert," Alis said. "If you want someone, take me."

"Oh, no, the mood has quite left me," Robert said. He rolled his head back. "Let's see," he mumbled. "There was something else I was going to tell you, what was it?" He scratched his chin. "Right. That affair you planned at the Candle Grove—that was a good idea. I'm going ahead with it. And since it *was* your idea, I'm arranging for you to be present. Consider it an apology."

He pushed himself up. "I'd better get this seen to," he said, "and then decide whether I must kill the physician." He bowed. "I bid you ladies good morning."

Then he left.

When he was gone, Muriele began to shudder.

"Sit," Alis said.

"No," she gasped. "No, not in that chair. Not on the bed, never—never again."

"Well, come into my room, then. I'll make some tea. Come on."

"Thank you, Alis," she said.

She let the girl lead her into her apartment, and sat on the bed. Alis went to the little stove there and began to kindle it.

"What is he, Alis?" Muriele asked. "What exactly have I made?"

Alis stopped and turned halfway, then went back to her work with the stove. "In the coven," she began, "we studied the rumors of a creature like this. But in all our histories, it is only once recorded that the law of death was broken—by the Black Jester. He made himself as Robert is, deathless and yet not truly alive. But once the law of death has been broken, it is a simpler matter to make others. One of the Black Jester's titles was *Mhwr*. Those he created were called the *Mhwrmakhy*. In the Chronicles of the Old North Kingdom, the Black Jester was called the *Nau*, and his servants the nauschalken."

"Those last are easier to wrap my tongue around," Muriele admitted.

She still felt his hands on her, his weight pressing down . . .

"Wait," she said, in an effort to keep her mind elsewhere. "If the Black Jester broke the law of death, how could I have broken it again?"

"It was repaired, at great cost," Alis said.

"But it can be repaired," Muriele said hopefully.

"We no longer know how," she replied. "Those who did it perished in the doing."

Muriele bowed her head, despair filling her up. "Then I deserved—"

Alis took three quick steps from the stove and slapped her, hard.

Muriele looked up at her in utter astonishment, the sting still on her cheek.

"No," Alis said. "Do not say it. Never say *that*, and do not *think* it." She knelt and took Muriele's hand, and there were tears in her eyes.

Muriele ached to cry, but could not find her own tears. Instead she curled up in the bed, closed her eyes, and searched behind them for a forgetful sleep.

Leoff answered the light rap at his door and found Areana there, looking puzzled and quite pretty in a dark blue gown.

"You sent for me, Cavaor Ackenzal?" she said.

"Yes," he said. "Please call me Leoff."

She smiled nervously. "As you wish, Leoff."

"Please, come in, have a seat." He noticed an older woman in the hall beyond her. "And you, lady, if you please."

Areana looked chagrined. "I'm sorry," she said. "It's just—I've never been in the palace, and it's all so—well, I'm nervous, as you can see. This is my governess, Jen Unilsdauter. I thought it appropriate . . ." She trailed off, as if unsure of what she meant to say, or worried she'd already said the wrong thing.

"You are most welcome, Lady Jen," Leoff told her. "Most especially if you can speak for Areana's parents."

"I'm no lady, young man," she replied, "but I appreciate a compliment."

"Please, sit, both of you."

When they had, he returned his gaze to Areana, who was blushing.

"Leoff," she began, "I—that is too say—"

He got it then. "Oh, no, you misunderstand, I think," he hurriedly assured her. "I didn't ask you here for—not that I don't find you charming . . ." He trailed off. "This is getting worse and worse, isn't it?" He sighed.

"Well, it's certainly becoming more and more confusing," Areana agreed.

"It's this, you see," Leoff said, patting the score on his worktable.

"This is why I've asked you here. You've heard about the perfor-mance to be given at the Candle Grove?"

"Of course," she said. "Everyone has. I am very much looking forward to it."

"Well, that's good," he said. "That's very good." He hoped he hadn't insulted her.

"And?" she queried. Leoff realized he hadn't actually explained.

"Right," he said. "I would like you to sing the lead role."

Her eyes widened improbably large. "Me?"

"Ah, yes," he said, rubbing his hands together. "Or at least audi-tion for it."

"I don't understand."

"I was struck by your singing voice at Lady Gramme's. It's not only lovely, but precisely the voice I'm looking for for this perfor-mance. I think you'll understand when you've read the part."

"The part?" she said, frowning in puzzlement.

"Yes, yes—it's a new sort of thing, somewhat like a lustspell but a bit more—um, elevated."

"I should hope so," the governess huffed.

"Oh, hush, Jen," Areana said. "You enjoy the lustspells as much as I do. We only pretend to disdain them, remember?"

"Yes, but a girl of your position—"

"Hear me out," Leoff said, "Please. It's the story of Lihta, from Broogh. You know the tale?"

"Yes, of course."

"You would sing the part of Lihta."

"You mean act it," Areana corrected.

"No, no, look here," he said, showing her the music. "You can read, can't you?"

"She reads very well," the governess asserted.

As Areana looked over the pages he saw comprehension begin to dawn.

"You see?" he said.

She looked at him doubtfully. "It's my Newland accent you want, isn't it?"

"In part," he conceded. "And I also believe that if this play is going to be for the people of Newland and Eslen, one of you should be in it. But you have to understand, I would never compromise my music for such a whim. You have a sort of—of—innocent boldness that any other singer would have to feign. In you it is pure."

Areana blushed again, more deeply this time. "Now I really *don't* know what to say," she said.

"Well, here, let's try a bit of it," he suggested.

"All right."

He chose Lihta's first air, which she sang beautifully, and then the trickier bit he called a spellsing, a sort of cross between talking and singing. Well before she was done, he knew his instincts had been correct.

"It's lovely," she said.

"When sung with such a voice, it cannot help but be," Leoff told her. "I truly hope you will consider the part."

"If you really think me suitable, I would be honored," she gushed.

"You are as perfectly suitable as can be," Leoff said, beaming. Then he coughed, and composed his features more seriously. "But I need to tell you something rather important. It may change your mind."

"And what is that?"

"Praifec Hespero has expressly forbidden the performance of this as written. When we defy him, he will be angry. I think I shall bear the brunt of his displeasure, and will certainly take all responsibility, but there is some danger to everyone involved, you included."

"Why should the praifec disapprove?" Areana demanded. "There is nothing unholy here, surely?"

"Not in the least, I assure you."

"Then—"

"The praifec is a man of the saints," the governess suddenly interjected. "We *certainly* cannot go against his word."

"But it doesn't seem reasonable—," Areana began.

"Areana, no," her governess warned. "You shouldn't get mixed up in this."

Areana faced Leoff. "Why do *you* take this risk?" she asked. "Why do you ask me to?"

"Because it will be magnificent," he said softly. "I know in my heart it is right, and I will not be deterred. I told you I would never compromise my music, and I never will, not when I know I have created something worth hearing."

Areana continued to stare at him, biting a little at her lip. Then she lowered her eyes.

"Jen is right," she said. "I believe you, Leoff. I believe *in* you. But I can't do this. I'm sorry."

He nodded, feeling disheartened. "Thank you for your time, then. It was good to hear you sing a bit of it once, anyway."

"The honor was mine, sir," she said. "And thank you for your honesty."

"Come," the governess said. "We might be in trouble even for coming here."

They left, and Leoff sat back down, disheartened, hoping all the auditions didn't go this way.

It was a bell later before the next arrived, and Leoff felt a ferocious smile widen his face when he saw who it was.

"Edwyn!"

Edwyn Mylton was a tall man, gangly as a scarecrow, with a face that seemed at first glance long and sorrowful until you got to the eyes, which positively gleamed with mischief and goodwill. Edwyn grabbed him in a bear hug, slapping him on the back.

"Court composer, eh?" he said. "I always knew you would make well in the world, Leoff." He lowered his voice. "Though it's a bit shaky around here, isn't it? Was there really a coup?"

"Yes, I'm afraid so—but my performance goes on, er—in a sense. How have things been with you? I never dreamed to find you turning up at my doorstop. I thought you were still playing for the dreadful Duke of Ranness, a hundred leagues from here."

"Ah, no," Edwyn said. "We had a bit of a falling out, me and the duke. Or perhaps I should say a throwing out—of me. I've been in Loiyes, at the court of the duchess there, a delightful if taxing creature. I heard about this performance from Rothlinghaim, who received your invitation but could not come. I hoped to present myself as a suitable replacement."

"A very suitable replacement," Leoff agreed.

"Well, don't keep me waiting, man, show me the piece."

"A moment, Edwyn," Leoff said. "I need to make plain a few things first—about the performance."

He explained to Edwyn the same things he'd told Areana, but with a bit more detail about the particular objections.

"But he can't actually *do* anything, this praifec, can he?" Edwyn objected. "He has no temporal power."

"No, but then again, he has the ear of the prince, whom I don't know at all. I cannot say what will happen when he finds out that I've deceived him."

"But won't he attend rehearsals?"

"I'm sure he will. But I think with careful planning, we can rehearse the piece the way he wants it and perform it as it should be done."

Edwyn nodded. "How serious do you think it will get?"

"At the very least I will lose my position. At the very worst I shall be burned as a shinecrafter. I expect something in the middle. I honestly believe the risk is much smaller, if not negligible, for my musicians, but I can in no way promise it."

"Hmmph. Well, let me see that. I'd like to know what all the fuss is about."

When Edwyn saw the first page, his face and body went still, and he said nothing until he'd read every last word and note. He looked up at Leoff then.

"Saints damn you, Leoff," he sighed. "You knew I would risk death to perform this."

"I'd rather hoped," Leoff replied. "Now, let's only hope we can find twenty-nine more such like-minded souls."

"You will find them," Edwyn said. "I shall help you."

By the end of the day he had recruited eight more players and had sent as many away. The next day went better, because word was starting to get around, and only those with stronger resolve showed up. He didn't worry that anything would get back to the praifec at this point—he trusted everyone he had invited, and the musician's guild was tight-lipped about its members and their business, as a matter of principle.

He was nearly ready to end his day when he heard another tap at the door. He opened it and found Areana there, this time without her governess.

"Hello," Leoff said uncertainly.

She held her head high. "If you haven't filled the part of Lihta," she said, "I would very much like to sing it."

"But your governess—your parents—"

"I have some money of my own," she said. "I have taken a room in town. I know my parents, and they will come around."

Leoff nodded. "That's wonderful news," he said. "I just want to be certain you really understand the danger you might be in if you join me in this."

"I understand, *cavaor*," she said. "I am prepared to face whatever punishment should be pronounced upon me."

"I hope that will be none at all," Leoff said, "but I thank you for your courage." He gestured toward the hammarharp. "Shall we begin rehearsal?"

"It would be my pleasure," she returned.

And all Leoff's doubts vanished—but for one.

CHAPTER ELEVEN

RODERICK

A S ANNE WHEELED HER mount from the road and into the forest, a wind blew through, resurrecting the dead leaves into aerial dancers pirouetting in vorticose ballet. A faint chorus of women's voices attended them, thin and without depth, as if the song had fallen from a great height and been stripped and broken as it fell until nothing was left but a memory imprinted in the air, with that fading, too.

She thought she heard her name and then only the thumping of Tarry's hooves and her breath, which seemed almost to hover around her rather than come from inside. The tree boles went by hypnotically, one by one, rows of columns that never seemed to end.

Tarry leapt a fallen log and nearly stumbled on the slope beyond, but he recovered, and then the slope evened out. For that brief moment when she seemed to float, sunlight seemed to explode around her, melting the trees down into green grass and misty rinns far below, and she was again on Faster, hurtling down the Sleeve, terrified, giddy, and blissful with life.

For an instant she held it, but then it was gone, and she realized with a leaden heart that that, too, was only a memory of something irrevocably lost. That life, that childhood, was gone forever, and even if she made it home it wouldn't be the home she knew.

Tarry squealed and stumbled again, legs buckling, and in a fog of golden light Anne hurled forward through the dancing leaves and fertile smell of promised rain. She hit the ground and bounced, heard something snap, and pain like nearby thunder detonated in her thigh. She felt the flesh skinning from her elbows and arms as she wrapped them to protect her head, and finally fetched to a stop against a stump amidst the scents of turned earth, blood, and broken roots.

For a time she forgot where she was, and puzzled at the branches above, wondering what they could be, as something beat toward her like an approaching drummer.

She saw a face she ought to know but couldn't quite place, before it—like the wind and her childhood—faded.

Something lapped around her like the tongue of a giant dog, or waves on the strand, irregular in rhythm, soothing. Anne tried to open her eyes, but they seemed infinitely heavy, so instead she looked through the lids and saw her room—except it wasn't her room. It resembled her room, but the walls were falling in, and through a great hole near the ceiling red light streamed in that terrified her even to look at, and nearby—from the corner of her eye—she saw the door opening, and someone stepping through who shouldn't be there, whom she couldn't look at, and she knew suddenly that she hadn't awakened at all, but was still in some Black Mary of waking.

She tried harder to wake, then, to force her eyes open, to pry apart the wall of sleep and step through. But when she did, she was back in the room, and the red light was stronger, the door swung wider, and the shadow stepped in. Her skin felt a thousand stings, as if she lay in a bath of scorpions, and she woke, and it all started again . . .

She sat up and heard a voice screaming, which she took a moment to understand was her own. Her chest heaved as she clutched at strange bedclothes and prayed this was finally an end to sleep, and not another trick of the Mary. Then she felt the pain in her leg where the arrow had pierced her, and looked around in a fresh panic. She'd awakened before, not knowing where she was, not recognizing anything, and then gradually realizing she was in a familiar place made strange by the linger of dream. But as she stared about the room, it did not become familiar.

The lapping of her dream turned out to be the fire in the hearth a few yards away. Heavy tapestry drapes covered the windows, so she couldn't tell if it was day or night. A wolf pelt lay flat on the floor, and near the fire there was a loom and a stool to sit at it. Other than that, there was only a door, wooden and solid with iron bands.

She threw back the bedclothes. She wore an amber dressing gown worked with golden roses on the hem. She pulled it up until she could see her leg, and found it bandaged. She felt clean, as if she had been scrubbed, and a lilac scent seemed attached to her.

Anne lay there another moment, trying to remember what had happened. She remembered Tarry falling, and after that very little that could be separated from phantasm.

Whoever had found her, it couldn't be the Hansan knights. They had never shown any interest in taking her captive, much less in bathing her and bandaging her wounds.

Experimentally, she swung her legs over the bed and eased down to the rug upon the flagstone floor. When she put weight on the damaged leg it ached, but not so much that she couldn't bear to limp upon it, so she limped to the window and pushed the tapestry aside.

It was twilight outside. The sun was gone, but clouds of royal purple trimmed in gold and verdigris lay across the eastern sky. A light rain was falling, misting the thick glass of the window, which was cold to the touch. Plains or pasture stretched out and away to a dark green haze in the distance that might be forest, all resembling a painting that had been dipped in water while still wet.

She let the tapestry drop and hobbled to the door. As she had more than half expected, it was locked. Sighing, she turned back to examine the rest of the room—only to recoil at a sudden movement at the edge of her vision.

She fixed her eyes in that direction and saw a woman staring at her. She had almost opened her mouth to demand who she was when Anne understood that she was looking into a full-length mirror.

Her reflection was gaunt and hollow-cheeked, and the area around her eyes seemed bruised. The thin frizz of red hair was weird and shocking. Her freckles had darkened and enlarged from long days in the sun—but more than that, her face had actually changed. Grown older, not merely metaphorically, but in fact. The very shape of the bone was different—her nose seemed smaller, and for the first time ever she caught a glimpse of her mother in her.

How long since she had seen herself in a mirror? How much could a woman change between sixteen and seventeen?

And she was seventeen now, though she had missed her birthday. She had been born in Novmen, on the eighth. It had come and gone without her ever knowing or thinking about it until now.

There should have been a party, and dancing, and cakes. Instead she couldn't even remember where she had been, because she didn't know the date now, except that it was well past the month of Novmen. Indeed, the Yule solstice had to be approaching—if that, too, hadn't passed her in the night.

Unable to gaze long on what she had become, she searched the room for anything that might be useful as a weapon, but the only thing she found was a spindle. She took it in her hand and limped back to the bed, just as somewhere near the vespers bell began to toll.

Before the next bell, the creak of the door opening disturbed her. A stooped little woman in a gray dress and black shawl entered. "Highness," she murmured, bowing. "I see you are awake."

"Who are you? Anne asked. "Where am I?"

"My name is Vespresern, if it please you, Princess Anne."

"How do you know me?" Anne demanded.

"I have seen you at court, Highness. Even with your hair shorn so, I would know you. Is there anything I can get for you?"

"Tell me where I am and how I came to be here."

"My master asked that he be allowed to explain that himself, Your Highness. He asked me to fetch him when you woke. I'll find him now."

She turned and closed the door behind her, and Anne heard a key turn the lock into place.

Anne went back to the window and unlatched it. The air outside was wet and chill, but it wasn't the weather she was concerned with, but rather what sort of building she was in and how great the distance to the ground. What she found wasn't encouraging. Gray stone walls winged away in both directions. She could make out battlements above her and a few more windows below. The drop was perhaps twenty yards, and that to a moat of ugly-looking water. There weren't any ledges she could see other than the narrow casements of the windows. If she tied her bedclothes together, she thought she might decrease the jump by half, and the water might break her fall, if it was deep enough.

She closed the window and sat on the bed to think. Her leg was really bothering her, and she wondered how long such a wound would take to heal. Would it mend entirely, or would she limp for the rest of her life?

About a bell later, she heard the key scraping in the door again, and, clutching the spindle, she waited to see who it was.

A man stepped into the room, and immediately she knew him. Deep down she'd known she would.

"Well," he said. "I mistook you for a boy once before, and did so again when I saw that hair."

"Roderick."

"Well, I'm glad you remember me now," he said. "After meeting you on the road, I wasn't so sure you hadn't quite forgotten me."

"Roderick," she repeated, searching for something plausible to say.

His tone sobered a bit. "You terrified me, you know. I thought you were dead."

"I'm in your father's castle, then?" she asked.

"Yes, welcome to Dunmrogh."

"I had friends back in the forest. We were attacked."

"Yes, I know—I'm sorry, they were all slain. Brigands, I suppose. We've had our troubles with them, lately. But look, Anne—it's impossible that you could be here. How in the name of Saint Tarn is it that you are?"

She studied his face, the face she had dreamed about for so long.

While hers had seemed older, his seemed younger, and not as familiar as it ought to. It came to her that she had really known him for only a few days, not even a month. She'd been in love with him, hadn't she? It had felt like that. Yet now, looking at him, she didn't feel the overflow of joy she'd been expecting.

And it wasn't just because she knew he was lying.

"Stop it, Roderick," she said wearily. "Please. If I ever meant anything to you at all, just stop it."

He frowned. "Anne, I can't say I know what you mean."

"I mean my letter," she said. "The one I sent from the coven. Cazio did have it delivered after all." She shook her head. "I don't know why I doubted him."

"You've left me behind someplace, Princess. I thought you would be happy to see me. After all, we—I mean, I thought you loved me."

"I don't know what love is anymore," Anne said, "and there's too much else in the way of me wanting to remember."

He took a step forward, but she held up her hand. "Wait," she said.

"I've no intention to harm you, Anne," Roderick said. "Indeed, quite the opposite."

"I ask you once again, don't lie to me," Anne said. "It won't do you any good. I know you betrayed me. I've been chased over all the earth by men who tried to kill me, but when I finally started chasing them, where did they come? Here. They're here, aren't they?"

Roderick stared at her for a moment; then he shut the door and locked it. He turned and walked back toward her.

"I didn't have a choice, can you understand that? My duty to my family—that's always first. Before king, before praifec, before love."

"It was no accident that we met," she accused. "You were looking for me, that day on the Sleeve."

He hesitated. "Yes," he said at last.

"And my letter—you showed it to them."

"Yes, to my father. And then I hated myself—I still hate myself for what you went through. The whole thing began as a charade, to get you to trust me. But I got stuck in it somehow. Do you know how I've dreamed of you these months? Everything faded when I thought you were dead. I wished to die myself. And then, by a miracle, I found you here." He put his right hand to his forehead. "The dreams, Anne. The dreams of you, of holding you—I cannot sleep."

Roderick's voice shook with desperate sincerity, and she suddenly remembered the day she had met him. She and Austra had gone into the tomb of Genya Dare, below the old horz in Eslen-of-Shadows, and they had written a curse against Fastia on a lead tissue and placed it in the coffin so Genya could take it to Cer, the avenger of women. Only she hadn't really cursed Fastia, but simply asked that her sister would be nicer. And on a whim she had added, "*And fix the heart of Roderick of Dunmrogh on me. Let him not sleep without dreams of me.*"

"Oh," she murmured to herself.

Roderick dropped down on his knees and reached for her hand so quickly, she did not have time to withdraw it. He clutched it desperately.

"No one knows you're here except for Vespresern, and she won't tell because she loves me more than my own mother does. I can save you from them, Anne. I can make everything up to you."

"Yes? And how can you do that, Roderick?" she asked. "Can you return Austra, Cazio, and z'Acatto to me? They are here, too, aren't they?"

He nodded, his face a misery. "They're going to do something to them, something in the woods to do with the Old Worm Fane. I can't do anything about that, Anne. You don't understand—I would if I could—but it's too late."

"Who are *they*?"

"I'm not sure, really. They're from everywhere, although a lot of the knights are from Hansa. They serve the same lord as my father. A lord of great power, but I've never heard his name or where he lives." He reached to stroke her face. "You have to forget them, if you want to live. I can't hide you here forever."

"Then you will help me escape?" Anne said.

"What good would that do?" Roderick asked. "They would only find you again, and this time you won't have anyone to protect you. They will kill you, and I will live in Hell. I can't allow that to happen."

"What is your solution, then?" Anne asked.

"You'll marry me," he said. "If you marry me, you will be safe."

Anne blinked in utter astonishment. "What makes you think—?" She bit off her reply, which was to end with *"I would rather die by hanging than marry you."* She thought a moment, and amended the question.

"What makes you think I would be safe as your wife?"

"Because then you could never be queen in Eslen," he said. "Yes, I know that much. They do not wish you to become queen. If you were my wife, you could not, according to the law of your Comven. And my father would have to protect you as his daughter-in-law. It's perfect, don't you see?"

"And my friends?"

"They are beyond saving. They die tonight."

"Tonight?"

"Yes. And we shall marry—while my father is away, distracted by the ceremony in the woods. I've engaged a sacritor to perform the union. He will register it with the Church in the morning, and we shall have the protection of the saints and my family."

"This is very sudden," Anne said. "Very."

Roderick nodded vigorously. "I know, I know. But you must believe in your heart as I do in mine that we were meant for each other, Anne."

"If that is so," Anne asked stiffly, "how could you have betrayed me?"

"The letter came to my father," he said, without blinking. He apparently had already forgotten admitting he had given it to his father himself. "He opened it ere I saw it." He gripped her hand until she thought it would break, and tears started in his eyes. "I wouldn't have told them where you were, my love. I would *not* have."

Anne closed her eyes, her thoughts churning, and she suddenly felt his lips against hers. She felt a wave of revulsion and wanted to push him away, but she knew now that he was her only chance. The curse had driven him past reason, and his insane love for her was the only weapon she had.

So, trying to remember how she kissed when she wanted to,

when she meant it, she reached her arms around him and kissed him back. It went on for far too long.

When he finally pulled his tongue out of her mouth, he gazed gently down at her. "You see? You feel it, too."

"Yes, I love you, Roderick," she lied. "But you can never betray me again. You must swear it. I could never go through that sort of hurt again."

His face practically split in two with joy. "I swear it, by Saint Tarn, I swear it and may he strike me down if I lie."

"Then let us be married," she said, "as quickly as possible. If what you say is true, we will have only this one chance."

He nodded excitedly. "The sacritor is in Dunmrogh village. He expects us a bell before midnight. I will see to the preparations. You rest now. I'll take care of you. You will be happy, Anne—I swear that on my life."

Then he was gone again, and the door locked once more, and Anne was alone, wishing she had soap and water to wash the taste and smell of him from her.

PART **V**

HARMONY

The Year 2,223 of Everon
The Yule Season

Wihnaht, in midmost Yule, is the longest night of the year. At midnight, the gates of the heavens are thrown open and the omens of the coming year make themselves known.

—FROM *THE ALMANACK OF PRESSON MANTEO*

Sefta, the seventh mode, invokes Saint Satro, Saint Woth, and Saint Selfans. It evokes bitter memory, love lost, the dying sunset. It provokes melancholy and madness.

Uhtavo, the eighth mode, invokes Saint Bright, Saint Mery, Saint Abullo, and Saint Sern. It evokes the fond memory, the blissful first kiss, the rising sun. It provokes joy and ecstasy.

—FROM *THE CODEX HARMONIUM OF ELGIN WIDSEL*

CHAPTER ONE

THE SONG IN THE HILLS

L EOFF PAUSED TO RUB his eyes. The notations on the paper before him had begun to blur together, distinct notes melting into meandering black rivulets.

There isn't time, he thought desperately. *There isn't time to get it right.*

But he had to. If he was going to step this far off the edge of the world, it had to be perfect. And it was—almost. Yet he knew something was missing, something he not only didn't have right, but didn't have at all.

Frustrated, exhausted, he put his head down on the hammarharp and let his eyes close, just for an instant. His thoughts lost their discipline and began to float about like dust motes in a sunbeam. Then the dust motes became thistledown, and he was lying on the still-green grass of early autumn not far from the charming little town of Gleon Maelhen. He'd seen a purple moon the night before—a true wonder he'd stayed up late into the night to observe. Now he was considering a nap to make up for that, until from off in the hills he heard a melody, played on a shepherd's pipe. It transfixed him, because it was so beautiful and haunting, yet incomplete . . .

"Fralet Ackenzal—oh, I've disturbed you."

Leoff jerked like a hooked fish, scattering his papers everywhere, realizing in a panic that he'd fallen asleep. If the praifec found him like that and saw what he was doing . . .

But it wasn't the praifec. It was the lady Gramme.

He stumbled to his feet. "Milady—," he began, all in a rush.

"That's not necessary," she said. "I just came to thank you."

"Then—"

"Yes," she confirmed. "My men found Mery, just as you said. And I promise you, no harm came to your friend."

Leoff reflected that he couldn't be sure of that until he saw Gilmer again, but word had it that the regent's men were scouring the countryside for the little girl. Gramme had been quick to understand the implications, and had begged him to tell her where Mery was. He'd relented, knowing he was risking his friend's life, but believing Gilmer and Mery had less to fear from Gramme than from the regent. Once Mery was with her mother, the prince could hardly claim she'd met with foul play at the hand of the queen mother, and if the lady Gramme was discreet, he would never know it was Gilmer who'd watched after her.

"I should like to see her, when it is reasonable," Leoff said.

"It is reasonable right now," Gramme replied. "I just wanted to speak with you first, alone. I wanted to know, honestly, why you put yourself at such risk, for no gain I can see."

Leoff blinked. "I—it just seemed the right thing to do, lady."

She stared at him, then gave a weary little laugh and before he could react, bent and kissed him gently on the lips. Then she straightened. "Mery's back in the hall. I'll send her in."

He waited, stunned, wondering what had just happened.

Mery came straight to his arms when he saw her, a far cry from the days when she'd hidden in his cabinets.

"How was staying with Gilmer?" he asked her. "Did you enjoy that?"

"He was something of a grump," Mery allowed, "but he was as nice to me as he could be, I suppose. This one time, we went to the village . . ." He listened as she told him about some adventure of hers, but despite the fact that he was overjoyed to see her, the melody was stuck in his head again, and as she spoke, he began playing at it, the missing notes taunting him like an infuriating itch he couldn't scratch.

Mery smiled. "That's pretty," she said. "May I try it?"

"Of course," he said. "It's not finished . . ."

He listened helplessly as she played it—perfectly, of course, but still just as incomplete as his version.

"That's not quite right, is it?" Mery said.

He stared at her. "No, it's not," he said at last.

"What if—?" She glanced up at him, then put her tongue in her cheek, placed her hands on the keys, and pushed them down.

Leoff gasped, absolutely stunned. "Of course," he murmured. "Saint Oimo, of course."

"That was better?" Mery queried.

"You know it was," he said, mussing her hair.

She nodded.

He reached over and gently touched the keys, then did what she'd done—instead of sounding the notes singly as a melody, he played them together, as a chord.

"That's perfect," he sighed, as the harmony faded. "Now it's perfect."

CHAPTER TWO

CONFLUENCE

CAZIO COUGHED AND SPIT. Through pain-blurred vision he saw bloody spackles appear on the leaves as his head thumped against the ground, and he had an odd sensation of weightlessness, so that for a moment he wondered if he'd been beheaded, instead of struck by the back of a fist.

He briefly considered continuing to lie there, but instead he painfully flopped back to a sitting position—difficult to do with both hands and feet tightly bound.

He lifted his eyes to again regard the man who had struck him. Without his face-concealing helm, the knight looked young—only a few years older than Cazio, perhaps twenty-three or so. His eyes were something between green and brown, and his hair was the color of the dust of the Tero Mefio—not the copper red of Anne's hair, but a paler and weaker sort of ruddy.

"I apologize," Cazio said, feeling with his tongue to see if any of his teeth were broken. "I cannot imagine why I called you an honorless, cowardly gelding. How foolish I feel now that you have proved me wrong. But doing is more effective than words, as they say, and nothing proves bravery better than striking a man who is bound and unarmed—unless, perhaps, it is the murder of a woman."

The man squatted next to him, grabbed him by his hair, and

pulled his head back. "Why can't you shut up?" he asked in thickly accented Vitellian. "By all the *ansu* together, why can't you just learn to keep your mouth closed?" He looked over at z'Acatto. "Has he always been this way?"

"Yes," z'Acatto answered blandly. "Since the day he was born. But you have to admit, he does have a point. That's why you hit him, because it's so frustrating when he's right."

"I hit him," the man said, "because I told him to be quiet."

"Then put a gag in his mouth and spare us all," z'Acatto said. "You the embarrassment, and him the beatings."

"Better yet," Cazio said, pulling his face toward his enemy's, even at the expense of losing some hair, "why don't you untie me and give me my sword? How is it that even though you cannot die, you fear to fight me?"

"Are you a knight?" the man asked.

"I am not," Cazio replied. "But I am Cazio Pachiomadio da Chiovattio, ennobled by birth. What father raised you, who will not fight when he is challenged?"

"My name is Euric Wardhilmson, and my father was Wardhilm Gauthson af Flozubaurg," the man answered, "knight and lord. And no son of his need favor any ragtag ruffian like you with an honorable duel." He pushed Cazio's head back farther, and then released it. "In any event, my men and I have been forbidden from dueling."

"That's very convenient," Cazio said.

"No more convenient than noticing *hundscheit* in time to step over it," the knight replied with a nasty smile. "Anyway, it hardly looks like you defeated Sir Alharyi in a duel. It looked more as if someone dropped stones on him from above, then cut his head off while he was down."

"That would be the gentleman in the gilded armor, back near the coven Saint Cer? The one covered with the murder-blood of the holy sisters? The one who attacked me in the company of another and with the aid of the Lords of Darkness?"

"He was a holy man," Euric said. "Do not speak ill of him. And if you must know, I am not ansu-blessed as he was. Only one of us at a time is given that honor, and Hrothwulf was the chosen." He nodded toward another of his captors, a man with hair as black as coal but with skin so fair his cheeks were pink, like a baby's.

"Well, send him over. I'll fight him—again, I mean. I'll sit him down on his ass a second time."

"I'm starting to like the old man's suggestion of a gag," Euric said.

"You haven't gagged me since I've been your captive," Cazio said. "I don't imagine you will now."

Euric smiled. "True. It's much more satisfying to show you how completely your words don't bother me."

"Which is why you struck me, I suppose," Cazio said.

"No, that was just for the pleasure of it," Euric countered.

"Don't make a fool of yourself, lad," z'Acatto said. "You let him talk because you're hoping he'll get you mad enough to untie him. You want to fight him as much as he wants to fight you."

"Well," Euric allowed, "I would like to see how he thinks he could beat me with that little sewing-needle of his, yes," Euric said. "But I'm on a holy mission. I can't think of myself when my task comes first."

"There's nothing holy about chasing two young girls all over creation," z'Acatto grunted.

"That's done with," Euric said, his eyebrows lifting in surprise. "Didn't you know? We found them just after we caught you. In fact, Hrothwulf thinks *you* killed them."

"Killed them?" Cazio blurted. "What are you talking about?"

"They had their throats slit, both of them, just over the hill from where we caught you. There were already ravens pecking at their carcasses. That's how Auland got hurt."

Cazio stared at him. "What, the fellow who lost his eyes? The one that died of blood poisoning before the day was even up? You really think a raven did that to him?"

"I saw it myself," Euric said. But he looked strange, as if somehow he doubted what he was saying.

"Although—" He broke off. "No. I saw them. Their heads were nearly off."

"You're lying," Cazio said. The girls had just gone over the hill to answer nature's call. He'd only taken his eyes off them for a few minutes. Still, he pictured the girls, brigand's grins cut in their throats, and suddenly felt a wave of nausea.

"You sons of whores," he swore. "You get of distempered dogs. I'll kill every last one of you."

"No," Euric said. "You'd be dead already, if we didn't need a swordsman. But the old man will do, I think, if you're so very impatient to meet Ansu Halja. Rest assured, you will die, and it won't be pleasant, so take this time to pray to the ansu you pray to."

He put a loop of rope around Cazio's neck and jerked him to his feet. Then he threw the rope over a low-hanging branch and tied it off, so he couldn't sit down without choking himself.

He left Cazio trying to think of new curses.

That afternoon, more men rode in, most dressed like men-at-arms, but more than a few like clergy. That brought a brief hope, but it didn't take long to see that they were friendly with the knights.

Cazio had little to do other than watch them work, and try not to fall asleep.

The camp was near a rough mound of earth and stone, the kind that in Vitellio were called *persi* or *sedoi*, and often had fanes built on them. Those taking holy orders were said to walk such stations in a proscribed order to be blessed by the lords. But whatever was going on here seemed decidedly unholy. The newcomers had captives with them, as well, women and children, and they set about planting a ring of seven posts around the mound then clearing back the vegetation. Others began constructing a stone fane upon its summit.

"Have you any idea what they're about, z'Acatto?" Cazio asked, studying his enemies as they went about their antlike business.

"Not really," the old man said. "It's hard to think without wine."

"It's hard for you to stand without wine," Cazio replied.

"So it should be," the old man replied. "A man should never be denied wine, especially one who's soon to die."

He was interrupted by a commotion of some sort. There was a good bit of distant shouting, and the knights mounted and rode out from the clearing, followed quickly by the five men dressed like monks. They returned perhaps a bell later, leading more captives. These were all men, one of middle years and three younger, the youngest looking barely thirteen. All of them were wounded, though none seemed seriously so.

The older man they tied as Cazio was tied, just a perechi away from him. Then they went back about their business.

When none of the enemy was near, the new captive glanced over at Cazio.

"You'd be the Vitellians, then," he said in Cazio's native tongue. "Cazio and z'Acatto."

"You know us, sir?" Cazio asked.

"Yes, we've a couple of friends in common, friends of the fair sort."

"Anne and—"

"Hush," the man said. "Pitch your voice very low. I think those are all Mamres monks, but some may be of Decmanis. If so, they can hear a butterfly's wings."

"But they're alive, and well?"

"So far as I know. My name is Artoré, and I was helping them to find you. It looks as if I've done at least part of my job, though I would prefer that the circumstances were different."

"But they escaped? The knights didn't see them?"

Artoré shrugged. "I can't say for certain. My sons and I held them off as long as we could, but the monks are deadly shots. They wanted us alive, or we wouldn't be."

"How can the Church be part of this?" Cazio whispered. "It doesn't make sense."

"All men are corruptible," Artoré said, "and the more easily if they can tell themselves they are doing holy work. But in fact, I don't know much more about this than you do. My wife would be the one to ask." He looked glum. "I would have liked to see her one last time."

"We'll escape somehow," Cazio promised. "Just watch. I'll find some way."

But as he pulled at his intractable bonds, he still couldn't imagine how.

❈   ❈   ❈

Neil sat his horse, his hands crossed on the pommel, thinking he didn't like the looks of the forest that lay before him. He didn't know much about forests to start with—there weren't any on Skern, and besides the pretty thin ones he'd passed through on his way to Vitellia, he hadn't seen much of them on the mainland, either. But once, when he was about fifteen, he'd gone north with Sir Fail de Liery to Herilanz. The trip had started as an embassy, but they'd been set upon by Weihand raiders. It had come to a sea fight which they'd won, but not without damage, and so they had put ashore for repairs. Beyond the narrow, rocky strand there had been nothing *but* forest, a holt of fir and pine and black cheichete that seemed to Neil like one vast cave. Facing your enemies on the open heath or the great wide sea was one thing, but fighting where concealment was everywhere was quite another. They'd gone in to find a good mast, and come out with half their number, pursued by a tribe of tattooed howlers that recognized no king or crown.

This forest had that look, only worse, for while the one in Herilanz had been of straight, clean-boled trees, these twisted and wove together like a gigantic bramble-bush.

It hadn't been hard to follow the Hansan knights. The land between Paldh and Teremené was a rural one, the kind of place where people noticed strange things. A group of foreign armored knights and men-at-arms traveling hard and asking after two girls was a bit out of the ordinary. Even though he was a stranger himself, it wasn't hard to start people talking if he was polite and bought something.

Near Teremené he'd met the knights at a bend in the road, headed back toward Paldh. By the time he realized who they were, it was too late to try and hide. Instead he could only ride forward, reckoning that they wouldn't recognize him. They didn't, and the girls weren't with them.

There wasn't much he could do then but keep going. Either they had found Anne and Austra and killed them, or they had given up the chase. The last seemed unlikely, and so it was with a heavy heart that he entered Teremené. It was there, with a few well-placed questions and paying three times what he ought for a beer, he'd discovered that a few of the knights, "the really unpleasant ones," had gone off north, and some even said they had captives with them, a couple of Vitellian men.

And now, a few days later, Neil paused in front of a dark forest on a horse he'd named Prospect, wondering how deep it was.

"Well, Prospect," he sighed, "let's see what sort of nightkinders haunt this place, eh?"

He switched the horse's reins and started in, but hadn't gone more than a few yards before something ahead caught his eye, a flash of gold, and then something running into the trees. It stopped behind one of the big oaks.

Grimly, he dismounted, pulling his blade, wincing at the balance in his hand. The horse wasn't a warhorse—he wasn't sure what would happen if he tried to fight mounted, especially in these woods.

A head peeped around the tree and he caught a flash of a familiar face. Then the head jerked behind the trunk. He heard a muffled shriek, and he heard footsteps crashing off through the forest.

Austra.

Sheathing the sword, he ran after her, puzzled, certain she had recognized him.

She wasn't trying to hide anymore, but was instead running as if all the demons of the sea were coming after.

"Austra!" he called, trying not to shout it too loudly, but it only seemed to spur her to redouble her efforts. Still, he was the faster runner, and here where the trees were big there wasn't much undergrowth.

She was perhaps ten yards ahead of him when a man on a horse suddenly cut across her trail. She shrieked and dropped to her knees.

The man had on armor but no helm. He'd swung one leg over the black mare he rode, the start of a dismount, when he saw Neil.

The armored man didn't have time to cry out. Neil launched himself like a javelin, hitting him at the waist. Still on the horse but not well balanced, he pitched over the other side and landed with a thud and a clank. The impact canceled Neil's forward flight and dropped him on his side of the horse, so he rolled beneath its belly, drawing his sword. The other fellow managed to get his mail-covered arm up in time to stop his first cut, but Neil heard bone snap. He was sure now that it was one of the Hansan men-at-arms, if not one of the knights. He knew he ought to fight by the code of honor, but so far these men had proved only that they disdained the code.

He cocked back to cleave the man's naked head off, and suddenly realized he'd forgotten the horse. He dropped and rolled as hooves pawed the air and stamped where he'd just been standing. He backed away from the raging beast and that gave the knight time to regain his feet. He opened his mouth, and Neil suddenly understood that he was about to call for help.

So he did the only thing he could—he threw the sword. It tumbled and struck the man across the chest and face. His shout came out as a yelp, and blood spurted from a crushed nose. Neil charged, ducking under the man's wild head cut, and punched him in the throat, feeling cartilage crunch. The knight flopped to earth like a scarecrow cut from its pole.

Unwilling to take any chances, Neil picked up the man's sword and decapitated him. It took two chops.

He turned, panting, to find Austra still whimpering, curled up on the ground.

"Austra? Are you all right?" he asked.

"Stay back," she gasped. "You're one of them. You must be."

"What are you talking about?"

"I saw you die!" she wailed.

"Oh," he said, suddenly understanding. "No, Austra. The cut wasn't that bad, and a lady had her men fish me from the water. I almost died, yes, but I'm not a nauschalk."

"I don't know that name," she replied. "But Cazio cut one's head off, and it was still moving." She was looking up at him now, her eyes flooded with tears.

Neil glanced back at the man he had just decapitated. He didn't seem to be moving. "Well, I'm not like that," he said. "Cut my head off, and I'm dead, I promise you." He knelt and took her by the shoulders. "Austra," he said, gently, "I fought them, remember? So you could board the ship. Why would I do that if I were one of them?"

"I—suppose you're right," she said. "But the shock, too many shocks, you know. Too much of this. Too much."

He felt pity for the girl, but he didn't have time to indulge it. "Austra," he asked, gently but firmly, "where is Anne?"

"I don't know," Austra replied despondently. "She's supposed to be with Artoré and his sons, and they were supposed to be going to Eslen, but then I saw them bring Artoré into the camp, and I thought one of the monks must have heard me, though I was a hundred yards away—"

"Austra, are there more of these fellows in the woods?"

She nodded her head.

"Okay, then—quietly, let's go somewhere safer, and then you'll tell me everything, yes? Sort it out in your head while we ride."

"We have to save Cazio," she mumbled.

"Right. We'll save everybody, but first I have to know what's going on, and I don't think it's wise we talk here. Come on."

In a knightly contest, Neil could rightly claim the victor's arms, armor, and horse as the spoils of victory. And though this battle had been fought on less-than-knightly terms, he reckoned the same still applied.

The fellow's sword was a pretty nice one, made of good steel and with a better balance and edge than the one he'd purchased in Paldh. In a melancholy mood, he named the new weapon *Cuenslec*, "Dead Man's Sword," and hoped it did not prove to be a prophecy that would continue to fulfill itself.

The byrnie of chain mail fit him, if a bit loosely, as did the breastplate and gauntlets. The greaves were too long, however. The helm was tied to the horse, along with two spears, but the beast was unapproachable.

In fact, the horse was something of a problem. It would probably return to camp, alerting the dead man's companions to his fate. Of course, they would know eventually, when he failed to return, but later was better than sooner. Still, he didn't feel like killing the poor beast. Instead he took the rope he tethered Prospect with at night, made a lasso, and after a few tries captured him. Then he tied the other end of the rope to a tree.

Thus equipped, he and Austra returned to Prospect and rode back out of the forest, over a little hill and beyond sight of both the forest and the road, which felt safer than hiding in the woods. There he listened as Austra told her story and described the scene at the *seid*.

"You shouldn't have left Anne," he told her.

"I don't see how you can say that, after she betrayed you," Austra snapped. Then, looking chagrined, she went on, "Besides, she was safe, or I thought she was. Cazio and z'Acatto weren't."

"Yes, but how did you reckon to take on those knights by yourself?"

"I thought I might sneak in and cut their bonds," she replied, "but so far I haven't been able to get close enough."

"And you haven't see Anne at all."

"No," Austra said.

"Do you think they've killed her?"

"I don't know," Austra said miserably. "They've got Artoré and his sons. They must have killed one of them, because they brought an extra horse. But I counted, and there wasn't a horse for Anne."

"So you believe she got away?"

"I hope so," Austra said. "This is all my fault. She would never have come here except for me."

"There's no point in worrying over that," Neil soothed. "Concentrate on what you can do, not what you *could* have done." He was surprised to hear himself say the words, and even more surprised to realize that he actually meant them—not just for Austra, but for himself.

Yes, he had failed, several times now. He would probably fail again, but the thing a man did—the thing his father would have told him to do—was to keep trying.

"If Anne's alive," he reasoned, "she's on the other side of the forest. We can't go through on the road, or they'll ambush us the way they did your friends. But we have to go through—we have to find out if she's still alive."

"But Cazio—"

"There are at least two knights left, one of them a nauschalk.

How many priests and men-at-arms? How many would I have to fight altogether?"

"Some of them come and go," she said. "But I think maybe five monks and fifteen fighting men."

"That's too many," Neil said. "They'll kill me, and kill you, and then kill your Cazio and z'Acatto, and we won't have served the queen—or Anne—very well. Our duty is to them first, do you understand?"

Austra bowed her head. "Yes," she agreed.

"And you won't try and run off again?"

"No."

"Good. Then let's get going, while we still have the light."

Austra just nodded again, but continued to stare at the ground. Neil lifted her chin with his finger. "I swear by the saints my people swear by, once we know one way or the other about Anne, I'll do what I can for your friends."

"Thank you," she said.

"Right. Let's go then."

He took them into the forest off the road and swung wide around it, keeping his bearings by the sun. To his relief, it was less than a bell before he saw light through the trees. The forest, it seemed, was great in length but narrow in breadth. By that time the sun was setting, but in the dim light he made out a castle—and farther away, a village.

"Do you know that place?" he asked.

She shook her head.

"Well," he said. "Let's ask in the village."

Neil took them warily along the road, though it was all but deserted. They only had two encounters; the first was where the road split into branches headed toward the village and castle respectively. The only light was a crescent moon, but they heard the rumble of a carriage coming from the castle. Neil could only make out a shadow, but reckoned it was still a few hundred yards away. He twitched Prospect onto the town road, and the noise of the carriage soon faded behind them.

The second encounter came on the outskirts of the village, when he made out four horsemen coming toward them. He tensed in the saddle, putting his hand on Cuenslec's pommel. In outline they didn't seem to be armored.

"Who's there?" a man's voice barked from the darkness—in the king's tongue.

Neil gripped his weapon tighter, for though the voice sounded familiar, he couldn't place it.

"Put that away, Aspar," another voice said. "Can't you see who it is?"

"Not in this light. I don't have sainted vision, like you do."

"Well met, Sir Neil," the lighter voice said. "I suspect we have a lot to discuss."

CHAPTER THREE

CEREMONY

ANNE FOUND HERSELF STARING again at the girl in the mirror, recognizing her even less than she had the last time she looked, only a few hours earlier. This time she wore a bride's wimple of pale gold safnite brocade that concealed even the few wisps of hair that remained to her. The gown was bone, with long fitted sleeves and edgings in the same color as the wimple. The face surrounded by all this seemed lost and strange.

Vespresern seemed rather pleased by the effect. "It fit you nearly without alteration," she said. "A good thing, too, as we had little enough time to spare. My lord is in a terrible hurry." She patted Anne's arms. "He does so love you, you know. I've never seen him go against his father in even the slightest matter, before this. I do hope he's right about everything."

Vespresern waited, plainly looking for a response.

"He is always in my heart and my thoughts," Anne said at last. "It's my greatest desire to bring him all the happiness he deserves."

She meant that much, anyway.

"It's rare that anyone in your position is able to marry for love, my dear," Vespresern blithered. "You cannot know how lucky you are."

Anne remembered Fastia telling her the same thing, on more

than one occasion—Fastia, who had married so unhappily. Fastia who had once played with her and made her garlands of flowers, whom she had left in argument, whom she could never apologize to.

Fastia, now meat for the worms.

Anne heard footsteps in the corridor.

"Here he comes," Vespresern said. "Are you quite ready, my dear?"

"Yes," Anne responded. "Quite ready."

"Here," the old lady said. "We'll bundle you up in this old weather-cloak. There shouldn't be anyone to recognize you, but safe is what we'll be."

Anne stood still as Vespresern draped the woolen garment over the gown. A knock sounded at the door.

"Who will that be?" Vespresern asked—disingenuously, in light of her former statement.

"It's Roderick," the answer came. "Is she ready? This is the time."

"She's ready," Vespresern said.

The door creaked open, and Roderick stood there, looking regal in a deep, rust-red doublet and white hose.

"By the saints," he said, staring at her. "I've a mind to see you in the gown this moment."

"That's ill luck," Anne said. "You'll see it soon enough."

"Yes," he said. "I cannot believe I was without you for so long, Anne. Now even a bell seems far too long to go without gazing on your face."

"I missed you, too," Anne said. "I spent long nights at the coven, wondering where you were, what you were doing, praying you still loved me."

"I can do nothing else," he said. "The saints have inscribed you in my heart, and there is no place for anyone else there."

You don't know how truly you speak, Anne thought. *Indeed, you do not.*

"Come, let us go," Roderick said. "Vespresern, you go ahead to spy the way. We'll go down the servants' stair and through the kitchen, then out the Hind Gate, where the stables are. I know the guard on duty there, and he will not betray us." He took Anne's hand. "You have nothing to fear now," he said. "Your troubles are over."

"Yes," Anne said. "I see that."

Roderick knew his castle and people well—they met nearly no one but an old man in the kitchen, baking bread, and the guard Roderick mentioned. The baker didn't even seem to notice them. The guard clapped Roderick on the back and said something in Hornish that sounded encouraging and perhaps a bit risqué. It seemed strange to her—the guard was Roderick's friend, as she and Austra were friends. How could someone so ripe with betrayal, so filled with it, be loved by anyone?

Perhaps they could not, in truth, in the heart. Perhaps that was the real reason Austra had left her—because in her soul she no longer loved her—perhaps even hated her. Not for any particular thing she had done, but because there was nothing left in Anne to love.

But let that pass. It no longer mattered. All that mattered now was finishing this, however it would finish.

Then they were alone in the carriage. Vespresern rode with the driver, wrapped in a heavy cloak. Outside the last of day's light was fading and shadows crept along the ground. The moon was a narrow horn thrust into the horizon. In another night it would be new.

"Kiss me, Roderick," Anne said after the carriage had rattled along a bit. "Kiss me."

He reached for her, and then hesitated. "Shouldn't we wait for the ceremony?"

"We've kissed before," she pointed out. "I can't wait, it's been so long—don't make me wait."

There was no lantern, and she could not make out his face, but she felt his fingers trace the line of her jaw, and then rest gently at the back of her head as she felt his lips on hers, warm and soft. She remembered that night in Eslen-of-Shadows, how his hands had burned on her like metal just come from the forge, how her breath had quickened and her heart had raced, and how she had loved him—and just for the tiniest instant she really remembered and really loved him again, the way only a girl can love for the first time.

Their lips parted, but she pulled him back, both her hands clasped behind his head, and kissed him with all the darkness in her heart, pushing it into him, filling him through his mouth until it rushed out. He moaned, but could not pull away from her as—in her mind's eye—she erased his face. Then, still gently, she pushed him away. He began to shudder and sob.

"I . . . Anne . . . ah, Saints!" his voice rose to a hideous shriek, and the carriage jarred to a halt.

"You are nothing, Roderick of Dunmrogh," she said. She opened the carriage door and walked out into the night, ignoring the protestations of the driver and Vespresern. She limped back along the road, toward the forest, or where she thought it was. She hoped her leg wouldn't start to bleed again.

As the moon rose higher, Anne felt more and more certain of her way, and though the crescent's light was vanishingly pallid, she found that with each step it seemed to brighten and bleed through the shadows. A bell sounded in the distance, and then another, and the music of it seemed to float by like a breeze. She was somehow both calm and angry. She wondered abstractly what precisely she had done to Roderick, but didn't feel too concerned about it. Something bad, and permanent—that was certain, she could feel it in her bones.

She stepped beneath the groping trees as the eleventh bell sounded, and there she stopped. She knelt on the damp earth and closed her eyes and pushed away the world.

When she opened them, she was in a different forest, but it was still night, the moon still a sickle above. In front of her stood a woman she had never seen. She wore an ivory mask and a black gown that glinted with jewels.

"The fourth Faith," she said.

The woman bowed her head slightly. "You have called me, and here I am." She lifted her head back up. "You should not do this, Anne. You are free—return to Eslen."

"No," she said firmly. "I'm tired of running. I won't run any-more."

The woman smiled faintly. "You feel your power waking, but you are not yet complete. You are not ready for this trial, I promise you."

"Then I will die, and that will be the end of it," Anne said.

"It will be the end not just of you, but of the world as we know it."

"I do not much care for the world as we know it," Anne confided a little haughtily.

The woman sighed. "Why did you come here?"

"To tell you. If you are so certain that I must live, then you will help me, I think."

"We are *already* helping you, Anne. My sisters and I have strained ourselves, woven as much into the web of fate as we dare. We foresaw this moment, and there are two paths. One is the path home, to Eslen. At this moment your mother is locked in a tower, and the man who murdered your father sits the throne. A moment ap-proaches there, also, and if you aren't there to greet it, the result will be terrible beyond imagining."

"And the other path? The one in which I face my pursuers and free my friends? The one I'm going to take?"

"We cannot see past that," she whispered. "And that is gravely worrisome."

"But you said you foresaw this moment."

"Yes, but not your decision. We feared you would take the unsee-able, and have provided all the help we can. I do not think it will be enough."

"It will be enough," Anne said, "or you will find another queen."

The monks had been piling wood in a huge cone all day, but soon af-ter it grew dark, they lit it. Cazio watched the flames lick hungrily up toward the oak branches above.

"Do you suppose they're going to burn us?" he asked z'Acatto.

"If they meant to do that, they should have tied us up to the logs. No, boy, I think they've something more interesting in mind."

Cazio nodded. "Yes. Something to do with those." He meant the seven posts the monks had erected earlier, but he also meant the newer, somewhat more worrisome detail they had added only a few moments before—three hanging nooses suspended from a low tree branch.

"You always said I would end in a noose," he told the old man.

"Yes," z'Acatto agreed. "I never imagined I would be joining you, however. Speaking of which, how is your plan coming along? The one you promised Artoré?"

"I've got the broad strokes of it laid out," Cazio said. "I'm mostly lacking in details."

"Uh-huh. How are you going to slip your bonds?"

"That, unfortunately, is one of the details."

"You work that out while I get some sleep." z'Acatto grunted.

They were silent for a while as Cazio watched the play of light from the fire. It seemed as if giants made of shadow were leaping from the trees into the clearing and then retreating again—doing foot-work, as a dessrator might. He glanced longingly at Caspator, where the sword lay with the rest of his effects.

His bonds were loosening again, but if experience was any guide, someone would be along presently to tighten them.

Cazio himself was tiring, and was almost dozing when it finally started. The monks were leading captives to the perimeter of poles around the mound and securing them there. It took the first of their screams for the drowsy Cazio to understand that they weren't tying them there.

"Oh, buggering lords, no," Cazio said, redoubling his efforts at the ropes. He watched helplessly as a girl who could be no more than five had her arms stretched above her and nailed there.

"No!" he screamed. "By all that's holy, what do you think you're doing?"

"They're waking the sedos," Artoré whispered. "Waking the Worm." He looked frightened, which he hadn't before.

"How can . . ." Cazio stumbled off, overcome by the horror of it.

"How can men do things like this?" he finally managed.

"I don't think we've seen the worst," Artoré predicted. "And I think I'd best bid you farewell now."

Cazio saw someone coming in their direction. He lunged at the robe-clad monk, but the rope went taut around his neck and jerked him back.

"Stop it!" he screamed as the man cut Artoré's leash. Artoré was faster than he looked. He head-butted the monk in the face. The man jerked back, and then moved with blinding speed, striking Artoré in the pit of his stomach. The man gagged and fell to his knees, and the monk took him in an armlock and conveyed him to the post.

"Z'Acatto?" Cazio said feeling his breath coming suddenly short.

"Yes?"

"Thank you."

"What for?"

"For desserata. For everything."

The old man didn't say anything for a moment. "You're welcome, boy," he finally answered. "I could have spent my life worse. I'm glad to be here with you."

A monk was coming for z'Acatto. Euric was coming for Cazio.

"Don't get too sentimental," Cazio said. "I'm still going to get us out of this, and then you'll feel silly."

The men were almost on them. Cazio tried to relax, so he could move quickly. He would have just an instant when the rope was slack, and he would have to use that instant well.

Euric smiled and punched him in the jaw. Cazio felt his teeth snap together, and suddenly he was choking. Just as quickly, the pressure released, and he stumbled forward, dragged by the knight who had him from behind in a wrestling hold.

"Can't kill *you* yet," Euric said. "You're one of the guests of honor. I thought I would have to play your part, and I was ready, too, but then we found you."

"What are you babbling about, you filthy sod?" Cazio snarled.

"Swordsman, Priest, and Crown," the knight said, unhelpfully. "And one who cannot die. We've got a priest, and a royal, though she doesn't know it yet, I'm afraid—and now we've got our swordsman. As for the undying—well, you've already met Hrothwulf."

"Is any of that supposed to make sense?" Cazio asked, as Euric hustled him up the mound and stood him up on a block beneath the gallows tree, then set the noose around his neck. Another man brought Caspator and stuck the blade point-first into the ground in front of him. Cazio gazed greedily at the weapon, so close and so unreachable.

Now he had a good view of all the victims nailed to the posts. He could see their faces in the firelight. Z'Acatto already hung with them, blood drizzling from his crossed palms, not more than six perechi away.

Artoré was there, too—and he'd been right. It *was* getting worse. Going widdershins—one by one—the monks were carefully cutting their victims open and pulling out their intestines. They stretched these to the next post and nailed them into the arms of the next victim, then cut his belly, too. As this happened, a sacritor on the mound began chanting in a language Cazio had never heard before.

Meanwhile, a new party entered the clearing, a richly dressed man and woman. The man was tall and austere, with graying mustache and beard. The woman looked younger, but it was hard to make out her features from this distance, partly because she was bound and gagged.

"There's our royal," a voice said, just near Cazio's ear. He turned and saw one of the monks step onto the block beside him and calmly place the noose on his own neck.

"I honestly never knew," Cazio distantly heard himself say. "Never. I have seen cruelty, and malice, murder, and casual mayhem. But I never in my worst dreams ever imagined such sick depravity as this."

"You don't understand," the monk said softly. "The world is dying, swordsman. The sky is cracking and soon will tumble down. And we're going to save it. You should be honored."

"If I had my sword," Cazio said, "I would show you what I honor and how."

The woman was placed on the third block. Her eyes were wild with terror.

He turned his attention back to the circle. It was half-complete, and z'Acatto's turn was coming. There was nothing Cazio could do but watch.

CHAPTER FOUR

KHRWBH KHRWKH

CAZIO CLOSED HIS EYES as the knife-wielding monk
stepped up to z'Acatto, but then forced them open again. If the
only thing he could do for z'Acatto was to watch him die, then he
would do that. So he set his teeth and promised himself he wouldn't
give them the satisfaction of any more outbursts.

Z'Acatto suddenly did something really odd. He jerked his feet
into the air, levering both legs out straight and kicking them as high
as his head—an impressive show of agility and strength for a man his
age. Then he swung them rapidly back down, slapping them into the
post. His face was strangely serene, despite the pain he must have
been feeling. The nails ripped through his hands as he arched forward from the force of the reversal, tumbling him to the ground. He
bounded up immediately, driving his bloody right hand into the
monk's throat. The fellow dropped the knife, and z'Acatto immediately scooped it up, then sprinted toward Cazio.

Almost everyone else was watching the invoker, so that his mestro had closed more than half the distance before a shout of alarm
went up. The monk next to Cazio wasn't bound, since he was a volunteer, and he quickly reached to extricate himself from the rope
around his neck. But with a muffled cry Cazio tucked his chin against
the noose, pulled his legs up, and kicked him with both feet. His own

noose went instantly tight, though, and suddenly he couldn't breathe as both his block and the one the monk perched on toppled away.

Black butterflies began to flutter in his vision, as the rope turned him forward again and he saw z'Acatto getting up from the ground. The long black shaft of an arrow stood quivering from the older man's back and he was cursing steadily and inventively. He scrambled up the mound as another hail of arrows fell around him. He was hit again, this time in the calf, but he did not fall.

Another turn, and Cazio saw the monk, hanging like he was, but with both hands on the rope above him, trying to pull himself upward with one, and loosen the knot with the other. Z'Acatto denied him success, cutting the churchman's throat in one long slash, then with the next whip of his hand severed the rope that was just short of killing Cazio.

Cazio thudded to the ground, gasping for air. He couldn't see z'Acatto anymore, but he felt his bonds part, and with a hoarse shout he bounced to his feet and yanked Caspator from the ground. He turned to find z'Acatto with a third arrow in his ribs, his breath coming in rapid gasps, his eyes going glassy.

"Stay down, old man," Cazio told him. "I'll take care of this."

"Yes," z'Acatto wheezed. "Excellent idea."

Euric and two men-at-arms were first on Cazio's menu. They were a few perchi away, charging, meat-cleavers drawn. Cazio was a little surprised he hadn't been made a riddle by arrows, as z'Acatto had, but a quick glance around the clearing showed the archers lowering their weapons, and he smiled sardonically as he realized they wanted him alive so they could hang him.

He set his stance, slipping the noose off his neck with his off-weapon hand.

Besides their broadswords, they all wore armor, though none of them had helms. Cazio put his blade out in a line aimed at Euric's face. The knight beat at his blade to remove it, but with a twist of his fingers Cazio dipped his point beneath the searching blade, quickly changed his line, and sidestepped. Euric's momentum took him past Cazio, as Caspator's tip caught one of the men-at-arms in the throat. Using the weapon as a lever, Cazio jumped forward and to the left, turning the man to place the corpse-to-be briefly between Euric and the other warrior. This gave him shelter to withdraw the blade and set his stance again. The unfortunate fellow fell, blood bubbling from the hole in his trachea.

"*Ca dola dazo lamo,*" Cazio forcefully informed his foes.

The second man-at-arms thrust past Euric, lifting his hand for a cut, perhaps forgetting they were supposed to keep Cazio alive long enough to hang. Cazio countered into the attack, a fast, straight lunge that hit the man on the underside of his wrist.

"*Z'estatito,*" he explained as the man grunted and dropped his weapon. Euric's blade was streaking down from his right, a blow apparently meant for his leg, so Cazio caught it in an outside parry, then thrust into the eye of the man-at-arms, who was still standing there, staring uncomprehendingly at his bloody wrist.

"*Zo pertumo sesso, com postro en truto.*"

He ducked Euric's vicious backswing, because his blade was still stuck in a skull. As he yanked it out, Euric charged inside the point, grabbing his neck and bringing the broadsword's pommel down in a vicious blow aimed at his nose. Cazio managed to turn his head so the hilt grazed along the side of it instead of striking it square, but that was still enough set the world singing. He returned the favor by striking Caspator's grip into Euric's ear, and both men fell.

Cazio scrambled up, and so did Euric. From the corner of his eye, Cazio saw three of the monks running toward him with ridiculous speed, and knew he had only a heartbeat left to act.

"You won't escape," Euric promised him.

"I'm not trying to," Cazio said.

And so—as he had practiced with z'Acatto only a few days before—he flung himself forward like a spear, his body nearly parallel to the ground. Euric's eyes went wide, and he threw his own blade up in defense, far too late. Caspator's point hit Euric's teeth with the full weight and momentum of Cazio's body behind it. They shattered, and the steel continued over the tongue and through the brain. Euric blinked, clearly puzzled by his death.

"*Z'ostato,*" Cazio grunted.

Cazio had barely hit the ground before someone struck him from behind and caught him in a wrestling hold. It felt like an iron yoke around his neck. Then he was yanked roughly to his feet, and he found himself surrounded. One of the crowd was the fellow in the noble clothing.

"That was extraordinary," he said. "At least we can be certain that you are a true swordsman, now. But now we need a new priest and regal. My wife seems to have had an accident."

Cazio looked up at the mound and saw that the woman had somehow fallen off her perch and been hanged. He hoped he hadn't done it in the struggle.

"We have to hang you all together, you see," he said.

Cazio spat in his face. "You sacrificed your wife, you rabid dog?"

The man wiped his face without any other obvious reaction. "Oh, I would sacrifice much more than that to bring this faneway alive," he said. Then he laughed, a bit bitterly. "I suppose I will have to, actually—I don't have time to find my son, and I'm the only one here with royal blood, I think."

"No," a familiar voice called. "There is one more here with noble blood."

They all turned, and Cazio saw Anne standing at the edge of the woods. Her voice rose in a commanding tone Cazio had never heard her use.

"I am Anne Dare," she said, "daughter of the Emperor of Crotheny, Duchess of Rovy. I command you all to lay down your arms and release these people, or I swear by Saint Cer the Avenger, you will all die."

For a few heartbeats, the clearing was silent except for the crackle of flames and the moans of the dying. Then the nobleman next to Cazio uttered a single barking laugh.

"You!" he said. "I've been looking all over for you, you know. All over. Slaughtered an entire coven to find you. My men told me you were dead—and now you walk right into my arms. Outstanding. Come here, girl, and give us a kiss."

"You will not mock me," Anne said steadily. "You will not."

"I think I will," the man replied.

Anne stepped steadily nearer to the man. "You are Roderick's father," she said. A part of her was trembling with fear, but that part of her seemed to be sinking away, melting like snow in spring. "Of course. Roderick's father and his Hansan knights. And why did you chase me over the great wide world, Duke of Dunmrogh? What fear was in you that made you do that?"

"No fear," the Duke said. "I was doing what my lord commanded."

"Which lord is that? Which lord commanded my death?"

"How foolish of you to think I would ever name him," Dunmrogh said.

"Foolish is the man who does not ask what his lord fears of a single girl," Anne spat. She felt, suddenly, the sickness around her, a pulsing fever in the very earth itself, and something turning slowly in the dirt, opening one eye. It was like that day with Austra, in the city of the dead, when they had escaped the knights, but stronger. She took a breath and felt herself expand with it. "He only fears a queen in Eslen," Dunmrogh said, suddenly sounding the slightest bit uncertain.

"No," Anne whispered. "Like all men, he fears the dark of the moon." She took another breath and felt it turn as black and thick as oil in her lungs.

"Hang her," Dunmrogh said.

She let the breath out—and *out*, feeling the Worm pull up through her feet and flow through her. Dunmrogh screamed like an hysterical infant, but she did not stop with him.

She sent it on—through the monks, through the men in armor, shuddering, hearing herself laugh as if she were mad.

Dunmrogh bent double and vomited blood. Some of the monks started toward her, but it was as if they were moving against a wind too hard to overcome. She spared Cazio and the fading z'Acatto, but every other man was her slave, bowing to her power.

Except one. One man was still coming for her; the knight, the one who had cut Sir Neil. Her will sleeted through him as if he wasn't there, and the Worm would not know him. He quickened his pace, drawing his sword. She was dimly aware of Cazio trying to stand, raising his own weapon.

Then something in her twisted and diminished, and she felt as if she were falling. The last thing she saw was the knight, charging to take her head.

Cazio saw Anne fall, even as the knight came into striking range. He wasn't sure what had happened, wasn't sure he wanted to know. The only thing he knew was that he was free, and Caspator was in his hand, and there was an enemy in front of him.

Unfortunately, this one had his helm on, and his sword was the weird, flickering, glowing one he'd seen shear through plate armor in z'Espino.

Cazio thrust into the knight's downward cut, parrying and attacking with the same movement, but his blade scratched only the steel of a breastplate. The knight reversed, slicing back up from the downswing, trying to split Cazio from crotch to shoulder, but Cazio was already moving aside and punching his hilt into the knight's visor, trying to knock it off.

His adversary whirled and his weapon soughed a third time, and though Cazio managed to get Caspator up to meet it, the force was square on, right on the strong part of his blade, and his knees buckled from the strength of it. The knight's mailed foot came up and kicked him under the chin, and the bright smell of blood exploded in his nostrils as he flopped onto his back.

The knight turned away, ignoring him, moving back toward the prostrate figure of Anne. Cazio struggled to his feet, knowing he would never make it in time.

Then two arrows spanged into the armored man, and he staggered. Cazio looked in the direction the shots had come from and saw a man on a horse charging toward them. The arrows hadn't come from him—he carried a sword in one hand and a wooden shield in the other. They came from another pair—a slight, hooded figure and a rangy-looking man in a leather cuirass.

Cazio tried to use Caspator to push himself up and noticed, with a shock, that the strong part of his blade had been notched halfway through by the weird knight's weapon. Caspator was made from Belbaina steel, the strongest in the world.

The nauschalk was stooping toward Anne's motionless body when Aspar's and Leshya's arrows found him. The pause gave Neil just the time he needed to reach him. He cut hard with Cuenslec, and felt the solid, satisfying shock run up his arm. He didn't understand why the rest of the men in the clearing weren't fighting, or even on their feet, but he wasn't going to question it. Some of them were starting to get up, anyway, and when they did, he and his newfound companions would be very much outnumbered.

His horse reared and shied, so Neil quickly dismounted, facing the knight as he rose back up, wielding the arcane blade.

"They say Virgenya Dare's warriors had weapons like that," Neil said. "Feyswords. Weapons for heroes, weapons to fight evil. I don't know where you got that, but I *do* know you aren't fit to carry it."

The nauschalk pushed up his visor. His face was pale and pink-cheeked, and his eyes were as gray as sea waves.

"You," he murmured, almost as if in a dream. "I've killed you once, haven't I?"

"Only almost," Neil replied. He lifted his shield. "But by Saint Fren and Saint Fendve, this time *I* will die or *you* will."

"I cannot die," the man said. "Do you understand? I can't."

"Forgive me if I'll not take your word for that," Neil replied. All along he'd been shuffling forward, finding his distance. Now he slowly began to circle, his gaze fixed on the eyes of the nauschalk, a red fire kindling in his belly as the rage began.

Then the nauschalk blinked, and in that instant Neil attacked, leaping forward and cutting over the shield. His enemy replied with a swift thrust from a stiffened arm to Neil's shield, a good fighter's instinct, for it should have stopped Neil's attack by keeping him at sword's length.

But the feysword sliced through the shield just above Neil's arm. He still had to arrest his blow to keep from impaling his face on the glowing weapon, but he twisted the shield down, taking the stuck feysword with it, and chopped a second time. Cuenslec rang against the armored joint of neck and shoulder, and Neil felt the chain links part. The visor clanged down with the force of his blow, and once again Neil's enemy had no face.

He dropped the shield before his opponent could carve the deadly blade through his arm and drew back for another blow, but the feysword whirled up too quickly. Neil let the assault come but faded back from it, so the attack missed him by the breadth of a hair. Then he made his own counterattack.

He had reckoned on the knight having to recover the momentum of his attack before making the backswing, but he'd reckoned wrong. The weapon must have weighed almost nothing, because here it came, shearing up into his attack. Only by scrambling quickly back did he avoid being gut-sawed.

Neil's breath was coming raggedly already, for he was still weak from his last fight with the fellow.

The nauschalk, seemingly not tired at all, advanced.

"What's happening here, Stephen?" Aspar asked as he got Ogre still and took aim at a monk. The churchman had been down on the ground when they arrived, and was now rising shakily to his feet. Aspar let fly. The fellow never saw his death coming; an almost motionless target, the arrow took him in the heart and he sank back to his knees.

Around the clearing, more and more of the formerly motionless figures were rising again. Aspar aimed at the most active.

"I don't know," Stephen replied. "I felt something as we were approaching, something strong, but it's gone now."

"Maybe they never got the instructions from the praifec," Leshya guessed. "Maybe they did something wrong."

"Maybe," Aspar allowed. "But whatever happened, it seems to be to our advantage. Stephen, you and Winna go get the princess. Hurry."

Neil's battle with the armored knight didn't seem to be going that well. The knight's sword flickered like the knife Desmond Spend-love had planned to use to assassinate Winna, the one—he now recalled—the praifec had confiscated for "study."

He shot a man and selected another target, but this one saw him in time and dodged the shaft. Then he was running toward them, faster than an antelope. To his left, on the other side of the clearing, Aspar saw another.

"Leshya, take the left one," he grunted.

"Yes," she said.

Aspar took careful aim and fired again, but the monk spun aside without stopping, and the dart just grazed him along the arm. He was closing the distance so swiftly, Aspar figured he had only one more shot coming.

He released it at five yards, and still the man nearly dodged it. It hit him in the belly and he grunted as he took a wild, unbalanced swing at Aspar with his sword. Aspar wheeled Ogre and avoided the blow, then spurred the beast to give him distance to shoot again, but the monk kept coming, much too quickly, leaping through the air. Aspar managed to deflect the sword with his bow. But the force of his antagonist's leap knocked him out of the saddle.

Aspar managed to untangle himself from the monk and kick clear to draw his dirk, but even as he regained his feet he found the sword slashing toward him, a bit slower than Aspar was used to from the warrior-priests, whether due to the belly wound or whatever had gone on just before their arrival, he could not say. He managed to duck the blow and step in, grabbing the swordsman's wrist and slashing viciously at his inner thigh with the dirk. A spray of blood hit him in the face, and he knew he'd got the knife where he wanted it.

The monk didn't know he was dead yet, though. He grabbed Aspar by the hair and kneed him in the face, and as the holter fell back in sudden agony, closed his hands around his throat and began to squeeze. Aspar stabbed the dirk into his ribs and twisted it, but he felt something cracking in his throat, and black stars blotted out the mad green eyes glowering down at him.

Then the strength went out of the man's fingers and blood poured from his mouth, and Aspar was able to push him off.

Just in time to see another of the fratirs, only a yard away, sword raised for the kill.

The nauschalk came at Neil, and it was all he could do to evade the blows. Fighting in plate armor was less a contest of sword-skill than it was about who had the best armor. Fully armored knights didn't really parry; they just took blows and gave them. But in this case, Neil knew from experience that even the superior armor he'd worn in z'Espino was no match for the glistering feysword. And though Neil had spent most of his fighting life in mail or leather hauberk—and thus knew full well how to parry—he didn't really dare do that, either, not when each blow against his weapon of mere steel left it diminished.

He had to keep the battle rage at bay and think, watch for one more good chance before he was exhausted.

The knight cried out and drove forward, just as Neil realized he'd been backed up to the mound. He stumbled, and almost lazily saw the radiant weapon descending toward him—then suddenly he knew exactly what to do.

He lifted his own blade in high, direct parry, taking the entire brunt of the blow on the edge, rather than on the flat, where a parry ought to be made. The force of the cut slammed his weapon down onto his shoulder, and then the feysword sheared through Cuenslec and into his byrnie.

Ignoring the shattering pain, he released his sword and caught the nauschalk's weapon hand with both of his, spun so that he had the arm turned over his shoulder, and snapped it down. The articulated harness kept the arm from breaking, but the sword fell glimmering to earth.

The knight punched Neil in the kidney, and he felt the blow through the chain, but he gritted his teeth, kicked back into the nauschalk's knee for leverage, and threw him heavily to earth. Then, before taking another breath, he grasped the hilt of the feysword, lifted it, and plunged it into the cut he'd already made at his foe's shoulder. The nauschalk shrieked, a wholly inhuman sound.

Gasping, Neil raised the blade once more and in one fierce stroke cut off the head.

❖ ❖ ❖

An arrow swifted by Stephen's face as he reached the unconscious princess, but he ignored it, grimly trusting that Aspar and Leshya could keep any attackers off them until they'd gotten her to safety. Not for the first time, he wished he had more proficiency in arms than his saint-touched memory sometimes freakishly gave him.

"Cazio!" someone shouted, and Stephen saw that the girl, Austra, was right behind Winna.

The man trying to stand near the princess glanced up at them. "*Austra, Ne! Cuvertudo!*" he shouted.

It was a modern dialect, not the Church language, but Stephen understood it well enough.

But the warning came too late. What remained of the monks and other fighting men had recovered from whatever torpor had afflicted them. They were rallying behind a man who wore the blue robe of a sacritor. Stephen counted eight bowmen, all monks of Mamres, and ten armed and armored men advancing on them.

Aspar raised his arm up in pointless defense, then flinched as an arrow hit the monk in the forehead with such force that it kicked his chin up toward the sky. Looking back, he saw that Leshya had made the shot from less then two yards away.

"Stop, or I'll shoot," she said flatly as the monk toppled like a felled poplar.

"Sceat," Aspar managed weakly. He scrambled to his feet, reacquainting himself with his bow, only to find the string snapped.

He saw the men advancing on Stephen and the rest.

"We can still escape," Leshya said. "Someone must know of what happened here."

"It will take only one of us to tell it," Aspar said. "And I maunt that's you." He swung himself up on Ogre. "Come on, lad," he muttered.

Neil used what seemed the last of his strength to sprint to join the little group clustered around Anne. He placed himself with Cazio, squarely between her and their attackers. Cazio shot him a feeble grin and said something that sounded fatalistic.

"Right you are," Neil replied, as the bows of the monks trained on them.

"Wait!" the sacritor called. "We need the princess and one of the swordsmen alive. Leave them, and the rest of you may go."

Neil heard horse's hooves behind him, and turned to see Aspar. The warriors were moving steadily closer.

Neil didn't feel the need to dignify the ridiculous suggestion with a response. Apparently, no one else did either. He cut his eyes toward the archers, calculating whether he could get to even one of them before they killed him. Probably not, from what he had seen of their skill.

"Yah," Aspar said, as if hearing his thoughts. "They're good shots. But they aren't getting any worse. We might as well go get them."

"Wait," Stephen said. "I hear horses, a lot of them, coming this way."

"That's not likely to be good news for us," Aspar pointed out.

Stephen shook his head. "No, I think it might be."

Aspar thought he heard horses, too, but he'd just noticed something else—a shadow moving at the tree line. When an arrow suddenly struck one of the archers in the back of the neck, he knew it was Leshya. The remaining monks turned as one and fired into the woods.

Aspar kicked Ogre into motion, determined to make what use he could of the distraction. He was halfway to them before they started firing. He saw black blurs, and a shaft thumped hard into his cuirass, driving though his shoulder and out the back, leaving him dimly curious as to how many pounds these fellows could pull. It didn't hurt yet, though.

Another hit him along the cheek, cutting deep and taking part of his ear with it, and that hurt quite a lot. Then Ogre screamed and reared up, and Aspar floated for an instant before slamming into the ground.

Stubbornly, he pushed himself up, yanking out his throwing ax, determined to kill at least one of them before becoming porcupined.

But they weren't paying attention to him anymore. Some twenty horsemen thundered out of the woods, armed and armored except for the fellow leading them, a young man in a fine-looking red doublet and white hose. He had his sword drawn.

"Anne!" the lad screamed. "Anne!"

He only got to shout it twice, for an arrow hit him high in the chest, and he did a backflip off the horse. The archers scattered with saint-touched speed, continuing to shoot at the horsemen. Aspar choose the nearest, threw his ax, and had the vast satisfaction of seeing it buried in the man's skull before his knees gave way.

When Aspar went for the archers, Neil and Cazio charged the swordsmen. Neil reckoned if he was in close enough combat, the archers would have a harder time making a shot. He wasn't sure what Cazio reckoned, but it didn't matter. Within a few breaths they were fighting shoulder to shoulder. The feysword was light and nimble in his hand, and he killed four men before the press bore him down. Then someone struck his head, hard, and for a time he didn't know anything.

A man's voice woke him. Neil opened his eyes and saw a troop of mounted men. The leader had his visor pushed up and was staring down at him.

He said something Neil didn't understand and gazed around the clearing, face aghast.

"I don't understand you, sir," Neil said, in the king's tongue.

Behind him, Anne moaned.

"What in the name of Saint Rooster's balls is happening here?" the horseman demanded.

Neil pointed to the man's tabard. "You're a vassal of Dunmrogh, sir—you should know better than I."

The knight shook his head. "My lord Dunmrogh the younger, Sir Roderick—he brought us here. I thought he was mad, the things he told us, but—sir, you must understand that I knew nothing of these events." He held up both hands as if somehow to include the mutilated corpses that hung on the stakes and the general carnage scattered about the clearing in a single gesture. His roaming eye settled on the corpse of the Duke of Dunmrogh, and his eyes tightened.

"Tell me what happened here," he demanded.

"I killed Dunmrogh," a weak female voice said. "I did it."

Neil turned to see Anne standing, supported by Stephen and Winna.

Her gaze touched him, and her mouth parted. "Sir Neil?" she gasped.

Neil dropped to his knee. "Your Highness."

"Highness?" the mounted man echoed.

"Yes," Anne said, turning her attention back to him. "I am Anne, daughter of William the Second, and before Dunmrogh or any other lord, you owe your allegiance to me."

It sent a chill up Neil's back, how much she sounded like Queen Muriele in that moment.

"What is your name, sir?" Anne demanded.

"My name is Marcac MaypCavar," he replied. "But I—"

"Sir Marcac," one of his men interrupted. "That *is* Princess Anne. I've seen her at court. And this man is Neil MeqVren, who saved the queen from one of her own Craftsmen."

Sir Marcac looked about, still plainly confused. "But what is this? These people, what happened to them?"

"I'm not certain myself," Anne said. "But I need your help, Sir Marcac."

"What is your command, Highness?"

"Take these people down from those stakes, of course, and see that they are given care," Anne said. "And arrest anyone not nailed to a pole or in my present company. Take control of Dunmrogh Castle, and arrest any clergy you find there, and keep that place until you have heard from Eslen."

"Of course, Your Highness. And what else?"

"I'll want horses, and provisions, and whatever armed men you can spare," she replied. "And carry my wounded to a leic. By tomorrow's sunrise, I ride to Eslen."

CHAPTER FIVE

THE CANDLE GROVE

T HE CANDLE GROVE WASN'T a grove, and though there were lanterns aplenty, there weren't properly any candles. When Leoff had first heard the name for Eslen's great gathering place, he'd imagined it to have been named in some ancient time, when bards sang beneath sacred trees in the fluttering light of tapers, but in his reading about its history he quickly saw the foolishness of that.

The first Mannish language spoken in the city had been that of the Elder Cavarum, then the Vitellian of the Hegemony, Almannish supplanted at times by Lierish and Hanzish, and most lately, the king's tongue. Areana called the place the *Caondlgraef* in her native tongue, and readily admitted she had no idea what it meant. It was just an "old name."

Still, whatever its origin, Leoff liked the appellation and the images it evoked of an older, simpler day.

Structurally the Candle Grove was a curious hybrid of the ancient *amptocombenus* of the Hegemony, the wooden stages traveling actors threw up in town squares to perform their farces, and the Church pestels where the choir sang or performed in acts the lives of the saints. Carved into the living stone of the hill, it rose in semicircular levels, each tier being one long curving bench.

A large balcony jutted out from the middle of the lowest three levels, forming a separate platform for the regals. There were two stages—one wooden and raised, with space beneath it for trapdoors through which actors and props could vanish and appear—and a lower, stone one where the musicians and singers were situated. The upper stage, following the usage of the Church, was called *Bitreis*, "The World," and the lower stage was named *Ambitreis*, "Otherworld".

Those were the two worlds Praifec Hespero wanted to keep separate. He was going to be disappointed.

Above both stages rose a half-hemisphere ceiling painted with moon and stars and appropriately called "The Heavens." The royal seating was covered, too. Everyone else risked rain or snow.

But the sky was clear tonight, and though it was chill, there was no dampness in the air.

Around the Candle Grove—above the seats, stage, and even "Heaven"—stretched a broad green common, and since noon it had been a feast-ground. Leoff thought the whole city and many from the countryside must have been there—thousands of people. He himself had sat at a long table with the regent at one end and the praifec at the other, and between them the members of the Comven, dukes, grefts, and landwaerds.

He'd made his excuses and come down early to make certain that all was ready. Now it was; the seats were filling with bodies and the air with the murmur of thousands of voices.

Not since his first performance, at the age of six, had he felt such a trembling in his limbs and such profound unrest in his belly.

He looked down at his musicians.

"I know you can do it," he told them. "I have faith in all of you. I only hope to deserve yours."

Edwyn raised the bow of his croth in salute, but most of them spared him only a quick glance, for they were furiously studying their music which was almost—but not quite—what they had been rehearsing.

The praifec had monitored his rehearsals, of course, and approved them, because Leoff had rewritten the work to the churchman's ridiculous specifications. The instrumental pieces were played as introduction to what the vocalists would sing, and then the vocals were done unaccompanied. He had added the material the praifec wanted, and cut parts he had written.

But despite all that, this would not be the praifec's performance. Tonight, the instruments and the players would sing together, and the modes and triads and chords would all be altered. And if what Leoff believed was true, after the first notes sounded, the praifec would be helpless to stop him.

He gazed up at the royal box. The regent was there, of course, and most of the people who had been at his table. But there were two others. One was striking and unmistakable—Queen Muriele. He still thought of her that way despite the recent revision of her title. She wore a gown of black esken trimmed in seal-skin, and no crown or diadem ornamented her head.

The other was a woman with soft chestnut hair, someone Leoff fancied he had seen at court once or twice. The two were surrounded by a block of the regent's black-clad guards.

"I thank the saints, Your Majesty," he said under his breath, "that you should hear this." He hoped she did not despise him for helping her enemies vilify her.

The regent, Robert Dare, raised his hand to indicate that he was ready.

Leoff made sure the musicians had his attention then set his fingers to the hammarharp and sounded a single note. The lead flageolet took it up, and then the bass vithuls, and finally all the instruments as they adjusted their tuning. When that was done, silence fell again.

Fingers shaking, Leoff once more stretched his fingers toward the keyboard.

"It is meant to be Broogh," Muriele whispered to Alis as the musicians began tuning their instruments.

"A very pretty stage," Alis noticed.

It was. It depicted a town square, overlooked by the bell tower in the rear, and a tavern on the left, with a shingle that read PAETER'S

FATEM. The tavern was cleverly cut away so that one could see the facade, but also the inside of it. A new, small stage had been built some four yards or so above The World to represent an upper bedroom in the building.

On the right side of the stage stood the famed bridge the town was named for, crossing a convincing canal along which dried flowers had been placed, dyed to resemble living ones. Behind all that, painted on canvas, were the long green fields and malends of Newland.

As Muriele watched, a young man came out and sat upon the edge of the fountain in the square. He was dressed in the subdued wools of a landwaerden and orange sash of a windsmith, suggesting he'd recently been confirmed as one by the guild.

The musicians had stopped tuning now.

"Damned lot of vithuls and croths," the Duke of Shale muttered, somewhere behind her. "I can't see why all that is needed. Should make a dreadful racket."

As Muriele watched, the tiny figure of Leoff raised his hands above the hammarharp and brought them down.

And such a sound rose as Muriele had never imagined, a swelling thunder of music with high clear notes ringing to the stars and low drone of bass like the deepest, most secret motions of the sea. It broke straight into her soul and enthroned itself. It was as if the most important thing in the world had been said.

Yet despite the immense beauty and power of that chord, it was somehow incomplete—aching for resolution—and she knew she could not rest, never turn her eyes away, could never know peace until she heard it made perfect.

"*No,*" she thought she heard the praifec say. But then she only heard the music.

Leoff grinned fiercely as the first chord filled the half-bowl of the Candle Grove and spilled out into the night, a chord that no one had played in over a thousand years, the chord Mery had rediscovered for him in the shepherd's song.

That for your wishes, Praifec, he thought.

Because now that he heard it, he knew no one, not the praifec, not the Fratrex Prismo himself, could stop him before it was done.

The boy rose from where he sat at the fountain, and his voice suddenly soared with the instruments, as one with them. The language was Almannish, not the king's tongue, which jarred just for an instant and then felt completely right.

"Ih kann was is scaon," he sang.

> I know what beauty is
> The wind from the west
> The far-going green
> The curlew's song
> And her,
> And her . . .

His name was Gilmer, and he sang of life, joy, and Lihta Rungsdautar, whom he loved. And as he did so a girl appeared from the tavern, young and beautiful. Muriele knew when she saw her that this was Lihta, for she had "tresses like sun on golden wheat" that the boy had just been describing. And then she, too, began to sing, another melody entirely, though it wound perfectly around his. They were as yet unaware of each other, but their songs danced together—for Lihta was as much in love with him as he with her. Indeed, this was they day they were to be wed, as Muriele learned when they finally did see one another and their duet became unison. The music quickened into a lively whervel, and they began dancing.

As the two lovers stopped singing an older man came onstage, who turned out to be Lihta's father, a boatwright, and he sang a song both comic and truly melancholy.

"I'm losing a daughter and gaining a debt," it began, and then out came his wife, chastising him for his stinginess, and they, too, sang a duet, just as the young couple began to repeat their song, and suddenly four voices were lifted in an intricate harmony that somehow opened like a book all the ages of love, from first blush through complex maturity to final embrace. Muriele relived her own marriage in a single moment that left her breathless and shaking.

The aethil of the town joined them next, and townspeople arrived for a prenuptial feast and suddenly an entire chorus was joyfully serenading. It was utterly charming, and yet, even as that first act ended— with the sound of distant trumpets, and the aethil wondering aloud who else might that be coming to the feast—Muriele still longed for the resolution of the first chord.

The music faded, but it did not die, as the players left the stage. A simple melody began, echoing the joyous one of the banquet, but now in a plaintive key, a vaguely frightening key. As it grew in volume, a palpable sense of unease moved from listener to listener. It made Muriele want to check her feet, to make sure no spiders were climbing her stockings.

It made her very much aware of Robert.

The second act began immediately with the arrival of Sir Remismund fram Wulthaurp, the music of his coming so dark and violent— with a skirling of pipes and menacing runs in the deep strings—that she clutched at the arms of her chair.

She noticed with a strange delight that the player presenting Wulthaurp looked a great deal like her brother-in-law, Robert.

The story unfolded relentlessly as the wedding banquet became a scene of dread. The props of stage—which before had been transparent as such—now seemed utterly real, as if the Candle Grove really hovered over the empty shell of Broogh, as if they were spying on the town's ghosts, reenacting their tragedy.

Sir Remismund was a renegade, chased from Hansa, seeking plunder and ransom where he could find it. He slaughtered the aethil in the street, and his men ran wild through the town. Remismund— on seeing Lihta—made advances, and when Gilmer protested, he was taken prisoner, to be hanged in the square at sunrise.

Remismund, too proud to take Lihta by force, retired with his thugs to the tavern. And that was the end of the second act.

And on went the music, without pause, pulling them all irrevocably with it. Even Robert, who must surely have understood what was happening, did nothing, which was more than remarkable.

Muriele remembered her conversation with the composer, about why the Church forbade such compositions as this, about the powers of certain harmonies and intervals. And now she understood. He had ensorcelled them all, hadn't he? It wasn't simply *like* a spell, it *was* one. And yet it couldn't be wrong any more than falling in love or revering beauty was wrong. If the composer was a shinecrafter, then there must be such a thing as good shinecrafting; for there was no evil in this.

The third act began with a comic interlude in which one of Remismund's men courted a tavern wench, to no avail. Then entered Remismund and his chief henchman, Razovil, the latter to take a letter for him. He dictated a dispatch addressed to the emperor, spelling in chilling terms how he would break open the dike and drown Newland if he was not paid a king's ransom. Razovil wore robes that much resembled those of a praifec, and his beard and mustache strongly evoked Hespero. Razovil suggested constant amendments to the letter to put a fairer face on the demand, saying that the saints were much in favor of this enterprise and that the emperor was subservient to the saints. It was funny, the back and forth between the two evil men, but it was also disturbing.

The tavern maid, having hidden when Remismund entered, heard the whole plot. After the scene, she fled the tavern to tell Lihta and her father the news. The word was sent out and the townsfolk gathered secretly to decide their course of action. Just as the meeting was about to take place, Razovil came looking for Lihta.

To keep him from discovering their plotting, she went with him to meet Remismund, where the conqueror made another plea for her love, singing thus far the most beautiful song in the play.

Mith aen Saela
Unbindath thu thae thongen
Af sa sarnbroon say wardath mean haert . . .

With a glance,
You loosen the bindings
Of the hauberk which guards my heart.

With a word,
My fortress is taken
And the towers crumble down

With a kiss,
I would make you my queen,
And amend my evil ways

Despite his earlier actions, he sounded deeply sincere, and Muriele thought perhaps that she had been mistaken about Remismund. Here was a man, not a monster. His earlier actions must have some justifiable explanation, if he could love and court so artlessly.

Lihta told him she would consider his suit and left. As soon as she was gone, Remismund sniggered and sang aside to Razovil:

How tender, how winningly guileless, gullible, *foolish*.
One night of love, and I'm done with her.

Then he and his churchish sycophant shared a laugh together, and the music became merry—and somehow demonic.

That ended the third act, as the instruments throbbed almost away. Muriele found that for the first time since the play had begun, she felt slightly released—that she could speak if she wanted to. She glanced over at Robert.

"I'm very much enjoying this play, Lord Regent," she said. "My thanks for allowing me to attend."

Robert glared at her.

"I think you misjudged my composer," she added.

Robert's breath was coming a little hard, as if he had been trying to lift something too heavy. "It's a meaningless farce," he said. "A silly show of bravado."

"No," Hespero averred, "it is a perfidious act of shinecraft."

"If you're looking for shinecraft, amiable Praifec," Muriele said, "you need look no further than our dear regent. Stab him with a blade, and you will see that he does not bleed, at least not the same stuff men do. I've come to think you quite selective in which diabolic forces you despise and which you cozy up to, Praifec Hespero."

"Hush, Muriele," Robert snapped. "Hush before I have your tongue cut out."

"As you cut out the tongue of the Keeper?"

Robert sighed and snapped his fingers, and suddenly a gag was forced into her mouth from behind. Once the first shock was passed, she did not deign to struggle. It was beneath her dignity.

The praifec started to say something, and then the instruments began building a tower of melody to welcome Lihta back to the stage.

The girl stood near the gaol where Gilmer was imprisoned and once again the two exchanged vows of love. Gilmer told her that he had heard the town would rise up at midnight. He spoke of his fears that they would all be killed, his frustration at not being able to join them, and most of all the pain of never having her for wife. He begged her to flee the town before it was too late. The croths and vithuls lifted his heartache into the air and offered it to the very stars.

Lihta followed his song with hers, and Muriele suddenly caught the echo of the tune that Ackenzal had played for her the first time she went to see him, the one that had brought such unwelcome and unaccustomed tears to her face. Now it brought the tantalizing sense that the final note was coming, the harmony that would at last release her from the first. But then the melody became unfamiliar again, as Lihta reminded Gilmer that his duty was her duty also. Suddenly they were singing the "Hymn of Saint Sabrina," the saint who protects Newland, and a thousand voices suddenly joined the pair, for it was a song everyone in the audience knew. It was a mighty sound.

The lovers parted with the hymn dying on the wind. But before exiting the stage, Lihta met the tavern girl again, who asked her where she was going.

"To my wedding," Lihta replied, and then she was gone.

The tavern girl, distraught, took the news to Gilmer, who sang in anguish while the girl tried to comfort him.

Then, unseen by them, Lihta reemerged, wearing her wedding gown of silvery Safnian brocade, the sum of her father's fortune. As

Gilmer wept, and the clouds gathered in the deep strings, Lihta went to Remismund. She met Razovil first, who made mock of her while at the same time suggesting several lascivious notions. Then she repaired upstairs, climbing slowly, stately, to Remismund's room above.

On seeing her, Remismund resumed his charming facade, told her he would bring her joy and riches, and then excused himself to set his guard on watch, as he was soon to be preoccupied.

When he sang that, Muriele gasped through the rag in her mouth as she felt again Robert's body upon her, his hands pushing up beneath her gown. Her gorge rose, and she feared she would vomit into the gag, but suddenly Alis' hand reached and gripped hers tight. The terrible memory passed from visceral to merely unpleasant.

Lihta was alone now, gazing out at the night. The eleventh bell struck, and somewhere in the distance rose the faint chorus of the townsmen assembling for their hopeless battle against Remismund's men.

Then, in the high strings, something began to glide down, a bird returning to earth in many turns, here lifting a bit, but always going lower, until it faded entirely.

Then, alone—almost imperceptibly at first—Lihta began her final song.

> When comes again the light of day,
> My love, I will have flown away . . .

Her voice was tears made sound, but now Muriele heard it, the triumph embedded in the despair, the hope that could die only when belief in hope died. It was the melody from that day, the one that had decided her to commission the piece.

Lihta's solo voice was joined by a single flute and then a reed, and then the croths with their sweeping glissando elegance. It no longer mattered what words she sang, really—it was only the fear, and the grief—and as the vithuls and the bass vithuls joined her voice, the desperate courage and determination. Tears poured down Muriele's face as Remismund reappeared, unheralded by any music, but swaggering into hers. Lihta was standing by the window, wringing her veil in her hands as he took hold of her, and for an instant it seemed as if the music faltered, as if Lihta's resolve had failed.

But suddenly her voice rose, climbing ever higher while below her the music arranged itself in a mountain, like the very foundations of the world and there, *there* it was, the perfect chord that brought rushing everything that had come before, the beginning meeting its end, its completion . . .

Its triumph.

Lihta leaned up as she sang, as if to kiss him, slipped the veil around his neck, and hurled herself out the window. Surprised, his hands occupied with her, Remismund had no time to react. Both plummeted to the street. And though Muriele remembered that the stage was not really very high, and that she suspected some sort of mattress lay disguised beneath the window, it did not seem so now. It seemed as if they fell, and fell, and died on cobbles far below.

And still the harmony hung there, Litha's voice taken up by the instruments as if to show that even death could not silence that song. A march began behind it, as the townsfolk rushed upon Remismund's men, who, disheartened by his death, fled or died.

And when silence finally settled, it lasted for a long time, until someone shouted—no one important, just a person high in the gallery. But it was a ragged, glorius, triumphant shout, and then someone joined him, and then all the Candle Grove came to its feet roaring.

Everyone, that is, save Robert and Hespero.

Leoff gazed at the dumbstruck audience, then turned his regard to the praifec, whose glare was the match for any basil-nix. Leoff bowed stiffly, and heard a single loud cheer. Then the crowd seemed to explode. He knew that this was the greatest moment of his life—the like of which he would never know again—and felt not so much pride as the most profound contentment imaginable.

He still felt it half a bell later, when—as he was congratulating his musicians and blushing from a kiss Areana had impulsively given him—the guards came.

◦   ◦   ◦

Robert's guard dragged Muriele and Alis unceremoniously through the crowd and pushed them into the carriage that was to carry them back to their prison. But all the way back to the castle, she could hear them—the people—singing the Hymn of Sabrina. She couldn't stop crying, and when the gag was finally removed, she sang with them.

That night, she could still hear them through her windows, and she knew that once again, the world she knew had changed profoundly—but this time for the better.

It felt—for the first time in a very long time—like victory.

That night she slept, and dreamed, and the dreams brought not terror—but joy.

CHAPTER SIX

YULE

ASPAR WINCED AS THE leic pulled the needle through his cheek a final time and tied off the gut.

"That's done," the old man said. "You were lucky in both wounds. The shoulder should heal well."

"I'm not sure any wound is lucky," Aspar said, relieved to find that the wind no longer whistled through his cheek when he talked.

"It is when another fingerbreadth could have brought your death," the leic replied cheerfully. "Now, if you'll excuse me, I've more of you to tend to."

"What about her?" Aspar said, pointing with his chin to where Leshya lay, bundled up in wools, her unconscious face pale even for her.

The leic shrugged. "I don't know much about Sefry," he said. "The wound was pretty bad, and I did what I know to do. She's in the hands of the saints now." He patted Aspar's unwounded shoulder. "You had better rest, especially if you're really so foolish as to try to ride tomorrow."

Aspar nodded, still regarding the Sefry. The ride to the castle was a memory seen through a fog of pain and blood loss. Winna had stayed with him, though, keeping him in his saddle. She'd left only a few moments ago, answering a call from the princess.

He understood that Sir Neil and the Vitellians were pretty banged up, but Leshya had the worst of it by far. They'd found her pinned to a tree by an arrow.

He put his hands on his knees and pushed himself up, went over to stand by her in the candlelight. His shadow fell across her face, and she stirred.

"What—?" she gasped, eyes fluttering open.

"Be still," Aspar said. "You've been hurt. Do you remember?"

She nodded. "I'm cold."

Aspar glanced over at the fireplace. He was sweating, himself. "I thought you'd taken off," he said.

"Yes," she murmured, closing her eyes. "Couldn't do that, could I?"

"I don't see why not."

"Don't you? But—doesn't matter. I didn't."

"Werlic. Thank you."

She nodded, and her eyes opened again. They shone like violet lamps.

"I have to go with them tomorrow," he said, "to Eslen."

"Sure," she said. "I know that."

"Well, the thing is, I need you not to die while I'm gone," he explained.

". . . Don't take your orders, holter," she said. "But stay here with me until you leave, yes?"

Aspar nodded. "Yah."

He settled on the floor next to the bed, and soon fell asleep. When he woke again, it was morning, and Winna was gently shaking him awake.

"It's time to go," she said.

"Yah," Aspar said. He looked over at Leshya. She was still breathing, and her color looked better. "Yah."

Cazio dribbled a bit of water onto z'Acatto's lips. In his sleep, the old swordmaster grimaced and tried to spit it out.

"Well," Cazio said, "that's a good sign."

"He has to drink," the healer said. "He's lost a lot of blood, and blood is made from water." The Hornish healer spoke Vitellian with a funny accent, as if he were singing.

"Blood is made of wine," z'Acatto contradicted, cracking one eye half-open. "The original wine, the wine of Saint Fufiono, that's what flows in our veins. Water is what they drown babies in."

The healer smiled. "A little watered wine wouldn't hurt," he said. "I'll find some."

"Wait," z'Acatto wheezed. "What country are we in?"

"You're in Hornladh and the Empire of Crotheny."

Z'Acatto winced and let his hand drop. "Cazio," he said, "do you know that no drinkable wine has ever been produced north of Tero Gallé?"

"We don't find our wines difficult to drink," the healer said.

"Please," z'Acatto went on, "I have no wish to insult, but that only means you have no sense of taste, at least not a cultivated one. How did I come to this hellish place? A man's last drink should remind him of all that was good in life, not send him to Lord Ontro weeping."

"First of all," the healer said, "you aren't dying, not that I can tell."

"No?" z'Acatto's brows lifted in surprise.

"No. You'll be long in bed, and longer recovering your strength, but I've stopped your bleeding, and none of your wounds seem likely to go septic."

"You're mostly bone and gristle, in other words," Cazio put in.

"If I didn't know better," the healer said, "I would say whoever shot you was intentionally trying to wound, not kill. Since no one is that good a shot, I'd say you have the saints to thank."

"I'll thank Saint Fufiono if there's some Vitellian wine around here," z'Acatto said, "and *much* thank the man who brings it."

"I believe there is some Gallean *Barnicé et Tarvé* in the cellar," the healer replied. "That will have to do."

"Eh," the swordmaster said. "That could work out until I can come across something better."

The healer left, and z'Acatto grumbled a little under his breath, then fixed his eyes on Cazio.

"We're both still alive, I've noticed."

"Indeed," Cazio said. "Although it's unclear to me exactly how."

"You're hardly scratched."

Cazio glanced down at the copious bandages and dressings that covered his body. "It's true," he replied, "All thanks to that practice we had." He then explained, as best he could, the events of the night before.

"Well," the old swordsman said, when Cazio had finished, "these are matters that . . ." He trailed off, and for a moment seemed to fall asleep, but then he perked back up. "When are we going home?"

"I thought you were the one who said I ought to get out and see the world."

"Well, we've seen plenty of it," z'Acatto replied. "Now it's time to lie in the sun and drink something from a good year for a while, don't you think? It might even be safe to go back to Avella by now, but if it isn't, I'm sure the countess would take us in again."

His eyes narrowed at the expression that must have crept across Cazio's face. "What?"

"Well," Cazio said, "as it turns out, Anne is Princess of Crotheny."

"You don't say?" z'Acatto snorted. "Don't you remember when the news came about William's death, how those girls got so upset?"

"Well, yes, but I thought they were just upset because their emperor had died. I didn't know it was her father." He remembered how when he'd first met Anne, he had held back his own minor title to impress her at the most opportune time. Now he felt silly about that, as about so many things.

"You might have told me," Cazio said.

"If I don't make you use your own brain, it will turn into mealmush," z'Acatto retorted.

"Anyway," Cazio pressed on, "her kingdom has been usurped and her mother taken prisoner. She's asked me to come along and help reclaim the one and free the other."

"Not your country," z'Acatto said, suddenly serious. "Not your business."

"I feel as if it is," Cazio said. "I've come this far—I think I'll finish it."

"There is no 'finishing it,' boy. What you're riding into is war, and that's something you don't want any experience with, I promise you."

"I'm not afraid of war," Cazio told him.

"Then you're a fool," the swordmaster spat. "Remember how I told you fighting a knight was nothing like one of your noontime duels?"

"I remember," Cazio said. "You were right, and thanks to your advice I've survived."

"Then listen to me one more time, even if it's the last time," z'Acatto said. "Whatever you imagine war is, you're wrong. It's terrible, and being brave doesn't help. It's not dying in a war that's the worst thing, it's *living* through one."

Cazio held his gaze firmly. "I believe you," he said. "And I believe you speak from experience, though you won't talk about it. But I feel this has become my duty, z'Acatto. I think I belong in this fight, and I think I should have earned enough respect from you that you wouldn't imagine I still make decisions like a boy. I may not know exactly what I'm walking into, but my eyes *are* open."

Z'Acatto sighed and nodded. "You've traveled farther than your leagues, Cazio," he said at last. "And you have learned some judgment. I finally see the character I knew you had in you starting to come through. But take my council on this. Go home with me."

"You can't travel now," Cazio said, "but when we've set things right in Eslen, you can join us there."

"No," the old man said. "As soon as I can travel, I'm returning to Vitellia. If you go north to this mess, you'll go without me."

Cazio drew his damaged blade and raised it to attention. "I salute you, old man," he said. "What you did last night was beyond belief. I will never forget it as long as I live."

"You're going," z'Acatto said flatly.

"I am."

"Then go. No more pretty words. Go. *Azdei.*"

"*Azdei*, mestro," Cazio replied. He was suddenly terribly afraid that he was going to cry.

◊ ◊ ◊

Neil knelt before Anne and tried to hold himself steady on one knee, but his body, racked by pain and exhaustion, betrayed him, and he fell. He caught himself with his hands.

"Ease yourself, Sir Neil," Princess Anne said. "Sit, please."

He hesitated, then stood and slumped onto the bench. Bright and dark spots danced before his eyes. "I'm sorry, Your Highness," he mumbled. "I'm just out of breath."

The princess nodded. "You've been through much, Sir Neil," she observed, "and some of it has been because of me. I did not trust you in z'Espino."

"That is clear to me, Your Highness."

She tucked her hands behind her back and regarded him with a solid gaze. "I wronged you," she said. "And you almost died. But I had my reasons. Do you doubt me?"

Neil found that he didn't.

"No, Your Majesty," he said. "I understand what your position was. I should have made more of an effort to convince you."

"I am not queen, Sir Neil," the princess said softly. "You should not address me as 'Majesty.' "

"I understand, Your Highness," Neil replied.

She lay a hand on his shoulder. "I'm glad you survived, Sir Neil. I am most glad."

Neil heard the apology there—an apology without weakness. A very regal sort of apology that sent a little thrill through him.

I serve someone worthy, he caught himself thinking. He hadn't known Anne before, not really. But he did know she hadn't been like this. Something basic in her had changed; she had been a girl. Now she was something much stronger.

"Ah, Cazio," he heard Anne say. Neil glanced up to see the Vitellian had joined them.

"Mi Regatura," Cazio said, a bit cockily. But then, as if the gesture pained him, he dropped to one knee.

Anne regarded him for a moment, then nodded and said something to Cazio in Vitellian.

"I must see someone else, now," she told Neil.

Neil made the sign of blessing, and Cazio made a similar sign, then they both rose. As Anne left, the Vitellian looked at Neil.

"I speak not well your tongue," he managed in an incredibly thick accent. "But I listen, no? You brave man. You brother." He held out his hand.

Neil clasped it. "It was an honor to fight beside you," he said.

"She—" the Vitellian pointed after Anne, struggling for words.

"Not the same," he finally managed.

"No," Neil breathed. "She is a queen now."

Anne gazed down at Roderick's corpse. Vespresern had already washed him and laid him in a winding-sheet. Now she stood weeping as Anne and Austra looked on.

"He died bravely," Anne ventured.

Vespresern turned hard eyes on her. "He died for you," she said. "I can't imagine you're worth it. He loved you. He was mad with love for you."

Anne nodded, but she didn't have anything to say. After a moment, she left, with Austra following her.

The two women went up to the battlements, so Anne could feel the wind. The threat of rain was long gone, and stars blazed in the night sky.

"I thought I loved him," Anne said, "and then I thought I hated him. Now I don't feel much of anything but pity."

"Why?" Austra said. "Anne, his father must have told him to court you. They planned to kill you all along, and Roderick was an instrument of that plan."

"I know. And if I hadn't cursed him with love, he would have killed me himself, I'm sure. But I did curse him, and cursed him again. He died for something he didn't even understand. Like that horse, remember? Duke Orien's horse? It broke its leg, and we were hiding in the hayloft and saw them kill it? You could see in its eyes, it didn't understand what was happening to it."

"I suppose."

"And if I had never been so foolish as to write him, still none of this would have happened. His love was first counterfeit, then shinecraft. Mine was neither—it was just a foolish girl's game. So whose shoulders should this all fall on?"

"You can't take it all on yourself."

"Oh, but I can," Anne said. "I must. I went *there* again, Austra. I saw the fourth Faith, and she told me that my mother has been imprisoned and my father's throne usurped. That's why we're leaving here tomorrow."

"That can't be true," Austra said.

"I believe it," Anne replied. "First they kill half of us and then they take our throne. That seems like a pretty logical course of events. But they missed me, and they're going to regret that."

Austra regarded her for a long moment. "I believe they will," she said. She started to say something else, but seemed to struggle for a moment. "I'm sorry I disobeyed you," she said finally.

Anne looked frankly at her. "Austra, you are truly the only person I can claim to love. I know that now. I can't even say that about my mother or Charles, not honestly. You are the only one I love."

"I love you, too," Austra said.

"But you can't disobey me again," Anne said, taking her hand. "Ever. I might be right, and I might be wrong, and you may try to convince me when you think I'm wrong, but once my word is spoken, it is *your* word, too."

"Because you're the princess and I'm a servant?" Austra murmured.

"Yes," Anne replied.

They set out the next morning—Anne, Austra, Winna, Aspar, Neil, Cazio, and twenty horsemen from Dunmrogh. The clouds were back, and a midday snow began to fall, the first snow of winter. It was Yule; from now on, the days would only get longer.

RESACARATUM

L EOFF GLANCED UP AS the praifec entered the little room that had been his home for the past two days. There wasn't much to it, the room—a table, a few candles, and no window at all. Of course, there wouldn't be, this deep underground.

"You're a very clever man," the praifec said after a moment. "And far more political than I would have imagined."

"I told you it would be magnificent," Leoff said, trying to sound brave.

"Oh, yes, and so it was," Hespero agreed. "Even I was moved by it—moved as if by shinecraft, in fact."

"It was music, not shinecraft," Leoff insisted. "All music is magical. You can't artificially separate—"

"Oh, I most certainly can," the praifec replied. "And I'm afraid the council of praifecs agrees with me. Leovigild Ackenzal, you are here convicted of shinecraft and high treason."

He stepped closer and rested a hand on Leoff's shoulder. The touch made the composer's skin crawl.

"No, my friend," the praifec said in his most avuncular tones, "enjoy your small triumph. It will have to last you the rest of your life."

Leoff held his chin high. "I'm not afraid to die," he said.

The praifec shrugged. "I'm not going to kill you," he said. "But in a moment, I will leave this room, and so will you, and you will be taken to a *place*." He put his hands behind his back. "Fralet Ackenzal, do you know the meaning of *Resacaratum*?"

"It means a reconsecration—to make holy again."

"Indeed. The world has become an unholy place, Fralet Acken-zal, I think you will agree. War threatens everywhere; terrible monsters wander about—why you've met one yourself, yes?"

"Yes," Leoff said.

"Yes. The world is in need of purification, and when that need arises, the Church is at hand. It's beginning now, in every country, every village, every house. The *Resacaratum* has begun. And you have the honor of being one of its first—examples."

"What do you mean?" Leoff asked, the hair on the back of his neck pricking up.

"You will be lustrated, Fralet—made pure. I fear the process may be painful, but redemption rarely comes without cost."

He gave Leoff's shoulder a friendly squeeze and left. And as he promised, someone came and took Leoff to a place.

He tried to be brave, but Leoff was not made for pain, and after a time he screamed, and cried, and begged for an end to it.

But it did not end.

ACKNOWLEDGMENTS

A special thanks to Terry Brooks for his support and encouragement. Thanks also to Elizabeth Haydon, Melanie Rawn, Katherine Kurtz, Robin Hobb, John Maddox Roberts, and Charles de Lint for their kind words about *The Briar King*.

Thanks to my readers: T. Karen Anderson, Nancy Baker, Kris Boldis, Marshal Hibnes, Chris Hodgkins, Lanelle Keyes, Eugenia Mansfield, Charlie Sheffer, and Nancy Vega.

Thanks to Jack Simmons, Ph.D., for his help with matters nautical. Any mistakes in such matters don't originate with him.

As always, thanks to my editor, Steve Saffel; editor in chief, Betsy Mitchell; and managing editor, Nancy Delia. Thanks to Eliani Torres for wading through my misspellings and other mistakes. Thanks also to editorial assistant Keith Clayton for tons of hard work.

Thanks to Kirk Caldwell for more beautiful maps, Stephen Youll for the cover art, and Dave Stevenson for putting it all together.

Thanks to Colleen Lindsay and Christine Cabello for putting me out there, in three dimensions and in cyberspace. Sorry I ruined a perfectly good assistant, Colleen, even if only for a day or two.

Thanks to Mark Maguire for managing production.

Across the pond, many thanks to Stefanie Bierworth and Peter

Lavery, not only for publishing this book in Britain, but for their hospitality—especially Peter, who put up with me as a houseguest.

Thanks to Dave Gross for his perpetual support and for being best man at my most recent wedding.

Belated thanks to Jacques Chambon, who edited my first books published in French. The world is a lesser place without you, Jacques.

ABOUT THE AUTHOR

GREG KEYES was born in Meridian, Mississippi, to a large, diverse, storytelling family. He received degrees in anthropology from Mississippi State and the University of Georgia before becoming a full-time writer. He is the author of *The Briar King* and the Age of Unreason tetralogy, as well as *The Waterborn, The Blackgod,* and the *Star Wars*® New Jedi Order novels *Edge of Victory I: Conquest, Edge of Victory II: Rebirth,* and *The Final Prophecy.* He lives in Savannah, Georgia.

HAIRUWARD
THE DEW RIVER
GLASTIR
SCHILDU
THE BAIRGHS
DHAERATH
SARNWOOD
MEY GHORN PL.
WHITE WARLOCK RIVER
MIDENLANDS
BROGSWELL
CRENREFF
PALE
THAURP
THEN RIVER
ROGHVAEL
AVENBROOK
WHERTHEN
TULHAEM
OFTHEN
ENGSWYS
BOGELIH
LEAN GABLE HILLS
DUNMROGH
EVER
FOXING MARSHES
DANFROC
HORNLADH
DAW RIVER
MAG-Y-TARF
TAFF CREEK
GULSIRITH HILLS
WHITRAFF
OWLTOM RIVER
DOLHAM
WALHAM FOOTHILLS
NORENHESS
DUTH-AG-PAE VILLAGES
REWN ALUTH
WATTAU VILLAGES
TERO GALLE
THE BLOODWATER SEA
N
W
E
S